Robert G. Barrett was raised in Bondi where he has worked mainly as a butcher. After thirty years he moved to Terrigal on the Central Coast of New South Wales. Robert has appeared in a number of films and TV commercials but prefers to concentrate on a career as a writer. He is the author of *You Wouldn't Be Dead For Quids*, *The Real Thing*, *The Boys From Binjiwunyawunya*, *The Godson*, *Between the Devlin and the Deep Blue Seas*, *Davo's Little Something*, *White Shoes*, *White Lines and Blackie*, *And De Fun Don't Done*, *Mele Kalikamaka Mr Walker* and *The Day of the Gecko*.

Also by Robert G. Barrett in Pan

ROBERT G. BARRETT

LES NORTON'S BACK IN

WHITE SHOES, WHITE LINES AND BLACKIE

PAN
AUSTRALIA

First published 1992 in Pan by Pan Macmillan Publishers Australia
This edition published by Pan Macmillan Australia Pty Limited
St Martins Tower, 31 Market Street, Sydney

Reprinted 1992, 1993, 1994, 1995

National Library of Australia
cataloguing-in-publication data:

Barrett, Robert G.
White shoes, white lines and blackie.
ISBN 0 330 27370 1.
I. Title.
A823.3

Typeset in 10/11 pt Times Roman by Post Typesetters
Printed in Australia by McPherson's Printing Group

e grabbed this book for you
aymond, because of the
over, it reminds us of you
nly joking buddy. Page
(always.)

your good friend

(Fluffy)

Looser. 2

The author would like to thank the following people for a laugh and their help in getting this book together: Al Baldwin, Surfers Paradise, Queensland; Paul Tjientjin, Dirranbandi, Queensland; and Sheila Martin, Granite Falls, North Carolina, USA.

As usual, the author is giving a percentage of his royalties to Greenpeace.

Here you go Ray, you
made me feel so guilty
I finally sent it.
hope you enjoy it and the
hotos.
ee you soon !!!   *V man.*

h — yeah I changed my name!

This book is dedicated to Marguirite Therese, the Jane Russell of Auckland.

The Hakoah Club in Bondi is a very, very nice club, frequented by very, very nice members and their guests; mainly Eastern suburbs citizens of the Jewish faith. Set where Hall Street rises past the post office, you walk up a small set of wide, white marble steps, through the glass door and into a cool, bright foyer; reception and phones on the right, doorman and guests' book on the left. The floor then gently rises past a small, angled fountain, set beneath a large copper Menorah candelabrum to take you into the main drinking and dining area. There's a poker-machine room on your left, a bar, a lengthy servery full of choice foods, staffed by polite staff, then a check-out lady and coffee machine next to a large cabinet full of cream-stuffed cakes and other calorie-drenched delicacies.

The hot-food servery faces another, crammed with beautiful, crisp salads; a number of chairs and tables in between. The salad servery is backed by a long padded seat in a kind of motley green and topped with indoor plants set in a frosted-glass surround. This faces across more chairs and tables to where a length of folding glass doors opens up onto another area full of chairs and tables full of middle-aged or elderly men and women, reading, eating or talking over coffee. Most of the men wear thick-rimmed glasses, and some have beards. The women are

1

dark-eyed, with lacquered hair and matching twin-sets with fat backsides and matching fat ankles.

Noisy but happy kids wearing yamulkas dart around the chairs and tables, and now and again a smiling teenage boy will walk through carrying a backpack or a soccer ball, his shin-guards still jammed precariously in his socks, to be met by teenage girls in track-suits carrying gymbags. The low, gold-painted ceiling and muted lighting make for a nice, relaxed, law-abiding atmosphere. Exactly the kind of place you would expect to find nice, law-abiding Jewish people of various nationalities, enjoying a quiet drink, a coffee, or a meal with friends.

Definitely not the kind of place you would expect to find a low-life thug, extortionist, robber and now part-time bouncer like Les Norton. A man who, in the short space of time he'd been in the Eastern suburbs, had probably rolled over more Jewish landlords and estate agents than Rommel's Panzer Division. But there he was. In a pair of jeans, Nikes, and a white Save-Antarctica T-shirt, seated where the long padded seat faces the folding glass doors, a slice of Sacher chocolate cake sitting on a table in front of him, next to a cup of coffee that strong, Norton reckoned, if it had been any stronger it would have jumped out of the cup and started doing push-ups.

Actually, Norton liked the Hakoah Club. A friend of his nominated him, so he joined; and it was one of the best moves he ever made. It was barely five minutes walk from his house, and although he wasn't all that interested in the heated pool, the saunas and spas, it was quiet, the beer was cold, and, being a good tooth-man, Les didn't mind the food; especially the veal bakony, the potato latkes and the banks of crisp, fresh salads, as much as you want at the right price. Now and again Norton might bump into one of his old landlords or an estate agent he'd brassed but he'd always give them a polite if somewhat thin smile. Norton's thin smile, though, would invariably be returned by one thinner than the cabbage soup their unfortunate relations got in the death camps during the Second World War.

2

However, on this particular occasion, Norton wasn't smiling that much at all, thin or otherwise. In fact for all the interest he was taking in his fresh coffee and slice of delicious chocolate cake, Les might as well have been sipping rusty tap-water and eating a five-day-old scone. Yes, thought Norton, as his gaze shifted disconsolately towards the ceiling just above his head, where cracks of red undercoat were pushing through the gold, that's just like me, isn't it. My heart and emotions bleeding through the cracks of my shattered life. Les Norton, the simple country boy from Queensland, was in the middle of another love affair turned sour.

To be honest, everything had been going along cosy and the whole thing wasn't even Norton's idea; it was Warren's. The caper with the old block of flats had gone over smoother than a bunch of carnations on Mothers' Day. The only people who knew the truth were Les and the two Romanians. He'd settled everything with the tenants; all he had to do now was wait for the insurance money, which was just a matter of two government departments getting their act together. How long that would take Norton didn't know, but he wasn't going to make any unnecessary waves. He had the money he'd ripped off from the bikies, and even though he was half joking, Price did weigh in the $50,000; probably to keep Norton completely on side.

Oddly enough, despite being completely oblivious to what had happened, Price seemed to have found a new respect for his trusted employee and friend. Even if at times he would wish Norton to the shithouse. Especially if Les took a turn working some nights and would remark to Price when they were leaving the club, always in front of Price's friends, 'You know what this place needs, Price? A few nice paintings. Give it a bit of class.' And always one of Price's friends would agree and Les would add, 'Now that you've got a bit of time, you should have a look around. You never know, you might pick a couple up at the right price, Price.'

And the silvery haired casino owner would just blink at

Norton impassively till Les walked him to his car. Then he'd say, 'One of these days, you red-headed cunt, I'm going to kick you right in the nuts. You know that — don't you?'

So everything was moving along splendidly. Norton had money, a night or two at the club just to keep his hand in, and plenty of time to train and just do his thing. Until Warren tipped him into Annie.

Annie was an Indian pommy who worked in her cousin Gianna's Indian takeaway food shop, Let's All Japardi, at Maroubra Junction. Annie was about twenty-two and no oil-painting, though she had a whippy sort of body and nice legs plus a fair sense of humour. The Indian girl with an accent straight out of 'Minder' got Les in at first. Warren had been having an affair with Gianna, who lived with her boyfriend, an electrical contractor who worked about ninety hours a week and was always too tired to go out. Gianna didn't mind doing a bit of porking on the side, and Warren wasn't adverse to porking someone's wife or girlfriend behind their spouse's back if it was offered to him. But the only way Gianna could get out was with Annie in tow as chaperone. So it always had to be a foursome. Which was where Les came in.

Gianna was the better sort of the two; a hot body, dark, sexy eyes and matching long dark hair. And Warren was getting a bit keen, sneaking her back to the house at every opportunity with or without Annie. But for the life of him, Norton couldn't seem to get keen on Annie. She was a good-hearted girl, always bringing food and other odds and ends round to the house, where unlike her cousin, Annie could come and go as she pleased. She'd buy Norton little presents and Les always felt self-conscious about accepting them because he knew Annie didn't make all that much money and he had heaps. Yet the more Norton would protest the more Annie would warm to him, thinking, Oh, isn't he such a lovely man. Not like those right cadgers I knew at home. Before long Annie had a hairdryer in the bathroom and a couple of pairs of stockings hanging in the laundry. But the keener Annie

4

got on Les, the more Norton was finding himself dropping off.

Norton wasn't quite sure what was turning him away from Annie and causing him all this torment. Being a dud root didn't help her much. In fact Annie wasn't just a low number in the sack, she was probably the worst root Les had ever had. Norton would hammer away, like he was putting up a thirty-storey office tower and Annie would lay there with her arms spread across the bed, eyes closed, mouth open catching flies, and a kind of 'ravish me, take my body, I'm yours' look on her face. She couldn't tongue kiss, she didn't like any trick shots, and blow jobs were against her religion. Norton even bought a new set of supercharged power-pack batteries for Mr Buzz and she didn't like that either. Norton was even forced to remark to Warren one morning that he didn't know what Gianna was like in the sack, but as far as Annie went, you'd have more fun bonking a speed-hump. Of course Annie might have been having the time of her life having multiple orgasms one after the other. But if she was, she certainly never let on and she never mentioned it to Les. She might have. But if she did, Les certainly couldn't remember. So that wasn't helping their relationship much.

Being a half-baked wog didn't worry Les. Or a pommy either. There was definitely no racism involved, though it wasn't a bad quinella if you were a bigot. The main thing gnawing away at Norton's soul though, was the smell. No matter what she did, Annie always ponged of curry. She'd call round after work with all these little do-dads from the restaurant, and as soon as Les opened the door it was like they'd just landed at Bombay airport. Norton reckoned he could smell her as soon as her car pulled up. Coming back from the beach or straight out of the shower and liberally splashed with 4711, Annie still smelled like fifty kilograms of chicken vindaloo. One night in a frenzy of unbridled passion and drunken lust, Norton stuck his face into Annie's ted and went for it like a hungry pack-wolf. Even it stunk of curry. And for all the difference it

5

made, Les might as well have been reading Annie the used-car section in the *Herald* classifieds.

No, sexually or otherwise, it definitely wasn't the happiest scene round Chez Norton at the moment, and something was going to have to give. Warren could move out and shack up with Gianna. Les would get a room in a boarding house. Or he'd sell the house and move to Dhinnabarrada Mission, Antarctica; anywhere to get away from the smell of curry. He began to hint to Warren that he wasn't all that rapt in the two vindaloo queens, and how long did Warren expect this thing between him and Gianna to continue? Besides, porking some bloke's girl behind his back while the poor mug's out working his ring off wasn't actually cricket, and Norton wasn't keen on being a party to such underhanded shenanigans. Also, if the boyfriend got wind and came round to punch Warren's lights out, the debonair young advertising executive could sort it out for himself. The band-aids were in the bathroom, next to the iodine.

But Warren didn't seem to take the hint, and continued to bonk blissfully away, everything all going over his head. Nevertheless, it was going to have to end. But bloody how? Which was why, on a pleasant Wednesday afternoon, the second week in March, instead of enjoying a piece of chocolate Sacher cake and coffee at the Hakoah Club, Norton was staring up at the ceiling, lost in pain and thought and wondering why life had to continually deal him such misery and tear his heart out.

It was probably for this reason Norton didn't notice the figure standing at his table holding a cup of coffee and an apricot Danish. A neat figure in his late twenties, around five feet six, slightly pudgy, wearing smart grey trousers, expensive grey shoes and a white shirt. A gold Longines quartz sat on his left wrist and a gold-banded diamond ring glittered on his right hand. Loose black hair covered his ears and collar, and wisped slightly over a pudgy but happy sort of face and pudgy but happy sort of mouth. A small yet thick nose had no trouble supporting a pair of brown steel-rimmed glasses, behind which peered a pair of inquisitive brown eyes set under thick, dark eyebrows.

'Hello, Les. How's things?'

Norton's gaze fell away from the ceiling. 'KK,' he answered, a little absently. 'How are you?'

'Not too bad. Mind if I join you?'

'No, no, go for your life.' Norton shuffled slightly in his seat and moved his coffee to one side of the table.

KK was Kelvin Kramer, a good Jewish boy if ever there wasn't one. The only word to describe KK was conman — with a capital K. He originally came from Melbourne, settled in Sydney with his family, who had money, then gravitated on his own to the Gold Coast. Surfers Paradise in particular. KK always had a scam going. A device to make your car run on water and give you at least a hundred miles per gallon. Cream to give men a bigger dick. Irresistible male scent that would have women throwing pussy at you like frisbees. An ointment for women guaranteed to give them bigger boobs, take the grey out of their hair, renew the fillings in their teeth and make them look at least twenty years younger. A Tibetan elixir promised to flush every impurity from your system, improve your memory, make you lose weight and fix your aching back. Just send $20 plus postage to box so-and-so, Surfers Paradise. Anything. KK would put his grandmother on a slave block if he thought there was an earn in it. It was rumoured he even sold a pair of ice-skates to a woman who had just lost both her legs in a car accident, and a saxophone to a miner with a collapsed lung. Scruples, ethics or a sense of fair play definitely weren't part of Kelvin Kramer's make-up, and despite coming from a fairly decent family, KK's standing in the Jewish community couldn't have been any lower if he'd been related to Joseph Mengle.

KK's other claim to fame was an American starlet and model he'd been squiring around New York for a while, Crystal Linx, a blonde bimbo with an enormous pair of boobs who'd posed for a heap of cheesecake and had a few minor parts in some B-grade thrillers. Crystal had cut

7

a single that blipped fleetingly on the charts, but despite this she was cutting another and possibly an album. Her main talent, however, was her monstrous set. Stories about KK were always turning in the media, and photos of him alongside Crystal in the glossies or whatever else turned up in Australia from overseas. He got nicked in London for fraud — sonar walking-sticks for the blind that got about thirty people run over — and he just got out by the skin of his teeth. Now along with being Crystal's squeeze, he was running around America promoting Queen Witchetty Grub Royal Jelly. One hundred per cent guaranteed to cure everything from dandruff to Legionnaires disease.

It would have been at least a year since Les had last seen KK. He came up the game a few times with his brother and a couple of mates for a laugh and a splash. Which was one thing you could say about KK, he loved a splash and was generally always good for a laugh. His brother Menachem, or Manny as most people called him, was a different kettle of fish altogether. Where KK was dark and pudgy, Manny was one of those hard, lean Israelis with scrubby red hair and piercing blue eyes. Manny had also been a lieutenant in the Israeli para-troopers, and was one tough, fit bastard. Eddie had known him for years and, being a warrior also, they were fairly good mates. Manny even trained with the boys a few times and it didn't take them long to realise he knew every trick there was to either disable you, cripple you for life or leave you dead on the spot, if you took him too lightly.

Oddly enough, Manny's name had just come up the day before at Eddie's house in Edgecliffe. Les was round helping Eddie put a new roller-door up in his garage, and Eddie mentioned that Manny had been nicked the day before in Perth with a case of Uzis, travelling on an Israeli passport as a member of the Mossad. Where Eddie got his information Les didn't know; there were quite a few things about Eddie Les didn't particularly wish to know. It had been hushed up, but at the present time, Menachem was well and truly a guest of Her Majesty's Commonwealth Police. Now here was his young brother, about a year on. Still, thought Norton, with all his doings between here, the US and the UK, Kelvin's probably a busy boy. It was a bit of a buzz to see him though, and momentarily took Norton's mind off what was troubling him.

'So KK,' said Les, as Kramer settled down with his coffee and Danish. 'What brings you here? Wait, don't tell me, let me guess. You got one of the lost Dead Sea Scrolls. Carbon dated, fully kosher and everything. And it's for sale at the right price.' Les smiled as KK stirred his coffee. 'You're not here for the apricot Danish.'

KK took a sip of coffee and looked evenly at Norton. 'I suppose I could ask you the same bloody thing.'

'I'm a member — already,'

KK had to blink. 'You a member. Christ! And they call me a conman.'

'Actually,' replied Les, 'I've just booked to see Yaffa Yarkoni in the King David Room. It should be a good night.'

'What are you going to do? Steal all her dresses.'

Norton conceded the point and tried not to grin.

'No,' continued KK. 'To tell you the truth, I've only been back a few days and I was supposed to meet my brother down here.'

'Ohh yeah, Manny,' faked Norton. 'How is he these days? I haven't seen him for a while.'

'He's ... good. But he hurt his back in a car accident and couldn't make it.'

Norton shook his head sympathetically. 'Shit! Bad luck. I like Manny.'

'Yeah. So I was supposed to meet one of his mates and he can't make it either.' KK shook his head also. 'It's stuffed me up a bit.'

'What do you mean — "stuffed you up"? Have they got the scroll, have they?'

'No, Einstein. Manny was supposed to look after me for five days. I've got Crystal coming out to Australia. You do know about me and Crystal Linx, don't you, Les?'

9

'Sure. Every time I'm in a Mt Druitt barber shop and I pick up *People, Picture* or the *Melbourne Truth*, her tits come belting out at you like Kenworth headlights.'

KK fixed on Norton through his glasses. 'Going by your big boofhead, I'd say you've been hanging round quite a few Mt Druitt barber shops lately.'

Again Norton was forced to concede the point. For some reason he'd let Annie give him a trim and he ended up looking like a cross between a baboon and a roadie for the Sisters of Mercy.

'Like I said, Bela Lugosi,' smiled KK, 'I've got Crystal coming out promoting her new single. We're staying in a block of flats my family owns in Surfers, which are empty at the moment. I'm doing the whole rattle on the Gold Coast. She gets in Friday and flies back to the States on Tuesday. Manny was going to be my minder.'

'Minder?'

'Yeah. You know, just help us handle the media crush while we do all the publicity shots and that. Get us in and out of the limo and make sure no mugs try to get their hands on Crystal's giant, enormous et-sa.'

Norton took a sip of coffee. 'Bad luck your brother hurt his back. Sounds like a bit of fun. Five days on the Gold Coast, galavanting around in the sun, sipping champagne. You still drink plenty of bubbly, KK?'

'All I can get.' Then the little Jewish conman sighed. 'But he's been hurt and his mate can't make it either. I'm more or less up shit creek.' KK took off his glasses, massaged the bridge of his nose, then put them back on again. 'I suppose I'll find someone.'

There was silence between them for a moment. A voice crackled out over the club intercom. 'Shlomo Podovodski, to the foyer please.' Suddenly Norton felt KK looking at him like he was a kangaroo caught in a spotlight.

'What are you doing?'

Les screwed up his face. 'Me?'

'No . . . the piece of fuckin' chocolate cake sitting on your plate, you goose. Yeah, you. What are you doing for the next five days?'

10

'How exactly do you mean... KK?'

'Do you want to come up and mind me and Crystal for five days? Someone told me you've got half a brain and you're not bad at bashing up drunks. I also heard there's not much doing at the game lately. You want to come up to Surfers for a few days. Get yourself a bit of an earn?'

'What's a bit of an earn?'

KK's expression didn't change. 'I'll give you $1,500 in the hand. Plus your exes.'

Norton couldn't believe it; it was truly the prophecy. And in here of all places. It was as if Moses himself had parted Norton's Red Sea of troubles. Five days away from the curry queen. In the sunshine, living it up, and a nice little earn thrown in; even if you didn't need it all that much. The way Norton was feeling lately, he'd have given KK $1,500 to take him with him. He could leave Annie a note saying he'd caught an infectious disease and was going into quarantine on Thursday Island. I'm not good enough for you, get yourself another man. Or, just don't be here when I get back. And your hairdryer. He might even ring Gianna's boyfriend long distance and tell him what was going on. He'd come round and give Warren a slap, and with Norton not being there, he wouldn't have to act the hero with some poor mug who was in the right in the first place. It would serve Warren right anyway, and just might put a stop to the whole sorry saga. Yes, this was truly a blessing from above; or wherever it comes from when you're in the domain of God's chosen people. That's it for me, thought Les, I'll never crack another anti-semitic joke again.

'Okay, Kelvin,' said Les, offering his hand across the table. 'You're on.' KK's handshake was a bit like grabbing five peeled prawns, but there was a modicum of warmth in it. 'What do you want me to do?'

'We catch the 10 a.m. plane tomorrow. I'll pick you up in a taxi at nine. Where do you live? It's just up the road somewhere, isn't it?' Norton told KK the address. 'You'll use my brother's ticket. And if anyone asks who you are, just say you're my brother. Not that you'll have to say much to anybody anyway.'

11

'Menachem Norton,' grinned Les. 'I like it already. Shit! What a day. I've been ordained.'

'That's right, Les. Just keep saying to yourself "I'm Jewish and I'm proud".'

'I'll go straight down and get myself a black frock-coat and a pair of white shoes. I'll be the only Orthodox Jew in a pair of white shoes. I mean, it is the heart of white-shoe territory where we're going. I wouldn't want to look out of place.'

KK wiped his mouth with a paper napkin. 'Listen, Les,' he said evenly. 'Do me a favour. When we get there, knock up on the jokes about white-shoes. All right?'

'Oh?'

'The people I move around with up there have heard it a million times. And it goes over like a boil on your arse.'

Something in the tone of KK's voice told Norton he meant it. 'Okay,' he nodded, 'I'll behave myself.'

'No white-shoe jokes.'

'You got it, KK. One black frock-coat. Hold the white St Louies.'

'Good. Well, I'll see you in the morning, Les.'

KK rose from the table when Norton pulled him up. 'So what about a little something up front? I'm skint at the moment. You wouldn't want your brother to lob with the arse out of his pants, would you?'

KK hesitated for a moment, then fished a wallet from his back pocket. His plump little fingers deftly flicked out five $100 bills, which he discreetly pushed across the table to Les. 'I'll give you the rest on Tuesday.'

Norton had the money in his jeans quicker than KK got it from his wallet. 'Thanks, mate. You needn't worry, I'll do the right thing.'

Ironically for all the banter, KK never doubted Norton's word for a moment. 'I know you will. Well, shalom, Les. I'll see you in the morning.'

'Yeah, KK. Shalom. It's been good to know you.'

The last Les saw of KK was him disappearing past the fountain in the foyer and out the front door. His spirits raised, Norton got a fresh cup of coffee and finished his

12

piece of chocolate cake. He left the club, took a stroll up to McKenzies Point in the sun, watching the joggers and the distant surfers and people on the beach while he had a think. And it was all good. Sensational in fact. He had an appointment at four with a hairdresser he'd taken out a few times — to get the job Annie had done on him straightened out. He was there on time, but the boss had gone home sick so Les got the junior. But no matter what she did, it could only be an improvement. She took up his sideburns, combed it into a kind of part in the middle and managed to square it off and even it at the back. In fact he came out looking that good he tipped her $5.

Les was home by five and immediately started putting T-shirts, a spare pair of jeans and some other clothes and odds and ends into a large overnight-bag. No white shoes, but he did throw in a pair of blue slacks and blue Italian loafers worth about $300 which he'd purchased from a gentleman in a hotel for $60. He also managed to cram in his ghetto-blaster. About the only good thing to come out of his affair with the curry queen was her other cousin, Benoit, who worked in an import record shop in Five-Ways, Paddington.

Benoit looked a bit like Annie, skinny with a chubby face. The boys carted him out a couple of times and he didn't really give a stuff what was going on because if it hadn't been Les or Warren, it would have only been someone else. Les slung Benoit $150, gave him half a dozen cassettes and told him to tape him up some good music. Benoit came back with some Stones, Paul Norton, the Herbs, some old soul tracks and this and that, plus a heap of Southern Boogie and Zydeco: Sugar Ray and the Bluetones, Anson Funderberg and the Rockets, Queen Ita, Nathan and the Zydeco Cha Chas, plus a heap of others. Norton hadn't heard all the tapes, but what he had so far he liked. Benoit told him some of that southern-fried boogie'd make him think his back ain't got no bone. And Les believed him.

He packed a few toiletries and things and that was about it. While he'd been packing Les had been thinking,

13

so he got a writing pad and biro and scratched out a brief note which he put in an envelope and placed on his dressing-room table. Feeling a bit peckish by now he got a bottle of Eumundi Lager from the fridge and drank that while he knocked up a spaghetti and waited for Warren to come home so he could tell him the good news. Or bad news. Whichever way Warren chose to take it. As he sipped his beer while the sauce was simmering, Les started thinking again so he made a quick phone call, getting straight through on the 'hot-line'.

'Yeah, hello.'

'Hello, Price, it's Les. How are you?'

'Les. How are you, mate? What are you up to?'

'Not much. What about yourself?'

'Just sitting here with my feet up, watching Rocky and Bullwinkle. Tea's just about ready.' Price moved the phone a little closer. 'So what's on your mind?' No one rang Price on the hot-line unless it was reasonably important.

'I bumped into an old mate of ours down the Hakoah Club today. Kelvin Kramer.'

'Ohh, little KK. How is the shifty little reffo shit?'

'He looked all right from where I was sitting. And he was cashed up.'

Norton told Price about the offer KK had made him in the club: going up, using his brother's name, staying at the family flats, he even mentioned about KK pulling him up over the white-shoe gags.

'So what do you reckon? He is a shifty, but it's a nice break, and an earn.'

Price thought for a moment over the phone. 'Yeah. Well, we both know that KK's a bit of a lad. But he's also a low thing when it comes to dudding people. But his brother Manny. That's a bid odd. We both know he's just been nicked in WA. And he's a heavy-duty dude. Eddie'd cut your lungs out and use them for leg warmers. But Manny'd eat them. He just doesn't seem the type of bloke who'd want to spend five days in the spotlight with the Yank bimbo.'

14

'Yeah, that's a thought. But it is his brother.'

'True. But Manny Kramer minder; it doesn't jell some-how. Still, go up, have a bit of fun. But just keep your meat pies open. There's a lot of shifty cunts up there. And a lot of money gets around at times.' Then Price laughed. 'No, it should be okay. Go up and have a laugh.'

'I will. But if anything doesn't seem too kosher, I'll give you a ring.'

'If you don't get me here, you'll catch me at the club.'

'Okay. I'll give you a call anyway. Might send you a T-shirt.'

'Do that. Anyway, here's tea. You wouldn't believe it either, we're having roast pork.'

'And me a Jew. See you, Price.'

'See you, Les. Have a good time.'

Norton returned to the sauce and opened another Eumundi Lager. While he was stirring slowly, he started thinking again. Bloody Price, he's a wise bloody old owl at times. Manny Menachem minder? Mmmh. Oh well, it's not like I'm bound to some iron-clad contract. If it gets too punishing I can just catch a plane home. I'm five hundred in front no matter what.

Warren arrived home around seven in jeans and T-shirt, much like Les. 'G'day Les,' he said, breezing into the kitchen. 'How's things?'

'Pretty good, mate. How was work?'

'Not bad. The Eumundi Lager promotion's coming along better than we thought.'

'That's good.' Norton took another swig of beer and grinned. 'It's a good drop. Bring as much home as you like.'

'So I've noticed. Is there one left in the fridge?'

'Might be.'

Warren opened a bottle of beer, took a pull and looked into what Les was stirring. 'That smells all right. What are we having?'

'Spaghetti à la No Names. You hungry?'

'Yeah. I am a bit.'

'Good. And get into it. It's the last decent feed you'll be getting for a while. I'm going away for about a week.'

15

'You are! Where?'

'Surfers Paradise.'

While Warren finished his beer, Les told him about the offer he'd been made, leaving out the bit about Manny. It was just a job and he was getting paid for it.

'Shit! Five days in Surfers perving on Crystal Link's megasonic gazonkas. Wait till you see those in the flesh. You'll think all your birthdays have come at once. Fuck, I wish I was going with you.' Warren put his empty in the kitchen tidy. 'Have you told Annie?'

'Why don't you have your shower and we'll discuss that after we've had tea. They're not coming around tonight anyway, are they?'

'No. Wednesday night they go to aerobics then do the books.'

'Good. Well, have a tub and we'll get into this.'

Warren scrubbed away the dirt and grime from a hard day at the advertising agency, spent mainly doing lunch and drinking coffee while they watched semi-erotic Italian game show videos. He changed into a grey track-suit, and it didn't take long for both of them to each demolish two plates of pasta. After that piece of chocolate cake at Hakoah, Norton didn't feel like sweets. So, after cleaning up they settled back in the kitchen over coffee. A bit of light FM drifting in from the stereo in the lounge.

'I'll get straight to the point about the Tandoori twins, Woz. I'm giving Annie the arse.'

'Ohh, that's nice. You know the poor girl's in love with you.'

'I realise that, Warren. And it's tearing me apart.'

Warren looked at Norton over his coffee. 'So what's brought this on?'

'She's a dud fuck. She stinks of curry. And she's a wog. Do I need another reason?'

'Well, that's putting it bluntly. You certainly haven't lost your tact.'

'No, fair dinkum, Woz. She's not for me. In fact this whole deal's not our go. You porking that bloke's sheila behind his back, it's not going to get you anywhere.'

16

Warren shrugged. 'I'll worry about . . . '

'But you needn't let it cruel your thing with Gianna. Keep bringing her round here, I don't give a stuff. What you do as a paying boarder in this house is your business. Just count me salmon and trout with Annie. That's all.'

Warren thought for a moment. 'Fair enough,' he shrugged. 'How are you going to tell her?'

'I've left a note.'

Norton handed Warren the brief letter he'd written while packing his bag. Warren opened it and started to read it out loud:

'"Dear Annie. I hate to have to tell you this, but I have just found out I have a girl pregnant back in my home town. We used to be engaged and I thought it was all over between us. Now she's about to have my baby. And I will have to marry her. I never told you about Yirrinbinni. I suppose I should have. I don't know how long I'll be at Fitzroy Crossing. At least till the baby arrives. In the meantime, find yourself another bloke. Someone who deserves you better than me. Love Les. PS. I have left your hairdryer and stockings in a plastic bag near the front door."'

Warren folded the letter up, put it back in its envelope and placed it on the table. 'Touching, Les, touching. Especially the part about her hairdryer and stockings.'

'Well, I didn't want to leave them laying around. You'd only start using them. So just give that to Annie. When are you seeing them? Tomorrow night?' Warren nodded. 'That'll do.' Norton looked at his watch. 'You fancy watching the movie? I've got to be up reasonably early tomorrow.'

'Yeah. So have I. We're having a power breakfast at eight-thirty.'

'Make sure you wear your power tie.'

They took their coffees into the lounge and settled down in front of the TV. If Warren had anything on his mind during James Bond in *From Russia With Love*, he never mentioned it. Their main topic of conversation was that Sean Connery was definitely the best James Bond.

They were both in bed not long after eleven. As Norton closed his eyes and scrunched his head into the pillows, he had to smile. Well, this time tomorrow night I'll be in Surfers Paradise. I wonder what it'll be like? His smile turned into a bit of a laugh. I reckon it'll be all right — despite what Price said. Les had been up at six a.m. to train with a couple of blokes down North Bondi Surf Club. A couple of very fit young detectives, who paddled skis and ran like they were being chased by internal investigators. He had no trouble getting to sleep.

Les and Warren bumped each other in the kitchen around seven. Warren was only having coffee; Norton wasn't all that hungry either, figuring he'd get fed on the plane anyway. Warren was gone before eight. 'See you later, Les. Have a good trip.' 'You too, Woz. Make sure Annie gets that letter.'

Norton got into a pair of jeans, Mambo T-shirt and joggers, checked his overnight-bag to make sure he had everything he needed and put the $500 KK had given him into his wallet. He then went to the secret panel in his wardrobe and looked at the stash he kept in there, drumming his fingers on a panel as he did. Will I? Or won't I? Yeah, why not. He took $2,000 out and stuffed it down the bottom of his overnight-bag. You never know, I might meet a good sort up there. Les went outside to make sure that no desperate could steal his old Ford, then went back inside and settled back, listened to the Rev. Dr Doug and waited. At five past nine a horn tooted out the front. That sounds like my brother. He tossed his bag in the boot, jumped in the back next to KK and they were on their way to Mascot.

KK was wearing the same trousers as the day before with a blue cotton jacket and reading a copy of the *Gold Coast Bulletin*. 'So how are you, Les?' he said, very casually.

'Not bad, KK,' answered Norton. 'How's yourself?'

'Good. Good.' KK continued to flick easily through his paper.

The taxi headed up the steep hill in Wellington Street, past the school, towards Bondi Road.

'So where did you say we'd be staying up there again, KK?' asked Les. Partly out of trying to make conversation, partly out of curiosity.

'My family owns a block of six units right on the beach at Surfers. About five hundred metres from Cavill Avenue. No one's in them at the moment. Crystal and I will be staying in one. You'll be in another.' KK looked up at Les and smiled. 'Five days in your own fully furnished luxury apartment; the beach at your door, five minutes from the heart of Surfers.' KK went back to his paper and shook his head. 'You should be fuckin' paying me.'

'You wouldn't take any money off your brother, would you?'

KK half smiled. 'When we get there, just remember what I told you about those white-shoe gags, Rodney Rude. Okay?'

'You're the boss, KK.'

They were in the first-class section of the plane twenty minutes before take off. Kramer continued to read his paper. There was plenty of room so Norton sat back and checked out the punters getting on the flight. About another three or four got in the first-class section; the rest were mainly couples, families or singles filing into the economy section, probably on package holiday deals. A team of football yobbos from Newcastle surged through, doing their best to let all the other passengers know the Muleville A Grade Mules or whatever they called themselves were on tour. Then a bunch of men, all in their late thirties roared in, wearing yellow Bonds shirts with 'Mac's Head Muff Divers Annual Tour Of Duty' stitched on the front pocket. 'No Muff Too Tough.' Norton checked his watch and shook his head as they drunkenly shoved each other down the aisle. The stewardesses shook their heads as well. Les also noticed the stewardesses steal a glance over at KK now and again, say something to each other and giggle.

Norton hardly had time to read a magazine, eat some

sort of ham quiche and drink the orange juice before they were approaching Coolangatta airport. He didn't have a beer and noticed that although the stewardesses offered them champagne, KK, the international playboy, wasn't bothering either.

'I thought you liked drinking champagne?' enquired Les.

'I do, Les,' replied KK indifferently. 'Champagne, not Flemington Blush, or whatever it is they throw at you on Australian airlines.'

'Fair enough,' agreed Norton.

The stewardesses flung themselves in front of the curtain separating first class from economy when they landed so those up front could get off before the riff-raff surged through. The next thing Les and KK were walking across bright, sunny and windy Coolangatta airport. Their bags were the first two on the conveyor belt. As KK went to get his, Les picked it up for him.

'It ain't heavy,' he winked. 'It's my brother's.'

KK shrugged, gave another half smile and nodded for Les to follow him across to the Hertz counter. Out in the hire section of the carpark, KK checked the car number plates then opened the boot of one to let Norton throw their bags in.

'Okay, Les,' he said, handing him the key. 'You can start earning your money. You know how to drive one of these?'

Norton looked at the brand new maroon XJS Jaguar with the spoiler on the boot, and shrugged. 'I'll soon learn.'

Inside, the XJS was pure air-conditioned luxury. Four-speaker stereo, power everything; the seat felt better than the one behind the desk in Price's office.

'So what's doing, KK?' asked Les, as he familiarised himself with the dash. 'Is this going to be our transport while we're up here?'

'No. We'll be getting around in a limo most of the time. I'll just keep this on standby in case I need to go to the laundromat.'

20

The Jag had five on the floor. Les backed out and gingerly moved through the carpark to the Gold Coast Highway, stopping for the light at the intersection.

'Left?'

KK nodded. 'Left.'

The light changed, Norton eased into the traffic, slipped the Jag into second, looked at the speedo and nearly shit himself. They were doing seventy-five. 'Christ!' he said out loud, and tried to ease down into third. There was no noise, no nothing and he'd barely looked hard at the accelerator. 'Bloody hell!'

KK grinned at Norton, then suddenly banged him on the shoulder with his rolled up paper. 'Go for it, Les,' he laughed. 'Let 'em know KK's back in town.' KK continued to laugh. 'Ahh, it's good to be back on the Coast.'

But Les didn't 'go for it' as KK told him. He would have liked to; it would have been something else to put his foot down and let that V-12 do its thing. But a $1,000 fine and doing his license for twelve months would have taken the shine right off his five days on the Gold Coast; plus who knows what might come up alongside his name on a Queensland police computer. So Norton just stuck to the speed limit and cruised along in comfort with the sun streaming in through the sun-roof while the little conman cackled away alongside him. Pointing out different high-rises he'd been involved with, or ones built by someone he knew, or others built by someone using Japanese money who'd slung either the council or some politician to get it all together. And there was no shortage of them. In fact that's all there seemed to be on either side of the highway: shops, restaurants, blocks of flats and monstrous high-rises. It was as if some giant in a pair of white shoes had taken fifty kilometres of beautiful coastline and dropped hundreds of AMP buildings all along the beachfront. Or as close to it as you could get. Surfers has sure changed since the last time I was here, mused Norton, as he looked out at all the development that had brought money and employment and its accompanying crime and corruption to the

21

Gold Coast. Yeah, they sure got what they wanted, but they lost what they had.

It was pleasant enough, however, motoring grandly along the ample highway, some FM station playing a bit of Jenny Morris, the sun beaming down, tapping the accelerator every now and again to effortlessly overtake any cars. Les couldn't help but chuckle a little to himself. When he'd left Queensland he was more or less on the run from the law with the arse just about out of his pants. Now he was back with $2,500 in his kick, driving a brand new Jaguar and about to meet an international film star. Has the country boy come good or what? Norton wasn't quite sure. Yes, it wouldn't be hard to get roped into this sort of lifestyle. Then he looked over at KK's oily, fat little face, cackling away behind his glasses. Yeah. For about five fuckin' days.

A sign on their left said Neptune's Casino, where KK said he and Crystal intended having a bit of a flutter on Saturday night; and a few kilometres further on to their right, just before the heart of Surfers, KK pointed out another sign, Hancock Avenue, and told Les to turn right.

'It's the block right at the very end, on The Esplanade.'

Norton turned slowly down a short street crammed with landscaped blocks of flats and high-rises standing almost cheek by jowl; each with the mandatory two pools in the back. At the end he came to a smaller block of brick colonial flats with a kind of Spanish appearance, facing them from the adjacent street.

'Pull up in one of those driveways out the front.'

The Jag rocked gently to a halt and Les cut the engine.

The block of flats was three storeys, two flats per floor, and all the garages spread round the bottom. What wasn't a kind of orange-coloured brick was painted white with ochre-tinted tiles and was neither super modern nor flash but seemed to have heaps of character. The two larger flats on top had sun-decks front and back with large sliding glass windows and doors. Where the garages finished were two white wooden gates, then a high brick security fence also in matching brick and tile. A solid security door in frosted glass and oak was set in the front, and above this a sign, red on white, said 'Zapato Blanco'. There was a high-rise on the left, another block of flats on the right with the beach right at the back door.

'Well, what do you reckon?' said KK, as they got out of the car.

'Very bloody nice,' replied Norton sincerely, as he opened the boot and handed KK his bag. 'I could handle living here. Very nice indeed.'

KK let Norton take the place in for a moment or two. 'Just remember what I told you about those white-shoe gags.'

Norton wasn't sure but KK seemed to be looking at him a little odd. 'If you've told me once, KK, you've told me a thousand times. I think I've got the picture by now.'

'But I've got some good news for you.'

'Yeah? You gonna give me that other grand now — are you?'

Kramer smiled. 'You've got the afternoon off. And tonight.'

'Yeah?'

KK nodded and checked his watch. 'There'll be a bloke coming round in about an hour I want you to meet. I'll be with him part of the time, he's in the music industry. Then after that.' Kramer made an expansive gesture with his arms. 'Enjoy.'

'Sounds all right to me.'

'You won't be able to take the car because I'll probably need it. You'll be sweet though. But tomorrow, we leave here at eleven to pick Crystal up in Brisbane at one. All the media rattle starts after that.'

'Rattle and hum, eh?'

'Don't worry, Les. You'll have plenty to keep you occupied till Tuesday. And keep your eyes off my girl's tits too.'

'That and the white-shoe gags?'

KK seemed as if he was trying not to grin. 'I think you've got it.'

23

Kramer gave Les a key, which he said was a master key to every door in the flats including the garage. Then he opened the security door and they walked up two flights of nicely carpeted brown stairs with white walls and indoor-plants to their flats, KK's on the right, Norton's on the left.

Holy shit! said Norton to himself, as he stepped inside and closed the door behind him. How good's this? The flat was two bedrooms, fully furnished, with an en-suite and queen-size bed in the master bedroom. Thick beige carpet lead past a massive bathroom and laundry into the loungeroom. The furniture was expensive and comfortable; paintings on the walls and a large glass table and chairs sitting in front of a modern kitchen. Thick, dark curtains drew back across floor-to-ceiling sliding glass doors to give a million-dollar view north and south of Surfers Paradise and out over the ocean. From Norton's point of view the beach was that white it almost looked like snow, and the water blue and inviting.

The only thing that struck Les as a little curious when he stepped out onto the sundeck was a kidney-shaped pool in the backyard completely drained. Oh well, he thought, who gives a stuff when you've got all that ocean; and a set of stairs at the edge of the sundeck told him you'd be there in less than a minute. A flick of a switch told him the remote-control TV worked perfectly, as did the stereo alongside, and a check of the kitchen told him it was fully appointed — there was even a jar of coffee, sugar and a carton of milk and several cans of soft drink in the softly humming fridge. The phone, sitting on a kind of bar-cum-table, worked also.

Oh well, surmised Les, I imagine KK would have a caretaker who'd know when he was arriving. Les had another look around then started unpacking and hanging up his clothes, putting his shaving gear and that in the en-suite. And to think I'm getting paid for this. He gave a little wink towards the sky. How sweet it is.

With the FM radio drifting in from the lounge-room, Les took his time unpacking, leaving his ghetto-blaster in the bedroom. He changed into a pair of grey canvas shorts and a white T-shirt, made a cup of coffee and stepped out onto the sundeck. There were a number of people dotted along the beach and a thick cluster near the flags in front of the surf club about five hundred metres or so north. A number of brightly coloured kites of various shapes and sizes drifted and fluttered in the breeze above the beach, and, if Les wasn't mistaken, some radio station was setting up a kind of a promotion with a DJ and dancers on the beach.

He made another cup of coffee then opened the sliding glass doors on the other balcony to let some air through and take in another view. Traffic swished past or slowed down, tourists on hired motorscooters, the odd tour bus, people walking or riding pushbikes. A very balmy, touristy scene in the warm, Gold Coast sunshine. Ahh Queensland, thought Norton, as he happily sipped his coffee. Monday one day. Tuesday the next.

Les was leisurely sipping his coffee when a large, dark green BMW saloon with tinted windows came down Hancock, stopped for the traffic then pulled up in the driveway alongside the Jaguar. Two men in their late twenties, one stocky, the other more Norton's size, got out wearing T-shirts, trousers and light cotton jackets. The stocky one opened the back door and as he did Norton got a quick glimpse of a gun sitting in a holster near his kidneys. A tallish man around forty or so got out, wearing a white shirt, brown trousers and matching shoes, and gold-rimmed sunglasses. He had straight blond hair combed across his face, and from the angle of his jaw and mouth he didn't look like the happiest person Les had ever seen in his life. He said something to the two younger men and they walked to the front door; the taller man noticed Les on the sundeck, said something and they all looked up. Norton caught their eye and came inside.

This must be KK's mate from the music industry, mused Les. S'pose I'd better play minder and let them in. Funny about the gun, he thought, as he went down the stairs. Then again maybe that's what they mean in the

25

pop music business when they say, this record's number one with a bullet. They'd barely rapped on the door when Les opened it.

'Hello,' said Norton cheerfully. 'You must be from the Mormon's. I'll have a *Watchtower*.'

All three looked at Les impassively, then the older man spoke. His voice was very clipped and completely lacking in humour, noticeably rolling the Ks and Rs as he spoke. 'I believe Mr Kramer is expecting me.'

'Yeah, sure. Come on in.' Les opened the door and stood to one side.

The older man turned to the others. 'Wait 'ere,' he said, then stepped inside.

Norton gave the other two a smile. 'Gotta keep the flies out,' he winked, then closed the door in their faces.

'Up here, mate.' Norton lead the fair-haired man up the stairs. 'You must be KK's friend from the music industry?'

'That is korrrect.'

Norton waited a moment or two as they walked up the stairs. 'Nice day outside.'

'Yes, it is rawther.'

Mmmhhh, thought Les. 'Korrect. Rawther. Wait 'ere.' I'm not all that smawt, but I reckon this bloke's from Sowth Efrika. They got to KK's door. Les knocked. KK opened the door, saw the blond man and smiled.

'Meyer, how are you? Good to see you.'

'Yes. You too, Kelvin.'

'Les, this is Mr Meyer Black.'

'Pleased to meet you, Mr Black.' Meyer nodded, but didn't offer his hand.

'I'll be spending part of the time up here with Mr Black. On business.'

'Okey doke.' Norton gave Black a smile, then turned back to Kramer. 'Anything you want me to do?'

Kramer shook his head. 'No. We'll be okay.'

'All right. Well, if you want to give me the keys, I might move the car into the garage.'

'Not a bad idea.' Meyer stepped into the flat. KK got the keys and handed them to Les.

26

'If you need me for anything, I'll be in the flat.'

'Good on you, Les.' Kramer gave Norton a smile and closed the door.

Norton jangled the keys as he thought for a moment, then trotted back down the stairs. While I'm shifting the car I might as well meet those other two young executives from the record industry. You never know, they might make me the next Slim Dusty.

Meyer Black's two business associates were leaning against one side of the BMW watching a couple of girls walk past when Norton came out the front door. They turned briefly, Les gave them a smile and a bit of a wave; they nodded just as briefly behind their sunglasses and continued watching the two girls.

The garage was grey concrete inside, fairly clean with more than enough room for the Jag. Les had it garaged and the roller-door locked in less than five minutes. The two executives had finished perving on the girls, so Les decided to go over and maybe say hello.

'So how's it goin', fellahs? All right?'

The two men moved away from the car and stood not quite in front of Les. Not quite menacingly, more an air of easy awareness.

'Yeah, not bad,' said the shorter one with dark hair.

Norton had come across this type of bloke before. Professional security men. Hard, fit, alert. They'd know all about knives, guns, fast driving, and if you took them too lightly in a bit of grappling you could come off awfully bruised.

'I'm Les, anyway.'

The stocky one looked at Norton a moment, then offered his hand. 'Steve.'

'Steve.'

'And this is Frank.'

'How are you, Frank?'

Shaking hands with Steve and Frank definitely wasn't like grabbing hold of two chocolate eclairs and they didn't come on with those bodgie California grips either. Norton was impressed.

27

'Kelvin says we might be seeing a bit of each other over the next few days. I was up there waiting for you.' Frank and Steve didn't say anything. 'With all this Crystal Linx rattle.'

'Ohh yeah, that,' said Steve.

'I'm just helping Kelvin and her with the press barrage and the fans. Get them home safely and that.' Norton shrugged. 'It's a few days' work.' Frank and Steve nodded, but didn't say anything. 'So how's the pop music business going?'

Frank looked at Steve for a second. 'Pop music?'

'Yeah. Kelvin told me Mr Black owns a record company in Brisbane. He's promoting Crystal's new record.'

'Ohh, the record company. In Brisbane.' said Steve. 'It's going good.'

'Keeps us busy,' added Frank.

'You been working for Mr Black long?'

Frank seemed to think for a moment. 'About a year or so.'

'Yeah. He doesn't seem like a bad bloke. I had a bit of a mag to him going up the stairs. He's South African, eh?'

'Johannesburgh,' said Steve. 'He was in the record business over there.'

'I'm from Sydney myself. Where are you blokes from? You gotta be Queenslanders?'

'Brisbane,' answered Frank, not with a great deal of interest.

'Brisbane, eh?' Les shook his head. 'Jees, I haven't been there in a while.'

Norton continued to make small talk long enough for him to figure out that Steve and Frank were handing out answers like gold watches and were probably wishing he'd piss off. He was about to say goodbye when Meyer and KK walked out the front door. Frank got straight behind the wheel, Steve opened the back door without bothering to ask Les to get out of the way. KK was leading; Norton handed him the keys and smiled.

'I put it in number two.'

'Good on you, Les,' said KK, taking the keys.

Meyer was waiting for him to get in first. KK made a quick gesture with his hands. 'Well, like I said Les. You've got the night off. I don't know when I'll be back. Just remember, it's all on tomorrow.'

'Okay. I'll see you in the morning.' Norton stepped back to let Meyer into the car. 'Nice to have met you, Mr Black.'

'Yes. You too, Les.'

Steve closed the door, got in beside Frank and in no time the BMW was across The Esplanade, heading down Hancock. Norton watched them off, giving a friendly wave. He took his time walking up the stairs to his flat, he took his time getting a glass of ice-water and he took his time drinking it out on the back sundeck in the breeze. So, Mr Meyer Black, thought Les, as he watched a handful of surfers catching a few swells that were closing out a bit in the slightly onshore wind. If you're in the record business, my Sowth Efrikan friend, Saddam Hussein's in the Salvation Army. You might be, but somehow that brief chat with your two gorillas makes me think different. You don't need pros with guns to go round sticking records in juke-boxes.

The longer Norton sipped his ice-water, the more he was convinced there was skulduggery afoot and he might make a phone call later on. Oh well, he shrugged, so what if KK is putting on some sort of a stroke. I can't see it involving me. If it does, I'm on the toe. He can do what he fuckin' likes. Les drained his glass and flung the ice out into the empty swimming pool. All I know is, I've got the night off and I'm all cashed up. And the afternoon too. So what will I do?

Les went to his bedroom, looked out the window then looked at his training gear. I could have a run and do a heap of sit ups. In this heat? How about I go for a nice long walk and check out the Gold Coast. Leaving what he had on, he went out to the kitchen where he'd left his sunglasses next to some money he'd absently dropped near the phone. Norton picked up a twenty cent coin and flicked it into the air. Heads north, tails south. Five

29

minutes later the flats were secure and Les was across the beach, heading at a brisk pace along the firm sand at the water's edge towards Main Beach.

Norton was right about the disco set-up. It was a local radio station along with some nightclub getting a promotion going, on the beach, right in front of the sprawl of shops and high-rises surrounding Cavill Avenue. He stopped for a while to watch about half a dozen young girls, mainly blondes, bumping and hoofing around in their bikinis to the usual Madonna, Prince, or whatever dance music. Three of the girls were all right, the others could have played half-back for South Sydney. The crowd on the beach seemed to be enjoying it, whistling and cheering as a couple of cops in shorts hovered round in case any mugs got too out of control. Not a bad turn-out for nothing on a Thursday afternoon in the sun, mused Les, and continued walking.

Walking along the beach was more than pleasant. The low tide ensured plenty of firm, damp sand and the light sou'-easter behind was welcome because it was certainly hot enough. There were plenty of others walking too; people of all ages, sex, nationalities, shapes and sizes. Some would smile, some would even give a quick greeting. All except the Japanese. They avoided eye contact as if their lives depended on it, and appeared absolutely terrified to say 'g'day'. Well, up yours too, thought Les. And your whaling companies, your drift-nets and your attitude towards the environment in general. Shitty little bastards.

About another three kilometres on, the crowd started to thin out then thickened a little as he got to Main Beach. There were still kilometres of beach ahead and although it was still pleasant, it was starting to get a little monotonous. Les checked out a few punters and girls on the beach then decided to have a walk round the back streets and head home.

He ran across The Esplanade, half walking, half jogging along the streets heading towards the highway. It was mainly blocks of flats, a few houses and no shortage of high-rises. He found a small shopping centre and bought a soft-drink, crossed walkways and stopped on a bridge over the Nerang River to watch several speedboats zooming across the water and around the canals beneath. There were more high-rises with each one seeming as if it was trying to out do the other. The ultimate was a purple, mauve, pink and blue monstrosity that appeared to be a hundred storeys high. It looked like something on the cover of one of those big, glossy, fantastic planet, science-fiction magazines; and if some bloke in a space-suit riding on the back of a pterodactyl came flying around the building carrying a ray-gun, Les would not have been in the least bit surprised.

In a back street, just off the highway, something a little nicer and with a lot more character caught his eye. Tucked in amongst the flats and high-rises was a small, two-storey boarding house. It had to be, because a sign out the front said, 'Boarding House. Mrs Llivac Proprietor. Vacancy.' It was white timber, and four blue poles held up a verandah right across the front, dotted with comfy old seats and chairs. The iron railing was red and blue and ran into a set of steps at one end. There were two glass doors in the front and in the centre was the main door with a fly-screen on it. If Norton wasn't mistaken, an old grey cat was asleep on one of the seats. Yellow and red bougainvillea meandered through the wooden lattice work beneath the verandah, with a sizeable garden in front of that and a white picket fence separating it from the road. There was a woman pottering around in the garden wearing a loose blue dress and a straw hat. She looked about forty, not a bad style, maybe a little plump with tarty blonde hair poking out from beneath her hat. She had healthy brown skin and a happy brown face which seemed to accentuate the bright pink lipstick round her mouth.

She noticed Les looking at the flowers, looked up and smiled. 'Hello there,' she said pleasantly. 'How are you doin'?'

31

If Norton wasn't mistaken, there was the hint of an American accent.

'Pretty good thanks. How's yourself?'

'Fine. Jes fine.'

'Nice garden you've got. You must put a lot of work into it.'

The woman pushed her hat back a little. 'Oh, all the dust and soot coming in off the highway doesn't help much. But I get by. Just as long as I keep at it.'

'In fact,' said Les, 'that's a nice house you've got all round. You must be the last boarding house left round here. How come the developers never got to you?'

'Goddam white shoes. They've been trying hard enough. But I'm quite happy the way I am.'

'Good on you,' laughed Norton. 'In fact, if I wasn't already booked in somewhere, I'd probably stay here myself.'

'You could do a lot worse.' The woman smiled generously. 'And I make the best deep-dish apple pie on the Gold Coast. And that's a fact.'

'I'll bet you do, maam,' grinned Les. 'I'll just bet you do. Anyway, I got to get going. Nice talking to you. Goodbye.'

'You take care now, you hear.'

Norton was still chuckling to himself almost a kilometre along the highway. Well, isn't it nice to know there's still some genuine people in the world. He strode on in the heat and before long he was back in the main drag of shops and high-rises approaching Cavill Avenue.

Les could hardly believe the difference. One minute he was chatting to a pleasant lady over her fence. The next thing it was traffic, stop-lights, noise, people surging along the footpath past hotels, arcades, a TAB. Photo shops, food shops, shops selling everything from a T-shirt for $5 to a house on a canal for quarter of a million. Asian spielers jumped out of jewellery shop doors at the Japanese tourists. Other spielers, mainly women, jumped out at everyone and they all seemed to zero in on Les. 'Can I interest you? Did you know that? Would you like to take

32

advantage?' By the time he made it to Cavill Avenue, Norton felt like he had a big question mark on his forehead and a beanie with a propeller sitting on top. Cavill Avenue appeared to be a huge mall with pine trees running down the middle. To the right was the Nerang River, the other way led to the beach. Les decided to walk down to the beach.

It was another surge of people, this time going past restaurants, discos, outdoor eateries, more shops selling T-shirts, other shops, Ripleys Believe It Or Not, all stacked one on top of the other; plus more arcades, a shopping centre and two currency exchanges jammed in amongst this. There was a post office on one corner and a hotel with mirrored windows on the other. A street ran off to the left. Les thought he'd check that out on the way back. Another white shoette collared him just as he crossed the corner; Norton told her to piss off.

Les strolled amongst the outdoor restaurants, stopping to watch some girls with a huge rag-doll tied to a pole, braiding coloured do-dads into people's hair. A country and western band was starting to set up, and a busker in an Akubra hat was wailing away near a sunken chess board next to a bronze statue of two kids examining a sea shell. Yes, well it's all happening in sunny Surfers, thought Les, as he strolled down to The Esplanade corner.

A McDonald's overlooked the beach on one corner and a Hungry Jack's on the other, with no shortage of punters, mainly tourists, stuffing themselves with Big Macs or Bacon Burgers De-Luxe. The disco on the beach had packed up and the high-rises were throwing shadows right across to the water's edge. Les thought he'd check out the street he'd seen earlier. On the way, he strolled into an arcade, bright, modern, mainly white marble, crammed with shops and lots of lush greenery. A huge white statue of Michaelangelo's *David* stood above a fountain, his wozzer pointing out over the shops, punters, chairs and tables and a bank of Chinese eateries where for $3 you could stuff yourself with Chinese food till it was coming out of your ears. Norton stood there for a moment or two and watched a swarm of people doing exactly that. He walked on to the street he'd seen earlier.

The whole street seemed to be crammed cheek by jowl with discos or nightclubs and more arcades. A sort of fair-sized bar called the Boulevarde, built out onto the footpath, caught his eye and he was almost tempted to have a couple of hundred beers after the long, hot walk. But something more appealing was right behind him. A nice little health-food shop with chairs and tables out the front called the Love Train. It was cool and green inside with all these lovely little posters on the wall: Remember Yesterday, Dream About Tomorrow, But Live Today. May You Always Have The Freedom To Be Yourself. The World Is Full Of Beauty When The Heart Is Full Of Love. I like the last one, thought Les sincerely. Tell it to that curry-eating bag back in Sydney. The people behind the counter couldn't have been any nicer. Norton ordered an Orange Julius, which went down in about two swallows. Then a Hunza pie and a Real Choky, which he took his time over at a table out the front while he watched the punters go past.

Yes, things could be a lot worse, mused Les. Heaps. I'm sitting in the sun, I've got money and a top place to stay. One certainly can't complain. The last piece of Hunza pie went down along with the Real Choky. He patted his muscled stomach. Well, that was all right for a snack. What about tea and what am I going to do tonight? Fuck cooking anything, there's too many grouse-looking restaurants around for that. And I suppose I'll be dining out with KK and Miss America mostly. But I'm going to have to have a drink. Imagine if friends popped in and there's nothing in the fridge. It would be embarrassing, to say the least. There was a bottleshop barely twenty metres directly in front of him. He bought two dozen bottles of Power's Red Stripe, a bottle of Jim Beam Green Label and two large Diet Pepsis. That should do till tomorrow. But I don't feel like lumping this back in the heat. He was about to start looking for a taxi when something else he'd noticed earlier made him smile. He strolled back up to the corner next to the hotel with the mirrored windows.

There were three pedi cabs sitting there, with the drivers, two men and a girl, either sitting on or standing next to them. Naturally Norton chose the girl. She was in her twenties, scraggly brown hair jammed under a sweat band, no make-up, wearing a pair of football shorts and a stained, loose fitting kind of singlet. Her mouth was set and Les couldn't tell what her eyes looked like because she was wearing dark sunglasses.

'You know Hancock Avenue?' he said.

'Sure do,' replied the girl, probably having been asked the same question a thousand times by the same number of yobbo male tourists.

'Down the end, on The Esplanade.'

'Righto.'

Norton got into the pedi-cab, placing his booze at his feet; the girl slipped the bike into low gear, got up on the pedals to do a U-turn out of the Mall, and the next thing they were on the highway heading south.

The red-headed Queenslander didn't quite know what to think as they whirred along in the traffic. He felt like a real yobbo tourist, a big bloke getting some sheila to cart his frame round for a laugh. Also, it felt terrific sitting back after that long, hot walk with the afternoon breeze blowing over his face. But the view, right in front of where Norton was sitting, was the best he'd seen since he got off the plane. The girl driving the pedi-cab had a backside that would break your heart; sitting on a long, muscled pair of brown legs that ran all the way up to it. There was just the right amount of condition in her tanned back, running across her shoulders into her arms; and under the singlet, there wasn't a part of her moved that shouldn't. Norton didn't get a look at her melon, but she had a figure that made some aerobics instructors he knew in Sydney look like Roseanne Barr.

'So how long've you been doing this?' he asked her.

'Ohh, about six months,' answered the girl.

'Hard way to get a dollar.'

'You're not kidding. Keeps me fit though.'

'I imagine it would,' answered Les, nodding his head enthusiastically, as the girl got up on the pedals again to go round a stopping taxi.

'But this is my last bloody night. Thank Christ!'

'Yeah?'

'Yeah. I'm out of here after tonight. And out of Surfers next Tuesday.'

'Fair dinkum? Where are you going?'

'Taree. You know where that is?'

'Yeah. I've driven through there a few times.'

'I got family there.'

'How are you getting there? Taking the pedi-cab?'

'No,' laughed the girl. 'I get the bus Tuesday morning. I share a flat with a couple of other girls. I move out. Another's moving in.'

'Sounds like a good way to see Australia.'

'Australia, yeah.' The girl had to get back up on the pedals to stop them getting crushed by a truck. 'Not bloody Surfers.'

They swung into Hancock and by the time they got to The Esplanade corner the view was still as good as ever. Better if anything. Especially when the girl got back up on the pedals as they took the driveway in front of the flats.

'How much do I owe you?' asked Les getting out of the pedi-cab with his booze.

'Six bucks'll do.'

'Here you are.' Norton gave the girl a twenty. 'Keep that.'

'Oh. Thanks very much.'

It was worth it for the bloody view, thought Les. That wasn't all he was thinking. 'You look a bit thirsty. I've gotta take this stuff upstairs. There's couple of cans of soft-drink in the fridge. Do you want me to bring you one down?'

The girl looked at Les for a minute. 'Okay,' she shrugged.

Norton was up the stairs, his booze in the fridge and back down with two cans of Solo quicker than it takes Angry Anderson to comb his hair.

'There you go,' he said, ripping off the ring-pull and handing it to the girl.

'Thanks,' she said. 'Thanks a lot.'

'You're welcome.' The girl took a hefty swallow. Norton watched her, taking a swig himself.

'What's your name?'

'Des.'

'Des. I'm Les.'

'Nice to meet you, Les,' smiled the girl.

'So this is your last night working in Surfers, Des?'

'Yep. Thank Christ!'

'I'm only up here for a few days myself. Working for the bloke that owns these flats.'

'Kelvin Kramer.'

'You know him?'

'Everybody does, don't they?'

'He's bringing out his girl, Crystal Linx. You know her?'

'The sheila with big boobs.'

'That's her. I'm helping them with the media rattle. Till she goes back on Tuesday.'

'Have fun.'

Norton sipped his drink. 'So how's the pedi-cab business, Des? How much would you make a night? If you don't mind me asking. I suppose you'd do all right?'

Des looked at Norton a second. 'I only lease the thing. It's not mine. By the time I pay the company and that,' she shrugged, 'I might make a hundred. Hundred'n'fifty. Whatever.'

'How about I make you an offer, Des?' The girl continued to look at Norton over her soft-drink. 'How about I hire your pedi-cab for the night? Only, leave the pedi-cab behind and we'll go by taxi.'

'What are you talking about?'

'Here you are.' Les handed the girl $200. 'I'll hire you. Come out with me for the night. It's got to be better than pushing that thing around in the traffic.'

The girl looked at Les through her sunglasses, then her mouth turned down. 'Who the ... hell do you think you

37

are? Here.' She flung the $200 back at Norton. 'Take your money and stick it in your arse.' Les managed to catch the two hundred. But not the can of Solo. It got him right in the chest. 'And your soft-drink too.' The girl glared at Norton dripping Solo. 'You mug tourists. You're all the same. Hire me for the night. What you're looking for, shithead, is in the local yellow-pages. Under M. For mug. Get stuffed.'

The girl got up on the pedals as Norton grabbed the handlebars. 'Hey, look, Des, I'm sorry. That's not what I meant. You've taken me the wrong way.' Des glared at Norton, but he had the handlebars in a grip of steel and she wasn't going anywhere. 'All I meant was, come out with me for dinner. And have a few drinks, if you wanted. I've got a heap of money. Kramer's paying for it all. You could have a nice meal and you wouldn't lose a night's wages. If you thought I meant something else, I'm sorry, Des. I really am.' Norton looked at her for a moment then let go of the handlebars.

The girl continued to glare at Norton from behind her dark glasses, then settled down a bit. 'Okay, fair enough. It's just that...'

'That's okay. I do make a bit of a mug of myself at times. But I'm still fair dinkum.' Les handed her the $200. 'Here, take the money anyway. And if you still want to come out for a bit of nosh...?'

Des looked evenly at Norton for a moment. 'Okay,' she answered, slowly nodding her head. 'You're on. But if you so much as...'

Norton made a gesture with his hands. 'On my bank manager's life. Dinner and drinks, anywhere you like. Home when you like.'

'I live down towards Main Beach. You know where that is?'

'I'll be in a taxi anyway.'

'Here's the address.' Des took a notebook and biro from beneath the seat. 'And my phone number.' She handed it to Norton and smiled. 'What time?'

'What time suits you?'

'Eight?'

'See you at eight.'

'Okay, Les.'

'Hey, before you go.' Norton reached down and picked up the can of Solo Des had flung at him. 'You want to finish your drink?'

Des looked at Norton grinning and grinned herself. 'How about I have some of yours?' She grabbed Norton's can of soft-drink, took a swig then handed it back to him. 'See you tonight.'

Les barely had time to wave before she turned into The Esplanade and headed towards Cavill Avenue.

Well, raise my rent, smiled Les to himself. How about that. I've got a nice dinner date for tonight. And nothing wrong with her either. Let's just hope she doesn't wear that singlet. But with my $220 in her kick, she could buy herself another dozen. Norton's smile got bigger. Who gives a stuff. Let's just hope she turns up. There is something about that girl I like. And it isn't just the view. He had another look at the piece of paper Des had given him. Les was still looking at it, sitting by the phone, as he pulled his joggers off in the lounge-room.

After that long, hot walk, the ocean, from out the balcony window, looked bluer and more inviting than ever. As soon as he had his shorts off, Norton had a towel over his shoulders and was jogging across the soft white sand at the back of the flats. The water was absolutely beautiful. No hint of a chill, clean and sweet. Like swimming in a mixture of velvet and perfume, mused Les as he splashed around happily. He caught a couple of waves and just had a wallow in general as he watched some surfers a little further out and the people walking past, all taking advantage of the afternoon's coolness by the sea following a fairly hot day. The big Queenslander felt good; the dinner date with Des making it better again. He followed this with a long, steamy shower and a close shave then rubbed a bit of cream on his moosh.

With his hair still wet and a towel around him Les went

to the kitchen, got a bottle of Red Stripe from the fridge and decided it was time to make a phone call. For some reason the STD pips didn't sound on the other end of the line.

'Yeah, hello.'

'How are you, Price? It's Les.'

'Les. Where are you ringing from? Up there?'

'Yeah, and it's all right too. What are you up to?'

'Ohh not much. Just sitting here watching TV. Bit of something on my mind.'

'Yeah. What's that?'

'I'm getting a bit sick of this Boris Battinof. He's no good. I think I might get Eddie to go pay him a visit.'

'Yeah, you're not wrong. He's a dropkick all right.'

'All the time — make big trouble for Moose and Skvirrel. I think I fix.'

'Sure you do. And Natasha too.'

'Yeah. His rotten sheila's just as bad.' Price gave a bit of a silly laugh. 'Hey, before I forget. I want you to do something for me while you're up there.'

'Sure.'

'You'll see a bloke right on the beach at Surfers. He runs the beach hire, and sprays people with suntan lotion. His name's Jim Martin.'

'Yeah?'

'He's an old mate of mine. Go and say hello for me, and ask him if he's had any oysters Amos lately.'

'Oysters Amos?'

'You got it.' Price chuckled away again for a moment or two then quietened down. 'Now what's going on?'

'Does the name Meyer Black mean anything to you, Price?'

Norton told his boss about his brief meeting with the South African and his two heavies. Describing him right down to his accent.

'Meyer Black, eh.' Price chuckled again. 'Yeah, I know him. I've done a bit of business with him myself. He's a nogoodnik. He's a smuggler. Among other things.'

'A smuggler?'

'Yeah. Gold kruggerands, diamonds, arms. He lives

40

up there most of the time. But he flits between Sydney, Hong Kong and South Africa. Calls himself an importer. I haven't seen him for a while, so I wouldn't be surprised what he's up to now.'

'So forget about the record business, eh?'

'Hah! The only record's Meyer's interested in is how many he can break making money. He loves the stuff. And he's absolutely ruthless too. If that greasy little reffo's mixed up with him, watch yourself.'

'You needn't worry. I've already thought of that.'

They chatted on a little longer. Price added what he could about Black. Les said to say hello to Myra and he'd give that message to the bloke on the beach. And he'd be in touch if need be.

So, thought Norton, after he'd hung up, Meyer Black — smuggler. Well, that'd be right. What comes out of South Africa? Gold, diamonds and arms, I imagine. Les snapped his fingers. That's probably why Manny was coming up. Maybe they were doing an arms scam and now there's a hassle because Manny's got himself nicked in WA. I notice KK didn't bother to introduce me as his brother either. Mmmhh. Anyway, I'll just keep acting the big, dumb minder. But I'll be keeping my big, dumb minder's eyes open. Les looked at the phone again and this awful, cunning, evil smile began to flicker round his narrowing brown eyes. Funny how those pips didn't sound. I think I might make another phone call while I'm at it. He went to the bedroom and got a piece of paper from his wallet. Gee, it was nice of Annie to give me her cousin's phone number, just in case I might have to ring her there sometime. Stopping himself from smiling, he pushed the appropriate buttons on the phone.

'Hello,' came a man's voice.

'Is that John?' Norton spoke a little softer and closer than normal.

'Yeah.'

'Mate, you don't know me. I'm an electrician. I worked on a few jobs with you and I always found you a good bloke.'

41

'Yeah, so?'

'Mate, I don't know how to tell you this, and maybe it's none of my business, but my wife said I should. Did you know your girl's seeing another bloke behind your back?'

'What!?'

'It's been going on for a while, mate. He lives at Bondi, and he's a real little cunt too.'

Norton could hear the bloke's teeth grinding over the phone and the steam hissing out of his ears. He gave him his address and said if he got there around eight on a Friday night he'd catch them at the front door. He told the bloke again he was sorry to have to do this, but it was mainly his wife's idea and they both didn't like to see a good bloke being dumped on.

'So that's it, John. You can work it out for yourself.'

'I will, mate, I will. You needn't fuckin' worry about that.'

Then the phone went dead.

Norton looked at it for a moment and took another swig of beer. Well, at least if he punches up Warren out the front, he won't wreck any furniture. And I can always wash the blood off the front steps. Besides, how many times have I told Warren he's gonna have to learn to fight sooner or later. Well, here it comes. Lesson number one. Always keep your guard up.

He finished his beer, went back to the bathroom, combed his hair and splashed a little Tabac on his face. The face looking back at him in the mirror definitely wasn't the face of a good bloke. Jesus, you're a cunt, Les. You really are. Suddenly Norton's face burst into a grin. No, I'm not. I'm Jewish. And I'm proud.

By the time he changed into a pair of blue slacks, the blue Italian casuals and a light denim button-down-collar shirt, then had another half a bottle of beer and watched the ABC news, it was about time to call a taxi. Ten minutes later it was bipping the horn out the front and Les was on his way to Main Beach.

The address the girl had given him wasn't far from the shops where Les had had a can of soft-drink during his

42

afternoon walk. He got out and told the driver to wait. It was a squat brick block of six with a low brick fence and a small yard out the front, not unlike some blocks you see around Bondi Junction. A short, steep flight of steps, with no landing, led up to Flat 1 on the bottom left. Les knocked then came back down a few steps. The door opened and a tallish sort of girl stood there; Norton couldn't make her face out because of the light behind her.

'Yes?' she said, looking down at him.

'Is Des there, please?'

'Who?'

'Des. The girl with the pedi-cab. She's expecting me.'

The girl continued to look down at Les. 'No one here by that name.'

Norton's heart sank slightly. I knew it. I just fuckin' knew it. 'This is Flat 1/177 . . .?'

'Oh come in, you big dope. You're looking at her.'

The girl stepped aside to let a slightly puzzled Les inside and closed the door. But it definitely wasn't the girl wearing the daggy shorts and sweaty singlet Norton had shared a can of soft-drink with earlier. This one was wearing a tight, sleeveless, yellow dress with a zig-zag front, cut just above her cleavage and matching high-heeled shoes. It came past her knees where a split up the side revealed two sensational tanned legs and no stockings. The scraggly brown hair was washed and braided to a softness that brushed lightly across her shoulders, and hidden behind those dark glasses earlier were the deepest, most beautiful green eyes Les had ever seen. They were like dampened emeralds in moonlight. She wore the barest hint of lip-gloss, plus enough eye make-up to make things interesting, and the tantalising scent of some fragrant, sweet body oil hung in the air from her neck and smooth brown shoulders, so shiny they almost glowed. Norton could hardly believe what he was seeing.

'Des . . . you look . . . different.'

'Well, I'm sorry if I didn't wear the old shorts and singlet. I'll get changed if you like.' Then Des gave Norton

43

one of those stupid, whimsical looks across the shoulder pretty women are apt to give men after they've just spent two hours making themselves look sensational and they know it. 'Anyway, I don't know what you're going on about,' she said, giving her head a tiny toss that made the braids catch the light as they danced silkily across her shoulders. 'All I did was have a shower, wash my hair and iron an old dress.'

'Yeah, right,' answered Norton, still half in a trance at her good looks and half wanting to kick one of the walls in he was that happy it was her.

'Come into the kitchen.'

'Okay.' Les followed her down the hallway, and if the view in the pedi-cab had been worth a million dollars, in the yellow dress and high heels it just increased about ten times in value.

The flat had a long corridor, the bedrooms and bathroom ran off to the right then a decent size lounge-room with the kitchen off it. The furniture was average and comfortable with a fairly modern TV and stereo; but it was neat and tidy and the carpet looked like it got vacuumed regularly.

'Would you like a beer — or something?'

'No, that's all right, thanks,' replied Norton, leaning slightly against the fridge. 'I got a cab waiting outside. There's no mad hurry though,' he added.

'I'm just about ready anyway.' There was a red hand-bag sitting on the kitchen table with a pair of white earrings next to it. Des picked them up and began working them into her ears.

'Where are the other two girls?' asked Les.

'Work,' said Des, giving Norton a bit of a checkout herself. And liking what she saw. 'They're both waitresses.'

'You ever done any waitressing?'

'Yeah. A pub in Townsville. Another one in Cairns.'

'Better than driving a pedi-cab?' Norton let a bit of cheeky smile cross his face.

Des returned Norton's half-smart smile. 'The tips aren't as good.'

You cheeky, rotten mug, thought Les. He felt like getting her in a bear hug and kissing her face off.

'Okay. I'm ready. Let's go.'

Des turned off the kitchen light and was about to do the same in the loungeroom, when Norton noticed a canary half covered over in a cage, and stopped dead. 'What the ...?' The canary was hanging upside down.

'You noticed, did you? That's Seymour. He belongs to one of the other girls.'

'Yeah. But what ...?' Norton continued to stare at the little bird; eyes closed, sound asleep, still hanging upside down.

'He comes from a farm out near Tambourine Mountain. They raised him with a couple of flying foxes.' Des covered the cage right over and looked at Les. 'So if you think you've got problems, sport, we've got a canary thinks it's a bat and hangs by its feet.'

Norton laughed and shook his head. 'You should make it a little cape.'

'We have. A black one with red lining. He puts it on at midnight.'

Des left the light on in the hall. Next thing they were in the cab.

'You know a good place for a feed?'

Des nodded and leant across to the driver. 'You know Grandma's House, in Martha Street, Mermaid Beach?'

'Sure do,' replied the driver, slipping the taxi into gear.

'That's where we're going.' Des turned to Norton. 'You'll like this place, Les. It's only been open a little while and the touros haven't got onto it. But the food's good. You like steaks, Les?'

'Reckon. The bigger the better. I'm that hungry I'd eat a greyhound and chase the mechanical hare. What about you?'

Des's beautiful emerald eyes lit up. 'After pushing that pedi-cab round all week, I'd jump into Bass Strait with a broken bottle and fight a white pointer shark for a lump of horse meat.'

'I know the feeling.'

They chit-chatted on a bit after that. The driver figured the big, red-headed bloke in the back had money and wasn't in any particular hurry so he took his time, getting caught at as many lights as possible while Norton and Des waffled on to each other.

Des did come from Taree. She was twenty-seven, but not wanting to throw the towel in at nineteen like her girlfriends and raise a tribe of kids, she'd spent the last few years travelling round Australia with a couple of quick trips overseas. She'd spent almost a year in Surfers; it was fun, and she'd managed to save a few bucks. But now she was looking forward to going home where her father had a panel-beating business. How long she'd stay there she wasn't sure. At least six months. This time she might even stay for good. Which Norton interpreted as: if the right bloke came along, settling down in a quiet country town and raising a tribe of kids after sewing all your wild oats might not be such a bad idea after all. No worse than pushing a glorified rickshaw around in the Queensland heat.

Les told her the truth about himself. He came from Queensland, worked as a bouncer in Sydney, where he owned a house at Bondi, and although he hardly knew KK all that well, took the five days in Surfers on as a bit of a hoot. After meeting her he was glad he did. He didn't mention the drug scams, murders and other things he'd been involved in; he lived a bit of a quiet life actually. Like her, he'd managed to squirrel away a bit of money and he might settle back down in Queensland himself. You're right, Des, home is where the heart is. As the meter ticked over they were getting on famously.

Then Norton looked at her evenly. 'Des, when I said earlier that you looked different, I really meant something else. You took me by surprise. You don't just look different, you look . . .' Norton was having trouble with the word; 'you look beautiful,' he said, with a smile and a bit of a shrug.

'Oh, get out.'

'All right, I'll put it to you another way. If just having a

46

shower, washing your hair and ironing an old dress makes you look like that, I'd love to see you when you put your mind to it.'

'Oh, you idiot.' Des tried not to smile, but the look on Norton's face when she gently slapped his shoulder gave her away.

'But there is something I've got to ask you.'

'What?'

'This "Des"? What's it short for? I'm just Les, and that's it. A good old Aussie name. But Des? What is it? Desmonda? Despina? Desiree. Des the next train stop at Central? What?'

'Desilu.'

'Desilu?'

Des looked at Norton impassively. 'You ever watched the Lucille Ball show?'

Les screwed his face. '*I Love Lucy*? About twice — maybe.'

'At the end it says, "Produced by Desilu Productions". Desi Arnaz and Lucille Ball.'

Norton shook his head. 'I still don't . . .'

'They used to call my mother the Lucille Ball of Taree. She looked just like her, only twice as dumb. And she used to watch the stupid bloody show all the time and it went to her head a bit. Till she had four kids. Me and three brothers. So somewhere along the way I got named Desilu.' Norton just looked at her. 'I don't tell many people. I told the other pedi-cab drivers it stood for Destry. Now every time I get a fare, they all yell out, "Destry rides again".' Norton tried not to laugh. 'So you reckon that boy named Sue's got troubles. And my surname's Donaldson. Desilu Donaldson. Great, ain't it?'

'Well, I think your secret's safe, Des. 'Cause I can't ever see them showing that thing on TV again.'

'No, thank Christ. There wouldn't be a TV channel in Australia stupid enough.'

'Couldn't be any worse than this girl from out my way. Her first name was Edna. And her last name was Bag. Know what we had to call her? Edna Bug.'

Des turned away and laughed. 'Oh you stupid . . .'

'Anyway. What about I call you DD? I'm mixed up with KK. And it sounds better than Les and Des all the time. What do you reckon?'

'Okay, Les,' smiled DD. 'You got me.'

The conversation drifted off a little, with DD looking out the window at the passing traffic, apparently deep in thought. It was a beautiful warm night. Now and again, through the gaps in the high-rises on Norton's left, you could see the moon sparkling on the ocean from a sky drenched with stars. Les couldn't have been happier. He had a date with a beautiful girl who liked a laugh, and if something should eventuate, so much the better. No matter what, it was still going to be a good night, just having her for company. He was up here for another five days, he was a moral to see her again before she left. You never know what might happen. I might even nick that Jag and run her back to Taree. In the meantime, leave her with her thoughts. Though I bet I know what she's thinking. How often do you go out with Steve Stunning plus he's got a big pocket full of chops.

DD was thinking something along those lines. Les was all right, no two ways about that; better than she'd expected. He dressed neat, didn't stink of beer and cigarettes and didn't seem the type who'd want to jump all over her after filling her full of drink and forking out for a meal. He still wasn't getting his $200 back. That was hers. If he wanted to get into her pants he'd have to spend a bit more time on her and a bit more than a handful of twenties. But there was something about the big dill. And what if he did? DD could think of much better things to hump her tu-tu against than the constant thumping of that seat on her pedi-cab. A nice meal with a nice bloke. Who knows what might happen? But no matter what, Les couldn't have come along at a better time; he was a gift. Which was why she took up his offer a little quickly. Because Desilu wasn't only thinking about Steve Stunning and his big pocket full of chops. DD was also thinking about the overnight-bag she'd found on the road

48

Wednesday night, coming back from Neptune's Casino, which contained 40 one-ounce deals of choice marijuana heads, rolled up in a Brisbane Broncos jumper.

She'd just dropped three fat Japanese off at the casino, almost busting her ring getting them up the ramp. Not having a fare, she was taking it easy as she headed back to Cavill Avenue when she spotted the bag in the gutter. It was picked up and stashed in the compartment beneath the passenger seat in about a microsecond. She never noticed the beige LTD that had almost run up the back of another car a little earlier, causing the driver to accidently knock the boot release next to the seat. The four men in the LTD were about half a kilometre up the highway before they noticed the boot was open and the bag, thrown loosely on top of some other gear in the back, was missing. A screaming U-turn and an angry, cursing search of the area failed to find the missing overnight-bag. Not that the four thick-set gents were worried about missing out on a good smoke so much. The stuff in the bag was to be swapped for something in powder form that was more to their needs and livelihood. DD didn't notice the four men in the beige LTD morosely driving along the highway a little later; and they didn't take any notice of the girl in the sweaty singlet, driving a pedi-cab as they went past her not far from the turnoff to KK's flat.

DD got a fare to Main Beach not long after, so she decided to call in home, have a quick cup of coffee and check out what was in the bag. DD nearly shit herself when she opened the football jumper. After she stashed it, got rid of the jumper and settled down a bit, her travelled mind went into action. DD had been around long enough to know a good smoke. If she could get that to Taree next week, she knew someone who could get it to Newcastle, who knew someone who could soon get it to Sydney. Forty deals? A quick sale. At least ten, possibly twelve thousand dollars. So here she is, stuck with all this potential money and still having to work Thursday and Friday night. But to suddenly tell the boss to stick his pedi-cab where the feathers are thinnest could possibly arouse suspicion, because they all knew DD was scratching for a dollar and would go bare knuckle with Mike Tyson for a fare. Then like a bolt out of the blue, Les turned up. Naturally she couldn't get back to Cavill Avenue and wave the $200 around quick enough. Somebody else could have her shift that night. Friday night, she'd say she was too crook or he was taking her out again. This went over quite well, and there was more calls of 'Destry's gonna ride again' as she handed the pedi-cab over and caught a taxi home to get changed. So Les certainly came along at the right time, and he was okay. In fact she was almost wishing now she hadn't referred to him as some big red-headed goose with more money than brains, when she saw her boss and later told her flatmates where she was going that night.

DD turned from the window and smiled at Norton. 'We're almost there.'

Les returned her smile. 'Good. I'm feeling pretty peckish.'

The taxi turned into Martha Street and stopped. They both got out and despite unknowingly getting dudded on the fare, Les tipped the driver $5. Grandma's House was a two-storey restaurant-bar, just back from the beach, in between a video store and a bakery, and a few other small shops. The front was painted white, with 'Grandma's House' splashed across the front in red. Under this was a cartoon drawing of Red Riding Hood, the Wolf and Grandma, all in a chorus line kicking their legs up.

'Hey, I like it already,' said Les.

'Wait'll you try the food.'

Norton pushed open a single door and they stepped inside. A bloke dressed much like Les was standing just inside. 'Good evening, sir,' he said pleasantly. 'Are you dining?'

'Bloody oath,' replied Norton. 'I just hope you've got enough in the kitchen. She eats like a horse.'

The bloke smiled at DD. 'How are you, Des?'

'Pretty good, Ray.'

50

There was an area with mirrored walls as you walked in, a long bar to your left and a DJ's stand at one end of that. Posters and photos of film stars covered the walls and a number of indoor-plants hung from the ceiling, which led to another area out the back. There were about a dozen or so people standing around having a drink; the DJ hadn't started, just a Jenny Morris tape playing. The place reminded Les of a little bar and restaurant he knew near Randwick Junction.

DD pointed to a set of stairs at the back of the bar, leading to the restaurant above. 'Up this way,' she said.

Norton followed her up the stairs, DD's shapely back-side in the yellow dress momentarily making him forget how hungry he was. For food at least. The restaurant was roughly the same size as the front area below. Windows looked out over the street opposite a busy kitchen at the rear, with more posters on the walls and indoor-plants. It was hot, busy, with heaps of atmosphere, and the smells coming from the kitchen made Norton feel like someone had turned a sprinkler on in his mouth. A wholesome blonde girl, wearing a Grandma's-House T-shirt, walked over.

'For two, is it?' she smiled.

Les nodded and they were lucky enough to get a nice cool table next to a window. There was a blackboard menu: mainly grills and seafood. The girl handed them a wine list and left.

'What do you fancy to drink?' asked Les.

'I'm going to kick off with an icy cold bottle of Corona,' said DD.

'Yeah, I might have the same,' nodded Les. 'Then we'll have a bottle of plonk.'

'Or two,' smiled DD.

'Two each, if you like,' winked Norton.

The waitress came back and they ordered the beers. By the time they studied the blackboard menu the beers were gone, so Les ordered another two.

DD went for the barbecued calamari with macadamia nut and mango sauce, and the house T-bone. Norton

51

chose the same, plus a dozen oysters Kilpatrick as well.
And a bottle of '74 Veuve Clicquot. They were making
quite a dent in the shampoo when the entrees arrived. Les
reckoned there wasn't enough d's in delicious to describe
them. DD matched Norton bite for bite, drink for drink.
Norton ordered another bottle of bubbly. They were
getting into that when two monstrous T-bones arrived,
surrounded by crispy, thin chips, onion rings and a bowl
of garden-fresh salad. Still spluttering on their sizzle
plates, they were as thick as a *Collins Dictionary* and
hanging over the edge of the plate and tender enough to
eat with a spoon.

'Christ! How good are these,' said Les.

DD gave Norton a thin smile. 'Just keep your eyes off
mine, pal.'

Again the pedi-cab driver matched Les bite for bite.
She even gnawed the bone and wiped her plate with a
piece of garlic bread. When she'd finished, there wasn't a
grease stain left on her plate, let alone a chip or a shred of
salad. DD was something else.

'You fancy sweets?' ventured Les.

'Bloody oath,' was the reply. 'Did you think I came
here just for a snack?'

Norton was in love.

They ordered Bananas Grandma. Which were two big
Queensland bananas, fried in butter and honey, sprinkled
liberally with shredded coconut, passionfruit and
chopped strawberries, plus scoops of ice cream and a
splash of Cointreau. Not only was it delicious also, it
finally stopped DD in her tracks along with Norton.

'I think a nice cup of coffee'd go well now,' said Les. His
head floating just a little from the champagne; the Cointreau had cut the string.

'Good idea,' nodded DD, her beautiful emerald eyes
starting to swim a bit also. 'Then we'll go downstairs and
rage it off. It starts to kick on about now.'

They finished their coffees, with possibly the odd,
strange look passing between them. Les paid the bill,
leaving the girl $20. Then they went downstairs. As they

52

were walking down the stairs, The Bondi Cigars' 'Howling at the Moon' came drifting up; not all that softly either. Hello, thought Les, what's this? The place had filled up a bit and a DJ in his thirties, wearing a green Hawaiian shirt was throwing on some records.

'Hey, you're right,' said Norton. 'This looks all right.'

DD took hold of Norton's shirt and put her face about an inch in front of his. 'Would these little green eyes lie?'

'Never in a million years, I would imagine.'

She blew him a little kiss. 'I'll have a Jack Daniels and Coke, thanks. And you can have anything you like.'

From then on the night was just a hoot. There was no dancefloor so the DJ didn't have to play heaps of punishing house music to keep zithead trendoids and gay posers happy. Instead he threw on all sorts of things, mainly rock 'n' roll. Of course not having a dancefloor didn't make much difference because everybody was dancing anyway, including Les and DD, while they topped up with bourbons and the odd pina collada.

They boogied to the Swinging Sidewalks' 'Now Now', rocked and bopped to Dire Straits' 'Heavy Heavy Fuel', hustled to Fontella Bass's 'Rescue Me', really worked the T-bones around to Bob Geldorf's 'Love or Something', and joined up with a bunch of other happy drunks in a boozy chorus line to Tina Turner's disco version of 'Nutbush City Limits'. That, and a bit of 'Right Said Fred', was the closest the DJ got to house mush all night.

Dancing with DD was sensational. Her body was whippy and light and her backside, when they bumped, harder than some forwards' Norton had packed scrums with; only a much nicer shape and smelled a lot better. By around midnight sweat was pouring down DD's face and her beautiful brown hair was plastered all over her head. Norton didn't look much better. In fact, between her yellow dress and his denim shirt, they both looked like they'd come through a carwash on a motorbike.

DD took a slurp of bourbon and held on to Les for support 'You know what I feel like now — a swim.'

'Yeah. Not a bad idea.'

'There's a pool back at your place, isn't there?'

'Yeah but...'

'No bloody buts. That's it, we're going back to your place for a swim.'

'Yeah but...'

'Stick your buts. I'm going to see Ray and get us a taxi.'

Les was about to say something but DD left him to weave her way over to the man at the door. Instead, Les went to the bar. DD returned and was watching him from behind as he stepped back to let a girl get served first even though he was there before her. Yeah, I thought so. A bit of a square. A real country boy. Shucks, man, do you think it proper we go back and have a swim — you havin' no bikini and all, maam. Well, just watch yourself back home, pal. As well as spending all that money, you might find yourself being raped on top of it. They had their last drinks while they waited for a taxi. Norton was going to tell her about the pool, but the DJ was getting half tanked by now and had turned the music up, so Les couldn't be bothered shouting. Not over Johnny Diesel's 'Soul Revival' anyway. Ray caught DD's eye and waved. They skulled their drinks, breathed a boozy goodbye to the bloke on the door that almost singed his eyebrows off, and the next thing they were in a taxi on their way to the flat.

'Lift your arm,' said DD.

'What?'

'Your arm — lift it.' Les did as he was told and DD snuggled up against his chest. 'Wake me when we get to your place.' She closed her eyes and made herself even more comfortable.

Well, what about this, thought Les, barely able to contain himself as he felt DD purring away against his chest. The young lady seems to be very much my way. Who knows what might happen on a balmy holiday night on the beautiful Gold Coast? Might be a different story though when she looks for the deep end of the pool to jump in. This time the cab driver could see the big red-headed bloke in the back wasn't interested in a grand tour of all the stop-lights on the Gold Coast Highway. They were out the front of the flats before they knew it. No sign of KK, thought Les, as he paid the driver. Not that I care all that much. If I make too much noise he can sack me. I don't give a stuff.

'Hey, this place is really nice,' said DD, stepping inside as Les opened the door and switched on the lights.

'Yeah, it's a good joint all right.'

DD had another look round when Les switched on the loungeroom light. 'Very nice indeed. Now where's the pool?'

'That's what I was trying to tell you.' He opened the fly-screen and they stepped out onto the sundeck. 'There it is.'

DD looked at the pool, screwed up her face and turned to Les. 'It's bloody empty.'

'That's what I was trying to bloody tell you. But you know how it is with you sheilas, it's like trying to get the last word in with an echo.' DD put her hands on her hips and looked up at Norton through her eyebrows. 'But if you want a swim. What's that out there?'

DD followed Norton's outstretched arm. The sea was awash with moonlight under a sky full of stars. Puffs of tiny white waves rolled in and the noise drifting up as they gently washed against the shimmering water's edge was as soft as a kiss. It was hot, there was no wind and after all the activity at Grandma's House the water did look inviting.

'Yeah, a bloody great ocean full of sharks, sea wasps and heaps of sand all up your Khyber.'

'But it'd still be nice. And there's two showers here.'

DD looked at Norton as a trickle of sweat ran down her back. 'You got a T-shirt?'

Les grinned. 'Small woman's or XWOS?'

Les gave DD his Mambo T-shirt and told her to throw her gear in the first bedroom. He got into his Speedos and a pair of training shorts, just in case Mr Wobbly should start jumping up and down as soon as he saw DD in her

55

knickers and a wet T-shirt, and grabbed a couple of towels. It was just as well, because DD looked pretty sensational just wearing it dry as she stood in the lounge-room. He handed her a towel. Next thing they were down the back stairs jogging drunkenly across the sand towards the water's edge.

'Well, you know the old saying, last one in's a rotten egg.'

Norton ran into the water, crashed through a few small waves then dived in. The water didn't have the slightest hint of a chill; if anything it seemed even better than it did in the afternoon. Les flopped around washing away the heat and sweat then stood up and turned towards the beach.

'Come on, DD. It's terrific.' There was no sign of her. 'DD,' he yelled out a couple more times. Suddenly the beach looked very empty. Wonder where she is? Les stood waist deep in water looking for her. He was about to call out again. Next thing.

'Aargh! Gotcha.' DD jumped up on his back from behind, same time as a wave hit him, knocking Les on his arse.

Norton got up spluttering water and was about to grab DD and give her a severe dunking but she was gone. 'You mug,' he yelled out. He managed to make out her laughing face in the moonlight, so he dived under the water, grabbed her ankles and lifted, sending DD backwards into an oncoming wave.

They wallowed around pushing each other, splashing water in each other's faces and carrying on like a couple of big silly kids in general. The T-shirt was clinging to DD now and her body looked more tantalisingly beautiful than ever. From DD's point of view Norton didn't look too bad either, the water and moonlight rippling over the muscles in his stomach and chest. The night's activities plus all the food and booze started to take its toll, and before long they were bobbing around in about a metre of water. DD had her arms around Norton's neck, he was gently holding her waist. Above them the moon and stars were literally sizzling in the sky. In a situation like this, it was a photo finish who kissed who first.

DD's lips were soft and sweet, the salt water adding a spice that spun Norton's eyes around. Their tongues met, waves hit them, DD's T-shirt floated up and her breasts were as firm as two honeydew melons, the cool water turning her nipples into hard, juicy raspberries. Their kissing intensified.

They didn't bother about the Burt Lancaster–Deborah Kerr scene in *From Here to Eternity*, getting sand everywhere you don't need it. They headed straight for Norton's bedroom and the queen-size bed. Les slipped DD's T-shirt off, along with his shorts and threw them in the en-suite. DD was wearing some sort of pink satin knickers that almost sent Mr Wobbly into a tail spin. Les kissed her down onto the bed then started kissing and licking the salt water from around her neck and nipples and out of her navel. DD was sighing and starting to make tiny groaning noises. He slipped her knickers down and DD groaned some more as she brought her knees and ankles together so Les could get them off altogether. DD's skin was still fragrant with body oil and it bit gently into Norton's tongue, along with the salt water as he moved from her navel down to her thighs. DD was groaning audibly now. She brought her knees up and Les moved his face in between her legs; it too was salty and fragrant and tasted better than a dozen Georges River oysters, straight out of the shell. Norton's head was starting to swim. He pulled off his Speedos, got between her and kissed her full on the mouth and neck. DD scrabbled her fingers into his hair and crushed her tongue into Norton's ear.

'Ohh fuck me.'

The big, red-headed goose with more money than brains did exactly what the lady wearing the yellow dress on the bed in the next room told him.

Les worked his way into DD and couldn't remember anything ever feeling so good; her lean, brown body was pure delight. She writhed and moaned; Les held her

57

round the shoulders and started stroking away, feeling her moving with him. He started going a little faster, but not for too long; it was too good to finish. DD would wriggle and moan. Les would slow down and DD would choke back a tear as he'd start up again.

'Ohh yesss.'

They worked their way all over the queen-size bed, scattering sheets everywhere. DD got on top, they had a brain-snapping sixty-niner. DD went along with it all, pushing Les if anything. Norton had a quick flashback to Terrigal. But this wasn't Sophia. DD was just a healthy, fit Australian girl who'd met a healthy, fit Australian boy she fancied. So she'd just met Les? So what? And she did say there was something about the big dill. But it couldn't go on forever. They found themselves at one end of the bed near the wall, Norton lifted her legs up and started putting in the big ones; DD grabbed him round the neck, threw back her head and shook it, sending a spray of water across the wall as she threw herself up with him. Then poor Mr Wobbly swelled up and exploded inside DD like a hand-grenade. Eyes jammed shut and the veins almost pumping out of his forehead, Norton arched his back, gave it his last then crashed face first into the pillow alongside DD. Bloody hell, thought Les. How good was that. He moved his face to get some air in. DD, baby, if only I could scream like you and tell everyone else how good it was too.

After a few moments his breath started to come back and DD was softly running her fingers through his hair. She had a half smile on her face that somehow reflected in her voice. 'Are you all right?' she said.

'Yeah, I think so,' answered Norton, not all that sure. 'But could you do me a favour?'

'Sure.'

'Have a look underneath the bed will you. I think my spine's stuck in the floor down there somewhere.'

'Righto. And while I'm there. Have a look round the ceiling and see if you can find my ankles. They flew past my head about ten minutes ago.'

They had a bit of a laugh at themselves and a cuddle, then Les suggested a nice cool shower. Save water, shower with a friend. Naturally the shower went a bit longer than normal. They got towelled off, Des wasn't in any hurry to get home so Les gave her another T-shirt, they straightened up the bed and got back in. As they did Norton popped a cassette in the ghetto-blaster. The first track was Happening Thang's 'Sitting by a Fireplace'. The words seemed to exactly set the tone of the moment.

It wasn't long, and between the pillow talk and laughter, knees started nudging, fingers started walking then hands started wandering and lips met. Mr Wobbly rose to the occasion, more than willing to do battle again. The next one was as good as the first and went almost as long. But it was the knockout blow for both contestants. When it was over, DD was snoring softly, much in the same position she'd been in on the back seat of the taxi. Les could hardly keep his eyes open, but he had a big smile on his face and couldn't remember feeling this good. Yes, he thought, if you could do that five nights a week, you'd only have to train three and you'd never have a smile off your face. Was it the best night Les had ever had? He wasn't sure. But it was that close it didn't make any difference. The tape cut out at exactly the same time as Norton.

Friday dawned warm and sunny; one or two puffs of cloud in the sky and a light nor-east breeze promising it would be a hot day before the clouds arrived in the afternoon. Les was woken by the blinds drawn, the ghetto-blaster playing softly and the shower running. He felt good, no hangover but just too relaxed to make a move. He half dozed off again when DD was standing in front of the bed in her underwear, drying her hair with a towel.

'Hello handsome,' she said brightly. 'How are you?'

Norton shook himself awake. 'DD. How are you? How long've you been up?'

'About ten minutes. I left you snoring your head off.'

'Ohh.' Norton grinned and gave DD a very heavy once up and down in her underwear. 'I was thinkin'...'

'Yeah, so was I. But I'm just a little sore, and I do have to get home, you know.'

'Yeah fair enough. Mr Wobbly feels like he's got a bit of bark missing too.'

DD crawled across the sheets and gave Les a kiss. 'So how about getting a cab together.'

'Okay. I'll just have a quick shower myself.'

'I'll make some coffee.'

Norton had a shower then got into a pair of jeans and a clean T-shirt. DD was in the kitchen with a cup of coffee waiting for him. Les thanked her, took a sip and could hardly keep his eyes off her. The yellow dress was all creased, her hair was still wet and all over her head, but she looked just as beautiful as the night before.

'Okay, DD,' he said 'I'll get straight to the point. When am I going to see you again? I'm in love with you.'

DD brought her coffee over a bit closer to Les. 'God, you're mad,' she smiled. 'But here's what's happening. Today I'm packing and I've got some people coming over tonight to look at some furniture. Tomorrow I'm selling more furniture and Saturday night I'm going out with the girls for a farewell drink.' She put her arms around Norton's waist. 'But from Sunday till Tuesday. I'm home alone, on my own, all by myself. Just me, a boring old TV set and Count von Seymour.'

'Don't worry about a thing, DD. It's all sweet. I'm there.'

Les rang for a taxi and they took their coffees out on the sundeck to watch Surfers Paradise come to life; seagulls hung in the air, people walked and jogged along the water's edge and the sound of the waves gently washing against the sand seemed to bring back pleasant, funny memories from the night before. Les noticed the curtains were still drawn in KK's flat and was about to say something about him to DD when a horn bipped out the front. DD got her bag and they were on their way to Main Beach. Les joked about meeting Crystal Linx, it should be a bit of a hoot which he'd tell DD about when he saw her on Sunday night. Next thing the taxi pulled up at her place.

'I'll walk you to the door.'

'I knew you were a gentleman, Les. That's why I went out with you.'

Norton didn't bother propping outside her door, he gave DD a squeeze at the bottom of the steps; she squeezed back.

'Honestly, Les, that was one of the best nights I've ever had. Thanks a lot. And I mean it.'

'DD, the pleasure was all mine. And I mean that too.'

DD's beautiful green eyes smiled right into Norton's. 'Les. In the taxi last night you told me I looked beautiful. And this morning you told me you were in love with me. How about leaving me with something else nice. That's if you really meant it.'

Norton smiled back at DD and thought for a moment. 'Let me put it to you another way, DD,' he said. 'If ever your pedi-cab needs a seat, I've always got a face.'

'You're gorgeous, Les.'

Norton grabbed DD, gave her a quick crushing kiss then he was back in the taxi waving to her as the driver did a U-turn back towards Hancock Avenue. Ahh Queensland, thought Norton, spreading himself into the back seat. Ain't it good to be back home. He took a look at his watch. Just on eight-thirty.

At nine o'clock Les decided it might be time to knock on Kramer's door and see what's going on. After two knocks, Kramer came to the door wearing a red terry-towelling shave-coat; his eyes were puffy and his hair was still all over his face.

'G'day, KK,' said Norton. 'I thought I'd better give you a call. Don't we have to pick up Crystal today?'

KK blinked at Norton for a second or two. 'Yeah... right. The plane doesn't get here till one though.'

'Okay. But by the time we get to Brisbane, and all that.'

KK thought for a moment. 'Yeah, I suppose you're right. I'll have a shower, Get the car and I'll meet you out the front in half an hour. We'll have some breakfast.'

'You got the keys?'

Kramer blinked again. 'Yeah, hold on.'

Along with his glasses, Kramer got the keys from somewhere; he handed them to Les then closed the door. Norton went back inside his flat, tidied the bedroom and folded his clothes while he listened to the radio. A bit of breakfast'd go well just quietly, he thought; after all the food last night, there was now a gap in Norton's stomach that needed replenishing. He was going to make another cup of coffee, but changed his mind. He was standing next to the Jag when Kramer came out the front door in a pair of white slacks, blue shirt and Reeboks.

'Where do you want to have breakfast?' asked Les, as they got in the car.

'There's a place on The Esplanade, just before Cavill Avenue called Peggy's. We'll go there.'

'We may as well walk.' Les hesitated to start the car.

Kramer looked at Norton like he couldn't believe what he was hearing. 'What do you think I hired this for — show?'

Norton was about to answer 'fuckin' oath' but they scarcely had time for two words when Kramer pointed to a driveway going into a big hotel complex on The Esplanade.

'In there. Stick it anywhere.'

Les eased the Jaguar up the driveway and parked it in the first empty space he saw that said STRICTLY PRIVATE. GUESTS ONLY. They got out of the car and a man in a pair of King Gee shorts, pushing a broom, came over with a concerned look on his face. He saw KK and smiled.

'Oh, good morning, Kelvin,' he said politely. 'Lovely day.'

KK slipped him $5. 'Ain't it just peachy. Keep an eye on this heap of shit while we have breakfast, will you?'

'Certainly. Would you like me to give it a hose?'

'Nahh! Don't worry about it.'

Peggy's was all dark green and white and very nice with lots of vines and trellises. Chairs and tables covered with crisp, white tablecloths spread out onto the footpath, and

62

a radio was playing softly through speakers on a wall. Kramer pulled up a chair and sat facing Cavill Avenue: Norton sat facing opposite him. Les barely had time to take in the beach, the surrounding high-rises and the punters strolling past when a woman about forty walked briskly over wearing a dark green dress with 'Peggy's' across the front pocket in white. She handed them both a menu.

'Good morning, Kelvin,' she said, very ladylike. 'How have you been? I haven't seen you for a while.'

'Not bad, Peg. How's things with you?'

'Fine, thank you.'

Kramer ordered orange juice, smoked salmon and scrambled eggs, toast and coffee. Les ordered the same plus a bowl of fruit-salad with King Island cream and extra toast. It was quite pleasant sitting out on the footpath in the sun; people were starting to mill onto the beach, and the traffic wasn't too heavy. Across the road Les noticed a bloke wearing a seaman's peaked cap with several tattoos on a lean body that brown it almost glowed. He was getting deck-chairs and surf mats from a kind of white concrete bunker built onto the beach, and stacking them neatly on the sand. He was whistling cheerfully as he worked. A couple of Japanese tourists walked up to him; he stopped what he was doing to give them a quick going over with suntan-oil from a spray-gun and compressor sitting on the sand.

'You know that bloke across the road?' asked Les, taking a sip of orange juice.

'Jimmy Martin? Everybody on the coast knows Jimmy. He's almost as well-known as me.'

'Evidently he's an old mate of Price's.'

'Is he?' answered Kramer indifferently.

The fruit-salad arrived and like the orange juice, it was chilled, fresh and plenty of it; the cream was that thick, Norton could stand his spoon in it.

'So what did you do last night?' enquired KK.

Norton chewed and swallowed one half of a strawberry that was almost as big as a blood-plum. 'Had a bit of a feed, then I bumped into a girl I knew from Sydney. So I had a few drinks with her and a couple of her friends. Had a pretty quiet night actually. What about yourself?'

'I had dinner at Mey... Mr Black's house. Played a little backgammon and we mainly talked business.'

'About betting Crystal's new record together?'

'Yeah. Crystal's new record.'

Norton thought he could detect a smirk behind the little playboy's sunglasses. 'I only spoke to him for a few minutes. But he seems like a nice bloke.'

'Oh, he is Les. He's a gem.'

'I just hope the record goes well for both of you. You deserve it.'

There was definitely a smirk in KK's eyes this time. 'We both, do Les.'

The eggs and that arrived and they ate almost in silence, which suited Les. For some reason he couldn't seem to warm to Kelvin Kramer. It wasn't because he was Jewish or anything stupid like that. In that respect, if anything, it was the other way around. Norton was the big dumb goy. He'd also shared a laugh and a joke with Kelvin when he'd come up the Kelly Club with his friends or whatever. But that was on a different basis. KK was then a customer: a punter. If a customer dropped the lowest joke going you'd laugh fit to bust. And if they carried on like a bit of a dill, you'd go along with that too. Now Les was in KK's employ; beholden to him, so to speak. And he was a full-on little lair; his whole attitude in general was full of mug. And for the amount of pissing in each other's pockets, even at breakfast, they should have both been wearing neoprene suits. If it had been anyone else, Les would have said what a great night he had, how good the restaurant was, get there. But not KK.

And KK definitely wasn't up there just to promote Crystal's new record. He had to be up to something. Though with all this media rattle coming up, you'd think if you were pulling a stroke the last thing you'd want would be publicity. Then that could all be past tense. Menachem might have been doing something with Black,

64

and KK was going along for the ride, and Les was the big, dumb heavy roped in at the last minute. But somehow Norton couldn't help feeling he was in for a use if he didn't watch himself, and he'd have to keep a close eye on the little shit, picking at his scrambled eggs sitting in front of him.

Then, on the other hand, Norton didn't know how lucky he was. KK couldn't have come along at a better time. And a use? Here he was having breakfast in the sun, he was $500 in front and sooner or later he was going to find time to sit back in that fabulous unit, listening to those tapes he'd brought up, with his feet up, having a beer looking out at a million-dollar view. And what about Desilu? If it hadn't have been for KK, he'd have never met her. So instead of casting aspersions on Kelvin, he should be kissing his feet. And it was only till Tuesday. Sunday maybe. Because no matter what, even if the sheriff was round at Gazpuncho Blonko, or whatever he called those flats, taking out all KK's furniture, Les was seeing DD on Sunday night. Norton chewed on another portion of delicious smoked salmon, winked up at the sky and took a sip of orange juice. Yeah, you're right, boss, I shouldn't be such a nark. Sorry.

By now a few more people began drifting into Peggy's: tourists, plus a number of people who knew KK. Flashy blokes with streaks in their hair, plenty of gold plating and young birds hanging off their arms. Flashy blokes with suntanned, flashy sort of wives. They were all casually but well dressed; definitely no bums. They'd see KK, put on a bit of a show for his benefit. There'd be heaps of 'God strike me's' and 'it's great to see you, old mate' and plenty of back-slapping. KK would bridge up in return. He never bothered to introduce Les: a bit of eye contact and one or two nods and that was about it. But with a bit of observation and by gathering snippets of conversation, Les figured they were mostly white-shoe rorters, the others were in the nightclub game. But KK was their mate, they slapped his back and KK lapped it up; even if to get from one table to the other you almost had to wade through the false camaraderie.

They'd been there a little over an hour, Les was on his third cup of coffee, watching the show go on around him. KK was at another table, his arm around some white shoe's neck who was wearing Mexican cowboy boots. KK looked at his watch, got up and walked over to Norton.

'Les, bring the car round, will you.'

Norton screwed up his face. If the car was any closer, you could piss on it. 'Bring the car round?'

'Yeah. Just pull up out the front. I'm still talking.'

'Yeah, righto, KK.'

Chauffeur Norton stood up and drained his coffee; KK left him standing to continue talking to the white shoe in the Mexican boots. Bring the fuckin' car around, eh? Les got behind the wheel, hit the ignition and eased the big Jag out of the hotel parking area. The bloke in the King Gee shorts smiled and gave him a bit of a wave. Les winked and smiled back; there wasn't much else he could do. The traffic along The Esplanade had increased noticeably now. Les had to chance it a bit to get out, only to pull up a few metres on to a screeching of brakes, bipping of horns and a loud 'Ya fuckin' goose' from a four-wheel-drive right behind him. Then the lights just ahead turned green, leaving Les sitting there with more traffic, more horns bipping and a lot more being yelled at him than 'Ya fuckin' goose'. Norton looked across at KK still talking and thought, You're not fuckin' wrong. KK heard the commotion, thrived on it momentarily then after waving goodbye to everybody, made a big show of paying the bill and ambled casually over to the car. For some reason Norton reached across and opened the door for him.

'Where would you like to go now, KK?' asked Les, wanting to pull the steering-wheel out of the dash and wrap it around KK's little Jewish head.

The smirk was well and truly back in Kramer's eyes. 'Home, James.'

Which meant driving about a kilometre up The Esplanade to find a street that ran left then back onto the highway into more traffic, all to save a 300 metre walk. 'I should have known, shouldn't I?' answered Les quietly.

Les moved off just as the lights turned green. There wasn't much traffic ahead, but plenty behind him still bipping their horns; especially the bloke in the four-wheel-drive who was right up his arse. About half a kilometre further on Les noticed a break in the traffic coming the other way. Fuck this, he cursed to himself. He tromped on the accelerator, getting about ten lengths in front of the cars behind him in around a second, slammed on the brakes, spinning the steering-wheel at the same time, and did a screaming U-turn back up The Esplanade, still finding time to give the bloke in the four-wheel-drive the finger as he sped past. KK barely blinked an eyelid. He came to life as they went past Peggy's, hoping some-one would notice him as he reached across Les and waved. Norton pulled up into the driveway of the flats to find a huge stretch limousine sitting there. He couldn't tell the make, but it looked like they'd taken Queen Victoria's rail-coach, painted it white and turned it into a lowrider. There was a chauffeur leaning against the bonnet; average looking, dark hair, wearing a grey suit, sunglasses and black gloves.

'What's this?' asked Norton.

'What do you think it is, you big dill?' replied KK. 'A fuckin' Mr Whippy van? That's what we're going to pick Crystal up in. We'll be getting around in that most of the time from now on.'

'What about the Jag?'

KK shrugged. 'I might even let you have it, now and again.'

'Gee — thanks.'

'In the meantime. Stick it in the same garage and give me the keys. I want to have a word with the driver.'

KK got out. Les put the car in the garage and started to feel a little easier. This was more like it, and a chance to get my hands on the nice Jag for a while as well. The driver was showing KK inside the limo when Les closed the garage door and walked over.

'Yeah, that's as good as gold, Tony.' KK nodded to Norton. 'Tony, this is Les. He's our minder for the next few days.'

Tony offered his gloved hand. 'Hello, Les.' His voice was cheerful, in a laconic sort of way and his handshake was warm. Les figured him to be just a driver for some car-rental company.

'How are you, Tony?'

KK absently looked at his watch. 'Well, I've got to grab a couple of things and I suppose we'd better get going.'

'Yeah. I wouldn't leave it too late,' said Tony. 'The traffic into Brisbane can get a bit heavy this time of day.'

'What about you, Les?'

'Yeah, I might grab a clean shirt.'

'We'll be back in twenty minutes, Tony.'

Les used his key to let KK in and they didn't say much going up the stairs: see you out the front. After three cups of good, strong coffee, Norton's mouth was starting to taste like an old tyre some dog had pissed on. He cleaned his teeth and had a think. All this media crush, yobbo fans and whatever. If I put a good shirt on I'm a moral to get it ripped. Bugger it. If they wreck my Mambo Musical Dog T-shirt I can soon get another one. Those shirts are worth money, even if I do buy them off thieves. He left what he had on. Tony was down the front, still waiting patiently alongside the limo when Norton came out the front door.

'Could be a busy day, Tony?' smiled Les.

Tony returned the smile and shook his head slightly. 'For you maybe, mate. Not for me. All I gotta do is drive this.'

'Don't knock yourself around — willya.'

Tony continued to shake his head. 'No way in the world, mate.'

KK suddenly came bounding out of the flats over to the car. 'Righto. Let's go.' Tony opened the door and they bundled in.

In the back of the limo was a TV, phone, bar, vase of flowers and other things spread round a padded, air-

68

conditioned area big enough to play ice-hockey in during winter. Les sat alongside KK with another seat somewhere in the distance behind the driver. It wasn't quite the same laid-back, sarcastic KK Les was used to, however. Maybe it was the occasion, but KK was babbling away at 100 mph, waving his hands around, jabbing at the air with his fingers. What's the song say, mused Les, 'He's just an excitable boy'. I'd like to get a look behind those sunglasses. But listen up now; the generalissimo was speaking. He told Les what he had to do. There would be a media crush. Crystal would be tired and probably irritable after the flight and not wanting to give any interviews. Les had to keep the media hacks off her back and especially any mugs trying to grab her boobs. Coming home the press would probably be on their tail, Crystal would want to go inside and get some rest. If they wanted a photo session and all that rattle she'd do it on Monday before she left for New York; or possibly Sunday. Give the lady a break, folks, it's been a long trip and she's just got off the plane. Later that night after dinner, they'd be going out in Surfers for a few drinks, they could take as many photos as they liked. But the interviews and the topless photos. Monday. Keep the pricks guessing. Make them wait. They're only shit anyway.

KK rattled on some more to the driver and Les, repeating himself half the time. With Norton it was going in one ear and out the other. He had the gist of it though. Get Crystal into the limbo unscathed, especially her gazonkas, and tell the mugs from the tabloids to piss off and leave her alone; she'd pull her tits out on Sunday. Easy. Though out on the ran-tan that night, amongst all the drunks in Surfers Paradise, could be a bit trickier. And just what is this Crystal Linx like? Christ! thought Les. I hope she's not as big a lair as her dopey fuckin' boyfriend.

Eagle Farm looked exactly like it did the last time Les had seen it, and the International Departures and Arrivals section the same as just about every other major airport in Australia. Except as they approached, there was a media scrum brandishing TV cameras, tape-recorders, microphones on poles that looked like long dusters, ordinary cameras and other things, spreading out from the footpath and across the road. A group of curious onlookers surrounded all of this. The car rocked gently to a halt. Oh well, thought Norton, adjusting his sunglasses, looks like the circus has hit town. I wonder if Annie will recognise me on the news tonight?

As soon as the press corps saw the limo pull up they converged on it like piranhas. Les thought he might as well have some fun so he jumped out first, pushed a couple out the way and held the door open for KK. The media scrum was the usual scruffy bunch of hungover, sardonic hacks of both sexes from the entertainment end of the papers and every cheap, tits-and-bums magazine in Australia. They were about thirty strong and surged forward, taking a few tentative photos and a bit of TV filler, their main target of course was Crystal Linx.

'Kelvin, what's going on?'

'Where's Crystal? How long's she out here for?'

'Can we get a few words, Kelvin?'

Kramer stood next to Les for support and held up his hands as more flashes went off. 'Jesus Christ! Give me a fuckin' break, will you, you pricks. She's not even here yet.'

'How long will she be on the Gold Coast?'

'Will you be doing a video?'

'When are we gonna see her tits? Hic!'

KK started towards the arrivals lounge with the press crowding after him. 'Now listen, you pack of fuckin' hyenas, shut up for two minutes and I'll tell you what's going on. You're enough to give anyone the shits.'

Despite his feelings towards KK, Norton loved the way he spoke to the media. No matter what he said they'd bad-mouth and misquote him. It was in their nature. Being nice to a journalist, especially from the tabloids, is like feeding and patting some mongrel dog that hates the world. No matter how you are, it's still going to bite you, piss on your leg and shit on your lawn. KK realised this

70

from past experience so he was just getting in first. Plus he had a hot item: Crystal Linx. He knew it, and they knew it, and if they didn't like it they could all go shit in their hat and piss off. And there was no chance of that. A photo of Crystal's giant, enormous set splashed across the front page of some cheap Oz tabloid was more important than the discovery of a cure for cancer or a solution to global starvation.

'She's here till Tuesday, okay? She's staying at my place in Surfers. After leaving NY in a snowstorm and being stuck in a plane for thirty hours she's not going to feel much like talking to a bunch of cunts like you. We're having a quiet weekend together. She is my girlfriend, in case you dills might have forgot. We'll sort out the promotion for her new song. Then on Monday, maybe Sunday, you can do all the shitty interviews and take all the cheesecake photos you want. You got that — schvantzs.'

'Do you agree with what Miles Eisenberg said in *Variety*?' trilled some female journalist from the Brisbane *Sun*. 'That Crystal Linx has done for the record industry what Pol Pot did for inner-city living in Cambodia?'

A half chortle went through the media. KK turned to Les. 'Tell these pieces of shit what I told you in the car, Les.'

'You heard the man,' said Norton. A couple of cameras flashed. 'Give these young lovers a chance to see each other again. And give the lady a bit of a break. Then on Monday, you won't only have your page-three girl, you'll have enough tits to fill pages four, five and six as well.'

KK looked at Les and blinked. 'Hey — I like your style, Les Norton. I might make you press liaison officer.'

'You'd better supply me with some Dettol and rubber gloves if I've got to deal with these turds.'

'Yeah. Follow me. Let's get away from the cunts.'

Les fell into step with KK towards the VIP section, putting as much distance as possible between them and the media. They stood near the door and KK pulled out a small cigar and lit it.

71

'We shouldn't have to wait long. Her plane arrived before we did, I've timed this splendidly.'

The VIP door opened and a couple of tennis players, one or two pro-golfers, a politician and a rally driver came through after each other, all pushing metal trolleys with their luggage stacked on top. None looked too happy when they saw all the baying press jackals gathered for the kill. But their looks of displeasure turned almost to disbelief when they were totally ignored. The door pushed open again and there was Crystal.

Norton had never seen her in the flesh before and she was still wearing sunglasses. But there was no mistaking that shock of teased, blonde hair poking out from under a big, floppy denim cap, the pouty pink mouth and the slightly plump face. She seemed a little taller than Les expected, then he noticed underneath the mandatory ripped denim jeans she was wearing blue suede spiky, high-heeled shoes. Despite the Queensland heat she still had on a full-length sheep-skin coat done up, her hands barely visible poking out from the thick wool inside.

KK tossed away his cigar. 'Get her straight in the limo,' he said urgently.

KK put his arms round her and gave her a kiss; she flashed a big, white, showbizz smile and kissed him back. There were two suitcases in the trolley, Norton picked them up and began shoving his way, none too gently, through the media crush, whose circuits had now started to overload with the arrival of Crystal. She clutched her handbag, held onto KK, then they both held onto Les and set sail for the safety of the limo with the press jackals in hot pursuit. Cameras were flashing, arc-lights came on as the TV cameras whirred, microphones were thrust at them and questions were shouted at Crystal from every direction. Naturally she was asked the mandatory question every entertainer or celebrity is asked as soon as they step off a plane by some genius in the Australian media.

'Hey, Crystal,' shouted some boozy hack. 'How do you like Australia?'

If KK treated the press a bit ordinary, his American

72

girlfriend was absolutely diabolical. Plus she blasted the Australian journalists with a thick Bronx accent and a loud, gravelly voice that almost singed the hairs on the back of Norton's neck.

'Howz would you like to go fuck your grandmother, dust butt.'

'Crystal, is it true that your record company cancelled your contract?'

'Is that your ass I can smell, or did a fuckin' cow shit in here?'

'Miss Linx, have you just spent a month in a European clinic?' shouted some woman reporter.

'Have you been getting fucked by any big black niggers lately, cactus cunt? Or do you always walk that way?'

They shoved through the one big crowd that had gathered now. Norton could hardly believe what he was hearing. Crystal blasted all and sundry all the way to the car. It was beautiful. Wait'll this hits the news, Les laughed to himself. Has this sheila given them an in-depth interview or what. Tony had the boot open, Les threw the two bags in and skipped round to open the door for Crystal as Tony got straight behind the wheel. Still leaving Crystal time to give the Australian press one last blast.

'Hey, Crystal. Is that right, your last two records laid a giant egg?'

'You know what I'd like to do,' said Crystal, putting her hands on her hips. 'After thirty hours stuck on that plane eating piss-ass airline food, I'd like to lay a big shit on each one of your pointy little hayseed Australian heads. You goddam motherfucking goofbrains.' She then gave them all the good old American finger. 'Sonofa-bitch! No wonder Sinatra still throws up everytime he thinks of you assholes.'

Les slammed the door and jumped on the seat behind the driver. From the rear window he could see the TV crews still filming the limo as they sped off. Crystal and KK sat there without saying anything: Crystal on the driver's side. They didn't carry on like lovers all thrilled to see each other and kiss madly. Instead there appeared to be an air of tension in the car. They were out of the airport, nearing the highway, before Crystal finally spoke.

'Well, KK darling. How did you like the press conference?'

'Crystal, all I said was be abrupt, make out you're tired, give a bit of cheek if you want and get to the car. But shit . . .'

'Ohh kiss my ass, KK. If anything, you're just as big an asshole as any of them. How the fuck I let you . . .' Crystal's voice trailed away as she appeared to notice Norton for the first time. 'So who's the big cheeseburger with the red hair?'

'Crystal, this is Les. Les is going to be looking after us till you go back.'

Norton gave her a bemused smile and a short, slow wave. 'Hello Crystal. Nice to meet you.'

Crystal gave Norton a disinterested, once up and down. 'So what are you, Les? Some good 'ol Australian boy, are you?'

'That's me, Crystal. One good 'ol Australian boy. With a root-beer to go. Hold the mayo. It's still nice to meet you though,' he added, the half smile still on his face.

'Likewise, I'm sure.' Crystal looked at Les for a moment then started undoing the front of her coat. 'Phew! Thank Christ I can loosen this shit up, I'm almost suffocating. Is it always this fuckin' hot here for Chrissake?'

Crystal undid all her coat and that was when Norton's eyes nearly fell out of his head. In proportion to the rest of her, Crystal had the biggest pair of boobs Les had ever seen. She was wearing a bulky red ski jumper yet they still pushed it out almost to breaking point. They were perfect, they never moved a centimetre. The limo would rock a little moving through the traffic and they sat there like two mini Ayers Rocks. Jesus! thought Les, fascinated, what about those. No wonder the tabloids go mad. Bad luck the pool's empty. Fuck it, if KK doesn't fill it I'll fill it

74

myself. If not, I hope she likes going down the beach topless.

Crystal could sense what Norton was staring at through his sunglasses. She gave her chest a slight shake; nothing moved. 'You like these, do you, Les? KK does. Don't you — darling?'

'I never really noticed, Crystal,' answered Norton. 'But yeah. I wouldn't mind one full of margaritas and the other full of Eumundi Lager. They're not bad — are they?'

Crystal didn't bother to reply. KK looked like he was going to say something for a second, not necessarily to Les, instead he seemed to be deep in thought, picking a little nervously at his chin and gazing out the window. The limo cruised towards the Gold Coast practically in silence, the air of nervous tension seemed to persist all the way to the flats. KK spoke briefly with Crystal a couple of times; Les couldn't hear what they were saying and didn't particularly want to. He was looking forward to the photo session on Monday, though, and was definitely staying in Surfers for that.

Before long they arrived at the flats. There were no TV crews, the networks had more than they needed for the six o'clock news and were probably rushing it to air at that moment. Just two cars with some reporters from a local paper and a tits-and-bums magazine. Crystal did her coat up tight, Les opened the door and stepped out. The journalists and the two photographers barely had time for a quick photo and an even quicker 'Go blow it out your ass motherfuckers' from Crystal. When she and KK were inside the flats with the door slammed behind them, Norton got the bags from the boot. Tony shut it, saying something about he'd be back at eight, then drove off leaving Les standing there holding the two suitcases.

'Well, fellahs,' he said with a shrug to the reporters. 'Not much good you hanging around. She's having a sleep, she's pretty shagged. But we're all going out on the town tonight. Get your photos and that then if you want. They're my instructions anyway.'

75

'Who are you?' asked one journo, his photographer raised his Canon reflex.

Norton thought he'd take a leaf out of KK's book. After all, wasn't he supposed to be family? 'Don't worry about who I am. But if you try and take a photo of me. I'll wrap your camera round your fuckin' head.'

The photographer lowered his camera. 'Did she say anything in the car?' asked the journo.

Norton hoisted the two suitcases. 'Yeah. Yo'all go get yo'selfed fucked now. Y'hear.'

Les slammed the door shut behind him. KK's door was closed when he got up the stairs. Les knocked and waited. Kramer opened the door and took the cases. 'You did good, Les,' he said, half closing the door. 'Tony'll be back with the limo at eight-thirty. We'll see you down the front then. We'll go for a meal.'

'Okay,' shrugged Les. 'If you...'

'Just keep any mugs away from the place. I'll see you then.' Kramer gave Les a quick wink. 'You did good.' The door closed.

The big, red-headed Queenslander stood there for a moment then went inside himself. Well, close the door and bring in the mat, he thought, kicking off his Nikes in the loungeroom. You did good, Les. Good? I did fuck all. Except try not to burst out laughing at the moll. And what about the moll? Tits or no tits, isn't she something else. And doesn't she give out a good pay. I'd like to be around when Crystal baby gets a roll on. The look on that sheila's face when she called her cactus cunt. Ha!

Norton went to the fridge, got a cold beer and took it out on the back sundeck. One thing for sure. If you were putting on a scam, the last person you'd do it with would be her. She's about as cool as a burning oil well. No. Les sat down on a big plastic banana-chair and put his feet up. I can relax now. If there was any scam going on, it would have been between KK's brother and that Black rooster. Now all I have to do is keep those two out of trouble till Tuesday; and get into plenty of trouble with the lovely DD while I'm doing it. He took another slurp

76

of beer. In the meantime, all I gotta do is keep an eye on this joint and hang round till eight, then fill myself full of more good food, and probably have a bit of a late one tonight. Heh-heh! How hard's that? Sipping on his beer, Les figured he'd at least have time for a quick swim. He had a look out the front; the two reporters had gone and there were no cars on the driveway. KK's curtains and blinds were still drawn all around and the place looked safer than Fort Knox. A high brick fence ran around the back; if anyone tried to jump over that, he'd be waiting with a lump of wood. He got down to his Speedos, grabbed a towel and jogged down to the beach, making sure the back gate was closed solidly behind him.

Once again the water was glorious; an easy little wave rolling in and a nice breeze blowing in over the ocean. The only thing missing was DD. Norton splashed around for a short time but duty called so he reluctantly trotted back to the flats; apart from the water, there was a smattering of shapely girls on the beach sunbaking topless.

After closing the back gate, Les noticed a shower near the pool, so he stood under that then got changed into a pair of shorts and a T-shirt upstairs. He got another bottle of Red Stripe from the fridge and was about to take it out on the sundeck when he thought he heard a car pull up in the driveway. Hello, who's this — more fuckin' reporters? He stepped out onto the front verandah and it was a white Econo-Van with 'Mermaid Pool Service' on the side in blue. Norton's eyes lit up. They're going to fill the pool — you bloody beaut. Wait a minute. I know those two blokes. It was Steve and Frank. Steve got out wearing white overalls, carrying an overnight-bag. He had a look around for a moment then noticed Les, stared for a second then smiled and waved. Les smiled back and made a gesture with his bottle. Steve said something to Frank, sitting behind the wheel, who looked up, smiled and waved also. Les acknowledged his wave. The boys are certainly friendly today, he mused. He was about to go down and open the door but by the time he thought about it Steve had let himself in. Les strolled out to the sundeck to see if maybe he wanted a hand; however, after waiting a couple of minutes there was no sign of Steve. Scratching his chin Les strolled back out to the front verandah, but rather than appear to be snooping or make a gig of himself he watched through the curtain. It wasn't long before Steve returned to the van still carrying the overnight-bag. He had another look around then climbed in the front and they drove off. Well, so much for getting the bloody pool filled, thought Les. Then again, KK's probably told him to piss off — he wants to do a bit of porking with Crystal, come back tomorrow. And I can't say I blame him. He took another swig of beer. That's the way they do things in sunny Queensland.

Norton spent the rest of the afternoon sipping one or two more beers on the shaded sundeck, keeping an eye on things while he listened to the FM stereo down low; he even managed to doze off for about an hour. Yes, it was a hard way to earn a dollar.

Later in the evening, the place still looked safe and sound, with no sign of the young lovers, so Les walked to a small supermarket around the corner in the main drag and bought fruit, milk, bread and a few other odds and ends to make a sandwich, getting back in time for a cup of tea and a biscuit and watch the six o'clock news.

There she was, all right; Crystal Linx in all her foul-mouthed glory, giving it to the media and anyone else who happened to be standing around. KK looked kind of cool and kind of nervy at the same time, until he hid himself away in the back of the limo. Behind his sun-glasses, Norton looked like Norton. In fact if you didn't know him, you'd think he was just some other big stone-faced minder doing his job. The Brisbane newsreader seemed quite bemused by the whole thing, and with all the bleeps and the accent, you couldn't tell much what Crystal was saying anyway. Les thought the whole thing was a great hoot and hoped Price and Warren saw it in Sydney. Then it was straight to Canberra and the Prime Minister saying yes, the United States grain subsidies were just about fucking the Australian wheat farmers completely and he would definitely be discussing it with the President when he arrived in Australia on Monday night for a three-day stop-over on his way to Japan. Norton didn't take a great deal of notice of this, he was still chuckling about seeing himself and Crystal on the news. He dunked an arrowroot biscuit into his tea. I can't wait to see what the papers say in the morning.

Wearing jeans and a red check button-down-collar shirt, Les walked down the front around 8.30 p.m. He had heard the limo pull up earlier but left it as long as he could as he didn't fancy being stuck with the driver who, from what Les gathered so far, wasn't the greatest conversationalist in the world. Tony was sitting behind the wheel, Les said a quick hello, got an even quicker one back, then leant against the door. There was no sign of any reporters. About fifteen minutes later, KK and Crystal came out the front door. KK was looking very Boz Scaggs in a white shirt, white belt and trousers; Crystal had on a bulky, blue polka dot shirt with huge dots, a red polka-dot tie, jeans and a blue, loose-fitting cotton jacket. Compared to in the car earlier her moodiness seemed to have vanished, and behind his glasses KK seemed positively ebullient.

'How are you, KK?' asked Les.

KK actually shaped up to Norton and gave him a slap on the shoulder. 'Wouldn't be dead for quids, old mate. Top of the world.'

'How are you, Crystal?'

'Fine, big guy,' she drawled.

Les held the door and they bundled into the limo and drove off. Les settled back to watch them. This time they sat a lot closer, KK even had his hand on Crystal's knee and she was very chummy also; a definite contrast to before. Which was understandable, thought Norton, being stuck in a plane for hours then having to run the gauntlet of the Australian gutter press as soon as you got off. Also, she would have had a rest, got cleaned up and KK probably would have given her one, maybe even two.

Without the sunglasses, she reminded Les a bit of Deborah Harry, only her eyes were narrower and her hair thicker and spikier. The other thing Les noticed was her boobs didn't seem as monstrous as before. They were covered up securely under the shirt and tie, but they didn't seem to thrust out everywhere like when he first saw them. Still, that would have been his first impression plus that big, bulky ski-jumper. They were still heaps big enough though and Norton imagined he'd probably have his work cut out keeping the mugs' hands off them later that night.

'Where are we going for a feed, KK?' he asked.

'A place called Fedora's. Just this side of Burleigh Heads.'

'All right is it?'

'All right! It's the fuckin' grouse. Taking you there is like giving a pig strawberries.'

'Remember what I told you, KK,' chipped in Crystal. 'I don't want some bunch of hillbillies rubber-necking me while I'm eating.'

'No chance, my dear. That's why I chose this place. I'm a regular.'

'I got a feeling it's gonna be the pits afterwards, running in and out of half a million discos with those goddam reporters on my ass. And I ain't stayin' out all night either.'

'No. But we have to celebrate.' KK threw back his head and laughed. 'Hey, do we have to celebrate.'

'Agreed.' Crystal laughed too. 'We do gotta celebrate.'

'You stitched up this record deal, have you?' asked Les tentatively.

Crystal blinked. 'What was that, Les?'

'I said, this music thing, your new record. You stitched it up, have you?'

Through his glasses KK blinked at Les also then threw back his head again and roared laughing. 'Oh yeah. I stitched it up all right. Like you wouldn't believe. Didn't I, Crystal?'

His girl got in on the act and started roaring with laughter too. 'Oh Jesus Christ! He stitched it up all right.

He sure damn did.' She bubbled with laughter almost fit to bust and looked at Norton. 'Oh my God, Les. You're priceless.'

KK had tears running down his cheeks. 'You're beautiful, Les. You really are.'

Norton looked at them howling away at what was obviously some private joke, shook his head and stared out the window. The things a man has to put up with to get a quid. The limo cruised on into the night. After a while Crystal and KK settled down, then they arrived at Fedora's.

The restaurant was right on the beach, sparkling white, brick and timber, all terraced gardens and palm trees and fenced off from the surrounding buildings. The beaming maitre d' was waiting at the door, tuxedoed up to the hilt, all flashy white smiles and oilier than a kerosene lamp. He ushered them to a table overlooking the ocean, treating Crystal as if she was Cleopatra entering Rome; and by the time some waiter had pulled Norton's chair out for him to settle his arse on, Les felt like a slice of snow pudding that just had custard poured all over it.

'Champagne, Mr Kramer?' asked the maitre d'. KK nodded. 'The usual?' KK nodded again. 'Of course.' The head flunky left them to study a menu each then returned with a bottle of '71 Moët in an ice-bucket.

'Want a glass of fizz, Les?' asked KK.

Norton thought for a second. If I've got to keep an eye on these two tonight, I'd better keep a clear head. Besides, that shit gives me an industrial strength headache the next day. 'No. Just a beer'll do thanks. A Crown Lager.'

'You are just a good 'ol boy — ain't you, Les,' smiled Crystal.

'That's all there is where I come from, Crystal,' replied Norton, returning her smile. 'Good 'old big 'uns. And big 'ol good 'uns.'

No matter what Les thought of the company, he couldn't knock Kramer's choice of restaurant. It was all blue and white inside with a beautiful view of the beach, a pianist tinkled a baby grand in one corner and there were

81

tasteful flower arrangements on all the tables, complemented by the subdued lighting. And if the service went overboard, so did the food. It was sensational.

Norton settled for a whole garlic mud crab and a tropical seafood cocktail for an entree. KK and Crystal had a grilled lobster each and mussels à la Parisienne for starters. There was heaps of garlic bread and salads. Les washed it all down with mineral water and finished with pecan pie and orange-coconut sauce. KK and Crystal had glazed blueberry cheesecake, which they didn't finish. Les didn't say a great deal, happy just to pig out while the two lovers got revved up on Moët and pawed at each other. Now and again some of the other diners would look over and make a discreet remark to each other. But they definitely weren't the 'Hey Norm, you know who that is over there' mob. The maitre d' got his photo taken with his arms around the two celebrities, and if his flashy smile had been any whiter, wider or oilier, it would have wrapped itself round his neck and leeched down his back.

All the earlier tension had completely vanished now, though Les figured the third bottle of Moët would have helped. He also figured Crystal definitely had a thing for the little Aussie conman. It may not have been blind passionate love, but it was definitely a thing. Norton had spent worse nights in worse company. Another thing he noticed. Although Crystal spoke with a thick New York accent, every now and again she'd slip into this Southern drawl, smooth as molasses in summer and sweeter than momma's drop-sugar cookies. Norton could have listened to it all night.

With the maitre d' doing everything but hold their hands, they left Fedora's around eleven and bundled back into the limo. KK and his girl were roaring a bit; Les just felt contented.

'So where to now, KK?' he asked, as they moved off along the highway.

'First up the Jade Terrace for a bit of reggae. Then we hit Surfers and let 'em know.' Kramer raised his voice. 'KK's back in town — yeah.'

82

Crystal slapped KK across the shoulder and started singing. 'The boys are back in town. The boys are back in town. Yeahoooowooayeah...'

By the time they went past the casino turn-off, Les figured out why Crystal's last two records had laid a giant egg. Even with studio help and the Sydney Symphony Orchestra behind her, Crystal couldn't carry a note if she and KK were carting it round on a stretcher.

The limo rocked gently to a halt outside the Jade Terrace, which was above the hotel with the mirrored windows Les had noticed the previous day. They climbed out of the car; KK had a beeper with him to let the driver know when they were ready to leave. There were big smiles all round from the doormen; one, a solid bloke going a bit thin on top, walked up the stairs with them. Les immediately liked the Jade Terrace. There was plenty of room, comfortable cane furniture, fish tanks, plants every where, and two balconies opened out over the street so you didn't choke on cigarette smoke. The bar in the middle was a sort of split-bamboo island. But the best part was the band. They were only a two-piece reggae outfit with a synthesiser but they made plenty of sound and the coloured singer had a huge white grin, dread-locks, and looked as if he'd just stepped off a boat from Trenchtown, Jamaica. All the staff knew KK and most of the people had an idea who Crystal was; those that didn't just wanted to know who the spunky little blonde was with the giant, enormous boobs.

It wasn't long and a bottle of champagne in an ice-bucket materialised at their table and Norton had his fist round a bottle of Fourex, which he sipped slowly. KK and Crystal hit the dancefloor and boogied drunkenly around; Les stood close by, quietly sipping his beer and talking to the bouncers who were a pretty good bunch of blokes. There wasn't even the slightest bit of trouble, because as well as yarning to Les, the bouncers were keeping an eye on KK and Crystal too, so Norton earned his money easy. Les could have stayed there all night; the band was great, it was a good atmosphere all round and there was any amount of nice-looking girls. Unfortunately it closed at midnight. KK hit the beeper and with the bouncer and the manager in step they swept down the stairs to the waiting limo.

After the Jade Terrace they hit just about every nightclub and disco in Surfers so KK could let the Gold Coast know he and his American starlet girlfriend were in town. The ridiculous part was, every place they went to was barely fifty metres from the next, yet KK insisted on taking the limo. Oh well, who gives a shit, thought Les. He's paying for it. Though Les was getting a bit sick of opening and closing the doors all the time. And every place they went to, it was the same thing. No matter if there was a queue a mile long or just a few out the front, whoever was on the door would welcome KK with open arms and usher them straight in. The manager or owner would be all smiles and find them the best table in the place, where KK would order a bottle of champagne, drink it, have a dance or two with Crystal, while he lapped up being the centre of attention, then after about thirty minutes they'd be on the move again.

The press were waiting for them at the first two places, Maxines and the Sand Castle, but as soon as they'd got enough photos, got sick of Crystal telling them to 'get the fuck out of here, you piss ass sonsofbitches' and found out they had to pay for their own drinks, they left them alone. The best part was, the manager or owner would always leave one or two bouncers with them so there was no drama at all. The yobbos would whistle and make a few derogatory remarks about Crystal's boobs, but that was as close as they got. Norton was doing it easy and could have got on the piss if he wanted to. But even having one at every place they went to was enough, because they went to plenty, the names going over Norton's head after a while: Blondie's, the Loft, the Love Boat, Rivers, Banana Splits, Cadillacs and more. One place the DJ was suspended above the dancefloor, another he played in the cut-away front half of a truck, another was built into a big sea shell. But they were all pretty much the same inside, mirrored walls and spinning lights going everywhere, they all played the same music and all full of the same boozy punters ogling Crystal while KK lapped it all up, playing Jack the Lad.

By about two-thirty, Les stank of cigarette smoke, was getting awfully tired and he didn't give a stuff if he never heard another Kylie Minogue, Madonna or Prince record again as long as he lived. He also noticed that even though KK was bubbling over with boozy joie de vivre, Crystal had stopped laughing at his jokes, no matter how hilarious KK thought they were. They'd just left some place called the Lighthouse and were in the limo motoring the fifty metres to the next one when Crystal finally snapped.

'All right, KK, that's fucking it.' She was half tanked, her hair was all over her head and the blue polka-dot shirt looked like a tablecloth in a cheap restaurant. 'How many more of these goddam flophouses do we have to go to? I have had e-fucking-nough.'

'Just one more. Then we'll go home.'

'Jesus H Christ!'

'How about you, Les? You havin' a good time?'

'Yeah, terrific, KK. All I live for is cigarette smoke, warm beer and house music.'

The last place was Squadron 9. All done up like an airforce hangar. Photos of aeroplanes all over the walls, half an old Tiger Moth hanging from the ceiling and the DJ in an Air Force uniform playing the usual schlock, now going into a Grease soundtrack medley. Norton felt like vomiting. That's fuckin' it. If I've got to put up with all this shit tomorrow night, I'm throwing the towel in. KK can get fucked. Again KK got the royal treatment and again he ordered another bottle of champagne; just about finishing it on his own. Crystal was staring daggers at him, and when they got up to go, Les had to help him to his feet and out to the car.

'Straight back to the fucking apartment,' Crystal snarled at Tony as soon as Les opened the door.

Sprawled in the back of the limo, KK was now a

blubbering, yammering wreck. His glasses were all over his face and his Boz Scaggs outfit looked like some wino had been sleeping in it. 'What a night,' he slurred. 'What a ripper of a bloody night. What a rip . . . ripper of a day all round. Wadabowd you, Les, old mate? Ripper, or what?'

'Yeah, mate,' replied Les solemnly. 'It was a ripper of a night all right. I've never had such a good time in my life. And you're a ripper of a bloke too, Kelvin.'

'Onya, Les.'

'And thanks for that grouse feed too. It was tops. Especially the crab with all that garlic and cream and butter all over it. It was a bit greasy but, Jesus, it was nice. I can still taste it.' At the mention of food, Kramer's expression seemed to change. He gave a rumbling belch and swayed against the seat. 'What about you, Crystal?' continued Les. 'Did you have a good night?'

Crystal stared moodily at Les. 'Did I have a good night? In and out of those fish markets all night. Having to hold your arm to get through all those drunken peckerwoods every time I went to the john to take a leak. Yeah, it was just peachy.' Then she looked at KK, staring into space and smiled. 'Oh I guess I had a good night. And the food was beautiful.' Crystal put her arm around KK and gave him a cuddle. 'And the company. There's just something about these Aussie boys.'

'Yeah. KK's a gem all right. And can't he put the champagne away too for a little bloke. Especially on top of all that rich tucker.'

Kramer stared at Les uncomfortably. His eyes started to bulge a little, he licked his lips and swallowed a burping hiccup. Norton thought he noticed a slick of sweat starting to glisten on his brow.

'Hey, Crystal,' said Les. 'Have you ever heard of the expression "Having an up and under"?' Crystal shook her head. 'A technicolour yawn? Having a laugh at the footpath?'

'I don't know what the fuck you're talking about.'

'Well, your boyfriend's just about to have all three, sweetheart.'

Les reached over and hit the automatic window button just as KK started to come to life; one hand over his face, the other on his paunchy little stomach. 'Aaaoowargh . . . glurg!'

Norton grabbed him, pushed his face out the window and Kramer let it all go. About five bottles of French champagne, a grilled lobster, cheesecake and one prawn he'd nicked off Norton's seafood cocktail. 'Atta boy, KK. Go for your life, son.' Kramer heaved again and splattered about another half a gallon of vomit all down the side of the limo. 'That's it, mate. Let 'em know KK's back in town.'

KK kept heaving all the way to Hancock Avenue, then dragged himself back in; his face looked like a kilo of octopus that had been off for a week. Crystal had some tissues in her bag and Les had a hanky so they managed to clean him up a bit. But Kramer was a shot bird. He just sat there moaning in Hebrew, English and Swahili.

'Yeah, Crystal,' grinned Les, 'there sure is something about those Aussie boys — isn't there?'

Crystal didn't reply. She kept dabbing at KK's mouth, trying not to get any on her jacket.

The big car came to a stop outside the flats. Les got KK out of the back seat, kicked the door closed and held him round the waist, his head lolling against Norton's shoulder. Tony got out and looked at all the vomit along the side of the car. He was about to say something to Les when Norton noticed another car in the driveway and two figures get out. One was tall and gangly with straggly black hair while his mate was shorter and had a beard. They almost ran over and the beard raised his camera.

'Hey, what do you want?' said Les, propping KK against the limo.

'What do we want?' smirked the tall one. 'Fuckin' photos, you dope. What do you think?'

Norton was tired, just a little edgy, he also had flecks of vomit on his good shirt. And that wasn't a very nice way to talk to people. The beard went to fire off a couple of quick photos when Les grabbed the camera, ripped it straight from round his neck, breaking the strap, then holding it by the lens, smashed it against the concrete driveway. Les gave it another whack then tossed it back to the beard.

'There. How's that for a photo.'

The tall one charged up to Les. 'Hey, what the fuck do you think you're doing?'

Norton backhanded the tall reporter, spinning him against the front of the limo, then grabbed him by the hair and speared him towards the Ford they came in, kicking him up the arse at the same time. The tall one yelped as he hit it head first. Norton grabbed him by the scruff of the neck, banged his head against the door again, opened it and flung him inside.

'And you're on private property, shithead. Now piss off, before I call the cops.' Les turned to the beard. 'You too, whiskers. Fuck off before I shove your camera up your arse.' Whiskers didn't need to be told twice. Holding what was left of his Leica, he was behind the wheel and out of the driveway by the time Les walked back and took hold of KK again. Kramer might have been an obnoxious little turd at times, but he'd just sprung for a terrific dinner and it was Norton's responsibility to keep the mugs away. Whatever his and Crystal's faults were, they didn't deserve to be made to look like idiots by a couple of shitmouth journos from a scumbo tabloid.

'Hey, you're not bad on your feet, are you — you big cheeseburger,' smiled Crystal, taking hold of the still half-comatose KK, who'd missed the whole thing.

Norton ignored her. 'Come on, let's get champagne Schlomo to bed.'

Tony didn't seem to take a great deal of notice at what happened. He was still looking at all the spew down the side of the limo. 'Hey, Les,' he said, 'you got a hose somewhere, mate?'

Norton hoisted KK and started towards the front door. 'All I gotta do is look after the flats, mate, you look after the car.'

They half dragged, half walked KK up the stairs. When

Crystal opened the door he seemed to momentarily come
to life and gurgled straight inside towards the bathroom.

'I'll be all right now, Les,' said Crystal, starting to close
the door. 'Thanks, Les.' Then she smiled a genuine, warm
smile. 'Hey, you're a bit of a honey. You know that, boy?'

'Why ma'am,' drawled Norton. 'Yo'all ain't so bad
yo'self.'

Crystal screwed her face up slightly. 'You sure you ain't
Suthin, boy?'

'No ma'am. Ahm from the Deep North. Goodnight,
Crystal. I'll see you tomorrow.'

Norton blinked around him after he switched on the
light in the loungeroom. Well, so much for Friday night in
Surfers, he thought, kicking off his shoes. Ahh, it wasn't
that bad. I've had a terrific feed, met a couple of good
blokes in that first place we went to with the reggae band.
So I gave flip from the press a smack in the mouth. So
what. And I got paid for it on top. The night was a piece of
piss really — easier than I thought. If it's all like that, I've
earned my money easy. But what about my clothes. He
sniffed his shirt and gave an audible 'phew'. His hair was
the same. Will I have a shower? No, fuck it, I'll have one
beer in peace then hit the sack. I'm knackered.

Les tossed his clothes in the bathroom, got into a clean
T-shirt then took a beer out of the fridge and went out on
the sundeck. There was a nice breeze coming in off the sea
which swept over him like invisible velvet; he noticed a
couple of lights on next door, but no sounds. Halfway
through his beer, Les couldn't believe how tired he suddenly was. Shit! Why not? It was almost 3.30 a.m. Les
didn't even finish his bottle of Red Stripe. He was yawn-
ing like a bear when he tossed it in the bin and turned off
the lights. A smile momentarily flickered across his face
as he crawled into bed and thought about DD and
Sunday night. Half a minute later Norton was snoring his
head off.

Les surfaced around ten, not feeling too bad at all. He'd
had six solid hours' sleep and not having drank much

there was no sign of a hangover. After getting cleaned up a bit, he made a cup of tea and took it out on the sundeck to find it was another hot, sunny day, with just the odd cloud in the sky and a light sou'-easter flicking across the tops of the waves. It was quite pleasant standing there in the breeze, but he still felt grimy and sweaty from the night before. Only one way to get rid of that, he thought. A bit of a gallop and a swim. There was no sound or movement from next door, no cars in the driveway, also no sign of Mermaid Pool Service to fill the pool either. Well, no one's going to miss me for a while. He got into his old training gear, wrapped a sweatrag round his head then after doing a few stretches by the back gate headed south on the soft sand, figuring to have the wind with him on the way back.

It was almost enjoyable jogging along on the soft sand, which was white and clean; the ocean, a few metres off to his left, was as blue and clear as ever and there were a number of girls sunbaking to have a look at as Les ground past. One good thing about running on soft sand, you don't need a Ca Va track-suit or a $300 pair of cross-trainers. All you need is stamina, and plenty of it. By the time Norton got around three kilometres he had to stop and ring out his sweatrag, and when he retraced his steps and arrived back at the flats, everything he'd had to drink in the last week was pouring off his face and running down his back. He found a grassy place by the back gate to do some sit-ups and push-ups, then walked down to the water and flung himself straight in, running gear and all. After the run, the water was that good it was almost indescribable; Les flopped around for almost half an hour and could have stayed in another three. But duty would eventually call.

He had a shower, got into a pair of shorts and a T-shirt then made an awful dent in a litre of fresh orange juice he had in the fridge. There was still no sound from the lovers next door and still no cars around. Les decided to walk up and get the papers and have breakfast at the same place they did the day before. The food there was excellent and

90

he couldn't see any of KK's white shoe friends wanting to put a mag on with him, even if they did recognise him.

Les was about to leave when a thought crossed his mind and a strange smile etched itself across his craggy face. He glanced at his watch. I wonder how things are at Chez Norton's right now? Only one way to find out, and I reckon he'd be up. Norton picked up the phone, pushed the appropriate buttons and took another swallow of orange juice.

'Hello,' came a very dismal, subdued voice at the other end.

'G'day, Woz. It's Les. How are you, mate?'

'Les. Oh, how are going?'

'Pretty good. So how's things with you? Has the house been burgled? Is my car still out the front? What's going on?'

'Ohh things are terrific, Les. Just great.'

'Nice to know you miss me. So what's doing? Did you give the lovely Annie my letter? How did she take it?'

'Terrific, Les. She was rapt.'

'I thought she might have been. Did she get her hairdryer?'

'Yeah. That's what really set her off. I thought I was going to get it wrapped round my head. Christ! Talk about swear.'

'Ahh fuck her anyway. As long it hasn't stuffed things up with you and Gianna.' Norton hedged a little. 'Everything still sweet there?'

Warren seemed to hedge a little too. 'I don't know how to tell you this, Les, but there's been a bit of trouble since you've been gone.'

'Trouble?' Norton raised his voice. 'What do you mean by trouble? You haven't gone to bed pissed and burned the fuckin' joint down, have you? You've blown up the stereo, haven't you. Full of fuckin' dope.'

'I wish to Christ that's all it was,' replied Warren. 'John turned up last night.'

'John?'

'Gianna's boyfriend.'

91

'Oh dear. What happened, Warren?'

'What do you think happened? He punched the shit out of me.'

'Good God, Warren. Are you all right? Tell me what happened, mate.'

Through swollen lips and a swollen nose, Warren told Les how he'd picked the girls up after work on Friday night; Annie still had the shits but was coming along for the ride anyway. They pulled up out the front and there was John. He got out of his car and started abusing the girls, who started screaming. John threw them in his car then went for Warren. Warren put up a fantastic effort, getting punched all the way up the front steps. He would have got punched through the front door as well, only in his rage John slipped on the top step and Warren was able to hit him in the face with a pot-plant off the ledge, splitting John's head open and knocking him down the steps. But not quite out. With blood all over him the girls managed to drag him away and into the car and Warren was able to get inside and lock the door. However, before he drove off, John got the pot-plant and threw it through the front window.

'What!?' bellowed Norton. 'You mean to tell me, I'm not out of the place five minutes and you're out the front brawling in the street. You've wrecked one of those grouse pot-plants dear old Mrs Curtin across the road gave me. And my bedroom window's broken as well. Christ! What must the neighbours think.' Norton was doing his utmost not to laugh. 'You're fuckin' good, Warren, I'll give you that. But fuck it. That's it. Pack your gear. Soon as I get home you're out on your arse. Go move in with your vindaloo queen.'

'Fair dinkum, I am sorry, Les. It's all my fault. I'll pay for it.'

'I'm fuckin' sure you will. Even if I've got to chase you all over Sydney 'cause you're still goin'.' Norton took another sip of orange juice. 'Ahh don't worry about it. Who'd have you anyway — after the reference I'd give you. So how are you? Are you all right?'

'Ohh yeah, real good, Les. Apart from two black eyes, a split lip, a swollen nose and a rotten headache I feel terrific. Plus my knee's fucked.'

'Shit! Jesus, bad luck I wasn't there — the cunt. I might go round and give him a slap for this. He's not too big, is he?'

'He's bigger than me. I know that.'

'Mmmhh! I might have to think on this, Warren.'

'Look, just forget the whole thing, Les. Let it go. It's over anyway.'

'Yeah, I suppose.' Norton took another sip of orange juice and looked out the sundeck to make sure the sky hadn't suddenly gone dark and there were no lightning bolts around. 'I wonder how the cunt found out? Hey, I'll bet it was that fuckin Annie.'

'Yeah, that's what I reckon. Though she seemed to have cooled off a bit coming over in the car.'

'Yeah, that's just the calm before the storm, mate. You know what Bullwinkle, the world's most intelligent moose, said. Hell hath no fury like a woman's corns. Never trust sheilas, mate. She couldn't have me so she crabbed it for you.'

'Did she ever — the bitch.'

'Oh well, bad luck. Though in a way it's partly my fault with that letter I suppose. Anyway let's not dwell on the past. Though no one likes getting a pasting. But things are going all right up here.'

Les told his flatmate about the weather, the unit, meeting Crystal Linx. Warren missed the news but he'd have a look at the papers when he went round the shops. He told Warren about DD and the top night they had and coming back for a gigantic bit of the other. Things were going along swimmingly. Sorry about his love life folding like that, but it could have been his front teeth.

'So that's about it, Woz. If I run DD back to Taree I might stay in a motel for the night, see what happens. But I reckon I'll be back by the end of the week. I'll see you then.'

'Okay, Les. See you when you get back.'

93

'See you, Woz.'

Norton looked at the phone, sipped some orange juice and tried not to laugh. But it was no good. And a swallow of orange juice went down the wrong way to make things worse. After Les choked and spluttered it all out he settled down a bit. Things couldn't have been creamier. No more Annie. No more tandoori twins in general. Bad luck Warren got a bit of a slap, but he wasn't hurt too bad. And that's what happens when you back-door blokes. Bad luck about the pot-plant. And the front fuckin' window. Hah! I can just see Warren getting that fixed. I'll have a beard down to my knees waiting. Norton finished his orange juice. But all this talk about fighting and whatever has put an edge on my appetite. I think it's time for breakfast.

Norton found a paper shop just past Cavill Avenue. They'd made the front page of the *Gold Coast Bulletin* and the Brisbane *Sun* and would have made the front page on the Sydney *Telegraph-Mirror* only they led with all the security arrangements surrounding the President's impending visit. Each paper said much the same thing under the usual, same but different, tabloid banners.

PLAYBOY'S PETULANT PET PELTS PRESS. Not bad mused Les. BIMBO BOOB QUEEN BOUNCES IN AND OUT OF BRISBANE. Reasonable. CRYSTAL LINX STINX. Now that I do like. Short and to the point, so they wouldn't have to tax their brains too much. 'American warbler and B-grade actress, Crystal Linx, let the Australian media know what she thought of them when she arrived in Brisbane, before embarrassed minders swept her into a waiting limousine.'

Embarrassed minders? That's odd, thought Norton. I could have sworn I was on my own and I was rapt in listening to her give it to them. The media then did its best to dump on her. There was a photo of KK and not a bad one of Les standing with the car door open while Crystal gave the press the finger. The rest was a beat-up of how she was a rotten singer, model and actress all

94

round. Kramer wasn't much better and should be in gaol and this latest record was the last chance to save his dwindling fortune. The usual vitriol and half-truths you expect when the media smells blood. Les kept the *Telegraph-Mirror* to read with breakfast, the headlines out of the others and dumped the rest in a garbage tin before walking round to Peggy's.

He found a shaded table to the side of the restaurant and ordered exactly the same as he had the previous day, plus a toasted cheese-and-asparagus sandwich. It was just as tasty and there was just as much as before; Norton took his time eating while he read the paper. Apart from his photo on page three, it was the usual crime scene in Sydney but mainly photos and stories about the US Secret Service arriving in Sydney and setting up security. There were plane loads of them in sunglasses and suits, and they'd brought everything with them but the fun rides in Disneyland and the New York Rockettes. Evidently this was the first time a US president would stay in Brisbane then visit the strategic facilities at Pine Gap. Not that Norton could have given a stuff one way or the other. The President wouldn't be stopping at Chez Norton and Les wouldn't be playing golf with him either. The only good thing in the whole paper was a couple of names in the lift-out racing section at the right odds that could be worth an investment later that day. He finished another coffee, paid the bill and was about to stroll round to the TAB, when Les remembered a small chore he'd promised to do for someone very dear to his heart, and it was just across the road.

The suntanned bloke with the tattoos was in between customers, sitting on one of his deck-chairs reading a magazine; next to him was another bloke, overweight, with a cap covering a balding head, talking into a cellular phone. The thing that struck Les as odd, however, was that if the suntanned bloke went back to Price's era, he had to be getting on for sixty. But in his seaman's cap, worry-free face and lean build, he didn't look much over thirty.

'Excuse me,' asked Les. 'Are you Jimmy Martin?'

The suntanned bloke looked up from what he was reading, studied Les for a moment, then nodded his head slowly and gave a very noncommital yes.

'I've got a message for you from a bloke in Sydney — Price Galese.'

The bloke looked at Les again then shook his head. 'You're not Norton, are you?'

'Yeah,' smiled Les.

'God strike me. I've heard about you.'

'Where from, Price?'

'Where bloody else.' The bloke in the cap shook his head again, then returned Norton's smile. 'God strike me. How is the old bastard anyway?'

'He's good. I'm Les, anyway.'

'Jimmy. Pleased to meet you, Les.' Jimmy took Norton's offered hand and gave it a solid pump. 'So what's the message from the old crook?'

Norton shrugged. 'All he said was, are you still cooking those oysters Amos?'

'Ho! Jesus!' This seemed enough to send Jimmy into a complete tailspin. He slapped his leg and threw back his head howling with laughter. 'God strike me. Did he say that — did he?'

'Yeah,' nodded Les, somewhat mystified. 'That was the message.'

'God strike me.'

Jimmy continued to roll around on his deck-chair, laughing like he was about to blow a boiler. His mate looked up from his cellular phone, gave his head a bit of a shake and continued talking. Norton was just puzzled. It was the most cryptic message ever, yet at Jimmy's reaction you'd have thought Norton just came out with the best gag of all time.

'So what's the joke, Jimmy?' asked Les. 'You're gonna have to tell me.'

Jimmy dabbed at his eyes. 'Price has never told you?' Norton shook his head. Jimmy shook his head also and stared at the sand for a moment. 'Christ! This goes back to 1959, '60.'

Jimmy, it turned out, had been a seaman for years and good mates with Price. Jimmy got a nest egg together and gave up the sea to become a successful restaurateur in Sydney around the same time Price kicked on in the gambling and started to set up the Kelly Club. Both being larrikins and knockabouts and plain good blokes, between the casino and Jimmy's popular restaurant they got to know just about everybody in the Eastern suburbs on both sides of the law, including a crime boss called Amos Nathan. Nathan used to run mainly strip-joints — sly-grog shops as they were known then — nightclubs, porn and just about anything to do with vice and sex. He wasn't interested in drugs and he left the gambling to Price and his bunch, but Nathan just about ran Kings Cross. The odd thing was, in twenty years of extremely dicey operations, Nathan barely had a strike against him. Nathan had oiled plenty of palms in both the government and the police department. The only thing they got him on in the end was tax evasion. And then they had to pay someone to shelf him.

One Saturday afternoon, Jimmy and Price had to go round to Nathan's house in Bellevue Hill with several cases of good scotch and a bag of American cigarettes, all at the right price for his clubs. One of Nathan's heavies opened the door with just a towel round his waist and told them to come inside. In the loungeroom, Nathan and another heavy were sitting around with no gear on plus four big-titted strippers, who also had no gear on, and several plates of choice Sydney rock oysters on the shell. It was what they were doing with the oysters, where they were sticking them and how they were getting them out, that spun both Jimmy and Price around: especially Price, being a good Catholic and all that. Nathan invited both Price and Jimmy to join the party. Jimmy was half keen to give it a whirl but Price shook his head and suggested they get on the toe, saying they had other deliveries to make and that. It was just as well they did. They'd barely got to the end of the street when three car loads of Vice Squad detectives came roaring down the street with a

97

warrant, banged on Nathan's door and arrested all of them on morals charges; even confiscating the oysters as evidence. In those days in Australia, bikinis were about a foot wide on the side, using the word 'bloody' was tantamount to blasphemy and the merest glimpse of a woman's breast, let alone a nipple, was enough to send ordinary citizens, church leaders in particular, into a foaming-at-the-mouth-tambourine-banging frenzy. So placing Sydney rock oysters in big-titted young ladies' private parts and sucking them out again was considered in extremely bad taste, no pun intended, and not a particularly nice thing to do on a Saturday afternoon; especially by square-headed members of the New South Wales Vice Squad. Amos and his team got off with a very heavy fine and a suspended sentence, and were lucky they didn't go to gaol. Nowadays, you can get the same thing on video, in glorious technicolour with a Dolby sound track.

Just as a joke though, Jimmy thought up this oyster dish for his restaurant, using chopped smoked salmon, white wine and spices popped under the griller and called it oysters Amos. And it was very popular with the customers. Till one night Nathan came in, saw it, ordered a dozen, and although he said he liked it, he also said he didn't want to see it on the menu again. So rather than have his restaurant fire-bombed, or be the only maitre d' in Sydney working tables in a wheelchair, Jimmy took them off the menu. Oysters Amos were off, in more ways than one.

'So that's the story of oysters Amos, Les,' smiled Jimmy. 'Does it make you hungry?'

Norton wasn't laughing as much as Jimmy had been, but it was still a reasonable yarn which he somehow couldn't quite picture Price coming up with late one night back at the club. 'No, Jimmy,' he replied. 'Not really. In fact I doubt if oysters au natural will ever be the same again.'

Just then a platoon of tourists lobbed up for a suntanoil spray, deck-chairs, surf-mats, the lot.

'Listen,' said Jimmy, taking hold of his spray-gun.

'Why don't you come round a bit early one day and we'll have a good yarn. Saturday's a bastard of a time. And I gotta get a quid while it's on.'

'Okay, Jimmy,' answered Norton. 'I got to get going myself. But I'll make sure I see you before I go back to Sydney.'

'See you, Les.' The compressor clattered into life and a fine mist of suntan oil wafted into the air.

Norton was still chuckling a little when he walked into the TAB just past Cavill Avenue. But he stopped chuckling when he had to work out the different betting tickets, the change of colours on the horse sheets, and the meeting codes to put a bet on in sunny Queensland. Somehow he managed to get a couple of all-ups going in Sydney, a quinella in Brisbane, and the daily double in Melbourne together and be back at the flat with some fresh milk and more orange juice to find the curtains still drawn next door.

So what to do now? thought Les. All these decisions so early in the day. One thing for sure, I don't need anything else to eat. He leaned against the railing on the sundeck and looked at the people lying on the beach and the others in the water. The water still looked inviting. Too inviting. There were no cars in the driveway: no noise from next door. Before he knew it, Les had a towel round his neck and was jogging across the sand to the water's edge.

He gave it another half an hour, wallowing around like a red-haired hippopotamus, catching the odd wave and thinking, when it was all boiled down, how lucky he was to come up here, eat his head off, do this and cop $1,500 at the same time. A couple of big-titted young girls walked past Norton, sprawled out in some shallow water; Les smiled at them and they smiled back. Ahh yes, how sweet it is, Norton smiled to himself. And this afternoon, I know how to make it even sweeter. Whistling happily, he walked back to the flats, had a shower and got into a pair of shorts. Still whistling, he moved the stereo speakers so they faced the sundeck, got a beer out of the fridge, put a cassette on and did what he'd planned the day before: stick his feet up, have a cold one and listen to the tapes he got made up in Sydney with the million-dollar view in front of him. No one to annoy him. The only mild disturbance a couple of willie-wagtails and the odd magpie either fluttering or walking around in the backyard.

What the music was, Les wasn't quite sure; some sort of toe-tappin' rock'n'roll with a raunchy, shuffling beat and an accordion. Some of the lyrics were in French. But he could make out some bloke saying,

> *Hot steppers dance Zydeco.*
> *Hot steppers dance Zydeco.*
> *Hot steppers dance the varnish off the flo'.*
> *Hot steppin' that Zydeco.*

Whatever you say, pal, agreed Norton, demolishing one beer and starting on another. He was lying back on the banana-lounge, listening to the music with his eyes closed when Norton sensed something. He opened his eyes and Crystal was standing on her sundeck looking at him. She had a dressing-gown wrapped loosely around her and her hair was still wet from the shower. He was about to say something when Crystal spoke.

'Where's that music coming from, Les?'

Norton indicated with his bottle. 'Just some tapes I got playing on the stereo. Hope I didn't wake you up.'

Crystal looked a little surprised. 'That's your music?' Les nodded. 'That's Cajun music.'

'I don't know what it is. But it sounds all right to me.'

Crystal cocked her head to one side. 'That's Queen Ita and the Bon Temps Zydeco Band.'

'I wouldn't have a clue,' shrugged Norton. 'I just like it.'

Crystal looked at him for a moment. 'Do you mind if I come in for a while, Les?'

'No, go for your life. Your key fits my door.'

A few minutes later, Crystal was standing on the sundeck, a T-shirt on under the dressing-gown, everything else heaving against the lot. Apart from a bit of a hard face she didn't look too bad.

'Would you like a beer or a cup of coffee, Crystal?'

100

'I wouldn't mind a cup of coffee.' Les went to get up.
'Stay there. I'll get it.'

Crystal found the jug and the coffee and a few minutes
later was back on the sundeck sipping a mug of coffee.

'Well, you've brushed up all right, Crystal. How's
champagne Charlie this morning? He looked like death
warmed up the last time I saw him.'

'He's not so good. He got up for a while earlier, then
went back to bed.'

'We going nightclubbing again tonight?'

'I would doubt that very much.' Crystal sipped her
coffee, then a big grin spread across her face as a new
track came on and she started bopping around a little to
the music. 'Hey, that's Boozoo Chavis.'

'It is?'

'I used to see him in New Orleans, Les. The big easy on
the big drink.' Crystal took another sip of coffee and
started singing along with the lyrics; considerably better
than in the car the night before.

Eighteen, nineteen, twenty years ago.
Uncle Bud beat the devil out of cotton eyed Joe. Uncle
Bud.
Down in Louisiana where the grass grows green.
They got more women than you ever seen. Uncle Bud.
Uncle Bud got cotton, ain't never been picked.
Uncle Bud got corn ain't never been shucked.
Uncle Bud got a daughter ain't never been touched.
Uncle Bud.
Uncle Bud got a daughter, her name is Joan.
Soft as butter, make her old man moan. Uncle Bud.

Crystal threw back her head and laughed. 'Where did
you get this music, Les?'

'I got a bloke in an import shop in Sydney to make it up
for me. Do you like it?'

'Like it?' Crystal shook her head and a far-away look
came in her eyes for a second or two. 'Shoot, Les, that
music reminds me of home. Good times, good folks, good
fiddles and good whisky.'

101

'Home?' Les looked quizzical. 'This is some sort of southern music. I thought you came from New York?'

'In a pig's ass I do. I've been there about three years. The Big Apple. Hah! The big sewer'd be more like it. But that's where the money is.' Crystal smiled a sweet smile. 'No, Les. I come from a little town called Granite Falls, North Carolina.

'North Carolina? Is that in the south.'

'Is North Carolina in the South?' Crystal looked shocked. 'Boy, have you got a sassy mouth. Keep on with uppity talk and ah might just have to whip yo' ass. Of course it's in the South. We're talking mint-juleps, magnolia blossoms and maghty fahn folks. It's the Red Cardinal state.'

'Red cardinal?'

'Yeah. It's a bird. The state bird.' Crystal pointed to one of the willie-wagtails bobbing around in the backyard. 'Like that li'l critter there. Only all red with a black face.'

'Oh.' Norton eased back on the banana-lounge. 'So tell us a bit about yourself, Crystal. And do it in that southern accent. It cracks me up.'

'Wah Rhett.' Crystal batted her eyelids. 'Ah declare, you do make a gal blush so. You want ah should talk suthin?'

'Ah'd surely be obliged, ma'am.'

Crystal laughed then gave Les a bit of a rundown on herself while she sipped her coffee and the cassette played in the background. She did come from the little town she mentioned where, with her giant, humungus boobs, she just about got driven mad. She was half singing in a band and doing other work and finally figured there were bigger things in store for her other than her tits, so she drifted down to a place called Baton Rouge, Louisiana, and joined up with a zydeco band — Big Gator Cha Cha. After a while she ended up in New Orleans, singing, doing a bit of modelling and cheesecake. It was here she met KK and his brother Menachem. She drifted up to New York to do more cheesecake photos and ended up cutting two

102

records. She met KK again in New York and ended up going with him. All the time telling her story she spoke 'suthin', and the accent had Norton fascinated.

Crystal looked into her now empty coffee cup. 'Les, have you met Kelvin's brother Menachem?'

Norton nodded. 'Several times.'

'If I tell you something about him, Les, do you swear you won't repeat it?'

'Sure.'

'I saw Manny kill two men one night with his bare hands. Two of the biggest niggers I ever seen.'

'Fair dinkum?' Norton wasn't the least surprised, but he was more than interested. 'Tell us what happened.'

'It was goddam quick, I know that.'

Crystal was working in a club in New Orleans. She's just met Kelvin, who of all things was in town getting a scam going with some old swamp woman in a bayou somewhere to make Cajun Slimming Herb Tea, or something equally devious. He was cheeky, liked a laugh, didn't mind spending up and Crystal liked him. 'Crocodile Kramer' she called him. One night Kelvin picked her up after work and he had his brother with him. They were walking back to the car parked near some alley when two huge black men holding knives jumped them. Again Crystal added how quick it happened. But somehow Manny shaped up to the first mugger like a boxer, grabbed his knife hand, pushed it up in the air, turned inside him, brought the knife hand back down and, bending the mugger's wrist, stuck the knife straight up into his heart. Norton gave a double blink as Crystal tried to show how he did it. The second mugger, Manny stepped to his left, slapped his hands around the huge black's right wrist, where he was holding the knife, stepped inside, blocked the mugger's right leg with his left, flipped him over his hip, then took the knife off him and shoved it into his heart. Both muggers were dead before their heads hit the sidewalk, and they hardly got time to make a sound.

'And he stabbed the both of them?'

'Did he ever. But you know the darndest thing, Les, he dragged both of them into the alley with the knives still sticking in their chests. Layed them out in front of each other and placed their hands around the other's knife. It was in the papers the next day. "Two men found dead in alley after killing each other in a knife fight".' Crystal gave a little laugh. 'They called it the Stagger Lee and Billy killing.

'That's journalists for you,' said Norton.

'Yeah. Ain't they the pits.'

'Oh, by the way. Did you see what the local variety had to say about you?' Les got the papers from the kitchen and handed them to Crystal. 'Not a bad photo of me.'

Crystal looked at the *Telegraph* first. 'What the fuck's this? "Crystal Linx Stinx." The goddam sonsofbitches.'

'Yeah, they're good, aren't they. I mean it's not as if you said anything to upset them.'

Crystal gave Norton a quick look then started reading. Les studied her over the papers, trying to figure her out. Was she really a foul-mouthed dropkick or just a country girl at heart who'd moved to the city and got hardened up a bit — something like himself in a way. Her story about moving from Granite Falls to New York via New Orleans was a hoot, and she didn't mind throwing in a laugh now and again. But even with the laughs and this southern gal bit, Les had a feeling she was holding something back. Yeah. Her tits, he laughed to himself, watching them straining against her dressing-gown. I wonder what she'd say if I asked for a private showing? They were still something else and Les was still looking forward to Monday's photo session. But what about Menachem's story. I knew he was bad news and that was the full-on Special Forces unarmed combat stuff she described. Right up his alley. And what about the way he left the bodies. How cool was that. No matter what happens up here, I think I'll keep sweet with his young brother.

'I don't believe these assholes,' snorted Crystal, handing Les back the paper and the headlines he'd saved.

104

'What a scuzzy thing to say about a fine suthin' belle like me,' she added, batting her eyelids.

'They just ain't got no class, ma'am.' Les took a sip of beer. 'So what are you going to say to them at the great unveiling on Monday, Crystal?'

'The great unveiling?'

'Yeah. When they take the photos on Monday and you drop 'em out for all to see. I was hoping to get a sneak preview round the pool. I even bought a two-litre bottle of baby-oil. One for each. I'm keen, Crystal.'

Crystal looked evenly at Norton's cheeky grin. 'We'll see what happens on Monday,' she replied slowly.

Norton was about to say something when he heard a voice behind him. He turned around: it was KK.

'Hello. What's going on here, behind my back?'

'Nothing much, KK,' replied Les. 'I'm just getting your girl drunk, that's all. So how are you feeling, killer?'

KK had a dressing-gown on and was holding a glass of Seltzer. 'Not real good,' he answered, shaking his head very slowly. 'Hey, Crystal told me what you did out the front last night. Thanks for that, Les.'

'That's okay,' said Norton. 'You never had your yamulka on, and it was Friday night. I thought you might've got the shits on religious grounds.'

Kramer winked; even that looked like it hurt. 'I might even give you a bonus when this is all over.'

Norton returned KK's wink. 'That would be very nice of you. So what's doing tonight? What do you want me to do?'

'You fancy eating around eight?'

'Yeah, sure.'

'We'll have a feed somewhere, then we'll go up to Neptune's for a bit of flutter. Show you what a real casino looks like. Not like that yabbie's nest you work in up the Cross for that thieving ex-milkman.'

'And afterwards I imagine we'll be going on another champagne tour of Surfers Paradise, KK? If they can get the limo cleaned.'

'No,' answered Kramer dryly. 'We won't be going

105

nightclubbing tonight, Les. Maybe one place is all. It's a quiet sort of joint and I want to see the owner. He's a good bloke. A couple of drinks then home. I'm not having a late one.'

'Suits me.'

'Hey, Les,' said Crystal. 'Do you mind if I borrow a couple of these tapes?'

While he was talking to Kramer, Les didn't notice Crystal take her cup into the kitchen and come back holding two cassettes. 'No, go for your life. There's about half a dozen there.'

'Just these two will do. Thanks, Les.'

Crystal turned and started towards the door. Kramer made a move too. 'I'll see you down the front about seven-thirty or so, Les.'

'Righto.' Kramer went inside, drawing the curtain behind him, leaving Norton alone on the sundeck.

Well, there you go, mused Norton. Dinner at eight. That shouldn't be too hard to take. He took another mouthful of beer. The only thing is, what am I going to do between now and eight o'clock? Decisions, decisions. Does it ever bloody stop. He took another slurp of beer, which finished the bottle, and gave a little sigh of exasperation. I may as well get a job as be like this. Les shook his head and looked at the empty bottle. Well, I suppose the first thing I'd better do is get another bottle of beer. Then put another tape on and do pretty much what I was doing before. What a bastard. Tough and all as it was, Norton did just that.

It wouldn't have been hard to drink every beer in the fridge, sitting on the shaded verandah, looking at the ocean while the music played. But after one more Red Stripe, Norton decided to hit it on the head. Even though tonight would be another piece of piss, turning up out the front three parts drunk just wouldn't be right. He ended up dozing off for about an hour, that wasn't hard to do at all. By then it was time to walk round to the TAB and see how his bets had gone: the quinella and the double both went down, but his all-up place bet fell in, leaving him just

on $230 in front. Which had him whistling away as he
made a cup of tea back at the flats. He thought about
giving DD a ring, but decided against it. She's a nice
enough girl and all that, thought Les. But she's still an
Australian one. If I ring her up and let her know I'm too
keen, she's just as likely not to turn up tomorrow night.
I'll ring her Sunday arvo. A slightly derisive smile flickered across Norton's face. I could ring Warren I suppose.
I doubt very much whether he'll be going out anywhere
tonight. Not where anyone knows him anyway. Poor
little cunt. I guess that was a bit of a weak act. But serves
him right, and a bit of a hiding now and again never hurt
anyone. It livens you up a bit — if anything. There were
other calls Les could have made: instead he took his time
under the shower and getting himself cleaned up. He was
out the front not long before eight and seeing as they were
going to Neptune's Casino he wore his blue trousers,
white Kelly Country Hawaiian shirt and the blue Italian
casuals. He didn't look too bad.

Tony was waiting, sitting behind the wheel of the limo.
Les gave him a friendly, warm smile, dripping with
falsity, and got a half smile back from the driver who said
nothing. Well, at least we know where we stand, mused
Norton, leaning against the back door. Around eight
o'clock, the royal couple came out the front door. Crystal
was wearing a loose fitting white top that buttoned across
her shoulder, something like a chef's coat, jeans and
denim cowboy boots. Kramer had on grey trousers, a
grey and black check shirt with a bit of gold-plating
round his neck and of all things, white shoes. Am I seeing
things? thought Les. I'm going to have to say something
here. Then again, if he's springing for another grouse
meal, he can wear sandals, black socks and a hanky on his
head with a knot tied in the corners if he wants to.

   'Hello KK, Crystal,' said Norton pleasantly, as he
opened the back door. 'How's things?'
   'Good, mate,' beamed KK from behind his glasses.
   'Jes fine,' smiled Crystal, giving her eyelids a flicker.

They settled in the back of the limo. Tony must have known where they were going in advance and the big car cruised gently off towards the highway.

'You picked a place for dinner?' asked Les. 'I wouldn't mind going back to that joint we went to last night. It was tops.'

'No,' answered Kramer. 'We're going up the other end of town. A place called the River Terrace. It's right on the river, the food's sensaish, and seeing it's such a delightful night, I thought we might eat out in the open. That sound alright to you?'

'Couldn't be creamier,' replied Les. 'A man just doesn't know how lucky he is — does he?'

'That's what I keep telling you, Les. Taking you to all these grouse restaurants is like giving a pig strawberries.'

Norton nodded slowly in agreement. 'And will you be seated in the same place coming home?' He reached over, pressed a button and the window whined up and down next to Kramer's head. 'Just testing,' smiled Norton. 'Make sure I can reach it in time.'

Kramer didn't reply. He just studied Norton impassively from behind his glasses. Crystal didn't say anything either. But the way she had her hands over her face and turned towards the window, Norton had an idea she would have liked to. Norton left them alone with their thoughts or whatever and before long they pulled up out front of the restaurant.

The River Terrace was about three kilometres the other side of Cavill Avenue, set unobtrusively between the high-rises and the other buildings. It was mainly green and white with palm trees and vines pushing through spreading jasmine and bougainvillea. There was one level as you walked in and another edged out onto a white concrete wharf built a few metres along the Nerang River. They didn't quite get the royal treatment like the night before, but it was that close it didn't make any difference. This time the maitre d' was a smiling brunette in a crisp pink dress who seemed to know Kramer; she ushered them downstairs to their table, which was set in an alcove

108

overlooking the river, something like a box-seat at the theatre. The lights from the surrounding buildings sparkled softly on the water, gentle music drifted out from the restaurant and the fragrance of jasmine and other flowers hung in the cool, silken night air. You couldn't help but be impressed. Christ! How good is this, thought Norton. It just gets better and better. I might even bring DD here tomorrow night. I wonder what the chomp's like?

The 'chomp' was equal to the surroundings. Kramer ordered champagne, a '63 Tattinger, which Les noticed he sipped rather than swilled; although Crystal gave the first bottle quite a nudge. Les ordered a bottle of Lowenbrau, because of all things the waiter reminded him of Jacko in *Brush Strokes*. Kramer had barbecued Moreton Bay bugs for entree, Crystal went for veal con funghi, then they both had another lobster each with the trimmings. Norton opted for the pan-fried barramundi in brandy and cream and a mud crab with sweet curry sauce that was almost as big as an armoured car. Everything was super delicious and definitely worth every cent of whatever it was costing KK.

It was delightful eating out in the open: no one to ogle or annoy them and the gentle breeze kept the air fresh and clean of any fumes or cigarette smoke. Norton got in on the conversation a bit, dropping the odd anecdote about the Kelly Club and growing up in Queensland. KK joked about a couple of scams he'd pulled off in England and going to college in Melbourne. Crystal talked about life in New York and growing up in North Carolina. The food, drink and conversation went down admirably and again Norton had spent worse nights in far worse company, and if this was how you earned $1,500 maybe the world wasn't such a bad place after all and KK wasn't such a bad bloke. Maybe. The lady in the pink dress was in constant attendance, and towards the end of the night asked if she could have a photo taken with them; this time including Norton. They had coffee but no sweets, knocked over some more Tattinger and Lowenbrau and around ten-thirty headed happily for the casino. Kramer was in reasonable shape mainly because Crystal had done his share of the drinking for him.

Having forgotten Neptune's was a hotel as well as a casino, Norton found the place to be a lot bigger than he expected when he opened the door of the limo to let Charles and Diana out. At first it reminded him of a pastel-coloured shopping mall, only more modern, a lot brighter and glitzier.

Tony parked the car, a sliding glass door hissed open, and they stepped through. It was quite immense inside, there were rows of shops and kind of arcades going off to the left and right, a glass lift glided smoothly up to a disco and another bar area or something and the whole complex beneath was surrounded by several stories of rooms and balconies festooned with hanging plants and vines. Gazing up and around, it looked all very swish and opulent. The gambling area for the average punters was straight ahead with another darkened and more secluded area below for the high-rollers. There was a throng of people on the move and Crystal's splash in the local papers must have been noticed by and large because quite a number of heads turned in their direction, including the uniformed security staff. Les was about to ask KK what he wanted to do when Kramer spoke.

'There's a bar just over there,' he indicated with a nod of his head. 'We'll have a couple to get us in the mood, then we'll attack.'

'Okey doke,' answered Les.

The bar to their right was called the Azmuth Lounge, and didn't appear too crowded for a Saturday night. There was no shortage of chairs and green marble tables. A green lounge ran round the outer perimeter dotted with several palm trees and a waist-level brass-rail ran round the bar. Stuck in the middle of this was a two-piece combo warbling some old Hall and Oates song. Norton ushered KK and Crystal to a table and sat them down; although there were two or three waitresses in floral dresses hovering around, Les said he'd go to the bar for the drinks.

110

'Let me have a shout, KK,' he said, 'it's the least I can do for those two top feeds you shouted me.'

'Suit yourself,' shrugged Kramer.

KK ordered a J and D scotch highball, Crystal wanted a double George Dickles on the rocks. Les wasn't particularly buying the drinks out of generosity or that he had changed his mind all that much about Kramer, but something caught his eye as they stepped into the Azmuth Lounge that KK never noticed and he doubted if Crystal would have anyway. Six rather stocky gents, all about thirty, were standing near the bar, casually and neatly dressed, something like Les. A couple were even wearing white shoes. They were all different heights and shapes, all tanned and solid and giving the appearance that they kept themselves in reasonably good shape; there may have been a couple of paunches from good food and drink but definitely no sloppy beer guts. Some had tattoos and streaks in their hair, and there was no shortage of gold-plating and junky gold rings. The solidest one had a crop of dark hair that started just above the ridge of his nose and looked thick enough to cut a fire trail in.

However, it wasn't just their stand-out appearance that caught Norton's eye on the night. Most everybody else that glanced over when they walked in seemed to have a look of bemusement on their faces: plenty of look-who-that-is-over-there, nudge-nudge, wink-wink. But as soon as this team saw Kramer their faces soured noticeably, and after working on the door of the Kelly Club, watching hundreds, probably thousands of punters coming and going, Norton could sense a bad vibe a hundred metres away through a dense fog. He went to the bar and ordered the drinks, plus a Jim Beam and coke for himself, and while making out he was checking his money, casually watched the six men in the bar mirror. They gave him a cursory glance but their eyes kept darting towards Kramer and you didn't have to be a lip-reader to know when someone was muttering 'fuckin' little cunt' out the side of their mouth. Les also thought he distinctly heard one bloke say something along the lines of 'Like to break his

111

fuckin' little neck.' Mmhh, thought Norton, as he walked back with the drinks. It appears not everybody on the Gold Coast has a pin-up of young KK in their locker at work. And those gents aren't the happiest chaps I've seen at the best of times. If Norton had been driving around on Wednesday night he would have noticed the same six blokes looking a lot less happier as they were searching up and down the Gold Coast Highway for a blue overnight-bag full of pot.

'There you go,' he said, placing the drinks on the table. Les sat down and raised his glass. 'Well, here's to a lucky night on the tables.'

'Yeah, cheers,' said KK.

'Here's mud in your eye,' winked Crystal.

Norton took another sip and turned to KK. 'It's funny,' he said, 'but I thought I saw a bloke over there I know from Sydney. Do you know any of those blokes at the other end of the bar, KK?'

Kramer turned around, had a brief look then turned around just as quickly. 'No,' he said emphatically. 'No one there I know."

'Yeah?' replied Les. 'Oh well. I must have been mistaken.' And I think your honest, straightforward answer, Kelvin, tells me everything I need to know. They won't start anything in here. But I might just avoid those chaps if I happen to be out and about with you and your lovely girlfriend and should see them somewhere. Six to one against aren't quite the odds I like.

The combo slipped into a tortured version of 'Radio Ga Ga' that would have brought a tear to Freddie Mercury's eye; and not just from copping a rather large one up the date either.

They had another two rounds of drinks and Les noticed the six men exit stage-right with one or two more sour glances in Kramer's direction.

'Well, what are we gonna do?' demanded Crystal, three double bourbons under her belt plus the champagne earlier. 'Sit on our goddam butts all night? I'm feeling lucky.'

112

'Yeah,' agreed Kramer. 'Let's go kick some arse.'

They finished their drinks and moved into the casino.

So this is the ultra swish Neptune's, is it? mused Norton, taking a look around. There were roulette wheels, baccarat tables, Black Jack, Sic Bo, people playing keno and other games spread out around green baize tables and green vinyl chairs under a chrome ceiling. A bank of electronic card machines ran around all this, plus several bars and waitresses in floral dresses moving around the punters and the croupiers in grey and white striped shirts with flat, red bow-ties. It was a fair sized area and the people were either seated or walking around while light music wafted down from the ceiling. Yes, it's certainly different from the Kelly Club, thought Les, not all that interested. Half the cunts in here wouldn't get in for a start. There were no good-looking hostesses in cocktail gowns and no well-dressed patrons. Half the punters wore un-ironed T-shirts tucked into daggy jeans and scruffy running shoes. Les even spotted a couple of chats in daggy track-suit pants. And I went to the trouble of ironing a shirt and polishing my shoes. I've been in better RSLs.

'Well, what do you reckon, Les?' said KK. 'Bit of class for a change, old son.'

'Yeah, terrific,' nodded Les. 'Who did they design the place after? Western Suburbs Leagues Club?'

Kramer was about to say something when Les thought he heard some bloke calling out 'Banzai. Banzai'. Crystal heard it too.

'Hey,' she said. 'Did I just hear some guy say, "Hands high. We're rolling"?' She looked to Norton's right. 'Hey, I did. That's a goddam craps table over there.'

Les glanced over to where a group of people, mainly men, were throwing dice. 'Can you shoot craps, Crystal?' he asked.

'Can I shoot craps?' Crystal looked at Les. 'Can Liz fuckin' Taylor do the Bridal Waltz? Has Buddy Holly stopped wearing glasses. Let's go.'

'I'm going to play Black Jack,' said Kramer. 'Will you look after Crystal while I'm gone?'

113

Norton was about to say yes. Instead he took off after Crystal, who made a bee-line for the craps table.

Norton wasn't all that familiar with craps. Price put a table in once, but it was too noisy, and worse, if the punters weren't careful, they could actually win. Billy and Les had a bit of muck around at the thing and were starting to get the gist of it when Price pissed the craps table off. The betting system was a little like two-up, you bet against the house, and you could bet with or against the punter who was rolling. It was more fun, though, to be with the thrower and hope he'd get on a roll, because while he was winning you won, and the more he won the more you did too. There were other ways you could bet. Like Hard Ways, where you had to throw the same two numbered dice or One Roll Bets, where the dice have to come up exactly as you call them, and Points. But if you're not throwing you just follow the roller, hope he or she wins, and make plenty of noise while you're at it. Although it is a fun game and very popular in America, it's rarely if ever played in Australia and there would be one craps table in a casino at the most. The closest thing in Australia to it would be Crown and Anchor.

There was a fair smattering of punters around the long, green table, if not actually a swarming throng. Crystal was standing near the win line. Naturally the game slowed up when she arrived on the scene; even if there was no display of cleavage in her white chef's jacket, you couldn't miss everything else. The boxman had just yelled, 'New shooter. High low to bet,' when his voice trailed off and the entire crew of dealers momentarily stopped. The assistant pit boss, in his grey suit and red tie, moved closer to the table as one of the crew, with one eye on Crystal called out. 'Hands... high. And... we're, we're... rolling.' Then the shooter rolled and, monstrous boobs or not, the game got itself back together because there was money involved.

Crystal took Norton's elbow. 'Here, do me a favour, Les,' she said, opening her bag and pulling out a thousand dollars. 'Get me some chips. And I don't mean a carton of

114

fuckin' French fries either, you big, dumb Australian peckerwood. Tens and twenties.'

'Certainly, oh sweet magnolia blossom,' answered Les dryly. 'How could one possibly refuse.'

Norton got the chips, returned to the craps table and handed them to Crystal, who was studying the roller. Although he'd established a point, Crystal soon figured he didn't have much of an idea what he was doing so she shoved a stack of chips on the Don't Come, meaning she could get in on the action without waiting for a new Come Out Roll to start. The roller threw, the boxman called out 'Sixes came easy'. No one appeared to do all that well but a pile of chips got pushed in front of Crystal. She left them where they were, three more blokes threw and more chips got pushed in front of Crystal. Before long it was her turn to roll.

'New shooter,' called the assistant pit boss, moving closer again. 'Lady's going to throw.'

'Hands high, hands high,' yelled one of the pit crew.

Crystal pushed all the chips she'd won, plus some more, onto the win line. She smiled round the table at all the punters, rattled the dice next to her ear then blew into her hand and winked at Les. 'Momma needs a new pair of shoes.' There was a quick flick of her wrist and bang! Up it came. 6 and 5. Norton gave a double blink.

There was a general hoo-ha from around the table, the assistant pit boss clapped his hands. 'And the lady is good.'

Crystal pushed all her chips onto the win line as the dice came back to her. Again she rattled them next to her ear, blew in her hand and winked at Les. 'Gotta get mah man off welfare.' Whack! Crystal did it again.

'Oh yeah,' cried the assistant pit boss. 'Rattle them bones, lady.'

Norton scarcely had time to blink when Crystal moved her chips round the table and had the dice up next to her ear ready for a One Roll Bet. Again she winked at Les. 'Devil's in hell, pappy's in heaven, looks like ahm gonna have to roll a seven.' The dice flicked across the table and

115

bingo! there it was, 4 and 3. There was a roar from the crowd, the assistant pit boss clapped his hands again; Norton shook his head and gave a double, treble blink. Crystal was on a roll. The best thing was so were all the punters that had followed her.

After that Crystal gave the dumbfounded Australians the biggest dice lesson they'd ever had, as Norton looked on in admiration. She made it look easy, rolling the dice and pushing chips all over the place, covering herself so that even if she lost she'd still win, and the place was coming alive with people now crowding round the craps table to see what was going on. Crystal would rattle the dice near her ear, blow into her hand some more and every time she'd throw come out with all this weird talk and corny sayings. Around her the Australians, if they weren't cheering, just stood there with their mouths open catching flies.

'Any you cats been to North Caroline? Well here's how the ladies roll a nine.' Crystal flicked her fingers again and zap! 5 and 4 bounced off the end of the table to land right on top of the C and E in the COME lane. 'Slam bam, thank you ma'am.' Crystal raked in more chips.

Norton stood with the rest of the mob, staring around like a stunned mullet, then he cursed himself. If Crystal hadn't taken him by surprise he would have got in on the action too. Then Crystal started to strut.

She wiggled her boobs and played for the crowd. 'Brother's a pimp, sister's a whore, looks like I'm gonna have to roll a four.' Ping! As sweet you like — 3 and 1. 'Ah don't pick cotton and ah don't talk jive. Now watch this, suckers, while I roll a five.' Two and 3 flipped over. The crowd howled. Crystal shoved more chips around. 'Box-cars' she cried out, and up came a pair of sixes. The crowd yelled for more, even Norton started to clap. Then as suddenly as she started, Crystal stopped. 'You gotta know when to hold 'em. Know when to fold 'em.' She pushed the dice back towards the boxman. Then she smiled round the table. 'See you next time I'm in town — suckers. Help me out here, Les.'

Seeing Norton was still on KK's time, what could he do? He helped Crystal scoop up the pile of chips, then went over and cashed them; twenty-six thousand dollars. Crystal dropped the money in her bag, picking out a thousand dollars which she handed to Les.

'Here, handsome, get yourself a new toothbrush.'

Norton looked at the roll of hundreds for a second. 'Thanks. I will,' he said, and put it in his pocket.

'That crap ain't worth taking back to the States anyway. Just don't tell my mockey boyfriend,' she added with a wink.

'Good as gold,' answered Les.

Norton ordered a couple of drinks, paid for them and they stood around quietly waiting for KK. Crystal had a look on her face, not like a cat that just drank all the cream: a fox. The hand holding her drink seemed to be shaking just a little and if Les wasn't mistaken a lot of adrenalin was pumping through the American girl from the South. Still, why wouldn't you be on a high after winning twenty-six grand? mused Les. He was trying to work out her facial expressions, however, when Kramer returned. Unlike Crystal's, Kramer's face looked like a piece of chewing gum someone had just stepped off on a hot footpath.

'How did you go, KK?' said Norton, knowing he needn't have bothered to ask.

'I could've done better,' he muttered, then looked at Crystal. 'What about you.'

Crystal shrugged delicately. 'I ended up about even.'

Kramer's hang-dog expression didn't change. 'What do you want to do now?'

'I ain't fussy, honey,' replied Crystal.

'I reckon we may as well piss off. I want to see a bloke for a minute and have a couple of drinks, then go home. I don't fancy a late night.'

'What ever you say, lambchop.' Crystal reached across and gently kissed Kramer's cheek.

Les and Crystal half finished their drinks then filed out of the casino to the stares and silent applause of the

117

crowd, the punters who had followed Crystal, and the pit crew; it would be a long time before they'd ever see anything like that again. Tony was waiting right outside the door with the limo. Shit, that was quick, thought Les. Has Tony got ESP? Then as they climbed in the back, Les noticed for the first time the tiny beeper on Kramer's belt. He simply tapped it and Tony knew exactly when to be out the front of wherever they were. Crystal told the driver to stop on the bridge they crossed over on the way in, she wanted to get some air.

It was quiet and cool in the back of the limo, Kramer especially. The silence was broken by Crystal taking in a deep breath and letting it out again.

'Well, I guess I won't be needing these anymore,' she said.

Crystal slipped her hand up her sleeve and pulled out two dice using her index and middle finger. She rolled them into the palm of her hand then eased them up onto her knuckles and rolled them backwards and forwards across the back of her fingers. Smoothly and easily she passed her left hand over her right and the dice disappeared. She turned her empty hands over a couple of times then flipped a dice up onto the back of each hand where she'd had them hidden in the crooks of her thumbs.

'You ever heard of the Baton Rouge Roll, boy?' smiled Crystal. Very, very slowly, Norton shook his head. 'No. You ain't from round these parts, are you, boy? In fact where are you Aussies from, boy?' Again Norton was forced to shake his head. Crystal held the dice up to the light. 'Ain't it just amazin' what a li'l 'ol bit of clear nail-polish will do.'

Norton noticed a shiny slick down one side of each dice. 'Did you switch the dice?' he asked, then wished he'd never opened his mouth.

'No, Les, I squirted them out of my pussy. Don't ever come to the South, boy. Folks there'll have you wonderin' which way is up.' Crystal tugged at her cuff. 'I had a little binny up my sleeve. Like the rest of them Aussie meatheads in there, you were all too busy watching my

118

boobs instead of my hands.' She gave her boobs a bit of shake. 'Gotta make the best of what you got, boy.'

The limo stopped on the bridge, Crystal got out, took a couple of deep breaths and had a look around. She shook the dice next to her ear again then blew into her hand. 'Momma likes to hump. Poppa likes head. But momma's little baby likes shortenin' bread.' She flicked her wrist and the two dice disappeared into the river. 'How about that. Snakes eyes.'

Back in the limo Crystal snuggled up to KK. 'Where to now, darlin'?' she mooched.

'A place in Cavill Avenue called CJ's.' Kramer looked evenly down at Crystal. 'So you just broke even, did you?'

'Would I lie to you, honey? Why, Kelvin, I declare.'

Well, I bloodywell declare too, thought Norton. What a sheila. How much balls must she have to put on an act like that, then switch the dice right under everyone's noses in the middle of a dice game in one of Australia' biggest casinos. No matter what he thought about Crystal and the abysmal way she spoke to him and just about everybody else, Norton now had a definite admiration for the girl from the South. And she knew to get out when she was in front too. It was certainly worth a word or two with Price and the rest of the boys when he got back to Sydney. Yes, Crystal baby, you might have a giant pair of tits but you've also got bigger balls than a lot of blokes I know, Les repeated to himself as he watched her open her bag and slip Kramer a roll of bills.

CJ's was a small nightclub Les had noticed earlier, just down from the post office in Cavill Avenue. It was all black and white and smoked glass out the front with 'CJ's Night Spot' in white across a grey background over the top. The club was two storeys above the shops and an arcade, where a short flight of stairs led into the arcade with the entrance at the rear.

The limo pulled up out the front and the passing swarm of punters stopped to see who it was, but before they had much chance Les had KK and Crystal up the stairs

119

and halfway down the arcade. There was a skinny sort of
bloke on a desk at the entrance who just had time to give
KK the usual big welcome before they bowled past about
half a dozen people waiting to get in. They filed up the
stairs past a bar on one level overlooking Cavill Avenue,
up another flight into the disco. The decor was black
carpet and black wallpaper with long wall mirrors in
between. The half-packed dancefloor was on your right
as you walked in where the punters were giving it heaps to
Sex Industry's version of 'Jail Break' under the strobe
and spinning lights. A long bar started opposite and just
past the dancefloor cornered off, splitting the club almost
into two sections. There was no shortage of chairs and
tables and a kind of lounge ran round the wall underneath the mirrors where more people were sitting, drinking and talking. Two hundred would have packed the
place; there would have been a little over a hundred in
there. For some reason Norton liked the place as soon as
he walked in. It wasn't too big or too small, it wasn't
smoky or gloomy and the punters looked all right too,
well dressed and not blithering drunk. Maybe the sign he
noticed as they walked in saying 'Patrons Must Be 21' had
something to do with it.

There was a bit of a sticky-beak in their direction at
first then everybody seemed more interested in what they
were doing; having a few drinks, boogying around or
chatting up girls or vice versa. Les and Crystal waited just
past the dancefloor as KK went to the bar. Norton
watched as the barmaid shook KK's hand, listened to him
for a moment, shook his head, listened again then got
some drinks. While they were waiting, Les checked out
some of the punters then had to smile to himself. Did I say
something about not a bad clientele? Standing a few
metres away in their yellow shirts were the same bunch of
blokes Les had noticed on the plane. The Mac's Head
Muff Divers. There were about ten of them and they even
had a couple of blowsy looking blondes in tow. Jesus! I
hope they don't go mad when they lamp Crystal's tits,
thought Les. They were a pretty big bunch. But they

120

seemed happy enough, throwing down the VBs, slapping each other on the back and laughing uproariously at everything and nothing. KK returned with the same three drinks they'd had at the Azmuth Lounge.

'Colby's not here,' he said, sounding a little disappointed as he handed them their drinks.

'That the owner you were supposed to meet?' said Les.

'Yeah. Colby Jones. I wanted to see him too."

'Ah well, it don't matter,' said Norton, taking a sip of his drink. 'He might turn up. Have a couple here anyway.' Norton also noticed quite a number of girls standing around; not bad sorts and not doing much except slew around, and one or two eyes slewed in Norton's direction. 'This isn't a bad little place.'

'Yeah,' agreed Crystal. 'I like it here.'

'Okay,' shrugged Kramer. 'We'll have a couple of drinks. Why not?'

They decided to move a little further away from the dancefloor. All the chairs and tables were full and they finished up somewhere between the bar and the Mac's Head Muff Divers. The DJ threw on 'Some People' by James Reyne and if KK wasn't in the best mood, Les was and so was Crystal. Norton was just about to ask her for a dance, mainly because he felt like it and also so he could say he'd danced with Crystal Linx, when he spotted something out the corner of his eye that sent a squirt of adrenalin into the pit of his stomach. It was the same team he'd spotted in the Azmuth Lounge: even in the soft light of the disco there was no mistaking their builds and presence, especially the one with the thick hair. They'd already noticed Kramer and if the looks in the casino were a little on the sour side, here they were positively rancid. Shit! This is lovely, thought Norton. Something's definitely not quite kosher here.

'Listen, KK' he said urgently. 'Drop the bullshit. Do you know that team over near the corner?'

Kramer looked around and looked straight back again. 'Oh shit!' he said, blinking through his glasses.

'Yeah, exactly. They were in the casino giving you the

same dirty looks. Now, I don't know what the story is, but I'm not taking on six blokes, KK. I reckon we ought to get out of here before something starts. Or I'm stalling anyway, I'm not getting my head kicked in for fifteen hundred bucks.'

'Yeah, you're right,' agreed Kramer. 'I saw them earlier myself but I honestly didn't think they'd be in here.' KK had also honestly forgotten he didn't have brother Menachem with him, who wouldn't have hesitated to pull out a rather large calibre pistol and drop all six of them without wasting a shot, if that's the way they wanted it.

'Hey, what's going on?' demanded Crystal. 'I am here too, you know.'

'Crystal,' said Les directly. 'Finish your drink. We're gonna have to go somewhere else.'

Crystal looked at Les. 'Somewhere else. What the fuck's wrong with this? We just walked in the goddam door.' She glared at Kramer. 'I'm not doing another one of your fuckin' champagne tours of Dogpatch. Fuck you, Kelvin.'

'It's not like that, Crystal,' said Les. 'It's just that there's a bit of trouble and we gotta hit the toe. So finish your drink. Sorry, mate.'

Unfortunately Norton had left his run just a little too late. As he tried to reason with Crystal, the tallest of the team walked over to the bar, making sure he almost walked right over Kramer as he did. He was dark haired and square jawed, not quite Norton's build but taller.

'Hello, KK' he said slowly and menacingly, standing back from the bar. 'Nice to see you. You greasy fuckin' little Jew cunt.'

Kramer blinked some more and gulped his drink. 'Nice to see you too, Terry,' he answered.

'Yeah, I'll bet it is. You fuckin' little arse.'

Ignoring the tall man's tirade, Les reached across and pushed Kramer's beeper. 'Come on, KK. Let's piss off.'

'And who the fuck are you?' said the tall bloke.

'Me. I'm no one,' answered Norton. 'And I'm out of here and they're coming with me.' He turned to Crystal and gave her an urgent look. 'Come on, Crystal.'

122

'Are you supposed to be looking after this little piece of shit and his slaggy moll of a girlfriend?'

'Whatever, mate.' Norton could feel his hackles start to rise and was close to giving the bloke a good smack, right in the mouth. But at the moment discretion was definitely the better part of valour. An orderly withdrawal was much better than getting kicked down the stairs by six big blokes. He might spot him again somewhere.

However, Crystal had heard the last remark and decided to put her head in. 'Hey, that's my boyfriend you're talking to, you pig-eyed sack of shit. And don't call me a moll either, you kangaroo-fucking, turkey-necked, Australian clamhead. Fuck you, boy.'

'I'll call you what I like, you soapy-looking, tunnel-cunted, Yank trollop.'

'Oh will you — you sonofabitch.'

Even if he got what he deserved, Norton couldn't believe it as Crystal threw her drink straight in the bloke's face. With a bit of luck, he might have been able to grab the pair of them and spear them out of the place down to the waiting limo. But now it was on no matter what; and as usual, Les was right in the middle. The bloke roared with pain and rage as he tried to wipe the burning spirits out of his eyes. Still hoping they might get to the door, Les made a lunge at KK and Crystal and it was a good thing he did because he didn't notice the solid bloke with the thick hair sneak round on his right and king-hit him with a sizzling left hook. As well as being well built, Haircut knew how to throw them too and if Les hadn't moved forward that tiny bit it would have broken his jaw and probably knocked him out. As it was, it knocked Les stupid. He let out an oath and slammed up against the bar, managing to cock his head just in time to cop a short right on the forehead and another left on his eye. Les was in a bit of trouble, because it doesn't matter how big and fit you are, if some big bloke belts you out of the blue when you're not ready for it, nine times out of ten, it's goodnight Irene. Especially if they follow up equally as good.

123

Norton tried desperately to get things back into focus. He could hear girls screaming and the crowd shouting as they moved back from the bar, but it was just a blur of sight and sound. He sucked in his breath, shook his head and threw a wild left that caught Haircut over the eye and followed up with another on his nose. Haircut looked surprised and they slowed him momentarily, but they weren't the best punches Norton had ever thrown; somehow he had to get himself together; that first left hook was a ripper. He thumped a rip up into Haircut's stomach, copping another right to his nose. But by now his mate had wiped all the drink out of his eyes. He was going to belt Crystal, who was holding on to KK, but he could always come back to them; get rid of their minder first.

Les just had time to cover up from the bloke's big right, but the left caught him on the eye. He got a left back-fist into the bloke's mouth that made him think, when another left hook caught him almost where the first one had landed. Haircut had leapt back into the fray. Shit, thought Les, his whole life starting to peel off before him as he slammed back against the bar. There was some skinny bloke on the door downstairs, the owner wasn't there to break up the brawl and KK would be about as much use in a fight as a tube of block-out in an atomic bomb blast. He might have been a chance with the two he was fighting, but out the corner of his eye Les spotted the rest of the team charging over. There was no way he could make it to the door on his own, let alone take KK and Crystal with him; the mob would have him before he got two metres. So this is it, mate. Norton braced himself and got ready to get the shit kicked out of him. Well, if I'm going down, I'll go down with what I've got left. With a desperate roar, Norton raised himself up and threw punches wildly at Haircut and his mate. But they were getting in a lot more than he was and now their mates were about to arrive on the scene. Don't kill me if you can help it, fellas, and try and leave something for DD on Sunday night.

Norton had done some rotten things in his life and

might have deserved a hiding, but somehow a star shone on the big red-headed Queenslander that night. A star in the form of the Mac's Head Muff Divers Annual Tour of Duty. No Muff Too Tough. As the gang had charged through the crowd to get at Les slugging it out with the other two at the bar, they bashed into the Muff Divers, spilling drinks all over their yellow shirts. There was no way the Muff Divers were going to cop this, being big lumps of blokes and half full of piss, and it was good enough reason to get into a good old brawl on your holidays anyway. Norton braced himself as the gang arrived to join in bashing him when he saw a flurry of yellow shirts leap on them from behind. There was a roar of cursing brawling men, and the whole seething mass crushed up against the bar, sending Les and his two assailants down under sheer weight of numbers. A couple of chairs sailed over the bar, smashing one of the mirrors and about fifty glasses, the bar staff and the punters moved out of the road as the place started to rumble like an earthquake had just hit it.

From beneath the tangle of gouging, cursing, punching and kicking men Norton managed to crawl out and find that KK and Crystal had moved round towards the dancefloor. He grabbed them both and shoved them towards the stairs. His head was still spinning but behind him he could see the gang was too busy fighting off the Muff Divers to come after them. As they got to the top of the stairs the skinny doorman was standing there wondering what was his best way of getting out of it.

'Come on, keep moving. Get the fuck out here,' ordered Norton, nearly taking the doorman with them.

They ran down the stairs and out along the arcade; Norton couldn't have been happier to see the limo waiting out the front. To the startled looks of the passers-by, he wrenched open the door and they bundled inside. Tony took one look at Norton and the horrified look on the others and hit the accelerator.

'Straight back to the flats,' barked Les.

'No worries,' answered the driver.

Norton took in a deep breath, sat back in the limo and tried to get his head together, though things were still pretty blurry. He hurt and he was angry. His good shirt was ripped to pieces and he'd lost one of his Italian shoes. He ran his hands over his eyes, felt the blood on his face and saw it on his hands. He could feel cuts all round his eyes and blood seeping out of his nose and the warm, salty taste of it in his mouth. His jaw ached and even when he closed his eyes everything kept flickering. But although he was wild and in a fair bit of pain, Norton also realised how lucky he was. If it hadn't been for those clowns in the yellow shirts he'd probably be on his way to hospital. Whatever he had, he was still blessed; a look in the mirror and feel around back at the flat would tell him just how bad it all was.

'Boy,' said Crystal, 'you is one hell of a mess. Them good ol' boys done whupped you bad.'

'Whupped me bad!' echoed Les angrily. 'If you hadn't tossed your drink in that bloke's face, I mightn't of got whupped. You... Dubbo!'

'Well, what did you all expect me to do — talking to a lady like that. I'm only sorry I didn't kick the big mother-fucker right in the balls.'

Les wiped some blood from his eyes and glared at Crystal; the way things were spinning around it looked like she had six tits. 'I only wish you bloody had now.'

'I'll say one thing boy,' said Crystal, 'you still fight good. And ain't you got just a great defence. I swear you never let one punch go past your head all night.'

Norton was about to tell her to get well and truly'd when he noticed Kramer sitting alongside her very quiet and very pasty faced. 'You're pretty quiet in all this, KK, you little shit. Who were those blokes?'

Kramer made a gesture with his hands. 'I swear to you, Les, I didn't think they'd be there. And I was getting ready to go, the last thing I want is any trouble.' He blinked through his glasses at Les staring at him. 'The tall guy's name is Terry Stinnett. He used to be a tally clerk in Sydney. Him and that team flog dodgy real estate up here

126

and rig horse races, among other things. They're bad cunts. I was in a racehorse scam with them and I pissed off out of the country with most of the money. And left them with a dud kite. I was going to settle with them but they found me before I got a chance to get in touch. You hardly ever see them at CJ's but they just happened to be there tonight. I'm sorry, Les. And I didn't mean for you to get hurt.'

Norton glared out the window. 'Must've been my lucky bloody night. And who's the bloke with all the hair that belted me first up?'

'I'm not real sure, but I think his name's Jasper.'

'Jasper eh,' hissed Norton.

The limo pulled up at the flats and very gingerly Les got out. Tony didn't bother, Kramer walked round, said something to him and he drove off.

'Why don't you come up to our apartment and we'll clean you up?' said Crystal.

'Yeah, righto,' grunted Norton, although another idea had started to hatch in his brain already. He was about to start walking when he stopped, looked down at his remaining shoe, then tore it off his foot and flung it up the street. 'I don't suppose I'll be needing that any more — will I?' He shuffled through the front door in his socks.

Crystal cluck-clucked and Kramer apologised again as they helped Norton up the stairs. When they got to their door, Les propped and leant against his own. 'Look, don't worry about me. I'll be all right. I can fix myself up.'

'Are you sure?' said Crystal. 'Your face looks like Les Hibbin's hat.' Kramer didn't say anything. Despite his sympathy and apologising he was glad not to have Norton bleeding all over his home-unit.

'Yeah, I'll be okay. I want to be on my own for a while anyway.' Les looked at the both of them; suddenly he felt very tired. 'So what's doing tomorrow? Are you doing those topless shots? What's the story?'

'I never intended doing any topless shots,' said Crystal. 'That was all horseshit. Those creeps from the press can go squat.'

127

'We'll be going out on Meyer's boat for the day,' said Kelvin.

'So you won't be needing me?'

'No. You can do what you like. We'll be leaving early, you just take it easy and we'll see you tomorrow night, or whenever.'

'Okay. Well, give me the keys to the Jag. Just in case I need to drive myself to hospital and get an x-ray or some stitches or something.'

'I'll get the keys now.' Kramer opened the door and stepped inside.

'Are you sure you'll be alright, Les?' said Crystal.

'Yeah. I used to be a lion tamer in another life.'

'Okay. But if you need anything, just knock.' Crystal went to touch Norton's face, then changed her mind. 'Goodnight, Les.'

'See you tomorrow, Crystal.'

Crystal disappeared into their unit as Kramer returned with the car keys. 'Here you are, Les. Take the car for as long as you like. You want some chops?'

'No. I'm alright.'

'Okay, Les. I'll see you tomorrow.'

'Yeah, see you then.'

'Hey, I am sorry about what happened, Les.'

Norton spat a gob of blood onto the stairs. 'Yeah. Don't worry about it.'

The door closed, leaving Les on his own. After a moment or two he let himself inside.

In the flat, Norton got out of his blood-spattered clothes down to his jocks, splashed some water over his face and checked himself out in the bathroom mirror. Les Hibbin's hat? How the fuck would she know about that? he thought out loud. But it wasn't a bad comparison, because the face looking back at him definitely wasn't Robert Redford. His top lip was swollen and although he hadn't lost any teeth, some were chipped and he could feel a few cracked fillings and cuts inside his mouth with his tongue. His nose wasn't broken, but it was that bent it didn't make any difference, and the thick,

128

dark blood coming from deep inside promised it would be around for a while and in the next few days start to look like blackberry jelly. His jaw wasn't broken either but when he opened and closed his mouth it clicked and clunked like a rusty gate. His right ear, where he'd copped that first left hook was red and swollen, very bloody sore and felt like it was going to burst; however, the cuts above his eyes were more gouges from rings than splits and wouldn't need stitching, but there were plenty of them. The rest was just bruising and he'd copped a couple of kicks in the ribs; they were nothing really. All in all not too good, but not too bad, and like he said earlier, it would have been a lot worse only for the Muff Divers.

The only thing that worried him was the concussion. Les opened and closed his eyes and rolled them around in their sockets. Everything was still slightly out of focus and flickering, and tiny pin-points of light exploded in front of him every now and again. He'd experienced this playing football. But at least playing football, someone came up over with the magic water and a sponge and freshened you up and half a dozen blokes didn't run in and start kicking the shit out of you. Yes, the street was definitely a different kettle of fish to the football field. But with some ice and a few band-aids he'd live to see the night out. If he started vomiting he'd get an X-ray on his head tomorrow. Norton stared balefully at himself in the mirror then had to smile. What did he say about getting a hiding after he'd set poor little Warren up. It does you good and even livens you up now and again. That has to be some sort of karma there and I suppose I deserve what I got.

But Les definitely didn't deserve the serve he copped. He had done nothing. All he was trying to do was leave. Maybe Crystal needn't have thrown her drink in the tall bloke's face, but he came over looking for trouble and he did deserve it, gobbing off at her like that. It wouldn't have surprised Les either if she did kick him in the nuts: Crystal had balls enough to do it alright. No. Norton didn't deserve the hiding he got, and he didn't deserve or appreciate getting pinged by some king-hit merchant while he wasn't looking. So the face in the mirror, as well as being a battered one, was a boilingly angry one also. Jasper eh, Les cursed to himself, gobbing more blood down the sink. You like king-hitting blokes, do you, Jasper? Well, I'll be finding you before I go back to Sydney, you bushy haired cunt. You and your mate Terry Stinnett. Either with a lump of pipe, a baseball bat or a good back-up. I can't see myself getting a back-up round here. But I know where there's a ripper not all that far away and I reckon I could get him down here without too much trouble.

There were some band-aids in the bathroom. Les put a couple over his eyes then filled a plastic bag full of ice from the kitchen, held it over his jaw and settled down in front of the TV for the while. But the late-night movie wasn't interesting Norton very much at all. The main thing burning on his mind was a square-up. Revenge. Norton wasn't vindictive or spiteful or anything like that. He just liked to even the score. What does it say in both the holy books? An eye for an eye, a tooth for a tooth. Well, how about both their eyes, all their fuckin' teeth and part of their jawbone as well? It was too early to make a phone call, but as sure as God made little green apples, he'd be making one first thing in the morning. He absently watched the TV screen while the start of a plan ticked over inside his head. Then the concussion came on again, and again Les started to feel very tired. He switched the TV off, spread a towel out next to his head and went to bed. Despite the pain, Norton slept all right.

Les woke up just before seven the next morning. He sat up in bed and blinked around the room as the memory of last night's events came back to him. He was happy to see the concussion had all but gone and everything had stopped flickering; his jaw was still bloody sore though. A check in the bathroom mirror while he cleaned his teeth showed plenty of colouring around his face and two reasonable black eyes, a fat lip, a thick ear and a nose that would have looked better on W.C. Fields. At least when he peeled the band-aids off his eyebrows the gouges didn't start bleeding. Apart from that, Norton was his usual good humoured, debonair self. That, and a searing hatred burning away in the pit of his stomach like a ship's boiler. He still had blood in his hair and round his chest and when he gobbed into the sink pieces of what looked like chopped up black jelly beans were still coming from back in his nose. One thing would fix that up and help his aches and pains: a swim. Les had another dour glance at himself in the mirror then wrapped a towel round his neck and jogged across to the water.

It was another perfect Queensland day: warm and sunny with one or two clouds drifting along before a noreaster that was as gentle as a kiss. From a distance, Norton would have looked like anybody else enjoying themselves on the beach, floating around in the surf, bobbing up and down beneath the easy rolling waves. But up close, Norton's face, as he schemed while he washed away his aches and bruises along with the blood, looked more like a very mean, very hungry crocodile that had just missed out on breakfast. He left the beach, had a shower in the flat then got into a pair of shorts and a T-shirt while he made a cup of tea. A look at his watch told him it was well and truly time to make that phone call. Mug of tea in one hand, he pushed the buttons and waited as it rang.

'Yeah hello,' came a familiar voice at the other end.

'G'day, Muzz. It's Les.'

'Les. How are you mate? Jeez, it's good to hear from you.' Murray sounded even happier than usual at the sound of his brother's voice.

'Not bad, Muzz. How's things with you?'

'Good. I was just thinking of ringing you myself, to tell you the truth. How's things in Sydney?'

'I'm not ringing from Sydney. I'm in Surfers Paradise.'

'Surfers. Shit! What the fuck are you doing there?'

'Getting my head punched in by a team of cunts. And I've got the shits.'

Les gave his brother a run down on how he happened

131

to be in Surfers, where he was staying, a little bit of what he'd been up to, then what had happened last night. Judging by the tone of his brother's voice, Murray guessed that not only was Les's cup of happiness not running over, it had completely evaporated and there was a big crack in it as well.

'Yeah, Muzz, I'm tellin' you those dirty, fuckin', white-shoe cunts would have near killed me, only for those other blokes jumping in. You ought to see my bloody head as it is.'

'Yeah. Sounds like it,' said Murray.

'So what's the chances of coming down and giving me a hand to sort these cunts out? Can you get away for a couple of days? I'll make it worth your while.'

'Aah you needn't worry about that. Yeah, sure. Elaine's taken the boys up to St George for a swimming carnival for a couple of days, so I'm on my own.' Murray paused for a moment. 'The thing is I ain't got a car. How about coming out and getting me?'

Les winced. Drive out to Dirranbandi and back. Shit! That's not quite a run up to the Blue Mountains on a Sunday. And it would also mean no date with DD tonight. Then again his head didn't look all that good and he'd probably frighten the shit out of her anyway. He looked at the car keys sitting next to the phone and drummed his fingers for a second. 'Look, give me an hour to think it over and I'll ring you back — okay?'

'No worries, Les. I'll still be home. I'll hear from you in an hour.'

'See you then, Muzz.' Les hung up the phone. 'Fuck it!' he cursed out loud. From here to Dirranbandi and back was around 1,400 kilometres. Then he'd have to run Murray back home again. Christ! How long would that take? He looked at the car keys again. In that brand new Jag? Mmhh. But Les had counted on Murray coming down because in the meantime he'd have to sniff around and find out where Haircut and his team drank so they could take them by surprise. Les didn't doubt for a minute he and Murray would kick the shit out of Stinnett and his team, but it was still six against two and they'd need to get the jump on them. No good asking K K and letting on to him what he had in mind; Norton still didn't trust the little weazle all that much. So how to very discreetly find out where Stinnett and his bunch hung out. Les gazed into his mug of tea, and the old grey matter swirled around inside his bruised and lacerated head. I reckon there's one bloke up here might know for sure. And I can have a nice breakfast while I'm at it. Les put his cup in the sink and went to his bedroom. He had one of those baseball-type caps with the adjustable back and 2MMM on the front in his bag. He pulled that down over his eyes, spread some coloured sun cream around his face and put on his sunglasses; unless you looked close, you'd hardly know he'd been in a fight. Norton locked the flat and strolled up to Peggy's.

Whatever the fight might have done to Norton, it definitely didn't dampen his appetite. He ordered scrambled eggs and bacon, pancakes and syrup, toast plus fruit-salad, washed down with fresh orange juice and two cups of coffee. It was still early so Les got a table out the front and while he was eating he watched Price's old mate Jimmy Martin whistling cheerfully as he set his gear up on the beach ready for another day. What did KK say? Everybody on the Gold Coast knows Jimmy Martin. Well, in that case I imagine it wouldn't be unreasonable to assume that Jimmy Martin would know just about everybody on the Gold Coast too. Les finished his second cup of coffee and sauntered over.

Jimmy was sitting in a deck-chair, reading a magazine, the same as he was on Thursday, and sitting next to him was the same bloke talking into a cellular phone, same as he was on Thursday also. Jimmy spotted Norton coming across the sand and smiled up from his magazine.

'G'day, Les,' he said cheerfully. 'How's things, mate?'

'Pretty good, Jimmy,' replied Norton. 'I was over the road having breakfast, so I thought I'd come over and say g'day. How are you?'

Jimmy waved his arms around at the sun and the sky.

133

'What could be better than this? You wouldn't be dead for quids, would you?'

'Better than cooking oysters à la Amos, I'd reckon.'

Jimmy tossed back his head and laughed as Norton nodded a hello to his mate talking on the phone, getting a wink and a smile in return.

'Hey listen, Les. You've got to tell me this,' said Jimmy. 'Was that your picture I saw in the local papers? You're not up here with KK, are you?'

Les nodded. 'Yeah. I'm staying at his block of flats just down the road.'

'God strike me. How did you get mixed up with him.?'

'By accident I suppose,' shrugged Norton. 'But it's all a bit of a hoot really. All I do is drive around in a limo, eating good food, drinking piss and keeping the mugs and the press away from him and his silly bloody sheila while she's out here making some pop record. It's a piece of piss to be honest. There's no trouble. She just bags the shit out of everybody, that's all. But she's quite a funny babe at times.'

Jimmy nodded slowly. 'And how do you find young KK?'

Again Norton shrugged. 'Take him or leave him, I suppose. I just know him from the game. But he's looking after me and it's got to be one of the easiest earns I've ever had.' Les gave Jimmy a wink and a smile. 'Not as easy as you've got it of course, James. But it's only till Tuesday then I go back to Sydney.' Norton looked at his watch. 'Anyway, I have to hit the toe. I've got to run around with them again today.'

'Aahh' said Jimmy, sounding a little downcast. 'I was hoping to have a mag to you.'

'Ohh don't worry, mate. I'll make sure I see you before I go. I want to have a mag to you myself.' Les snapped his fingers. 'That was something I meant to ask you the other day. I've got another message to deliver. Would you know where I can find a bloke called Terry Stinnett?'

Jimmy looked evenly at Les. 'Where do you know him from?'

'I don't,' replied Norton. 'It's just one of the sheilas at the game gave me a card to give to him. You know, one of those silly greeting cards. She showed it to me, it's quite funny. She just said if I should bump into him somewhere to give it to him. She said he's a tall bloke with dark hair. Got a mate called Jasper. I wouldn't know them for a bar of soap.'

Jimmy pondered for a moment. 'I'm not sure, Les. Terry and his team work weekends flogging real estate and that. They used to drink a bit at Fisherman's Wharf. I haven't seen them around much lately.'

'You'll find them every Monday night at the Boulevarde in Begonia Street,' said Jimmy's mate, folding up his phone.

'I'm sorry,' said Les. 'I didn't quite catch that.'

'The Boulevarde. It's a bar in Begonia Street, just round from Cavill Avenue.'

'Opposite a little health-food restaurant?'

'That's the place,' nodded Jimmy's mate. 'They're in there every Monday night at nine. One of their team's brother works on the door and they do their divvying up or whatever in there. They drink down the end of the bar near the back door. Terry's tall like you said. Jasper's shorter but solid with a thick mop of hair. You can't miss them.'

'Thanks, mate,' smiled Norton. 'Thanks a lot. That saves me a lot of trouble.'

Then the bloke looked at his watch. 'Jesus Christ! Is that the time? I got to get going myself.'

'Not sticking round in the sun?' enquired Norton.

'No,' said the bloke getting to his feet. 'I've got to catch a plane to Cairns. Business.'

'Okey doke. Well, I'll get going. I might see you tomorrow, Jimmy.'

'Righto, Les. See you then.'

Les smiled at Jimmy's mate. 'Have a good time in Cairns.'

Norton was whistling to himself, and the day seemed even sunnier as he strolled back to his flat. Well, how

135

about that, eh. Terry and the boys have a quiet drink on Monday night a the Boulevarde. How nice. And I think it's only fitting that I join them for a cool one myself. Me and Murray. Which definitely means driving out home and getting him. Then snookering him round here somewhere just in case there's a bit of trouble after we have the said quiet drink. Les rubbed the swelling on his jaw. Especially with Jasper. So I can't involve Muzz and I can't really put him up in the flat. Mmmhh.

Norton was mulling this over when, as he got near the flats, he noticed a white Ford sedan on the driveway out front. Hello, who's this? Fuckin' reporters I'll bet. Then he noticed Frank and Steve, Black's heavies, sitting in the front. For some reason Les propped behind the wall in front of a high-rise and waited. A minute or two later Crystal and KK came out, got in the Ford and drove off. No limo, no BMW? thought Les. Then what did Crystal say? The topless shots weren't on. They're just keeping inconspicuous. Fair enough. When the car was out of sight, Les trotted up the stairs to his flat to find a note shoved under his door: 'Les. We didn't want to wake you up. We hope you are feeling all right. If any reporters or that come round will you tell them Crystal's sick and I've taken her to a friend's place to rest. See you tonight or whenever. KK'

Yeah, right, KK, thought Norton, screwing up the note and tossing it in the kitchen-tidy. I'll do just that. He picked up the phone and pressed the buttons.

'Yeah, hello,' came the same voice.

'It's Les, Muzz. Okay, I'll come out and get you.'

'You fuckin' beauty. I mean . . . that's good. When do you reckon you'll be here?'

Les looked at the car keys then at his watch. 'I reckon around four or so.'

'What are you driving? A fuckin' F15?'

'No. A new Jag. I'll pick you up at your place. Then we should have time to duck in and see the oldies.'

'They're up in St George with the kids and Elaine.'

'Oh. Oh well, I'll catch up with them next time.'

136

'Listen, Les, instead of calling out my place, how about I meet you in the Rotary Park at the back of town next to the river. The less people know you're in town the better. And you never know who might call out my joint.'

Les thought for a second. 'Yeah, you could be right. Can you get there okay — not having a car?'

'Yeah, no worries.'

'You might have to stay here a couple of nights. I told you that.'

'Yeah, that's okay.'

'All right. Well, I'll see you next to the Balonne around four. Then we'll get back here, sort these white-shoe cunts out, and maybe have a drink or two and a mag after. For a week if you want?'

Murray chuckled over the phone. 'Sounds alright to me. I'll see you this arvo, Les.'

'See you then, Muzz.'

Norton sat looking at the phone for a few moments and an idea formed in his head. Well, he thought, finally getting up and walking to the bedroom, no good sitting around here picking my toes. The sooner I get going the sooner I get there. He threw a spare T-shirt and jeans into his overnight-bag. Some fruit from the kitchen and his remaining four tapes; wishing now he'd never given Crystal the other two. He made sure he had all his money then locked the flat and walked down the front.

Apart from a few passers-by and the general traffic, there was no one around, and definitely no reporters or photographers. Probably after all the abuse from Crystal and the smack in the mouth he'd given one of them they decided to brush her. Les had the garage open, the big Jag purring gently on the driveway and the garage locked again in about two minutes. He smiled to himself as he hit the blinker to go right along The Esplanade towards Main Beach. I think this is the quickest way to that nice lady's boarding house.

Norton parked just off the main road and strolled round the front. Mrs Llivac wasn't in the front garden but the same grey cat was asleep on one of the lounges on the front verandah. The front door was open, Les trotted up the stairs and rang a bell next to the fly-screen door. A few seconds later Mrs Llivac came down the hallway. The landlady didn't look half bad in a pair of jeans and an old sleeveless shirt; a white scarf holding her hair in place suggested she'd been doing some housework. She looked at Les for a moment then smiled.

'Oh hello,' she said pleasantly. 'You're the young gentleman I was talking to out the front on Thursday.'

'That's right. How are you, Mrs Llivac?'

'I'm fine. Come on in.' She opened the fly-screen door. 'What can I do for you?'

'I'd like to rent a room for three days. If that's all right?'

'Sure. No problem at all.' Mrs Llivac wiped her hands on her shirt and started to fuss a little. 'Come into the office.'

Les stepped inside Mrs Llivac's boarding house. A hallway with rooms on either side ran down to what looked like the kitchen and dining-room area. There was a loungeroom to the left with comfy old furniture and the same blue carpet as in the hallway. A TV, fishtank, lamps, paintings on the wall and other home comforts were all freshly dusted and spotlessly clean. The office next to the door and the loungeroom consisted of a bar with a pay-phone on top, a few tourist brochures in racks and a dozen or so pegs, some holding keys, on a wall to the left, next to a window facing the street.

'A friend of mine, a Mr Thomas, is driving down from the country,' said Les. 'He told me he wanted to stay somewhere away from all the hustle and bustle. So I suggested here.'

'Oh he'll like it here. It's lovely and quiet,' assured Mrs Llivac.

'It looks very nice all round,' said Les. 'I like your fishtank too. I've got one at home just like it.' He pulled a wad from his pocket. 'I'll pay you the three days in advance, if that's okay? How much?'

The landlady seemed a little surprised. 'Well, it's $45 a night with breakfast. Is that all right?'

138

Les peeled off the money and handed it to Mrs Llivac. 'There's two hundred dollars just in case he stays an extra night. I'm not sure what time Mr Thomas will be arriving. It could be very early this morning and he has to call into my place first. If you let me have the keys, I'll give them to him, save waking you up.'

'Sure. That's no problem at all.' Mrs Llivac wrote out a receipt and handed it to Les plus the keys. 'It's room number 3 on the right. Would you like to have a look? They've all got their own shower and TV. They're very nice.'

'And you make the best deep-dish apple pie on the Gold Coast, right?' smiled Les.

'Why, that's right,' beamed Mrs Llivac.

'No, I'll take your word for it. I have to get going, to be honest. I'm here on business. But it's a Mr Thomas, and he's a very nice man.'

The landlady breathed a very heavy once up and down at Norton. 'If he's a friend of yours I'm sure he must be.'

'Okay, Mrs Llivac,' smiled Les, jangling the keys. 'Thanks very much. I'll probably be around to see Mr Thomas.'

'Any time. Oh, I don't even know your name.'

'I'm sorry,' Les smiled syrupily again. 'It's George. George Menzies.'

'Thank you Mr Menzies. Bye.'

'Goodbye, Mrs Llivac.'

Well, chuckled Norton, as he got behind the wheel of the car and took off his cap and sunglasses, brother Murray should be quite comfortable in there. It's out of the way but not too far from the Boulevarde. And not too expensive either. But there'll still be a nice little drink for Muzz when it's all over. I'll see to that.

Les got onto the highway, drove past Cavill Avenue and pulled up at a garage not far from the Neptune's Casino turn off. He filled the tank, put a little extra air in the tyres, made sure everything else was all right and grabbed two bars of chocolate with his change. He didn't need a road map. Les, like the rest of his family, knew

139

every short-cut and back-road between Dirranbandi, Brisbane and the New South Wales border. He looked at his watch and moved off along the highway. Not too much later, Les had taken the turn-off to Tambourine Mountain and was cruising along in air-conditioned comfort towards Beaudesert.

Motoring along in the big English saloon was even better than Les had imagined; the car handled like a dream, with power to burn. Getting up Tambourine Mountain, past the old mill near Lamington Park, was a breeze and he wasn't even pushing it. He didn't bother putting on his tapes just yet, the Jag had one of those scanners and was picking up all sorts of things on Brisbane and local radio stations: country and western music, light pop, some talk-back show with an old bloke from Bundaberg playing a gum leaf. But Les wasn't all that interested; driving the Jag was a hoot in itself.

Especially when he got past Beaudesert and kept it in third going up Cunningham Gap, duelling with some bloke in a Nissan Pulsar and another on a motorbike. As they zoomed in and out of the trucks they were passing like something out of *Smokey and the Bandit*. The bloke on the big Bridgestone eventually won the race but the Pulsar soon disappeared in Norton's rear-vision mirror. Boonah went past; the next stop would be Warwick to top up again; the twelve pounding cylinders didn't mind a bit of petrol. Yeah, this is grouse thought Les, as he effortlessly hit 170 kilometres per hour going past another truck. In a way I'm glad I've got to go and get Murray now. He winked to himself in the mirror. Norton — you've done it again, you devil.

Then about fifty kilometres out of Warwick, it suddenly dawned on Les what a dill he was. He had a night lined up with a good-looking girl who he truly fancied. A girl who he could have taken out and had a sensational meal somewhere then gone back to the flat and got into some more sensational porking as well; with them both laughing their heads off while they were at it. Instead, he was driving like a maniac towards the middle of the

140

Queensland outback to pick up his brother, then drive back like a maniac again to get into a monstrous brawl in some bar, where, win, lose or draw, he was still going to cop more damage to his already battered dial. DD would be all frocked up for a big night, looking like a million dollars and he was standing her up to get into a fight. Okay, so he got a bit knocked about. It wasn't as if they'd killed him. Any normal bloke would have copped his lumps, hit the brakes and turned back. There'd probably be another day, another place. Unfortunately Les Norton definitely wasn't your normal bloke. He rubbed his jaw and looked at his two black eyes in the rear-vision mirror and the evil gleam emanating from them. No, definitely not. But the night might not turn out a complete disaster with DD. He'd ring her when he got to Dirranbandi and say . . . well, he'd think of something to say. And there's a chance he'd be back by twelve. She'd probably be up doing nothing. A bunch of roses, apologies all round. He'd work it out somehow. And there was still tomorrow and Tuesday. And who knows what?

On the other hand, it would be good to see Murray again. Bad luck Les'd miss out on seeing the oldies. But what about Grungle? Norton smiled. Wouldn't it be good to see that little fat shit again and give him a bit of a rough up? Bad luck they couldn't take him back with them. But knowing how often Murray washed him, after seven hours in the car it would smell like a dozen Indian fakirs with diarrhoea and shit all through it. But it would be good to see the dog again too. Christ! Grungle was part of the family as much as anyone else.

Norton topped up at Warwick; next stop would be Goondiwindi, 200 kilometres away. As he got out of town, Les slipped in the first tape and the top track was 'Hope Valley' — Sugar Ray and the Blue Tones. Shit! How good's this, thought Les, as it blasted out of the four speakers. 'Can't you see I'm bound. To that homestead ground. No matter where I go. No matter where I roam. Hope Valley you're my home.' Change that to Dirranbandi, chuckled Les, and we're laughing. This went into

'Tyre Trouble' — Happening Thang, then 'Go Girl' — The Tri-Saxual Soul Champs. Christ, Benoit, I don't know where you found these tracks but they sure move! Driving to the music Les casually looked at the speedo and he was doing 200 kilometres per hour. Yet for all the vibration and noise, he may as well have been in a lounge chair watching TV.

The road was long and straight, hardly another car and not a cop in sight. It was a breeze. All he had to do was brake now and again for some roadworkers or cockies grazing their sheep or cattle along the side of the road. The long paddock as they called it. Then Les began to notice the countryside had changed dramatically since the last time he'd driven through there, moving hot beef or whatever. Where there were once millions of trees, it was now just expanses of nothing. What were left were just dead, grey claws, groping towards the burning blue sky.

He braked for more council workers and not far past them went beneath a railway overpass across which someone had painted STOP POISONING THE TREES. Christ, you're not wrong! thought Les, as more expanses of bulldozed and dead trees went past on either side of the road. It was truly depressing and such a ridiculous waste of Australia's dwindling resources. I wonder what it is about trees that politicians and cockies hate so much? mused Les. Christ! Imagine if poor little Reg Campbell in Coffs Harbour saw all this. He'd have a stroke. Still, from what Reg tells me in his letters they're doing their best to fuck the land round there as well. So he's probably used to it. Then there was the road kill. Everything from kangaroos to wallabies, goannas to emus. You name it, it was laying poleaxed on either side of the road; along with the rosellas, cockatoos, kookaburras. If there'd been any bunyips around they would have been splattered along the road as well with the crows picking at them. Les shook his head. What a bloody shame.

The tape cut out just as Goondiwindi came into sight. Good old Goondi' smiled Les, as he cruised through the town centre with its myriad signposts pointing everywhere

142

from Mungilla to Mt Isa. He topped up again, had a snakes, then stretched his legs while he perved on not a bad sort working in the garage. Brown hair, blue eyes and tits shoving out everywhere. Les hit her with a bit of a corny joke as he paid her and loved it as her boobs bounced around when she laughed. Just past the garage was the sign: 'St George 111 kilometres.' Les debated about turning off at Talwood then cutting across to Thallon and Woondo. If you were the Leyland Brothers in a four-wheel drive maybe. But in that low-slung Jaguar, going through dry creek beds, over pot holes, logs, boulders and Christ knows what else? He nosed the Jag towards Bungunya and Yeegallon. From there it was more dead trees, dead animals, one or two cars and the odd road-train. Hubert Sumlin's — 'Bring Your Love To Me' cut into 'I Got The Wheels' — Paul Norton. Now that has to be a good song, chuckled Les. Then just outside of St George, there it was: 'Dirranbandi 87 kilometres.' Les dropped the Jag back into second and put the hammer down.

'The old home town looks the same. As I step down from the train.' Norton was laughing to himself as for some reason the words of that corny song drifted through his mind. 'Down the road I look, and here comes Mary. She's a dyke. And her brother's a fairy.' Isn't that what the girls at the club used to sing?

But about a hundred dead animals later there was no mistaking beautiful downtown Dirranbandi. The one main street, almost as long as it is wide, the pub on the corner opposite the railway station, the bank, post office, police and ambulance station. A butcher's shop, a few more shops, a row of trees down the middle with the town garage at the end, and that was about it. Les was going to skirt round Cowildi Street, but thought, bugger it. He had to see the old home town again and he'd only be here a few minutes if that. Nothing had changed. It was just as hot, dry, dusty and deserted as ever. Being a Sunday, what few shops there were were closed, making it even quieter than normal. Even the police and ambulance

143

station were both closed up. Yeah, nothing had changed. But hang on. There were changes. Dirranbandi now had a video store and the old Cafe de Luxe had changed hands and was now the Cafe Costa-del-Sol, with a bull-fighter painted a little amateurishly across the front window. Les was full of mixed feelings as he drove through town. On one hand it was good to see the old home town again with all its memories, plus his family and friends. And don't they say home is where the heart is? On the other hand, after living in Sydney and all the other places he'd been to, Les realised what a dead, fly-blown row of nothing it was, stuck out in the middle of absolutely bloody nowhere. What did that football coach from Chinchilla, that they all hated, used to call the place? Dirranbandi. Land of the four Cs. Cattle, cotton-fields, cane toads and cunts. Bullshit! It was still home, and if possible, he'd be having one beer at the pub before he left. But now it was time to pick up Murray and get going again.

Les turned left past the garage at the end of town and drove to where the Rotary Park sat on the right just before the bridge over the Balonne River with its usual slow-flowing, murky grey-brown water which was fairly high for this time of year. The trees on either side were leafy and green, weeping willows dropped their branches into the water as they vied with the she-oaks, red-gums and whatever for space along the muddy banks, the whole lot sitting quietly and peacefully in the shimmer-ing, outback Australian sun. Les looked around the swings and the hurdy-gurdy and the old painted steam-roller, but there was no sign off his brother. He switched off the motor and got out of the car.

After the air-conditioned luxury of the Jaguar, it was almost like jumping into a blast furnace; the heat near enough knocked Les over. 'Shit!' he cursed out loud, jamming his cap down further over his eyes and his sunglasses tighter onto his face. Jesus, I hope I'm not getting soft. This never used to bother me once. Les found

144

a seat in the shade, swatted flies and listened to the birds while he waited for Murray. Though knowing his brother, it wouldn't have surprised him if he jumped down from a tree or came up out of the river for a joke. Two hundred or so dead flies and the last of his fruit later, a brand new two-tone green Holden utility drove into the park. There was no mistaking the grinning square jaw and broken nose, sitting under a battered Akubra hat behind the steering-wheel. The ute pulled up alongside the Jag and out climbed Murray in his familiar moleskins, sleeveless denim shirt and dusty brown R.M. Williams.

'Hullo, Les,' he said, the grin on his face spreading wider. 'How are you, mate?'

'Muzz. Jesus, it's good to see you.'

There was the usual bone-crushing handshakes, pushes and shoves and rib-cracking embraces as the two Norton brothers greeted each other.

'Bloody hell, Muzz,' said Les, stepping back to take a good look at his brother. 'You're lookin' well, mate. I reckon you're getting younger if anything.'

'You don't look too bad yourself — for a city boy. Dunno about that poofy lookin' red T-shirt you've got on though. What's fuckin' Mambo? Ain't that some wog dance? No wonder those blokes give you them two black eyes.' Murray nodded towards the Jag. 'Still, I suppose it goes with your nice pink, yuppy car.'

Les laughed and pulled his brother's Akubra down over his eyes. 'You fuckin' hillbilly.' Les then nodded towards the Holden utility. 'Did you manage to borrow a car?'

'No' replied Murray casually. 'That's mine.'

'Yours?' Les screwed up his face. 'I thought you said you didn't have a car?'

'I lied,' was Murray's laconic reply.

'Lied!' Les couldn't believe what he was hearing. 'What do you fuckin' mean — you lied?'

'I lied,' repeated Murray, just as laconically. 'I had a second car all the time. Not a bad one either, is it? You like it?'

'Like it!' Norton's face went florid. 'You fuckin'
moron. I've just driven seven hundred fuckin' kilometres
and knocked back a root with a good sort tonight to come
out here and get you. And you had a car all the time.
You...' Les cocked back his fist. 'I oughta.'

'Now hold on a sec,' said Murray evenly. 'Before you
go off the deep end, I needed you out here bad.'

'Bad,' gritted Les. 'It'd want to be bad. Real fuckin'
bad.'

Murray looked directly and seriously at his brother. 'A
bunch of wogs tried to kill me on Friday, Les. I'm dead-
set lucky to be alive.'

The steely look in Murray's dark brown eyes told Les
something was definitely wrong and he calmed down a
little. He wasn't over rapt in the idea of someone trying to
kill his brother either. 'What happened, Muzz?'

'I'll tell you. But before I go on, old Joe Bracken's
dead.'

'Brumby Bracken. Shit! What happened to him?'

Old Brumby Bracken was the town eccentric; he got his
nickname from when he used to break in brumbies in his
youth. His wife and family died in a car accident and old
Joe just went bush, living out under the stars, coming into
town maybe three or four times a year in the last twenty
years. He was harmless enough and had been a good
friend of the Nortons. It was just that old Brumby's lift
stopped going all the way to the top floor when his family
died.

'Snake bite. But these wogs shot him up with machine-
guns thinking he was me.'

'Wogs? Machine-guns? Out here in Dirranbandi? Murray, you're getting a bit over my head here, son.' Then for
the first time Les noticed something. 'Hey, where's
Grungle?'

'He's crook.'

'Crook?' Norton's face darkened. 'Those fuckin' wogs
didn't...'

'No. Nothing like that.' Murray gave a bit of a laugh.
'Poor old Grungle took the trifecta. Elaine had a lump of

146

cornbeef in the fridge   about a month I reckon. So she ends up giving it to Grungle and he gets food poisoning. He's laying out the back, moaning and groaning and a branch falls of a tree and splits his eye open. He's got the shits good and proper, so he chased this rotten big cane toad and gets a squirt of venom in the cuts round his eye.'

'Bloody hell!'

'So I left him at home. Just as well. He's droppin' farts at the moment'd clear Lang Park if Queensland was leading New South Wales 30–0.'

'Strewth!'

'Funny thing,' chuckled Murray, 'he kept scratching at his eyes, so I cut the leg off one of the kid's wet-suits and made a sort of mask for him so he'd stop ripping the scab off all the time. You ought to see him. He looks like a burglar. Elaine calls him Beagle Boy number 700. Like in those Donald Duck comics we used to read when we were kids.'

Even though he was disappointed at not seeing his old mate, Les had to laugh at this description of him. He could just imagine Grungle's little piggy eyes staring out behind a mask. 'Ahh shit! that's bad luck. I was hoping to see him. I do like that horrible fuckin' dog of yours, you know.'

'Don't we all, mate? He's family. But don't worry, there's always next time.'

'Yeah,' shrugged Les. 'Next time. Anyway who are these wogs you reckon tried to kill you? What's going on?'

'No reckon a-fuckin-bout it. I should be dead. And I'm fair dinkum.'

'All right, I believe you. Hey, just one more thing before you start. I noticed on the way in we got a video store and the old milk bar's now a Spanish restaurant or something.'

'Ohh that,' chuckled Murray. 'The video store's run by an ex-British Airways pilot. He's Australian, his name's Greg McCiver. He's not a bad bloke and actually his missus comes from out this way. I've had a few drinks with him. He's been hijacked four times and he reckons after flying in and out of airports all over the world, he never wants to see another plane or an airport again. All he wants is peace and quiet.'

'He's picked the right place.'

'And the restaurant. That's the de Silvas'. They're good people and they like it out here too. The old man Enrico's got a property a bit further out towards Whyenbirra where he raises Brahman bulls for the rodeo circuit. He bred Razor Face.'

'Shit! He's never been rode.'

'Ask a few of those boys up at Cloncurry about him. But they're a good bunch, and if you want a good feed while you're here hop in there.'

'What about . . .?'

'You needn't worry about the cops. They're new blokes now anyway. But they're all up at Chinchilla. Two tribes of Abos are in town celebrating 40,000 years of culture and tradition. All getting pissed and trying to kill each other. So rather than let them wreck the town, the cops have herded them all into the local football stadium, flagons and everything, and letting them kick the shit out of each other in there. Some TV mob from the city's videoing it.'

'Nice to see our indigenous peoples are still maintaining their cultural identity,' said Les.

'That's what we pay 'em for,' winked Murray. 'So if you want to stroll around town it's all sweet. But after I tell you what happened and what I got in mind, I reckon the less people know you've been in town the better.'

'Okay, Muzz,' said Les seriously. 'What happened, mate?'

'What happened?' Murray shook his head slowly. 'Christ! What didn't fuckin' happen.'

The police were away and Murray was left in charge as honorary town sheriff, due to his position in the Parks and Wildlife service. All the Kooris were away watching the fighting, barracking for their tribe or whatever, and cotton harvest was in full swing so there wasn't a great deal to do. Not that there ever is in Dirranbandi. He was

148

in town Thursday afternoon watching the 2.50 p.m. goods-and-passenger train pull in, when he noticed four serious looking blokes pull up in a green army-style Land Rover. They were all wearing black singlets, shorts and hats, and Murray tipped them to be workers off one of the local cotton farms. The only thing unusual about them was they all had bushy black hair and thick black moustaches and wouldn't have looked out of place driving taxis or running a restaurant in Beirut. They were all fit and hard and had no trouble lifting up a wooden crate, about the same size as a family refrigerator they collected from the train and gently placing it in the back of the Land Rover. They had a bit of a look around, didn't notice Murray watching them and drove off out of town towards the Balonne River. Murray didn't think all that much of it, had a few beers at the pub that night then hit the sack.

Still not having a great deal to do the next day, and with the family away, Murray decided to kill two birds with the one stone. There were four old abandoned opal mines, all next to each other, about five kilometres past and 17 kilometres in from the bridge, which were now a hazard; a couple of horses and some cattle had fallen in there and it was only a matter of time before somebody got killed. It was Murray's job to blow them up. The council bought the explosives and the idea was to implode it so the whole lot would cave in. Murray drove out and set up all the charges. While he was there, Murray thought he'd call in on old Joe Bracken, make sure he was all right and ask him if he wanted to watch the fireworks. Joe's camp was about three kilometres away next to the river. Murray left his ute at the mines and walked through the scrub to Joe's camp.

Brumby's camp looked like one of those old McCubbin paintings, a blackened billy hanging over a campfire, a tarpaulin slung over a log between two trees for a tent, a tea-chest, a few other odds and ends, and that was it.

There was no sign of old Brumby. Murray called out a few times then opened the tent flap. There was old Joe,

149

lying on his bunk, foaming at the mouth and turning blue.
Murray didn't need to know he'd been bitten by a snake.
The thing was still curled up under his bed; a six-foot
taipan. It started to uncoil slowly at the sight of Murray,
and Wildlife and Parks officer or not, he grabbed his
machete and hacked its head straight off, then threw it in
the river. But poor old Brumby was just about a shot bird.
Murray found the bite on his leg, slashed it with the
machete, sucked some of the venom out then tied a
tourniquet around it. There wasn't a great deal more he
could do for the time, but back in the ute he had some anti-
snake veno in his first-aid kit. If he could get some of that
into old Joe he might be a chance. A pretty slim one
though, because instead of a McCubbin painting, old
Brumby was starting to look more like Gainsborough's
Blue Boy. It would be no good dragging Joe back through
the scrub, the poison would only spread through his body.
Murray propped his old mate up as best he could and
started running back to the opal mine.

Murray had got about a kilometre when he heard a
noise on his left. It was the same bushy haired blokes he'd
seen at the railway station, only this time there were six of
them and they weren't wearing singlets and shorts. They
were all dressed in full desert cammies and carrying
machine-guns. Murray automatically stopped, but
before he could say a word one of the men barked an
order in some foreign language and all men raised their
weapons. After the episode with the snake, Murray's
adrenalin was still pumping and something jogged his
reflexes. He dived sideways and rolled backwards, just as
a deafening burst of machine-gun fire tore into all the
trees and scrub where he'd been standing. He rolled
further and another burst from all six weapons ripped
into the ground and kicked up rocks and logs barely
centimetres away from his head. Murray waited a
moment or two and heard the same man bark another
order. Instead of charging at him, they knew what they
were doing, they fanned out around him heading him
towards the river.

Murray waited another second or two, took a deep breath then ran, crawled and rolled back to old Brumby's camp, with whoever it was chasing after him, firing bursts of machine-gun fire. How they never killed him Murray didn't know. But if Les didn't believe him, his brother lifted up his shirt and showed him the bandages where two bullets grazed his waist next to all the cuts and scrapes. Les shook his head, scarcely able to believe what he was seeing. None the less, whoever they were, they were still dealing with a Norton. An unarmed Norton. But a very angry Norton who knew what he was doing and knew his way around the bush.

There was a slight ridge just in front of Joe's camp. Murray dived over the top as another hail of bullets chopped into it, rolled down the embankment on the other side and into Joe's tent. Old Brumby was still lying on his bunk foaming at the mouth and Murray knew he was pretty much a goner no matter what. If the poison didn't kill him the blokes chasing Murray would. Murray grabbed Brumby off his bed, dragged him out the other side of the tent and threw him in the river, then dived behind some rocks, scrambled a bit further away just as the six men came charging down the ridge.

Whether it was the water or what that freshened old Brumby up, but he started waving his arms around and drifting along with the current it looked like he was swimming. All six men saw him splashing around and opened up with their machine guns. They didn't just shoot him: they blew him to pieces. The machine-guns had drum magazines, and shells were just pouring out all over the place. Joe's body rolled over and over from the force of the bullets, bits and pieces flying off everywhere. The six men kept firing till there was nothing left but torn pieces of clothing, scraps of flesh and gut and a deep, red stain slowly disappearing into the muddy water of the Balonne.

While this was going on, Murray crawled a bit further away and watched. Two of the men fired another burst into the water then, convinced it was Murray they'd just killed, the same man barked another order and they turned their attention to old Brumby's camp. There wasn't much but what there was they tore apart. They smashed up or ripped to pieces whatever of old Joe's meagre possessions they could find, threw it in a heap then set fire to it with some kerosene they found. When it burnt down they kicked the ashes into the river, along with anything else that was left, including all their empty casings. They cleared old Brumby's campsite, spread some rocks and bushes around and, by the time they finished, you wouldn't have known anyone had been there. Convinced their low deed was done and they'd covered their tracks enough, the same man grunted another order and they started walking back along the river in the direction of the bridge. Murray gave them a few moments while he patched his wounds up with a bit of mud and leaves, then followed.

They had a camp about two kilometres away, almost next to the river. Murray found a slight ridge fifty or so metres away and checked it out. The Land Rover was covered in desert camouflage and by the shape of the netting he could make out the wooden crate was still in the back. Even then it was almost invisible. There were three small tents, a table and chairs, and away from the campfire their machine-guns were stacked on their stocks, army style. Even without the six men standing about in their cammies and boots, the camp had a full-on paramilitary look to it.

By now Murray's wounds were starting to seep through the mud and leaves, so rather than leave any sign of a blood trail he started back to the opal mine. He drove straight home, cleaned himself up and bandaged his wounds, and kept what had happened to himself.

The next day he still didn't say anything to anyone in town or anyone that called out to the house. When he knew the sun would be behind him, Murray took a trail-bike down the opposite side of the river towards the camp. Even with a pair of Firebird 8 x 30, fluorescent red, objective-lens binoculars the camp wasn't easy to find; whoever they were, they were professionals.

152

Murray found a safe spot to hide and zeroed in on the campsite. By the time the sun came round two hours later, Murray knew just about all he needed to know, and left as silently as he came. He still didn't say anything to anybody, didn't tell his wife or kids when they rang from St George that night. He had a few beers at the pub later that night, came home early and changed his bandages and thought about what to do. Only in about a ten times worse mood than his brother was when he got belted at CJ's on Saturday night. Murray had been up about an hour still planning what to do when Les rang that morning. Now here they were.

'So what do you reckon about that, Les? Blow up about me dragging you all the way out here if you like. But' — a touch of sadness crossed Murray's eyes — 'if it hadn't of been for poor old Brumby, you'd have never have seen me again.'

Les stared at his brother and shook his head. 'Jesus bloody Christ!' he said slowly.

'And it's a good thing I never had the dog with me. They'd have blown him to bits for sure.' Murray spat into the dust. 'Plus I lost a fuckin' good hat.'

Les could hardly take his eyes off his brother as the words 'never have seen me again' sunk in a bit further. 'Have you figured out who these roosters are?'

'Yeah.' Murray nodded his head emphatically. 'They're some kind of Muslim terrorists. I sprung these flashes on the sleeves of their cammies and a stack of rolled-up prayer mats. I couldn't see all that much, but when I got home I rang a bloke in Brisbane and checked out the weapons. They're Soviet Degtyarev PRC 56s. You don't buy them in Woolies. By askin' around the garage and that I figured out they got here around lunchtime Thursday. They'd have only just set up their camp and picked up that crate from the station. Friday they'd have been sussing the area out. They wouldn't have known old Brumby was there yet, then they sprung me.'

'Yeah,' nodded Les. 'They sure sprung you all right.'

'What they're doing out here I haven't got a clue. But I

sure as hell ain't real keen on the wog bastards trying to kill me and turn our old mate Brumby into yabbie bait.'

Les scuffed at a rock near his foot. 'So what are you gonna do, Muzz?'

'What am I gonna do?' The look of sadness in Murray's eyes at the death of old Brumby was replaced by one of pure, icy hatred. 'I'm gonna kill all six of the cunts. You gonna give me a hand?'

Les thought for a second, got to his feet, folded his arms and looked down at his brother. 'Well, I'm here now, aren't I?'

Murray jumped to his feet grinning. He shaped up in front of Les as if he could barely contain himself. 'Good on you, mate. I knew you would.'

'Hey, but just hang on a sec, Muzz. You can't go racing out into the bush and take on half a dozen terrorists armed with machine-guns like you're goin' out pottin' rabbits. I hope...'

'Mate.' Murray held up his hands. 'Don't worry about a thing. I've got it all sorted out. We'll do it early tonight. Take us three hours tops, no more. The bodies gone, the truck, the lot. They'll disappear.'

'Three hours?'

'I promise you.' Murray gave his brother a wink. 'You just meet me here tonight at seven. I'll tell you what's going on. And I'll show you something that'll blow your mind.' Before Les had a chance to reply Murray looked at his watch. 'I'm gonna get going and get all this together. I'll see you here at seven. Have a walk round town and that if you want. But I'd keep it a bit low-key if I were you. Just to be on the safe side.'

'I will,' replied Les. 'The less people know I called into town and helped kill six blokes the better, I s'pose.'

Murray smiled. 'Go and have a feed at that Spanish joint though. No one knows you in there. And the food's the grouse.' Murray shook his head. 'Then, after Elaine's cookin' I reckon anything'd taste good. She nearly poisoned poor fuckin' Grungle.'

Les looked solemnly at his brother then grabbed his

154

hand and shook it almost like never before. 'Jesus, it's
good to see you, Muzz.'

'You too, Les, you too. Anyway, I'm off. I'll see you
back here at seven.' Murray got into his Holden ute and
drove back towards town.

Les stood there for a little while watching the disappearing dust cloud. By now he'd had enough of swatting
flies in the heat. He got back into the Jag, turned on the
air-conditioning and had a bit of think. Well, wasn't this a
bloody nice turn of events. Not only have a bunch of
ratbag terrorists almost killed my brother, now I'm going
out to get into a gun-fight, or who knows bloody what
with them. They'll disappear. Yeah. And if they don't we
just bloody might. And finish up joining old Brumby as
yabbie bait all along the fuckin' Balonne. Chill memories
of the shoot-out with the IRA at Yurriki flashed across
Norton's mind. Christ! I hope it's not anywhere as hairy
as that. But Murray seemed super confident. And this
time we'll have the drop on them. Les drummed his
fingers on the steering-wheel. And what's this thing he
reckons is going to blow my mind? Old Muzz can get a bit
carried away at times. I just hope to Christ he knows what
he's doing. Les suddenly laughed mirthlessly to himself.
Better ring DD and tell her not to wait up.

Les continued to stare out the window as the air-
conditioner hummed in the background. After a few
moments a rumble in his stomach told him he hadn't had
a feed since...? And that new Spanish restaurant
sounded all right according to Murray. He glanced at his
watch, he had a good hour. And it might be a good idea to
ring DD. Shit! What the bloody hell am I going to tell
her? With this, his hunger, and the forthcoming gunfight
on his mind, Les started the car and drove into town.

Sunday evening in Dirranbandi was definitely Sunday
evening in Dirranbandi; a few cars parked outside the
pub, a few crows crying to each other as the sun went
down, a couple of stray dogs walking around in the dust
and no people. There were no cars outside the post office

at the other end of town and none outside the restaurant. Norton parked the car opposite; he didn't bother to lock it, but he left his cap and sunglasses on and changed into a plain, white T-shirt. Even with a new name and the bullfighter on the window, the old Cafe de Luxe still looked its same dusty self. There were the two petrol bowsers out the front between the skinny wooden poles holding up the chipped fibro awning with the loose slats, and the same junk collecting flies in the window. It was open, but there didn't appear to be anybody inside. Les walked up to the post office. Shit! This is going to be nice, he thought, as he got the phone number out of his wallet and rummaged around for some change. He shook his head sombrely as he dropped the coins in the slot then dialled the number.

'Hello,' came a girl's voice at the other end.

'Yes. Is Desilu there, please.'

'She's not in at the moment. She's around at a friend's house. Who's this?'

Norton had a quick think then dropped his voice. 'I'm a friend of Les Norton, he asked me to leave a message for a Miss Desilu Donaldson.'

'Oh yes. She was expecting a call. What...?'

'Les was supposed to take her out tonight, but there's been a bit of an accident with the car and they're at the hospital.'

'Oh dear.'

'Les said not to worry, they're not hurt all that much. But they're at the hospital sorting things out with the police. Les couldn't get away and he asked me to ring up.'

'Oh.'

'He just said to say that he might be a bit late getting round there, that's all.'

'That's bad luck. Is there a number Des can ring?'

'There is, but I can't think of it right off. Some place in Tweed Heads. I'm not from up here myself.'

'Oh.'

'So will you tell her that. And Les will ring her when he gets a chance. But he's all right and not to worry.'

'I'll see that she gets the message. Thank you.'
'Thanks very much. Goodbye.'
'Goodbye.'

Norton hung up and looked at the phone, still shaking his head slightly. Not bad for off the cuff. But hospital. Shit! I hope that isn't another omen. Like when I joked with Warren about him getting bashed up and I copped it that night myself. Norton stepped out of the phone-box and looked up at a few golden streaks spreading across the fading blue of the outback Queensland sky. You wouldn't do it to me, would you, boss? Norton shook his head again. Oh well. If I've got to go, at least I'll go on a full stomach. He put the number back in his wallet and walked down to the cafe.

The new owners hadn't spent a fortune doing up the old Cafe de Luxe since they took over. The same old glass counter on your right as you walked in with the longer, laminex counter running past that. The same old three round mirrors on the wall behind it saying 'Milk Drinks and Sundaes. Sweets and Confectioneries. Peach Melbas and Banana Splits'. The same three laminated plywood cubicles on your left, the same red laminex tables fading to white in the middle, the aluminium edges dented and scratched, and the same uncomfortable wooden seats. There were even the same old thirties-style mirrors hanging on the wall above. The only things new were, instead of the old pinball-machine, a video one, and a couple of Spanish travel posters and a few empty Chianti bottles stuck to the wall. Between this and the other counter were three more tables and white plastic chairs. However, at the end of the counter was a blackboard menu next to the kitchen, from which were wafting some pretty tantalising cooking smells. Very tantalising indeed. Les studied the blackboard menu — there were the usual steaks, chips, pies, hamburgers etc., plus a few Spanish and Mediterranean dishes — then Les took a seat in one of the cubicles with his back to the street. A minute or two later a plumpish woman about forty came out wearing a plain blue dress with big white buttons down the front and a

157

blue apron. At first she could have passed for an Italian momma except her eyes were a flashing dark brown and her jet black hair was held on top of her head by a red wooden comb that looked big enough to ravel wool on.

'Buenos nochas,' she smiled.

'Hello,' Les smiled back.

Norton went for the taramasalata, capsicum salad and seafood paella. And a can of Golden Circle orange and mango to wash it down. His soft-drink and plate arrived, followed a few minutes later by the taramasalata and the capsicum salad. Murray wasn't kidding about the food. It was just about unbelievable. Les couldn't figure why the cafe wasn't packed. If it had been in Sydney, the yuppie let's-do-lunch set would have been kicking the doors down to get in.

The taramasalata just about sizzled on your tongue. The cod's roe was mashed to perfection with just the right amount of crushed garlic, the black olives were as plump as gooseberries and if the carrot and celery sticks had been any crisper, he'd have needed both hands to break them. The capsicum salad had been lightly fried to perfection, the white pepper was freshly ground, the olives were plump again, there was just the right amount of chopped parsley, and Les knew virgin olive oil when he tasted it. The paella? What could he say? Beautiful mussels, scallops, king prawns and the thinnest fillets of fish. It wasn't murdered with too much garlic or turmeric, and there were genuine strands of saffron spread across the long-grain rice. Les wiped a solitary grain of rice from his plate with the last of his bread and washed it down with the rest of his soft-drink then rubbed his stomach with satisfaction. A nice cup of coffee'd go well now, he thought. Les caught the lady's eye and ordered.

While Les was eating, a few people had drifted in and out; buying milk, chocolates, cigarettes, whatever. They barely glanced at Les; in his cap and sunglasses he probably looked like any other truck-driver having a meal. He noticed a small pile of magazines on one of the tables between him and the counter. He picked a couple up just as his coffee arrived. Christ! Ten out of ten for the coffee as well, thought Norton, after he'd stirred in some sugar. Oh well, the condemned man's going out on a good feed, Les mused as he sipped his coffee and flicked through the two magazines.

The magazines were Spanish. Well, that figures, thought Norton. Adds a little 'ambience' to the restaurant besides the empty plonk bottles and the old posters. But if the words were different the pictures were the same as in any el cheapo Australian tabloid. Drunken rock stars caught with their pants down, police raids, gory murders, plane crashes. Plenty of tits and bums and ads for clothes, cars, after-shave, erotic videos etc.

Norton ho-hummed through the first and started flicking idly through the second. Much the same fare though some photos of a sky-diver losing his parachute, a shipwreck, and a big heroin bust in Marseilles caught his eye. Something on a page with a big, glossy ad for men's clothes caught his eye too. Jeans, shirts, shoes etc. But not having much of an idea of Spanish, Les shrugged it off and flicked to the next. Norton didn't have to speak Spanish to recognise what was on the next two pages — Crystal Linx splashed across both of them. Hello, chuckled Norton, it's the girl herself. Then he started giving the double page spread double blinks.

There was a smaller photo of Crystal on the left in all her glory from the waist up. Giant, enormous tits just sitting there with two lovely pink nipples jutting out in front. The two other, larger, photos were a lot different, however. They were taken through a tele-photo lens on a lawn near a swimming pool, with what looked like some kind of a white painted villa out of focus in the background. Crystal was side on, sitting topless on a cushioned banana-chair, wearing a black string bikini with her hair in a pony-tail. Opposite and talking to her was a tanned, fit blonde also sitting topless on a cushioned banana-chair, wearing a blue, rolled down one-piece costume. The other photo was Crystal laying on her back asleep on a banana-chair. What caused Norton's double blinks was, compared to her girlfriend's and the ones in the smaller photo, Crystal's tits looked like two fried quayle's eggs smeared with peanut oil. Norton sipped his coffee and stared at the photos.

It seemed to be some kind of resort or a very exclusive villa. Apart from Crystal and her girlfriend there were hardly any other people around and Les could just make out a sign. '*Privado. Prohibido tomar fotographias*'. You didn't have to be a United Nations interpreter to figure out what that meant. He flicked to the front cover. *Ferbrero*. The magazine was barely a month old. Les stared at the Spanish by-lines and the story, but apart from maybe a word here and there it all went over his head. Those photos didn't though. Those tits lying on the banana-chair definitely weren't the ones in the smaller photo on the left. Or the ones that came bursting through the door at Brisbane airport on Friday. Or the ones he'd been perving on in the casino and in the restaurants or at his flat. They were sweet bugger all. Barely a handful in both of them sitting on two rolls of midriff. As a pin-up you wouldn't have given her a feed. And Norton was blowing up about the swimming pool at the flats being drained. If he'd have seen those, he'd have drained it himself.

Norton stared at the photos and finished his coffee. Privado. Prohibido fotographias. What did that woman journalist say at Brisbane airport? 'Crystal, have you just spent a month in a European clinic?' Something else made Les scratch at his chin. Drained the pool himself. Mermaid Pool Service. The empty pool? Norton slowly shook his head. Something besides Kelvin Kramer definitely wasn't too kosher here. Les gently tore the two pages out and put them in his pocket.

He paid the bill, thanking the lady for a fine meal, bought a Cherry Ripe and walked back to the car. The two old petrol bowsers out front of the cafe caught his eye — might be a good idea to fill up again. He topped up the tank, thanked the smiling Spanish lady again then drove back to the little park near the bridge. The sun was well and truly setting when he pulled up. He moved the car in a bit further, this time under some trees, got out and sat on the bonnet facing the river and chewed on his Cherry Ripe while he waited for Murray. Although he'd be up to his neck in trouble before long, Les kept thinking about those photos he'd now placed in his overnight-bag sitting in the car. Somehow the main thrust of his thoughts kept drifting back to the empty pool at that block of flats in Surfers. Les was still thinking on this when he thought he heard a slight noise behind him. It wasn't much and Norton was too deep in thought to turn around when a quiet voice almost next to his ear nearly made him jump off the bonnet.

'Well, here I am, Les. Right on time.' It was Murray.

Les blinked. 'Murray! Shit! Where the fuck did you come from?'

'From my place,' grinned Murray. 'Where else?'

It wasn't just the quietness of Murray's approach that surprised Les, nor the fact that he was wearing dark blue, long-sleeved overalls, it was probably the first time he could ever remember seeing his brother without a hat. Murray was sitting on one of the strangest looking motorbikes Les had ever seen. It looked more like an aqua-scooter with a long black seat, one fat wheel at the front and two at the back about a metre and a half apart. Behind the seat and across the two back wheels was a covered metal carrying space, like a big tool-box. All along the sides, across the carrying space and just about everywhere, right up to the handle-bars, was covered in solar-cells that didn't quite look like solar-cells. There was a light at the front and several on the back that weren't turned on, and its junky, angled yet smooth finish gave the thing a very futuristic appearance.

'What the fuck's that?' asked Les. 'It looks like something out of the Transformers.'

'This,' Murray gave the handlebars a pat, 'is a SPATV. A solar-powered all terrain vehicle.'

'Yeah?' Les walked inquisitively around the strange looking vehicle. 'Where the bloody hell did you get it?'

'The kids made it.'

161

Les blinked. 'Your kids? My nephews?'

'Bloody oath!' Murray climbed off the SPATV, folded his arms and looked at it proudly. 'You're not going to believe this, Uncle Les, but Wayne and Mitchell are half-baked computer geniuses. They hate fuckin' TV — thank Christ! And they're bored shitless with videos. So me and Elaine got them a computer each. And they're like two mad scientists. They've even got me in, playing silly bloody war video games and working out rocket trajectories and all this other space-age shit. They drive me nuts at times.'

Les shook his head. 'Well, I'll be buggered.'

'They knocked this thing up out of an old jet-ski we used on the river and a dune-buggy I got from the council.' Murray ran his hands along the sides. 'But you see these solar panels. They've re-invented them. They're halogenous as well. So they hold twice as much power.'

'Yeah,' nodded Les dumbly. 'I thought they might have been.'

'And have a look at this.' Murray opened a panel near the back carry space. 'You see that. That's a motor out of a little weed-eater and a tiny generator. When the batteries run down, you kick that in for half an hour, it charges them up and they never go flat.'

'Shit! It's only little, isn't it?'

'Yep,' agreed Murray, closing the panel. 'They're all worrying about inventing electric cars. These are the go — motorbikes, with a little engine to recharge the batteries.' Murray opened another panel to show Les the petrol tank; a two-litre plastic bottle. 'It's expensive to run though. A couple of litres of two-stroke lasts you about six months.' Murray shut the panel and stood back. 'It's completely noiseless, virtually pollution free. It does about 80 kilometres on the flat and you can just about drive it forever. What do you reckon?'

Les stepped back to have another good look. 'I don't believe it. Geniuses in my family.'

Murray winked at his brother. 'We might even patent it. Wouldn't the oil companies spew if something like this hit the market?'

162

'Just a bit,' nodded Les.

Murray watched for a moment as Les ran his hands over the solar panels. 'Well, I suppose you want to know what my plan is for tonight?'

'Yeah,' answered Les. 'I wouldn't mind having half an idea of what you're getting me into.'

Murray opened the carry space at the back, took out a pair of overalls same as his and tossed them to Les. 'Here. Get into these. There'll be a bit of blood and guts floating around tonight — and I wouldn't want to see you get that nice white T-shirt dirty.'

While Les got into the overalls, Murray explained his plan. It sounded simple. 'We go out on the SPATV, take us about thirty minutes from here to their camp. We pull up about half a k away and walk. There's a little ridge just above their camp. We shoot the six of them, dump the bodies and all their junk in the back of their Land Rover and drive up to the old opal mine. All the charges are still set up. We put the vehicle and the sons of Mohammed in the middle. And bang! Up goes the opal mine and down go the boys — about sixty feet. Truck, wooden crate, prayer mats, the lot. With about two hundred ton of rock and soil all over them. No one'll ever find the bastards. Like I said, they'll just disappear.' Murray grinned at his brother. 'What do you reckon?'

'Sounds terrific, Murray,' said Les, buttoning up the front of his overalls. 'And what are we going to shoot them with — laser-powered ray-guns? It's gonna be pitch fuckin' black in about another five minutes.'

'Almost as good.' Murray reached back into the carry space and pulled out what looked like some kind of cut-down assault rifle. 'You'll love these, Les. Ruger Mini-14s.' Murray grinned. 'You ought to see what they do to a pig or a wild dog. Forget about what those fuckin' tea-towel-heads did to old Brumby. When we're finished with the bludgers, there won't be enough left to bait a mouse trap.'

Les looked at the Mini-14 in his brother's hands. 'Hey, did you buy these off Eddie?'

'Yeah. About six months ago.'

163

Les nodded. 'I thought so. He mentioned something about you buying a couple of rifles off him. He didn't say much though.'

'That's what I like about your mate Eddie. He don't elaborate.'

Les took the Mini-14 from his brother and familiarised himself with its feel. It was roughly a metre long from the rear pistol-grip to the end of the barrel. It had a solid wooden stock, with another pistol-grip at the front and a sliding metal shoulder stock at the back. Under the front sight, folded alongside the stock, was a metal bi-pod. Just by holding it and moving it from side to side, Les knew it was some weapon all right.

'You know anything about Ruger Mini-14s, Les?' asked Murray.

'Yeah sure,' answered Les. 'Me and Warren always keep about half a dozen laying around the house in case the woman across the road might drop in for a cup of tea.'

Murray ignored his brother's reply. 'All right, well I won't go into all the full-on ordnance bullshit but they're fuckin' unreal. They're a sort of modified version of the M1-Garand or the M-14 the Yanks first used in Vietnam. It takes a .223, same as the M-16, but these are semi-automatic, they ain't rock 'n' roll.' Murray took a slightly curved magazine from the SPATV and clipped it beneath the rifle in Les's hands. 'That's a thirty-shot clip. I'll give you four. Not that you'll need them but... you never know. Now...' Murray took what looked like a black, stainless-steel bike-pump from the carry space and started screwing it on the end. 'Silencer,' he smiled. 'Or 'suppressor unit', as the yanks like to call them.' This made the rifle about fifteen inches longer. Murray's smile got bigger. 'But like they say on TV, "And that's not all".' From the carry space he took what looked like half of a fat pair of binoculars, with a couple of buttons and switches on it and a short length of cable. 'You're gonna love this, Les,' he said, as he expertly began sliding, screwing and clamping it on top of the rear sights. 'It's a IEHSLNS.'

164

'I thought that's what it might have been,' said Les, looking at it like it was a Chinese menu written in Cantonese.

'Image Enhancing Heat Seeking Laser Night Scope. From Otics Defence Accessories, Durango, Colorado. US of goddam A. In other words, Les, night-sight, makes you see in the dark. And makes sure you don't miss.'

'Christ! Where the fuck did you get this shit?' asked Les. The Mini-14 was now a little heavier and slightly bulkier, but by no means awkward or unwieldly.

'Off this bloke in Brisbane. There's gonna be a big war in the Middle East soon, Les, and this is part of the night-fighting gear the Yanks are going in with. Our blokes haven't even got this yet.'

'Bloody hell!'

Murray took the front of the gun and pulled down the bi-pod. 'They're Harris bi-pods too. Best you can get.' Murray stepped back and looked at the weapon in his brother's hands. 'Well. What do you reckon?'

Les cradled the weapon, took it by the two pistol-grips, held it up to his shoulder and looked along the sights. 'Hey, not bad, Muzz. I feel like the Terminator.'

'Now come over by the river.'

Still carefully holding the rifle, Les followed his brother over to the riverbank. Murray picked up two pieces of broken branch, rubbed them vigorously together for a few seconds then flung one out into the murky blackness of the Balonne. Les heard the splash and even though the moon was out, in the darkness he was stuffed if he could see the piece of branch floating on the water.

Murray pressed a button and clicked a switch on the night scope. 'Now take a look.'

Les peered through the sight and could hardly believe his eyes. It wasn't quite as clear as broad daylight, more like you were watching every thing on a black-and-white TV with not the best reception. But for pitch blackness it was quite amazing. The river was now a distinct grey. He could pick out leaves, ripples on the water, and the

165

movements of insects and animals near the river bank. The branch Murray had thrown in the water was clearly visible as it slowly drifted along, and the part Murray had rubbed appeared to be glowing. As Les zeroed in, a red dot appeared everywhere he aimed the cross-hairs of the night scope.

'Okay, Les,' he heard his brother say, 'rip off five shots.'

Les eased back the cocking lug, slid the safety off, held both pistol-grips and gently squeezed the trigger. There was a bit of a thump in his shoulder that the folding stock easily absorbed, a pop-pop-pop-pop-pop sound and the piece of branch disintegrated in the night scope in a distinct spray of water and flying pieces of wood. The only sound was the whack-whack of the bullets hitting the branch and echoing off the riverbank in the darkness. Les took his eyes from the sights, smelt the cordite in the air as he peered into what was once again darkness, then turned to his brother.

'Jesus! How good was that?'

Murray's grin flashed white in the night but there was pure evil in his eyes. 'Like I told you, Les, those tea-towel-heads want to fuck round with the Nortons, they got two chances. None and Buckley's.'

Les followed his brother back to the SPATV. Murray showed him one or two more things while Les further familiarised himself with the Mini-14. But it didn't take him long to realise you could get a baboon out of Taronga Zoo and make it an expert marksman with one of these outfits. Murray explained a few things more Les would need to know, then looked at his watch.

'Well, what do you reckon, we get going?'

'Yeah, righto,' agreed Les. 'The sooner we get this shit sorted out, the sooner we can be back home, sitting on our arses with a cold beer.'

'Okay then,' grinned Murray. 'Let's make a move.'

Les put the Mini-14 back in the carry tray, closed the lid, hopped on the back of the SPATV and they headed off.

Murray drove back out of the park and across the bridge, went about three kilometres along the road then turned right into the scrub along an old trail Les remembered as a kid. There was scarcely any sound from the strange little vehicle, except the crunching of dirt and twigs and a slight whining from the motor, something like a dodgem car. Knowing just about every inch of the narrow trail, Murray kept the lights off. He didn't drive fast, barely twenty kilometres an hour, and the fat tyres took the bumps easily. The wind in Norton's hair was just a soft breeze and if it hadn't been for the fact they were going out to slaughter six men it would have been no more than an enjoyable drive through the moonlit outback night. Les wondered if the terrorists would have a guard posted, but doubted it; after shooting up old Brumby they'd have figured he was just some old hermit and think no more about it. There was a slim chance they might find the old opal mine in the scrub, but if they did they probably wouldn't take much notice of that either. Murray seemed to think the six men wouldn't be around all that long doing whatever it was they were doing and they'd be keeping low key, then moving along. Though what six Arab terrorists were doing in Dirranbandi of all places was anybody's guess.

Neither man said a word; Murray appeared to be concentrating on the trail and Les was alone with his own thoughts. Before long, Murray pulled up on the SPATV with no more noise then a pushbike, about half a kilometre in from the river.

'Okay, Les,' he said, keeping his voice down, 'they're about half a k over there. Follow me.'

Silently, Murray opened the carry tray and took out the two Mini-14s. He adjusted all the attachments, making sure everything was ready to go, and handed one to Les along with three extra clips of bullets which Les placed in his overalls. Then Les noticed Murray take what looked like a flare pistol in a leather holster out of the carry tray and strap it round his waist. He didn't say anything to Les as he did this, just gave him an odd smile.

'Okay, Les. Let's go. I'll tell you what to do when we get there.' Les nodded and they set off.

Both brothers knew how to walk slowly and silently in the bush, whether it was day or night. Les could feel his adrenalin rising now and was starting to get a bit of a buzz. Whether it was a cruel, callous streak in him he wasn't sure, but he was now looking forward to this, and the gun in his arms had a feel about it he couldn't quite put into words. Besides that, it would be nice to waste the six rotten bastards who tried to murder his brother. Like Murray said, you don't stuff with the Nortons. Not on their home turf especially. They came to a bit of ridge, Murray made a gesture with his hand and very slowly, very quietly, they half crawled, half walked to the top of the rise.

The six men were sitting around a small campfire about thirty metres away, about five metres down with the river just a few metres the other side of their camp. In the light of the campfire and a Tilley lamp sitting on a table, Les could see the Land Rover, their neatly stacked weapons and the tents. The six men were sitting on two logs, spread out a little, laughing, talking and drinking coffee. There was a small radio sitting on the table tuned to some station, softly playing pop music. It was a friendly, cosy little scene. Murray studied them for a few moments then pulled down the bi-pod on the Mini-14, settled it in front of him and studied them through the night scope for a moment or two more.

'Okay, Les,' he finally whispered. 'You take the three on the left, I'll do the others. I'll give you a tap, switch on the laser sight and as soon as you pick your target, start firing.'

'Okay,' whispered Les.

Les too pulled down the bi-pod and set the Mini-14 on top of the ridge. He switched on the night-sight and zeroed in on the six men, swivelling across to the three on the left as Murray directed. With the heat and light from the lamp and the campfire it was as clear as a bell. Les could make out the patterns on their uniforms, the flashes on their sleeves, the expressions on their faces; he could even see the wisps of steam coming from their mugs of coffee. It almost looked as if you could reach out and touch them.

Les picked his three men and waited for Murray's signal. The six terrorists seemed happy enough, throwing back their heads every now and again to laugh out loud. Les almost — almost — felt a little sorry for them. Then Murray tapped him on his right shoulder. Les switched on the laser and a dot appeared where the cross-hairs were focused on the first one's forehead; he decided to work from right to left. Murray looked at him curiously for a second and was about to say something when Les gently squeezed the trigger; and this time with the bi-pod down, there was hardly any shock at all.

The only thing Les could compare to what he saw through the night scope was old black-and-white TV footage of President Kennedy getting shot in Dallas, Texas. The whole top of the terrorist's head lifted off in a thick puff of black and grey as he tumbled back over the log, tossing his mug of coffee up in the air. His mate next to him seemed too shocked or too taken by surprise to move. Les swivelled the cross-hairs to just near his heart and squeezed the trigger twice. It looked as if some invisible giant punched him in the chest. The front of his shirt tore open, he flew backwards over the log, hitting the ground on his back and landed with his feet draped over the log he'd been sitting on. Les could hear shouts now as the third man leapt to his feet spilling his coffee. He hesitated for a second, not knowing whether to grab for the machine-gun or make a break into the bush. That was all the time Les needed to move the cross-hairs and the laser dot onto his stomach and put three rounds straight through his ribcage. Les heard the man scream as he toppled down on his side. He moved the dot to just above his nose and blew nearly all his head off.

While this was going on, Murray was doing pretty much the same thing. He took the first terrorist out with a round straight in the face, which smacked into his mouth, then went up slightly and blew the whole of his head away. He put a couple of rounds in the throat of the one alongside and another at the base of his neck, almost decapitating him. The last one, though, he shot twice in both legs as he stood up, then once in the shoulder as he fell down between his two mates, landing against the log they'd been sitting on.

Les swivelled the night scope across all six bodies. There'd been surprisingly little noise; just the pop-popping of the silencers, the whack of the bullets hitting the men and a few quick screams. Les could see the one Murray had shot in the legs desperately trying to move, and faintly hear him moaning and coughing with pain. He was about to put one into his head when he felt Murray's hand on his arm.

'Not bad shooting, old mate, eh.' Murray had a grin from ear to ear. 'I told you it'd be all sweet.'

'One's still alive.'

'Yeah, I know. That's their leader. I want to have a bit of a yarn to him. Come on, let's go down and see what we got.'

With the Mini-14 still at the ready, Les followed his brother down the ridge to the camp site.

If it had all looked good in a kind of hazy black and white through the night scope, in glorious, living techni-colour it was a different thing altogether. Even in the flickering light of the campfire and the Tilley lamp, Les could scarcely believe the carnage; there was blood and pieces of bodies everywhere. The first bloke Les had shot was laying on the ground, the back of his head looked like a boiled egg with a big piece missing. The one next to him, with his feet over the log, had one eye closed, the other rolled back and his mouth gaping, the front of his shirt was torn open and all his chest had been blown out his back. The third one's insides were all over the place, his neck was still attached with a bit of jaw bone, an ear, a few teeth and that was about it. Around the log on the other side of the campfire was the same grisly, awful scene. One terrorist had no head at all, just a stump pumping blood. Another was sprawled against the log, his head still joined to his neck by a few shreds of flesh and sinew, but it was sitting in a puddle of blood forming at his waist. The third one lay between them like a broken puppet, his back against the log. Blood was pumping out of his shoulder and legs, spreading around him like a crimson rubber bathmat. There was no sound. Just the radio softly playing on the table and the terrible moaning of the terrorist still barely alive.

'Shit!' Les was finding it hard to believe the bloodbath in front of his eyes. He looked from the bodies to the rifle in his hands. 'Jesus, Murray! What have we done with these things?'

'I dunno,' shrugged his brother. 'But I think we won.'

Les shook his head and spat on the ground. He almost felt like being sick.

Murray moved over and stood in front of the terrorist still bleeding against the log. He was pretty much as Murray had described. Bushy black hair, thick moustache, a stubbly beard. His dark features were now pale with shock and pain; sweat was dripping down his face.

'G'day, mate,' said Murray cordially, almost friendly. 'How are you feelin'?' The terrorist spat something out in a foreign language and glared defiantly at Murray. 'Not very bloody friendly, are you?' Murray rested his rifle against the Land Rover then turned back to the terrorist. 'So what are you doin' in Dirranbandi?' Again the same look of defiance. Again the terrorist spat and cursed something at Murray. Murray nodded his head sagely. 'Yeah, I didn't think you'd tell me.' He stepped back from the terrorist and took the pistol out of its holster. In the light from the Tilley lamp it looked more like an old Derringer with one thick, short barrel. Murray broke the weapon like a revolver, took a shotgun cartridge from his overalls, slipped it in, snapped it shut, cocked it, then stepped back a little further.

The terrorist knew what was coming. Again he spat at Murray, his eyes still glaring defiantly through his pain. 'If I am to die,' he said, 'it is the will of Allah.'

'Fair enough,' agreed Murray. 'But I don't think it was Allah's will you comin' out here and tryin' to kill me and shootin' up my old mate Brumby Bracken. If you ask me,

171

mate, that's makin' it a bit willin' all round.' Murray held the pistol up and aimed it at the terrorist.

The terrorist continued to glare at Murray through his pain, then took a deep breath. 'Allah o akbar,' he cried.

'Yeah,' nodded Murray. 'You're right again. He is great. So give him my love when you see him. You arsehole.'

Murray squeezed the trigger. There was a roar and a flash as his hand kicked up and the terrorist took the full charge straight in the chest. Then right before Les's eyes, the front of the terrorist burst into about twenty blinding pin-points of bright green flame that momentarily lit up the faces of Les and Murray. The terrorist gave one dreadful scream, writhed up as the front of his shirt caught on fire, then slumped back dead against the log. There was an awful spluttering, sizzling sound for a second or two then it all went out. Les stared at the wisps of black smoke rising from the terrorist as the smell of barbecued flesh and something like burning urine, only stronger, caught in his nose, then slowly turned to his brother.

'What the . . .?'

'SSSS,' grinned Murray. 'Single Shot Street Sweeper. Kondor Arms, Durban, South Africa.' Murray held the shotgun-revolver up for a moment before slipping it back in its holster. 'The shell? That's called Dragon's Breath. The Yanks again of course. It's twelve gauge, but it fires pellets of burning phosphorous at 4000 degrees Fahrenheit. Anything it hits, it sets on fire. I've been dying to see how it works.' Murray turned to the terrorist à la shis-kabob then back to Les. 'Seems to. What do you reckon?'

'What do I reckon?' After the rest of it, this was all Les needed. 'I reckon you're putting him in the back of the truck. This is bloody horrible.'

Still grinning, Murray slapped his brother on the shoulder. 'Get out, it ain't that bad. We've seen worse fights down the pub.' Murray glanced at his watch. 'Anyway, let's get it all loaded up and see if we can figure out what we got here.'

172

Les was shocked, sickened and disgusted. But his adrenalin was still pumping noticeably and deep down he was curious as to what six Arab terrorists were doing in Dirranbandi. Besides, his night was stuffed and he wasn't going anywhere anyway. 'Yeah, why not,' he answered.

Murray said he'd throw the bodies in the back of the Land Rover if Les wanted to pull down the tents and gather up the rest of the junk. After what he'd just seen, this suited Les admirably. Murray started pulling the camouflage netting off the Land Rover while Les started on the tents, stopping only to check out the terrorists' weapons. They were solid, fairly heavy things, with a long barrel and a bi-pod attached. There was a short wooden stock, a drum magazine and a metal pistol-grip in front of a clumsy-looking wooden stock. Les thought he'd leave them for Murray, who would probably sell them somewhere.

The terrorists lived pretty frugally, a few mats and blankets, some towels and small overnight-bags; definitely no bottles of Monsieur Rochas or hairdryers. The small tents were no trouble to pull down; Les stacked and folded them loosely with the poles on top. He was about to check the overnight-bags when a leather satchel caught his eye. He opened it to find a sheaf of papers and folders, so he took it over by the table to study them in the light of the lamp while the still undamaged radio played some country and western song softly in the background.

The contents of the satchel were mainly in Arabic, a language Les didn't know but he could recognise the script. However, there was one white folder in English. Across the front and on the five pages inside was the seal of the Secret Service, United States of America, marked Top Secret. 'Classified' was stamped across the front. It was some kind of itinerary. Les screwed his face up as he tried to sort it out. 'Air Force One leaves Washington USA 0800 hours 3.9. Arrives Honolulu 1615 hours 3.10.' There was some sort of reference to Buckskin and how long he'd be in Hawaii. Then it went on about Air Force One arrives Mascot, Sydney, Australia, to be

173

met by Prime Minister of Australia. There was some jargon about Black Top Six and Red Bird Five arrives 1415 hours previous. Personnel on Air Force One to be briefed . . .? It was all in military jargon. Les looked into the night and thought of something. What had he seen in the papers and on TV that he didn't take all that much notice of? The President of the United Sates was arriving in Australia for a three-day visit on his way to Japan. Les had almost forgot. Air Force One was the presidential plane. Les read on as best he could and the facts and figures began to fall into place in a jumbled kind of sense. Buckskin was the code name for the President, Black Top Six was some kind of Secret Service command centre; Air Force One leaves Sydney, arrives Eagle Farm Brisbane 1040 hours. There was more jargon about times and dates, Delta Red Six, Blue Star Five. More about Buckskin. Then on about Air Force One leaving Brisbane and arriving at Pine Gap 1120 hours. Buckskin and Australian PM to be briefed by Generals Maunsell and Schneeberger before inspecting facilities. It went on more, but Les knew everything he needed. Slowly he walked across to his brother.

Murray had the six dead terrorists in the back of the Land Rover with their boots sticking out over the rear tray, from which blood was dripping down. Somehow he'd managed to manhandle the wooden crate out and smashed the top off with the butt of his Mini-14. He also was looking at some papers in the light of a torch he'd had in his overalls when Les walked over.

'Hey, Murray,' said Les, 'you're not gonna believe what I found.'

'Yeah,' replied his brother absently. 'Have a look at this.'

Les stared into the crate while Murray held the torch. It was a thick, well-built metal cylinder about two metres long, with a shoulder rest and two twin-mounted metal boxes covered in buttons and gadgets about half a metre from the front of the metal cylinder. Les didn't have to be a member of the United States Secret Service to recognise a portable rocket-launcher when he saw one.

174

'You know what this is?' said Murray, moving the torch back to the papers he was holding.

'Well, it's not a fuckin' Porta-Loo,' answered Les.

'It's a Bofors RBS 70 Ray Rider surface-to-air missile. It's a fuckin' SAM. Here, look, it's written here in Swedish, English and about five other languages. This is the instruction manual.' Murray waved the papers around. 'I don't fuckin' believe it.'

'I do,' said Les. 'Have a look at this, Muzz.' Murray shone the torch on the folder while Les read parts of it out to him. 'This is the itinerary of the President and the Prime Minister flying around Australia. Have a look what it says there. Sydney to Brisbane, then on to Pine Gap.' Les looked directly at his brother. 'What's between Brisbane and Pine Gap, Muzz?'

Murray thought for a second. 'Beautiful downtown . . .'

'Close-a-bloody-nough. These pricks were going to shoot down the President's jet with that rocket launcher.'

The two brothers stared at each other in the light of the torch for a moment, then Murray spoke.

'I also found out who the pricks are, too.' He held up a blood spattered shirt he'd taken from one of the bodies. 'Iraqi Republican Guard.'

Norton looked at the flash on the shoulder. There was a red triangular patch with a red, white and black flag beneath, and three green stars in the middle. Though it had that much blood all over it, it could've been any colour. 'I'll take your word for it.'

Murray threw the shirt into the back of the Land Rover. 'They've camped out here to pick up that rocket launcher from the station. Then they would have either fired it from here or moved somewhere else on the day, or whatever.' Murray spat into the bodies. 'The dirty cunts.'

'There's something else in the car too,' said Les.

'Yeah I know. Give us hand to get it out.'

They manhandled another wooden crate out, about a metre long. Before Les got a chance to say anything, Murray grabbed his rifle again and smashed it open. It was a rocket, brightly painted in red and yellow, a little

175

less than a metre long with two sets of three stabiliser fins front and back. Murray lifted it out, looked at it in his arms for a moment then lay it on the ground. While he was doing this, Les picked up a couple of pieces of broken wood. Les also didn't have to be in the US Secret Service to recognise the skulls and crossbones in black with the three orange markings around them. And he didn't need a master's degree in French to know what *Fabrique Militaire Atomique* meant. Or *Société Européenne de Propulsion. DARD 190. Dangereux. Radioactif.*

Les handed one of the pieces of wood to his brother. 'Shit! You know what this is, Murray. A fuckin' atomic bomb.'

'Not an atomic bomb, Les, it's a low-yield nuclear-tipped missile. Look at all those markings in between the stabilisers.' There were more words in French, more numbers in yellow and orange along the red and more symbols for radioactivity. 'The kids have got books on these things at home and they're always farting around with war games on their computers. That's what it is, all right.'

'Bloody hell!' exclaimed Les. 'What are we going to do with the fuckin' thing?'

'Dunno,' answered Murray slowly, continuing to stare at the deadly little missile. 'But let's get the rest of this shit loaded up and we'll work it out.'

They left the rocket and launcher where it was while they threw the rest of what they could find in the back of the Land Rover over the six dead terrorists. Murray hid their machine-guns in the bush with a rug over them, saying he'd come out and get them through the week and clean up anything else that might be left lying around. Their radio was a fairly good one; Murray left it on the table next to the Tilley lamp saying he'd throw it in the SPATV later. Satisfied everything was packed up, Murray told Les to wait while he went back and got the SPATV and had a think what to do with the missile and launcher. Les watched his brother walk off into the darkness, then sat down on one of the logs the terrorists had been sitting on. With the radio playing in the background, the crying of the night birds and a beautiful canopy of stars above his head, Les stared into the dying flames alone with his thoughts.

Despite the dreadful, sickening violence of the night and the gruesomeness of what was in the back of the Land Rover, plus what he'd left behind in Surfers Paradise, Les didn't know whether to laugh or cry. He settled on laughing; there wasn't much else he could do. It's times like these you need one of those cellular phones, he mused. I could ring someone up, say how are you going, what are you up to? And they'd say, not much, Les. What are you doing? And I'd say. Ohh not much. I just helped kill six terrorists out in the middle of bloody nowhere and we're just going to dynamite the bodies and I'm sitting here with a nuclear rocket, wondering what to do with it. Bit of a quiet night actually. Les shook his head. What would someone say if you rung them up and told them that? They'd tell you to stop playing with your dick. But shit! Wouldn't the papers love a story like this. Especially if I'd taken some colour photos. Yeah. Then I'd probably spend the next ten years in the can and the rest of my life looking over my shoulder for some crazy Arab out after my arse for stuffing up their plans. There's another thought. Me and bloody Murray just saved the President of the United States and the Prime Minister from getting blown to bits. Fat lot of thanks we'll get for it. Then knowing what a couple of boofheads both of them are, people'd probably say why did you bloody bother and they'd even be more dirty on us. You can't win either way. Les gobbed into the flickering coals and listened to the hiss. No. I think the less people know about this bloody caper the better. I know what I can do though. I can check that Land Rover, make sure it's going all right. We didn't even look for the keys.

The keys were in the ignition. Les started the motor, turned on the lights and checked out the four-wheel drive and that. Satisfied all was in order, he switched off the engine and stepped out of the cabin, straight into the silently approaching lights coming down the ridge, which heralded Murray's return. Murray pulled the SPATV up next to the Land Rover and got off.

'Have you worked out what to do with the rocket?' asked Les.

'Yep. I sure have,' nodded Murray. He looked at the missile for a moment then turned to his brother. 'Well, firstly, I don't want the fuckin' thing — unless you do.'

'I'm bloody sure I don't want it,' said Les. 'Make a terrific doorstop. But thanks anyway.'

'Okay. Well, I don't fancy burying it, just in case some dope might come across it with a metal detector and dig it up. And it's no good throwin' it in the river. It could get washed down stream or leak or anything.'

'Fair enough.'

'And I'm sure as hell not putting the fuckin' thing on the back of the Land Rover when I dynamite it. Imagine if the thing blew up.'

'Christ!'

'So you know what I reckon we ought to do with the bloody thing, Les?'

'What?' Les suddenly got this feeling he shouldn't have asked.

The look on his brother's face turned into this weird grin. 'I reckon we ought to let the fuckin' thing off.'

Les looked at his brother as if he'd just turned into a werewolf. 'What did you say, Murray?'

'We'll let the cunt off. I'll fire it straight up in the air. I've never seen a nuclear explosion — except on the movies.'

'Neither have I,' protested Les. 'And I don't fuckin' want to either. You ratbag.'

'Get out, you big, weak sheila. What's wrong with you? It'd look grouse.'

'Murray. You can't . . .'

'Bullshit! Come here, look, I'll show you.'

'Murray for Christ's . . .' But Les had seen this look on his brother's face before when he'd get a bee in his bonnet about something, and knew there'd be no stopping him.

'Anyway, what are you shitting your pants for. It's only a low-yield thing. It's not like there's gonna be another Hiroshima.'

Les shook his head, knowing the futility of even trying to reason with his brother. 'I don't believe this. I honestly don't fuckin' believe it. You are stone, raving fuckin' mad.'

Murray simply shrugged. 'Runs in the family — don't it.' Murray walked over and got the Tilley lamp from the table and placed it on the ground next to the Bofors Ray Rider. He took the torch from his overall pocket, studied the instruction manual then had another good look at the missile. 'Piece of piss,' he said, looking up at Les. 'I told you I've been playing war games with the kids on their computers. This is the same thing. Easier if anything.'

Murray slid open a kind of metal hatch on the back of the Bofors launch tube and got Les to give him a hand to slide the missile in, then closed it. There was a small panel on the launch tube between the shoulder rest and the digital fire control system. Murray slid that open, pushed a couple of buttons, inserted a short, thick length of cable through a small, square hole then closed that too. With Les's help he leant the Bofors Ray Rider against the roof of the Land Rover, then opened another panel on the digital fire control system. Murray pushed another button and the control panel lit up in red and white like a small chess board full of glowing digital numbers.

'See that, Les?' said Murray, pushing at the buttons and numbers. 'You set your altitude proximity guidance control. We're on land, not at sea, so I don't have to worry about that gyro-stabilized mirror. Just make sure the ballistic reticle connects the terminal mode to the engine thrust.'

'Yeah, and the leg bone conecka to the thigh bone,' said Les, half wishing he was somewhere else.

'Yeah, something like that,' chuckled Murray. 'Now I'm not going to get an optical signature, so I'll just set this for...' Murray pushed some more buttons. 'Ten thousand metres. That ought to do. Okay. Now give me a hand to get it up on my shoulder. The bloody thing's heavy, ain't it?'

With Les's help again, Murray got the Bofors onto his right shoulder with the front of the launcher resting on the roof of the Land Rover. He looked through the sights up into the stars and flipped open the firing button near the thumb joy-stick. The weapon was now armed and in full launch mode.

'Which way are you going to aim, for Christ sakes, Muzz?'

'Straight up.'

'What if the thing don't go off and comes back down?'

'Shit! That's a thought.' Murray took his eye from the sight and seemed to take a bearing from the river. 'Okay. Give us a hand to move it round the other side of the car. I'll aim it towards those cunts out in Chinchilla.'

'Yeah, good idea, Muzz,' said Les, helping to move the Bofors to its new position. 'I never liked those bastards. Remember when they beat us in the grand final?'

'Remember it. The bludgers. They didn't only beat us. They flogged us as well. I could hardly walk for a week.'

'Tell me about it,' agreed Les. 'I had to take three days off from work myself. It was only because Big Harry Proudfoot trod on a rusty nail two days before and couldn't play. And Jimmy Monshall got sent off.'

'Yeah,' said Murray, getting his face back behind the sights. 'Didn't we miss them.'

'And those bastards knew it too. Yeah, go on, Muzz. Aim the fuckin' thing towards Chinchilla. Liven those Kooris up, too.'

Murray placed his hand back on the thumb joy-stick and screwed his eye further into the sights. 'Well, twinkle twinkle little star. How I wonder where you are. I think I'll just pick the closest one. That one looks all right.' Murray gave a bit of a sardonic chuckle. 'I hope Dick Smith's not flying around in his helicopter tonight. Not at ten thousand metres over Chinchilla, anyway. Righto Les. Stand back, son. Here we go.'

Les didn't have to be told twice. Leaving Murray

180

holding the Bofors Ray Rider up against the Land Rover, Les got back about five metres from where the blast would come from the rear of the launcher and waited; for what, he didn't quite know. One thing Les did know, here was his brother, a Queensland hillbilly living out in the middle of nowhere, who could work out computers and guidance systems. Les had been living in the city all those years and was flat out programming a VCR. He didn't have long to wait.

The Bofors seemed to quiver for a second, then a red glow came from out the back, followed by a roaring *swoosh*, something like the sound of a kid's skyrocket, only about a hundred times louder. A cloud of dust, leaves and high octane smoke swirled round the Land Rover as the nuclear missile launched itself in a blinding red and white glow that screamed up into the night sky, leaving a thick, smoky vapour trail disappearing towards the stars.

Murray let go of the Bofors, stepped back and joined his brother staring up into the night, trying to pick a tiny red pin-point of light amongst the billions of stars. 'Well, at least it wasn't a dud.'

Les didn't reply. Alongside his brother he stared up into the sky waiting for what, he didn't know. His adrenalin was still moving around after the killings and his nerves were a bit on edge. Now Les began to feel awfully apprehensive. They waited for what seemed like an eternity.

'Hey, Murray, are you sure you set that thing for ten thousand metres?'

'Yeah. Positive.'

'Seems to be taking a bloody long time to get there.'

'Give it a chance.'

'Christ! I hope the bloody thing doesn't land on Chinchilla. I was only half joking, you know.'

Murray rubbed at his chin as he gazed up into the sky. 'I wasn't.'

Les stared up at the stars, trying to follow the vapour trail and pick out the rocket's glow. At not quite 12 o'clock high, more like 11.55, another, bigger star seemed to form between the others that quickly enveloped the surrounding ones in a blinding, silver glow. The silver quickly turned into a huge, equally blinding orange, red and black cloud of rolling, roaring flames lighting up the sky. The cloud spread and got brighter, like a thousand sun flares all rolled into one. From where Les was standing, if the explosion was ten thousand metres up, the epicentre had to be twenty kilometres across; though it seemed to be spreading towards the horizon. The rolling furnace of flames intensified and brightened to finally reach a terrifying climax that momentarily bathed the landscape in an iridescent, soft glow. From a distance it looked something like a thunderstorm, only instead of black, blue and mauve, it was orange, red and black, all turning in on itself.

Then the sound hit. It too was like a thunderstorm, only instead of a distant, rumbling boom it was more an explosion followed by a great crackling hiss. Like a monstrous pair of speakers blowing up on full bass and treble. The dreadful sound lasted for a few moments then, behind the orange glow, it seemed as if the sky was filled with a glowing white criss-crossing as the shock waves hit the sound waves, vaporised themselves around the nuclear explosion and hung in the sky. The cauldron of boiling fire rolled on for a few more moments till the crackling sound diminished and then there was just this orange glow in the sky, something like the aftermath of a late summer storm, only surrounded by a lattice-work of white shock waves. In a strange way it was almost beautiful. It was also quite terrifying. Christ! thought Les. Is that what the end of the world's going to look like? I sure bloody hope not. And these nutters managed to get hold of one. And there's another hundred thousand or more bigger ones sitting in silos all over the world. Bloody hell! Les didn't know what to think. Awestruck, he turned to his brother.

'Well, what do you reckon, Muzz?'

'What do I reckon?' Murray continued to stare up at

the orange glow still flickering across the night sky. 'I reckon if we hadn't come along, they'd have got the both of them for sure.'

'No, Muzz,' replied Les, gaping back up into the sky. 'You definitely deserve all the credit.'

Murray smiled at his brother. 'Why thanks, mate.' Then Murray turned back to the glow in the sky, put his hand over his heart and saluted. 'God bless the President. God bless the flag. And God bless the United States of America.'

'What about our bloke?'

'Ahh fuck him.'

'Fair enough.' Les turned to his brother. 'So what do you reckon we ought to do now? General Norton. NATO computer genius.'

'What do I reckon?' Murray turned and looked evenly at his brother. 'I reckon we ought to get to the shithouse out of here. Because if that's a low-yield one, I don't ever want to see the fuckin' real thing. And I reckon half of Queensland saw that. So let's piss off. We still got to blow that opal mine and get rid of our mates yet.'

Les didn't need to be told twice. In no time flat they had the Bofors, the pieces of wooden crates, and anything else they could find thrown in the back of the Land Rover and tied down with rope. Plus the Tilley lamp out and on the front floor. Typical bloody Murray, thought Les, as he followed the SPATV through the scrub in the lights of the Land Rover. Gets some shit going for a lark then we all have to bail out. He's no different to when we were kids. Though for some mad reason Les still couldn't help but laugh as he bounced along behind his brother.

After about ten minutes of bumping up and down trails and gullies through the barren scrub, Murray pulled the SPATV up in front of the old abandoned opal mines. In the lights of the two vehicles it looked like four holes spread out around a barren, dusty clearing, surrounded by several heaps of mulloch, rocks, old machinery and other rubbish. Murray guided Les through a gap in the

183

mulloch heaps into the middle of the clearing. Les stopped the Land Rover, turned everything off and got out. With the lamp in his hand, he walked over to Murray, framed in the headlight of the SPATV, and gave it to him.

'That's perfect, Les,' he said. 'Right on the button.' Murray lit the lamp, put it on the roof of the Land Rover and walked back to Les. 'Righto, hop on. There's a bit of a knoll behind this mulloch heap. We can watch it from over there.'

They bumped through about two hundred more metres of scrub, up a slight rise to the knoll and pulled up next to a few big boulders, sheltered by a couple of stumpy red gums above. Les got off and sat down behind one of the boulders; in the short distance he could see the lamp flickering in the clearing now surrounded by swarms of moths and other insects. Murray took a remote-control from the carry tray, sat down next to Les and flicked a switch which made two red buttons glow in the darkness.

'This'll probably be small potatoes after that other shindig,' said Murray. 'But it should look all right. Anyway, here we go,' he added and pressed one of the red buttons.

There was a deep, muffled explosion that seemed to shake the ground around them and the clearing under the Land Rover lifted up as four bursts of sparks and flame shot out of the old mine shafts, momentarily lighting up the surrounding scrub. These were quickly snuffed out, along with the lamp as the whole clearing and the Land Rover collapsed in a great cloud of dust. The sound of the explosion echoed dullishly across the scrubby landscape.

'Well, that one worked okay,' said Murray. 'Let's see how number two goes.'

Murray pressed the other red button as Les peered into the dust swirling round in the moonlit darkness. This time it sounded like a crescendo of explosions, slightly louder. The four mulloch heaps seemed to burst out, tumbling and crashing into the hole where the clearing had been in another great cloud of grey dust and smoke.

184

They watched it settle for a minute or so, then Murray tapped Les on the arm and tossed the remote-control back in the carry tray.

'Come on. Let's go down and have a look.'

They bumped their way back down to the scene of the explosions and peered into the smoke and swirling dust through the headlight on the SPATV. Where there had once been mine shafts and mulloch heaps was now a clearing strewn with rocks and rubble, settled in a bit of a basin shape. Somewhere, about twenty metres below, was the Land Rover, the six Arabs, their prayer mats and all their other junk, plus the lamp.

Murray turned round to his brother and grinned. 'Ashes to ashes, dust to dust, if the devil don't get you, the Norton boys must. What did I tell you, Les, I said they'd disappear. Unless you want to go and dig them up. I'd take a bloody big shovel though.'

'No thanks, Muzz.'

'And it's all kosher too. With respect to the dead of course. I just did my job as a good citizen and a government employee. And not a bad one either I might add. For a public servant.'

'What about the other one?' asked Les.

'Well, that was in my own time, wasn't it? You can't expect too much,' Murray slapped his brother on the leg. 'Well, come on. You want a lift back to your car or do you want to stay here gawking at this all night?'

Les grabbed his brother by the overalls, giving him a bit of a thump up under the ribs. 'Warp ten, Mr Sulu. And don't spare the hologenous solar cells.'

Murray spun the SPATV around in the dust and smoke and headed for a trail that lead back to the park by the river.

Both brothers knew there'd be no time and no real need for lingering goodbyes as Les left town. Unlike a conventional machine, the SPATV was virtually noise-free as they bumped along in the night and Les was able to tell Murray pretty much what he could expect in Surfers Paradise. He told him about the boarding house, where

185

the Boulevarde was, a bit about the six blokes they'd be getting stuck into drinking in the back bar. Les would meet him there at nine-thirty a.m. but no matter what he'd ring Murray at six at the boarding house. After the fight they'd both go their separate ways and Les would meet him back at the boarding house for a 'debriefing'. Then they might both move into a good hotel down at Burleigh Heads for a couple of days and get on the piss; all on Les. There might be some recriminations after the fight, but stiff shit, they'd both be out of town if it came to that. And as for KK and his girl, once Les had sorted out one or two things with them, they could both go and get stuffed. There was a little more, but Murray quickly got the picture.

The journey back took considerably less than going out. Murray wheeled the SPATV into the park and pulled up next to the Jag, still sitting quietly beneath the trees next to the silver ribbon of the Balonne, running slowly past in the moonlight.

Les immediately peeled off his overalls and tossed them in the carry tray. Apart from his face and hands he wasn't all that dirty, just hot and sweaty and a bit uncomfortable, especially where the dust and grime had mingled with the sweat and trickled down his neck. He opened the Jag and handed Murray a thick envelope.

'There's the keys to the boarding house, Muzz. The address, my address and phone number, plus where the Boulevarde is. I'll ring you at six, Monday arvo, but if you need me, ring. I won't be far.' Les grinned. 'You'll like Mrs Llivac too. She's a seppo, and she told me she makes the best deep-dish apple pie on the Gold Coast.' Les gave his brother a slap on the shoulder. 'She'd want to. This place is costing me a fortune. There's also $300 in there for petrol and tucker too.' Les looked evenly at his brother for a moment. 'And I don't know, Muzz, but I just got a feeling there might be a bit of an earn in this for you too.'

Murray took the envelope and put it in his overalls. 'Okay, mate,' he said. 'I'll see you in Surfers. If I need you

186

I'll get in touch.' He held out his hand and looked his brother right in the eye. 'Thanks for that bit of help, Les. You couldn't have come along at a better time.'

Les gripped his brother's hand. 'Don't worry, Muzz. You'll earn your keep tomorrow night. But we'll be sweet. We mightn't have those Mini-14s but we'll have the two of us again.'

Murray gave Les a wink. 'You never know what we might have. See you tomorrow.'

Les watched Murray wheel the SPATV out of the park and head towards home, then got in the car away from the mosquitoes, turned on the air-conditioning and gave him about five minutes while he wiped some of the sweat and dirt off with his spare T-shirt. He started the car, let it idle for a moment or two then headed off himself, knowing he still had an all-night drive in front of him.

The restaurant was closed and there didn't seem to be any people around, but the pub still appeared to be open and if Les wasn't mistaken there was a small group of drunks standing out the front, staring up at some touches of orange still lingering in the sky towards Chinchilla. Well, why wouldn't they, thought Les, taking a left at the post office. They were only about twenty or so kilometres away from us. He rejoined the road to St George and drove on into the night.

Norton wasn't tired, more mind-weary than anything else. It hadn't been a bad quick trip home. How often do you get to shoot three blokes, watch an atomic bomb go off and blow up an old mine, all on top of huge feed of Spanish paella. The thought of food suddenly made him belch and the pleasant taste of garlic and prawns lingered across his tongue. Les was going to switch on the radio or a cassette but changed his mind. Besides trying to settle down after what he'd just been through he wanted to have a think. And despite the killings and the nuclear explosion, Norton's thoughts kept turning to the overnight-bag on the seat next to him and the pages inside he'd torn out of that Spanish magazine. There was something there that definitely wasn't kosher. What it was Les couldn't

187

quite figure out. He drove on into the night, turned right outside St George and kept thinking. But the more Les tried to add two and two together, the more it wouldn't come up four. However, by the time he got to Goondi-windi and a lot more thinking about his present compan-ions and the others he'd met in Surfers Paradise, two and two may not have been coming up four but it was coming up very close to the square root of sixteen. Very, very close indeed.

Les found a truck-stop the other side of the quiet outback town, filled up again and got a couple of bars of chocolate. He was about eighty kilometres towards Ingle-wood when he saw the convoy of flashing blue lights approaching in the distance and slowed down. The first three cars were green RAAF Holdens followed by a black Chevrolet Biscayne; lights flashing, sirens howling as they roared past the Jaguar. Now I wonder where they might be heading? mused Les. Good one, Muzz. You're a genius all right. How I let you talk me into things at times I'll never know. I just hope to Christ you can make it to Surfers on time.

With this now on his mind, as well as everything else, Norton howled on along the outback roads. He filled up again at Warwick, yawned a couple of times and found he was starting to get a bit tired. As he drove off, he turned the air-conditioner on full blast and dropped a cassette in the car stereo at just about full blast too. Of all things, the first track was 'Six Days on the Road' — George Thoro-good and the Destroyers. Christ! thought Norton, turn-ing it down just a shade, if that didn't wake you up, nothing would. Good one again, Benoit, he chuckled to himself.

That cassette had finished and 'Down the Road' — Richard Clapton — was cutting out as Les went through completely empty Beaudesert and headed towards the coast. He switched the radio on and scanned around. No news or major news bulletins at that time of the morning; just country and western music from here and there and a bit of pop stuff. Norton left the radio on a Brisbane

188

station and drove steadily through the winding, rising plains up into Tambourine Mountain.

The sun was coming up and Norton was well and truly stuffed and sick of thinking about things when he pulled up outside Zapato Blanco Apartments just before six a.m. He got out of the car, stretched and yawned as another beautiful, sunny day in Surfers Paradise opened up around him. There was no sign of life from the flats, just a few cars going past, early morning joggers, cyclists, people walking dogs etc. As he opened the garage door, Les noticed the dust, mud and squashed insects all over the Jag. That's what I'll do. I'll hose all that off before I go to bed. Yeah. Like fuckin' hell I will. Norton put the car in the garage, slammed the door and dragged his arse upstairs. He took his Nikes and socks off and that was about all. Had a glass of water while he took in the magnificent, million-dollar view of the sun rising over the sparkling blue sea and across the beautiful white beach for about five seconds then crashed straight onto his bed — out like a light.

Norton blinked his eyes open around midday and gazed up at the ceiling, more or less trying to figure out where he was, what had happened and how he got there. Then along with the sound of the waves rolling in through the window as they washed up along the beach it all began to sink in. Oh shit! He moaned to himself. Did that really happen last night? The memory of the nuclear blast and the torn and bloodied bodies of the six terrorists flashed across his mind and he jammed his eyes shut and sunk his head back into the pillows. Yeah. It bloody happened all right. Then it also dawned on him it was Monday and he had a fair bit on that day and the night too. Especially the night. He took a few deep breaths and got up.

Oddly enough, Les didn't feel too bad at all. His back and neck were a little stiff, but he'd had six hours of good, deep sleep and it was nothing at all like waking up with a hangover. Along with his body, his T-shirt and shorts stunk of sweat and grime; he got out of them and went

189

into the en-suite, cleaned his teeth, then splashed a bit more water over his face. Norton's rugged good looks staring back at him from the mirror were definitely a lot more rugged than good looking. The swelling in his nose had gone down a little and he'd stopped gobbing up congealed blood, but he still had two delightful black eyes and more colour round his face than a tank full of tropical fish. However, the gleam radiating from Norton's brown, if rather blackened, eyes promised all this would be squared up tonight; with a bit of luck.

He walked out to the kitchen, had a glass of orange juice and some fruit and made a cup of coffee, which he took out onto the back sundeck where he noticed the curtains were still drawn and there was no sign of life from next door. Les sipped his coffee and gazed out over the beach across the empty swimming pool in the backyard. Yeah, Les chuckled to himself. The good old empty swimming pool. Recently unserviced and completely ignored by Mermaid Pool Services. It was an absolute peach of a day. Hot, sunny, scarcely a cloud in the sky; a gentle surf rolling in and an equally gentle breeze from the south whispering across a fair smattering of people swimming or sitting along the beach. Definitely not the day for a stinking hot, gruelling run on the soft sand, with sweat pouring out of you in buckets, making you think you were going to dissolve, and wishing to Christ you were doing something else. Les grabbed a towel, his sweatband and sunglasses and did just that; because if anything would take the stiffness out of him and get the old grey matter going that, and a swim afterwards, would. He locked up the flat and walked down to the beach. Les didn't bother with any stretches, he just clamped the sweatband on and headed south for fifteen minutes then headed back.

The run was just as punishing and miserable as the other one but it gave Norton plenty of time to think and plot things out. By the time he got back and had a nice long swim then a shower afterwards, he felt on top of the world, if not a little hungry. Also a plan of action, a nasty little scheme, and one or two other things he still wasn't completely sure of had fallen into place. He got into another pair of shorts, his last clean, white Wilderness-Not-Woodchips T-shirt, and headed up to Peggy's for breakfast, stopping to get a paper and sort a couple of other things out first.

Early Monday afternoon in Surfers Paradise seemed just like any other day; people surging along the footpaths, spielers jumping out of doorways, traffic, tourist buses, the start of another week for the locals relieving the tourists of as much money as possible in as short a space of time. Norton found the paper shop on the main drag the other side of Cavill Avenue. A quick scan across the local and interstate headlines said nothing about strange lights in the sky or little green men landing in outback Queensland. It was mainly the usual bullshit from Canberra, some singer on the Gold Coast had allegedly faked her own kidnapping and the police wanted to allegedly break her neck, and more alleged corruption on the local council. The *Telegraph-Mirror* said on page three the US President would still be arriving in Australia. Les bought a copy, tucked it up under his arm and walked a few metres up the main drag to his next stop.

The shoe store was roomy and bright and almost next to another arcade. There were heaps of everything, from training and aerobics shoes to Doc Martens to the full-on gleaming white Gold Coast specials. What wasn't on display around the walls was laid out on tables in the middle, a lot of which were on special. Norton was in there about a minute before a smiling young girl in a white dress with dark hair came over.

'Can I help you?' she asked politely.

Les returned her smile. 'Have you got any R.M.Williams riding boots? Flat heel, elastic side?'

'Should have,' replied the girl. 'What size?'

'Ten. Brown if you could.'

'Just a minute.'

The girl returned with the boots and handed them to Les along with a pair of socks. Les tried them on, walking

191

round the store a couple of times without bothering to check anything out in the mirror. They fitted perfectly, though as Les expected, being brand new they were a little slippery on the carpet.

'They'll do fine,' said Norton, sitting back down and slipping them off. 'Don't worry about the carton. Just put them in a plastic bag for me, would you?'

'Certainly sir.'

Les put his Nikes back on, left the socks on the seat, then paid the girl cash, thanked her and left.

What Norton was looking for next he found nestled away amongst the food shops, clothes shops, souvenirs and what have you in the arcade next to the shoe store. One of those Minit-Tipit stands, where they cut keys, re-sole trainers and vulcanise new heels and soles on leather shoes.

'Yeah, mate?' asked the spiky red-headed bloke in the red uniform, looking up from some keys he'd just cut.

'Could you put some rubber soles on these for me?' Les took the brand new R.M. Williams out of the plastic bag and laid them on the counter.

The red-headed bloke ran his hands over the soles and around the boots. 'Don't feel like slippin' on your arse, do you, mate?' he said, with a bit of a cheeky grin.

'No. I sure bloody don't,' answered Norton. He returned the bloke's grin, though where the bloke's was more cheeky there was definitely some evil in Norton's.

'Can you give us about an hour?'

'Sure, mate. Good as gold.' Les got his ticket and left the arcade.

Norton then retraced his steps through the crowds along the footpath to the Hertz Car Rental office across Cavill Avenue and on the opposite side of the highway.

'Yes sir?' said the fair-haired young lady behind the counter. In her crisp black and yellow uniform and with the air-conditioning on, she looked quite fresh and attractive.

'I'd like to hire a Ford LTD for about three days,' said Norton.

'Certainly, sir,' replied the girl. She reached beneath

the counter for a brochure and the appropriate papers. 'I'll just explain our rates to you and that. You know it's a little extra with the insurance?'

'Yeah, that's okay,' nodded Les.

The girl fiddled around with some papers, punched something into a computer then got on the phone while she checked Norton's driver's licence and other ID. Rather than make a big splash by pulling out a wad of notes, Les paid with his Visa Card. There were a few things to sign, a couple more formalities and some chit-chat about the weather and holidays while they brought the car around. The girl smiled and thanked Les as she handed him the keys, telling him the number and where it was, out the front a few metres up from the office. Les thanked the girl also and left.

The LTD was dark blue with plush grey upholstery and smelled new inside. Ahh yes, mused Norton, having a bit of a fiddle with the radio, the air-conditioning and the power-windows. This should get me back to Sydney in exactly the style a gentleman of my calibre deserves. And rather swiftly too, if need be. The big V-8 motor hummed into life.

Les took a left on Cavill Avenue, came round and parked in the street facing the flats about halfway up. Now, isn't life strange? Norton half joked to himself. Here I am, just about back where I started half an hour ago. He sat listening to the radio for a few moments and noticed there was still no sign of life round the flats — reporters or otherwise. Still, this isn't getting my stomach filled. Norton locked the car, gave it a last, satisfied look as he jangled the keys into his pocket then walked round to Peggy's for a late breakfast.

Well, I don't know about that song 'Breakfast at Sweethearts' but breakfast at Peggy's wasn't too bad. Les had a contented smile on his face. He'd finished the paper and a second cup of coffee, plus the usual pile of food, only this time with extra fruit. He'd noticed Jimmy Martin across the road, not all that hard at work amongst the people on the beach, but didn't bother going over to say hello; he was quite happy to sit there a little incognito in his cap and sunglasses while he enjoyed his breakfast. Norton glanced at his watch. Well, I reckon my boots should be just about ready by now. But I've got one more stop on the way. He paid his bill and left.

The Boulevarde in Begonia Street was open for the lunchtime trade; Les checked it out for a few moments from in front of the health food shop across the road. Outside it was one long, flat bar on street level, set in amongst the other buildings. The entrance was on the left, two small open-air balconies came out into the footpath, surrounded by stained glass and leadlight windows with a full-length stained-glass window where the building ended next to the wall of some other club or disco. It had a laid back, kind of upmarket style about it, definitely not your house-music-disco-rip-the-kids-off scene. Les waited for a break in the traffic then jogged across the road straight inside the front door to the left.

There was quite a number of casually dressed punters standing or sitting around, either having a meal or a drink. Les didn't bother to take off his sunglasses as he moved easily around, making out he was in there looking for someone while he checked the place out. It was all very nice. Soft lighting from old-fashioned lightshades, oak panelling, more stained-glass and mirrors round the walls, and vines in baskets hanging off the ceiling. There was an empty DJ's booth and vacant dancefloor to your left as you walked in and a long bar in the first room with white German-style beer pullers with wooden handles and empty glasses hanging upside down from wooden racks above. The barmaids were fit and efficient-looking in black minis, white shirts and cute paisley vests. The male bar staff wore white shirts and ties as they drifted around the stools and tables, picking up glasses or whatever.

Norton cruised around the first room, through a kind of folding glass door into what he figured must be the back bar. This room wasn't quite as big as the other with a small bar on your left as you entered, a short hallway that led to the toilets and a food servery with another, slightly bigger bar, next to the open-air balcony on the opposite side of the room. There were stools and tables scattered around, a cigarette machine in the corner and a full-length mirror running above a small wooden bench from it to the stained-glass window in the opposite corner that Les had noticed from across the road. The bar on the left was closed, but there were a few punters sitting around the one next to the balcony and the window in the corner. It was a smaller version of the one in the other room with the German beer pullers and the glasses racked upside down.

Very, very nice, Norton half nodded to himself. He glanced over at the full-length mirror. I imagine that's where Jasper and his mates should be drinking tonight. A nice quiet spot to do a bit of plotting and scheming. Very nice indeed. I reckon me and Murray should be able to wreck this joint in about five minutes tonight. Maybe a minute or two longer. Les placed his hands under one of the stools in the middle of the room and gently lifted it a little off the floor. Yes, I should be able to swing one of these around without too much trouble. Les had another glance around the bar, giving it all a slight nod of approval. So this is the scene of tonight's events eh? I like it. He half smiled at one of the barmaids as he walked out, leaving as unobtrusively as he entered, had a quick look at his watch and strolled round to the Minit-Tipit man.

'There you go, mate,' said the bloke in the red uniform, quite pleased with himself as he laid Norton's boots on the counter. 'They ought to last you a bit longer now.'

Les ran his hand along where the bloke had done a good, solid job, vulcanising a thin, hard rubber sole along the bottom. 'Yeah, they sure will,' answered Norton. 'How much do I owe you, mate?'

By the time the bloke had rung the ticket up on the till and turned back to Les, Norton had his Nikes off, sitting on the counter and the R.M.Williams on his feet. The bloke blinked a little at the Nikes.

'Put them in the plastic bag, will you, mate,' said Les.

195

'I'll wear the boots home.' The bloke blinked at Les and kind of shook his head as he placed Norton's trainers in the plastic bag. 'And get yourself a drink too.' Les gave the bloke five dollars more than was on the ticket, tucked the bag up under his arm and walked out of the mall.

If Norton had looked like your usual mug tourist getting around earlier, now walking back in a T-shirt, shorts and R.M.Williams riding boots with no socks, it was as if the biggest mug in Australia had just hit town. Les checked himself out in a shop window going past and he looked like a cross between Li'l Abner and Gumby. And every spieler, spiv and dropkick within cooee knew it. He hadn't even made it to the post office corner before he'd been almost goosed and rolled, gigged at and offered everything from a solid gold watch to a block of land guaranteed to treble his investment plus a boat and a week at Neptune's Casino thrown in. By the time Les had crossed Cavill Avenue he felt like sinking one of his R.M.Williams in the next white shoette's persistent snatch and right up the next smarty's arse. Norton made it to the flats with his temper in check, just. But he'd managed to scuff up the rubber soles and break the boots in a bit.

There was no sign of life out the front or upstairs, and Les wasn't sure whether to be curious or not. Oh well, he shrugged. Who gives a stuff. The less people to annoy me at the moment the better. He went straight up to his flat, got out of the R.M.Williams, placing them under his bed, then walked round in his bare feet for a while: thinking. Something else had been playing on Norton's mind, badly. He got a glass of water and put some ice in it then looked at his watch. Oh well, he sighed to himself. I've got to do this sooner or later. Let's hope the Norton luck hasn't completely deserted me. You never know. I might be able to wriggle my way through this. Les took a sip of cold water, picked up the phone and pushed the buttons.

'Hello,' came a girl's voice at the other end.

'Could I speak to Desilu, please?'

196

There was the pause Norton was expecting and the girl's voice cooled and slowed down noticeably. 'This is Desilu speaking.'

'Hello, DD. It's Les. How are you?'

'Oh Les. How nice to hear from you.'

Norton could hear the icicles of sarcasm dripping from the line at the other end.

'Yeah. Did you get my message last night?'

'Yes. Yes, I did. Some dope rang up, said you'd been in an accident and you were all right and you'd ring back. Thanks for ringing. It was more than generous of you.'

'Yeah. Well, that's why I'm ringing you now.'

'Oh, are you? Gee! Doesn't the time fly.'

'Yeah. Look I know...'

'Listen, Les.' DD's voice was slow, deliberate and definitely lacking in humour. Norton held the phone away from his ear a little and prepared himself for the blast. 'We had a pretty good time the other night and you're a great bloke. Just like a lot of other great blokes around. You're up here for a good time and you got a better offer. Well, good on you. But I sat around here till twelve-thirty, like a stale bottle of piss. All dressed up, ready to go out. It was tops. I felt like a nice dill, and I just can't wait to do it again. Now you decide to ring me up the following afternoon. Thanks heaps. I had a terrific night. Accident! Bullshit! Up yours sport — as far as you can get it.'

'Jesus! You haven't even given me a chance.'

'A chance. Ha! You had your chance, pal. And blew it. So listen Les... whatever your name is. Do me a favour will you?'

'Yeah, what DD?' answered Norton, knowing exactly what she was going to say.

'Get stuffed and go to the shithouse. And goodbye. I've got things to do.'

'All right, okay,' cut in Les. 'If that's how you feel, terrific. You reckon I'm bullshiting about last night. Beauty. I couldn't be bothered arguing with you — boofhead. So what are you doing now, besides sitting around with the shits?'

197

'What am I doing?' huffed DD. 'I'm packing the last of my stuff. And later on this evening I'm going out with a friend. Then in the morning I'm catching a bus home. On my own. Alone. Out of here and away from jerks like you.'

'Well, bloody good for you, DD. I hope you have a ripper trip and don't get a crook back. But I'm going to tell you something before you go — you ugly, horrible, skinny-looking bag.'

'I . . .'

'I'm going to be round your place at four o'clock this afternoon.'

'You . . .'

'And if you're not there, you scrawny rickshaw-driving scrubber, I'm going to kick your door in and piss down all your front steps. And I might even piss all over that budgerigar, or whatever it is, while I'm there. You got that, boofhead?'

'I . . .'

'Four o'clock this afternoon. Desilu Doodleson, or whatever *your* bloody name is, Les Norton will be calling. And be there. Or bloody else.'

Norton gave it about a second or so then banged the phone down. Not all that hard. But hard enough to sound hurt, offended and angry. It was the only play he had. DD had certainly got her two-bob's worth in and if Les had of grovelled and begged forgiveness, she would have immediately told him to go to the shithouse again. She was too steamed up. Les had to backfoot her. And what did his dear old dad always say? What does every Australian woman read, constantly? *Vague Magazine*. DD would be sitting there, wondering quite what was going on. She'd certainly upset Les, which was exactly what she'd intended to do and done an absolutely splendid job at it too. He'd gone through the roof. Had she judged the big goose a bit hastily? Oowah! Norton stared at the phone. Well, what else could I bloody do. And shit! It's not as if I took some sheila out behind her back. Christ! With a girl like her you'd have to have a pumpkin for a head if you did. Les gave a dry laugh. Of course I could always tell her the truth; that's if she's there. On the other hand, she might just think, who does this big mug think he is, and not be there. As for kicking her door in, I'm not that big a dill. Les couldn't help but gaze at the phone. Shit! Wouldn't it be a bastard to miss out on something like that. It could be a long, lonely drive back to Sydney. Though somehow I've got a feeling DD'll be there at four o'clock. Even if it's only to throw a jerry full of piss over me and tell me to fuck off. Another dry smile formed on Norton's face. Oh well. At least I'll get a chance to say goodbye. Les shook his head. Australian women. Ain't they just the most adorable creatures? Anyway, no good sitting round here like a lovesick puppy. There's things to be done. Like getting rid of last night's evidence. That Jag doesn't actually look like I've been driving it quietly round the streets of Surfers Paradise. Norton got up, went to his room and changed into a dirty T-shirt and shorts, then still in his bare feet, went downstairs and got the car out of the garage.

Being half asleep at five in the morning and having a master key both to the flats and the garages, Norton had inadvertently put the Jag in a different garage than normal. It was the same size as the other one, though in that one Les had noticed a hose and bucket amongst the bits of junk laying around. Apart from a couple of old banana-chairs and one or two empty cartons, this one was about bare. Where he'd nosed the Jag in, there was a bench against the wall with a few things strewn around; being a bit of sticky-beak, Norton went over and glanced through what was there. There wasn't much. The most noticeable thing was a piece of solid grey sponge rubber, about half a metre square by about thirty centimetres thick, next to a couple of tubes of Super-glue. The slab of sponge rubber looked like it had a piece hacked from one end. A piece of that might do to clean the car with, thought Les. Norton looked at the slab of sponge rubber, then he thought of something else. Then he looked out the open garage door and started to smile. What was it

KK had said to him in the limo on the way to Fedora's that night? Something about stitching up a record deal with Crystal. An answer to an innocent remark by Les that had cracked up both KK and Crystal. Next thing, Norton's smile had turned into a grin. Yeah I'll bet you did, you little cunt. I'll just bet you did. In fact, I fuckin' know you did.

Norton quickly got the Jag out of the garage, leaving the door open for the exhaust fumes to escape, and moved it down in front of the other one. Just as quickly, he ran upstairs, got a kitchen knife from one of the drawers and ran back down again. It took him about five seconds to hack off a piece of sponge rubber about a foot wide. With that and one of the tubes of Super-glue, he got out of the garage, locking the door behind him. With a flick of his wrist, the lump of sponge rubber landed up on his front sundeck, followed by the knife and the tube of Super-glue. Norton then opened the door tó the usual garage and in a few minutes had the hose connected, a bucket filled and with a rag and some detergent he'd found was washing 1,500 kilometres of dust and insects off the Jag, whistling quite happily to himself, at times even laughing out loud. Well, he mused, I don't think you have to be Einstein to work out what's going on now. The only thing is; where's the earn? The good, old earn. And I don't mean the one on the mantelpiece holding grandma's ashes. The one I promised Murray. Norton scraped a locust and two Bogan moths off the bonnet and smiled up at the sky. Now you wouldn't have me make my loving brother and his beautiful family go without, would you? Norton scraped at the remains of the insects, then winked at the sky. No, I didn't think you would.

Les was still whistling and thinking when a plain white Ford pulled in the driveway. Frank and Steve were in the front, KK and Crystal were in the back. Leaving Frank behind the wheel, Steve got out and opened the back door.

They couldn't miss Les hosing the Jag, so all three walked over. KK was wearing jeans and a T-shirt, same as

200

Steve; Crystal was wearing a loose-fitting red floral dress. Both were carrying small overnight-bags.

'G'day,' said Norton. The hose had a kind of gun on the end. Les put it down and started wiping the windshield.

'Hello, Les,' said Kramer. 'How are you feeling? Did you get our message?'

'Yeah,' nodded Les. 'No one's been around.'

'And how are you today, Rocky?' gibed Crystal. 'Ready for another whirlwind one-rounder?'

'Yeah,' smiled Norton mirthlessly, 'I can't wait for you to line me another one up.'

'Don't sweat it, big guy.' Crystal still had half a sneer on her face. 'Here. I brought you a present.' She opened her overnight-bag and handed Les a small plastic bag. Les opened it. Inside was a roll of Elastoplast, a bottle of iodine and a rock cake in a smaller paper bag.

The tired smile still on his face, Norton looked at Crystal. 'What's with the rock cake?'

'Eat it, Dempsey. It'll harden you up.' Norton was about to tell her where she could stick it, when Crystal turned to KK: 'I'm going inside. I've had enough of this goddam sun. I'll see you upstairs.' Without waiting for an answer she disappeared inside the flats.

'I hear you had a bit of bad luck the other night,' said Steve.

Norton took off his sunglasses and gave Steve a look at his two black eyes. 'Yeah. I suppose you could call it that,' he said, and put them back on.

'Sorry me and Frank weren't there. We'd have given you a hand.'

'I'm sorry you weren't either,' said Les. 'But thanks all the same.' Norton gave a shrug. 'Still, it could've been a lot worse.'

'What do you intend to do?' asked Steve.

Norton shrugged again. 'What can you do? It's just one of those things. I just got to cop it sweet. Who gives a fuck anyway. I'm out of here tomorrow.'

Steve looked evenly at Norton. 'I don't know much about where you come from in Sydney, Les, but believe me, Surfers Paradise isn't all glitter and glamour and have a nice day, like on the tourist brochures. There's no shortage of cunts up here.'

'So I believe.'

Steve turned to Kramer. 'We have to get going, Kelvin. Mr Black's expecting us back. I imagine he'll ring you this evening — or whatever.'

'All right then' nodded KK.

'See you, Les.' Steve gave Norton a friendly wink. 'Look after yourself.'

'Don't worry, mate,' lied Norton. 'Ain't nothin' gonna happen between now and when I leave tomorrow. Believe me.' Les returned Steve's wink. 'See you, Steve. Cheers.'

Steve got in the Ford alongside Frank and they drove off. Norton put the plastic bag Crystal had given him on the roof of the car and continued working.

'So what have you been doing, Les?' asked KK, watching Norton, the stolid and dutiful servant wiping away at the Jag. 'And what's with the car? You don't have to. The fuckin' thing's going back today.'

Norton the dutiful servant and battered minder shrugged. 'I spent last night at some friend's place. They got a farm out the back of Murwillumbah.'

'What did you do out there?'

'Not much. Sat around, had a mag. Smoked a couple of joints, listened to a bit of music. I didn't feel like doing a great deal.'

'No. I don't suppose . . .'

'Anyway, I got some shit and mud on the car getting out there, so I thought I'd clean it off. I wasn't doing much, just hanging around feeling sorry for myself.' Les wrung the cloth out into the bucket. 'What about yourself? What have youse been up to?'

'Us?' KK blinked at Norton through his glasses for a second. 'We spent yesterday and last night at Meyer's place. And went out on his cruiser this morning. Had lunch with him. Just playing it very low key. Keeping away from those fuckin' reporters.'

Les nodded. 'There has been a couple of car-loads

come round. I told them to piss off. I just didn't want to say anything in front of Crystal. I wouldn't like to upset her.'

'No. She's not real rapt in Australian journos at the moment. Not after what they said about her in the papers.'

'Yeah. Like I said to her, I couldn't understand that.'

'There's been a bit of a change of plans too, Les.'

'Yeah?'

'Crystal's flying out at nine tomorrow morning. Which means we'll be leaving for the airport around seven. Are you still capable of fending off any mug reporters tomorrow, between here and Brisbane?'

'Yeah, sure.'

'And we'll fly back to Sydney from there.'

'Yeah, no worries, KK. Good as gold.'

Kramer stared at Les pottering around with the car and shook his head. Any doubts he might have had about Les being a twenty-five-carat boofhead were completely swept away. Norton had had the shit kicked out him, been used and abused and except for a couple of shitty meals had been treated like shit in general. Yet here he was, washing the car, still fending off reporters and ready for duty first thing in the morning again. Anybody else would have told him to stick his job in his arse and split. But not Norton. Kramer had to shake his head again. What a nice mug. I might even give him a cheque for the rest of that money I owe him.

'Hey, listen, KK.' Norton stopped and looked up from what he was doing. 'There's something I have to tell you.'

'Yeah, sure, Les.'

Norton pointed to his black eyes. 'Apart from this, I've had a pretty good time up here, KK. And I appreciate you giving me the work. Shouting me all that grouse food. Plus that flat thrown in. It was real good of you.'

'Shit! That's all right, Les.' KK couldn't help but shake his head again. Brother, you are definitely getting a cheque.

'So I just didn't want you to think there were any hard feelings, that's all. Or I've let you down or something.'

'Ohh, shit no, Les.'

'And after all. This is part of the job — ain't it?'

'Yeah. Well, I suppose you could say that, Les.' A cheque? I should give him a cheque? This schvantz is good for an IOU.

'So seeing as you've done me a favour — and I think you know Crystal tossed a few bucks my way the other night too, don't you?' KK smiled and nodded. 'How about letting me return the favour?'

'I . . . ?'

'Seeing as we're leaving early tomorrow, how about letting me shout you and Crystal a couple of quiet drinks somewhere tonight? Go out about nine. Be home by eleven. Have a couple of drinks, a yarn and a few laughs? On me.'

Before KK knew it he was nodding his head. 'Yeah all right, Les,' he said. 'I'll see Crystal. But I'm sure she'll want to come.' KK smiled at Norton. 'Where are you thinking of taking us? Neptune's Casino?'

Norton returned Kramer's smile. 'No. There's a little place just up the road from here. The Boulevarde in Begonia Street. You know it?'

'Yeah.'

'It should be pretty quiet there Monday night. And I know one of the sheilas who works there.' Les shrugged. 'We'll just have a few quiet drinks and be up bright and early in the morning.'

'Yeah, okay, Les. That sounds good.' Kramer was almost dumbfounded. Why aren't there more mugs like this in the world?

'Good.' Les went back to wiping the car. 'So what are you doing now, KK?'

'I'm going upstairs to pack a bit of gear, and just take it easy for the rest of the afternoon.' KK winked at Norton. 'I have to put a bit of a smile on Crystal's face before she goes back too.'

Les winked back. 'Half your luck.'

Kramer started towards the flats. 'I'll see you later on tonight, Les.'

'Righto,' answered Norton. 'I'll keep an eye on things round here. And I'll give you a tap on the door around eight-thirty or so. See what's happening?'

'I'm sure Crystal will be cool.'

'I hope she's at least got a smile on her face.'

'See you, Les.'

Norton waited till Kramer got to the door. 'Oh KK,' he called out. Kramer turned round at Les still working on the car. 'What time has this got to be back?'

'About six. Whatever.'

'I might take it for a bit of a spin. Dry the water off.' Kramer just waved indifferently and the door closed behind him.

Les stared at the flats for a moment or two, dropped the wet rag in the bucket then took the plastic bag Crystal had given him from the roof of the car and took out the rock cake. I wonder, he mused. An all-in brawl in a bar. A stool comes flying through the crowd and hits Crystal Linx right across the back of the head. Who'd see where it came from? And who'd give a stuff for that matter.

Norton stood on one leg, was about to put his foot under the rock cake and changed his mind, deciding to give it to the willie-wagtails in the backyard. Figuring he'd put on the dutiful servant act long enough, Norton disconnected the hose and flung the lot in the garage. He closed the door, locked the Jag and went upstairs.

The first thing Les did was to get the stuff he'd tossed up onto the balcony. Now what have we got here, he half chuckled to himself as he took it into the kitchen. One piece of rather thick sponge rubber. He tossed the rubber onto a shelf in the kitchen next to the micro-wave oven. One plastic bag containing a roll of Elastoplast, iodine and a rock cake. He dropped that on top of the sponge rubber. One tube of Super-glue. Of course. Les dropped that on the sponge rubber. And one fairly sharp kitchen knife. Not thinking, Les dropped the light-hanndled knife onto the sponge rubber. It bounced off, hit the side of the micro-wave oven, then flicked across and the point stuck in the crook of Norton's arm just near his elbow.

205

'Shit!' cursed Les. The knife clattered onto the floor and Les watched a thin trickle of blood forming on his arm. Well, doesn't that serve me right for being a dill. He picked the knife up and placed it, carefully this time, on the sponge rubber. The cut on Norton's arm wasn't bad, the knife had barely dug in. But if he didn't cover it, it would keep bleeding and be an annoyance. Les walked to his room, got a pair of scissors from amongst some other odds and ends in his bag and came back out to the kitchen. Good thing bloody Crystal gave me that iodine and Elastoplast, mused Norton, wiping off the blood with his T-shirt. He cut a strip of Elastoplast off, daubed some iodine on the cut and pressed the strip of sticking plaster on top. Les looked at his bit of 'first-aid' for a second then started to laugh. I wonder? I just bloody wonder?

Still wondering and still laughing, Les walked out onto the sundeck with the rock cake, broke it up and tossed it down into the backyard. In a few minutes seven or eight different birds were picking at it. Les watched their beaks pecking furiously up and down in the grass as they squawked at each other, then looked at his watch. Well, he thought, it sure would be nice to sit here all afternoon watching the little birdies. But if I'm going to be round a certain person's place at four o'clock, looking reasonably clean and with a plausible story going, I'd better get my finger out. I can sort that other shit out in the kitchen when I get back. Les slid the fly-screen door closed, stripped off and got under the shower.

About half an hour later Les was standing in front of the mirror freshly shaved, wearing clean jeans, his Wilderness-Not-Woodchips T-shirt and the R.M. Williams boots, and liberally daubed with Tabac. He'd changed the strip of Elastoplast on his arm and put a couple of strips over the cuts above his eyes and another over a cut on his nose, which he'd also liberally daubed with iodine.

Well, he thought, putting on his sunglasses and jamming his cap down on his head. I definitely look like I've been in some sort of an accident. Now I'll probably go round and

get into another one. Still, who knows? He locked the flat
and walked down to the Jag. As he shut the door to his
flat, Les thought he heard music and a little laughter
coming from next door. Oh well, at least someone's
having a good time in Surfers this afternoon. A minute or
two later he was on his way to Main Beach via the
shopping centre in Surfers Paradise. He may not have
had left or right bower, but it doesn't hurt to have an ace
in your hand. And the way things were going, Les was
going to need all the tricks he could muster.

He parked on a bus-stop and it didn't take him long to
find what he was looking for — a flower shop. The young
blonde girl behind the counter was most helpful and in no
time at all she had a dozen long-stemmed red roses with
six carnations in the middle, carefully wrapped and
placed in a large, white plastic bag tied at the end so you
couldn't tell what was in it. The girl smiled and Norton
winced like he'd been hit in the stomach with a baseball
bat when she told him the price. He paid her cash and
trotted back to the car. Christ, thought Les, looking at
the flowers in the plastic bag on the seat next to him. I
could've got a pile of CDs, enough bourbon to stay drunk
for a week and a half a bag of dacca for what they cost. I
wonder if I meant it when I told that bloody rickshaw
driver I loved her? Either that or I'm not used to this
Queensland sun. The Jag hummed into life again and Les
headed for DD's house, parking just across the road.
    Norton stared across at her place and drummed his
fingers on the steering-wheel, thinking for a few moments.
Now, what would Basil Fawlty do in a situation like this?
Well, knowing old Basil, he'd tell the most outrageous lies
imaginable straight off the top of his head, and act
completely indignant at the same time. Les gave one of
those grudging nods of approval. And that's exactly what
I'm going to do. So look out, DD, here comes Basil
Norton. With the plastic bag behind his back, Les jogged
across the road, up the front steps and knocked on
Desilu's door. It opened about a minute or so later.

207

DD was wearing no shoes, a pair of loose-fitting grey gym shorts and a fawn Rainbow-Warrior T-shirt. She also wore no make-up, no trace of a smile and her hair was all over head. Tall, tanned and fit, she still looked good enough to eat. Norton couldn't help it, but his heart gave a little flutter as soon as he saw those beautiful emerald green eyes.

'I'm early for once.' Les smiled, bent his wrist and showed DD his watch which said ten minutes to four. Desilu wasn't all that impressed. 'Well, are you going to invite me in?'

DD stared right at Les. 'Does your watch have a minute hand?' Les nodded. 'Well, it'll go round twice, then you'll be back out here. Okay?'

'Yeah. Good thing I caught you in a good mood, isn't it?'

DD moved aside, let Les in and closed the door. Norton walked straight to the kitchen, DD followed then stood next to the sink. She gave Les a brief once up and down then stared at him impassively.

Les nodded at her T-shirt. 'Well, at least so far we're environmentally friendly — if nothing else.'

Norton's feeble idea of a joke almost, almost, got a reaction from DD. But not quite. 'Have you got something you want to say, Les?' she said, sounding a little tiresome.

Norton stared back at her for a moment then went into full Basil Fawlty mode. Arms waving, neck stretching, chin jutting out: the works.

'Yes, I've got something to say all right, DD. As a matter of fact I have. So I'm a bloody liar, am I? I got some mug to ring you up and string you a line of bullshit, did I?' Les tossed the white plastic bag onto the kitchen table. 'A liar eh. You skinny, horrible-looking beast. A liar.' Les whipped off his cap and sunglasses and tossed them onto the kitchen table next to the plastic bag. 'Well, what's that?'

DD gaped at Norton's black eyes and bruised face, stuck with strips of Elastoplast and liberally daubed with iodine. She gave a double blink then a little gasp. 'Good Lord, Les. What happened to your face?'

Les looked at DD as if he couldn't quite believe what he was hearing. 'What happened to my face?' he said. 'What happened to my face!' Then Les went into Basil Fawlty warp-ten, and his face reddened. 'What do you think happened to my face, you inbred bloody wombat? I hit the dashboard of a stretch bloody limousine, that's what happened. How do you think I did it? Fell off the bloody ski-lift at Thredbo, you stupid cow?'

'I . . .' DD was visibly shocked.

'A liar eh? A bloody liar. And what's that?' Norton lifted up the left sleeve of his baggy T-shirt and peeled back half of the strip of Elastoplast.

DD stared at the hole in Norton's arm them put her hand over her mouth. 'What . . .?'

'I was on a pethidine drip all night, that's how much pain I was in.' Les continued his tirade. 'They kept me under observation then gave me a CAT scan. They thought I had a fractured skull. But it was all right. I only got concussion and a broken nose.'

DD's face dropped along with her defences. 'Oh no.'

'Yeah. I got out of hospital this morning, got home, didn't know where I was. I tried to ring you up and the phone's engaged. I crashed out and the first thing I do when I wake up is ring you again. And what do I get? A great torrent of abuse. No wonder I had the shits.' Les gave DD a good view of his wounds, then looked more hurt and indignant than ever.

DD seemed to shrink a little and her face sank. She made a gesture towards Norton. 'Gee, Les, I didn't know. I . . .' Norton gave a little sniff and turned his face away from her. 'Look, why don't you sit down?'

'Hah!' Norton tossed back his head. 'Not much point in me sitting down.' He showed DD his watch again. 'I'm out the front bloody door in about another half a minute.'

'Oh you are not. You know I never meant that. Now come on. Sit down and I'll make you a cup of tea or something.'

Les stood there for a moment, a mixture of hurt and defiance on his craggy face. 'All right then,' he said. 'I wouldn't mind sitting down for a little while; to tell you the truth, I still don't feel the best. I almost blacked out a couple of times driving over here.' Norton sat down, tilted his head to one side and poked his bottom lip out and looked up at DD. It was the full-on little-boy-lost look, with just a touch of Basil Fawlty thrown in and the look of a good man completely shattered. 'I don't know, DD. I just thought you'd be a bit more understanding, that's all. I really did.'

DD moved away from the kitchen sink, put her arms around Norton's neck and shoulders and kissed him on the head. 'I'm sorry.'

Norton faked a wince of pain. 'Just watch my eyes there.'

DD took her arms from around Norton's neck and ran her hands lightly over his face; the gentle woman's touch which Norton loved. Then she kissed him softly on the lips. 'I am sorry, Les.'

Norton hesitated for a moment, the bottom lip still sticking out, then he placed his hands on DD's waist. 'All right,' he said 'But gee, I'm just upset you'd think of me like that. That's all.' He looked up at DD. 'Are we still mates?'

DD's face brightened. 'Yes, we're still mates. Of course we are. Anyway, I'll make a cup of tea and you can tell me exactly what happened. It must have been dreadful. Funny, I didn't see anything in the local papers.' DD switched on the kettle and pulled up a chair facing Les. 'So what happened?'

'What happened?' Norton blinked and started slipping into the other Basil Fawlty mode. 'Well it . . .' He stopped and ran his hand across his eyes. 'Before I go on. You wouldn't have a couple of asprin or something, would you? I left the tablets they gave me in the hospital back at the flat. I've still got a low headache.'

'There's some Panadol in the bathroom. I'll go and get a couple.'

Norton's eyes followed her shapely backside as she went to the bathroom and his mind went blank. What happened? Shit! What did fuckin' happen? Jesus! For Christ's sake, Basil, don't fail me now. DD returned with two Panadol, poured a glass of water, handed them to Les and sat back down. Norton swallowed the pain-killers with nearly all the water.

'Right. What happened? Okay. We were driving along the highway down near Tweed Heads. Crystal and KK were sitting in the back. I'm in the front next to the driver and didn't bother to put my seat-belt on. We'd just been having dinner. Anyway, while we're inside, the driver's been hitting the bottle while he's waiting. It turns out he's a piss-pot. Even though he's got five kids. Anyway, to make a long story short we take off, and we're cruising along the highway and some bloke in a... big black Mercedes takes a wrong turn and plows straight into the front of the limo. Crash!'

'Good lord.'

'They're okay in the back. But boofhead Les, not having his seat-belt on, I hit the dash. I'm stunned. And the driver shits himself. He'll lose his job and cop a fine. Because in an accident, no matter whose fault it is, they still breath-test you. Especially up here in the Sunshine State.'

'Tell me about it.' DD's eyes were brimming as she looked at Les. She placed her hands on his.

'So half stunned and like a mug, I offer to get behind the wheel and say I was driving. It was the other driver's fault anyway. So the cops and the ambulance arrive. They breath test me and I'm sweet. Apart from being covered in blood and not knowing where I am, that is. So they take me to hospital and in I go. And by this time I'm pretty stuffed. Don't know where I am. But I told Kramer to ring you and say I was all right. I didn't want you to worry.'

'Oh Les.' DD's face was dripping more compassion than Mother Theresa. She bent over and kissed Norton on the face.

The kettle boiled. DD made a pot of tea, poured them a cup each and put them on the kitchen table. Les took a sip, licked his lips and decided to keep the Basil Fawlty roll going. So far so good.

'Anyway,' he said, taking another sip of tea. 'The offshoot of the whole thing is the other driver is some bigshot alderman on the Gold Coast council. He's half pissed, but the cops aren't game to pinch him. Or let the papers find out. Harris or something. Bit of a heavy dude evidently.'

'Harris?' DD's face looked quizzical. 'There's a Henshaw.'

'That's him,' said Les. 'Big fat bloke.'

'That's Henshaw.'

'And his wife was with him. Beryl... Belinda...'

'Maxine,' said DD.

'That's her. Dark-haired sheila. She had a wig on... Anyway, she throws a mickey and goes all hysterical and threatens all sorts of dramas unless I sign a statement to say it was nobody's fault. Just an accident. So I'm in the hospital, got me head in a CAT scan, and I'm signing some statement. The cops were okay though.'

DD's eyes continued to drip sympathy as she sipped her tea. They were also glowing just a little with admiration. All the time she knew Les was a good bloke. How could she...?

'Yeah. So it turns out everything's sweet and I saved the silly bloody chauffeur's job.' Norton took another sip of tea and gave a derisive sort of laugh. 'The other off-shoot of the thing though, Crystal being a big star and all that and Kramer being who he is, this Henshaw bloke and his wife have invited us back to their place for dinner tonight. So it looks like I have to go.' Norton took another sip of tea and poked his bottom lip out again. Not all that much. But enough. 'Not that it should make much difference. You're going out somewhere. With a... friend.'

DD's face coloured. 'Well, I... didn't...' Then she smiled at Les. 'And he is only a friend.'

'Must be nice to have friends. Not like poor bloody

212

me.' Les took another sip of tea and decided it might be a good time to change the subject. 'So where's the other girls?'

'Fisherman's Wharf. There's a big boat function on. They started at three and finish at twelve.' DD shook her head. 'I'm glad it's them and not me.' Suddenly DD seemed to notice the white plastic bag. 'What's in the bag?' she asked.

'Oh that.' Norton shrugged nonchalantly. 'Just a few sandwiches. I was feeling a bit hungry, so I brought something to eat.'

'I could have...' DD's face screwed up. 'They're not bloody sandwiches. What...?'

DD opened the plastic bag and pulled out the bunch of roses with the carnations in the middle. Wide eyed, she held them out in front of her, stared at them, then looked at Norton.

'Les.' She was starting to gush a little. 'What? I mean. God, you didn't have to. Why did you...'

'Why?' Norton tried to look indignant and do another Basil but some emotion deep inside him gave the big Queenslander away. 'Have you ever thought when I told you I loved you the other morning I might've meant it? And I didn't want to lose you.' Les looked directly at DD. 'And that lift to Taree's still on tomorrow morning, if you want it.'

DD looked at the roses and held them gently. She kissed Les again, only with a lot more affection this time, then looked around the room. 'What am I going to do with them?' she said absently.

'I don't really care,' shrugged Norton. 'Just don't do what the last girl I gave a bunch of flowers to did.'

DD peered at Les, just a hint of jealousy in her eyes. 'Do you make a habit of this — do you?'

'No,' answered Les. 'I just gave her a bunch of flowers, something like those. And she went into her room, took all her clothes off, and came back and lay on the table naked with her knees up. And I asked her what was that for? And she said for the flowers. I was a bit young at the

213

time and I said to her. What's the matter, haven't you got a vase?'

DD looked at Les and swung the bunch of flowers back over her head, trying not to smile. 'If I didn't know you better, Mr Norton, I'd hit you right across the bloody head with them.'

Les shrugged again. 'You may as well. I couldn't feel any bloody worse than what I do now.'

DD put the flowers in a big blue vase and placed them on the kitchen table. 'God! Wait till the girls see these.'

Les could see DD was mesmerised. She was a shot bird. Norton had won hands down. He'd not only taken her every trick, he'd hardly given her a chance to turn a card over. Yeah, well, some blokes have got it. And some haven't. Then there's me. Les stretched uncomfortably in his chair and faked a yawn with a touch of pain.

'I'll tell you what,' he said, 'those Panadols on top of that cup of tea are starting to work. Jesus, I feel tired. Do you think I could lie down somewhere for a little while?'

'Where?' asked DD, a little quietly.

'I don't know,' shrugged Les. 'On your bed for a few minutes'd be nice. But don't let me fall asleep. I have to be back home by seven to get ready to go to that dinner.'

DD's eyes smiled, but her lips didn't. 'You're not lying down on my bed, sunshine.'

Norton shrugged again. 'Fair enough. I didn't mean anything by it. Just on the lounge for a while'll do.'

'All that's in my room,' said DD, 'is a bed, a bare mattress, an old blanket and a skinny pillow.' Then DD did smile. 'But Karen's room's got a nice big double bed and a stereo. I don't think she'd mind if you used it for a little while. As long as you took your boots off.'

Norton tried to look weary, slightly puzzled and in pain all at the same time. Somehow he succeeded. 'Okay. You want to give me a hand up? I'm knackered.'

DD took hold of Norton's arm and helped him to his feet. 'Come on, you poor old thing. Nurse Donaldson will look after you.' Les let her help him along the hallway, to

214

the first room on the right. DD pushed open the door. 'God, you really are a mess, aren't you?'

'You better believe it,' replied Les solemnly. 'At least the nurses were very nice to me.'

'Oh they were, were they?'

Karen's room was airy and bright with one or two rock posters around the wall and the odd indoor-plant. An old double bed with a wooden railing at one end and a white cover ran alongside a window, a dressing-table was against one wall and a small table with a ghetto-blaster on it next to the bed. Norton kicked his boots off and settled back against the pillows, his arms by his sides. DD switched the radio on and sat on the edge of the bed, resting her hand on Norton's knee; an ad for some car-yard on the Gold Coast was about the only sound in the room.

Les rolled his neck around the pillows and closed his eyes. 'Ohh yeah,' he crooned. 'How comfortable's this bed.'

'Feeling all right now, are you?' smiled DD.

'Yeah, reckon.' Norton scrunched his head back into the pillows and smiled. The bed certainly was comfortable, better than he'd expected. A bit too comfortable. He snapped his eyes open. 'Hey DD, don't let me go to sleep. I've got to be out of here by six.'

'That's all right. I have to start getting ready myself around then.'

'Ohh yeah, I forgot about that. What time's Steve Stunning coming round to take you out?'

'About eight.'

'Fair enough. It'll take you at least two hours to look any good.'

DD looked at Les. Les looked at DD. You could almost say they were both looking at each other. The commercial break on the radio ended, the DJ gave a time call and the next song cut in. It was an old Bob Dylan ballad — 'Tight Connection to My Heart'. Apart from being a nice enough song, the words seemed very appropriate. Especially, thought Les, the bit about the bloke getting beaten up wearing a powder-blue wig.

215

DD started to rock her shoulders gently, and softly sing along with the lyrics: 'You've got a tight connection to my heart.'

Before he knew it Les was crooning back. But in a much worse voice: 'Has anybody seen my love?'

The Captain and Tenile they weren't. But it seemed to work well at the time. Both people exchanging looks, both people knowing they were moving along very dangerous ground. The song hadn't finished when Les made a kind of beckoning gesture with his hands and his eyes and possibly just a tiny bit of his heart as well. DD didn't have to be beckoned twice. She lay against Norton's chest, her hands on his shoulders, her eyes about two inches from his. Les slid his hand over her back and placed it gently round her neck. Norton's eyes and nose might have been a bit belted about but there was nothing wrong with his lips. And there was definitely nothing wrong with DD's. They met, softly at first then intensifying, each kiss as exquisite as the last. Les held DD's shoulders and massaged them, DD scrabbled her hands through Norton's red hair. Someone's tongue zipped out — it might have been DD's. Before he knew it, Les had his hands up under DD's T-shirt, over her brown, smooth back and around her breasts. In all the carry-on in the kitchen Norton hadn't even noticed DD wasn't wearing a bra. He tenderly massaged her breasts and let his fingers run over her nipples. DD's tongue went that far down Norton's throat he thought he could feel it in his toes.

DD broke away from him and sat up on the bed. 'Environmentally friendly or not, this T-shirt's coming off,' she said.

'Yeah, mine too,' croaked Les. 'Stuff the wilderness. I never did like trees.'

Next thing Les and DD were grabbing at each other, kissing, caressing, as their passions and emotions came to the boil. DD was sighing; all Les wanted to do was kiss her sweet face off. It wasn't long before their T-shirts weren't the only things that came off. Norton got a brief glimpse of a pair of orange and black knickers as he eased

216

them down over DD's legs; about a micro-second before he had his jeans and Speedos off and Mr Wobbly was out of his cage, roaring, banging his little hands on his chest, telling the world he was raring and ready to go. DD gave Les a few delicate kisses before her mouth opened up and her tongue nearly sent Les into a frenzy. Norton ran his tongue over DD's breasts, down over her navel and returned the favour. Their lips met again. DD brought her knees up and Les got between her.

The first few shoves sent poor Les cross-eyed. If Thursday night was good, this was nothing short of sensational. But now they knew each other and had a feeling and understanding for each other which made it so much better again. It's hard to say if they were in love. But if anyone had looked in the window, by all the sweat and movement and the way the bed was rocking, they would have soon realised that Les and DD were definitely, very definitely, mates again.

Norton went for as long as was humanly possible; sweat was running down his spine, tingles were running up it. DD was under him, moving with him, squealing and just having a good time in general. However, it couldn't last forever, though Les would have liked it to. It finished with DD holding onto the bedstead behind her, her legs up round her head and Les gripping the top of the bedstead above her head, going for it like there was no tomorrow. Les gave a final roar, DD screamed and it was only by a stroke of luck they didn't rip the back right off Karen's bed.

Both being non-smokers, they didn't lie back and have the cliched 'cigarette after'. But DD found a towel and a bottle of cold mineral water, which had to be twice as good. They lay there in each other's arms, listening to the radio, enjoying each other's company and drifting into a bit of pillow talk as the late afternoon sun spilled in through Karen's window.

'Well, for a bloke half dead in a car accident, Mr Norton, you made a sudden and dramatic improvement,' said DD, gently picking at a scar on Norton's chin with her index finger. 'Miraculous, really.'

'It must have been those two Panadols.' Norton rubbed the back of DD's neck with one hand and her backside with the other. 'I think I've got a reaction to them.' Something told Les it might be an idea to switch back into Basil Fawlty mode. 'Anyway, you needn't talk. I only came round to explain things and say hello. Then I felt like . . . a bit of a rest.'

DD smiled. 'It could've been those red roses. I think I've got a reaction to them. And to a certain red-headed bloke as well.'

Norton's face suddenly turned into a dirty grin. 'I can always go and get another bunch of roses.'

If Norton's grin was dirty, DD's was absolutely filthy. 'I can always go out to the bathroom and get you another couple of Panadols. I'll bring back the whole box, if you want.'

'Did you happen to say 'box', Miss Donaldson?'

Number two finished about quarter to six in a lather of sweat and all the cold mineral water gone. DD was asleep alongside Les, looking like she'd just been pack-raped by a West Indian cricket team. Next to her, Norton was feeling like having a bit of a sleep himself and wondering if he might not have over-done it this afternoon and left nothing for tonight. He gritted his teeth and smiled mirthlessly to himself. No way. This afternoon's wasn't a bad effort, but it wouldn't stop him from going flat out for ten minutes in a pub brawl. He looked at his watch and tapped Desilu on the shoulder.

'Hey DD, I have to use your phone. All right?'

'Mmmhhh? Yeah, okay.' Desilu mumbled sleepily.

Norton climbed into his Speedos, got the phone number out of his wallet and walked quietly out into the loungeroom. It felt a little strange sitting there with hardly anything on, and he half expected one of the other girls to walk in at any moment. Certain Desilu couldn't hear him from Karen's room, Norton pressed the buttons and waited.

The phone rang for almost a minute before it was answered, and the woman's voice at the other end

218

sounded kind of strained or as if she'd had to run to the phone. But Les still couldn't mistake the soft, mid-west American accent.

'Hello. Boarding House.'

'Yes. Could I speak to Mr Thomas, please, Mrs Llivac. It's Mr Menzies.'

'Yes. Yes... just a moment. I'll... put you through to his room.'

'Thank you.'

There was a bit of a clicking sound, then a very cool, very laid-back voice answered. 'Yeaahhh. Hello.'

'Muzz, it's Les.'

There was a bit of a chuckle at first. 'I thought it might have been you. How are you, son?'

'Good.' Les smiled. He could just picture Murray lying back there grinning. He was also relieved to find his brother had arrived safe and sound. 'So you got here all right?'

'Yeah, no worries. I left not long after you. Got here about eight this morning. Did you see the helicopters?'

'Helicopters? I saw a convoy of Air Force cars screaming towards town.'

'I saw four helicopters this side of Goonda.' Murray chuckled over the line again. 'I think our little fireworks display must've stirred some of the natives up a bit.'

'You don't think anybody saw it, do you?' answered Les sarcastically.

'One or two maybe.'

'Anyway you got here okay, that's the main thing. How's the boarding house? You getting on all right with Mrs Llivac?'

'The landlady? Yeah, she's all right. Good as gold.'

'Good. Okay, now you know where this place is and how to get there?'

'Yeah. The Boulevarde on Begonia Street. Quiet lookin' sort of joint. Stained-glass windows. Couple of balconies. Bar out the back with a long mirror and a big glass door or somethin' in the corner. Bit swish actually.'

'You know it?'

'Yeah. I checked it out this arvo.'

'Ohh, good on you.' As well as being a little surprised, Les was also happy to see his brother was right on the ball. 'Well, that's the bar they'll be in out the back. You just be there having a drink and I'll start the ball rolling.'

'No worries. So what are you up to anyway?'

'I'm round a girl's place, she's asleep. I'll tell you about it when I see you tonight.'

'Okay. So what time do you reckon?'

'Get there about nine and when it's all over I'll see you back at the boarding house at eleven. And we'll sort things out from there. And keep your fingers crossed, Muzz. I got a feeling there just might be a nice little earn in this for you.'

'Sounds good to me,' answered Murray. 'You know how tough things are out in the bush at the moment.'

'Yeah, you're all starving. Especially the Nortons.' Les heard his brother chuckle again. 'Okay then, Muzz, I'll get going, I got some things to do. And I'll see you at nine o'clock. Okay?'

'No sweat, Les. I'll see you tonight. And wear your dancing shoes.'

Now Les had to chuckle. 'Count on it, Muzz. See you tonight.'

Norton looked at the phone for a moment then returned to Karen's room. Desilu looked to be still asleep though she'd put her knickers and T-shirt on. Norton put on his T-shirt and jeans and slid alongside her. He flicked some hair off her forehead; Desilu lazily draped an arm round his waist.

'Listen, DD,' he said softly, 'I have to get going, mate.'

'Yeah, okay,' mumbled Desilu sleepily.

Les looked at her for a second and raised his voice a little. 'Are you asleep or awake?'

'Desilu blinked her eyes open. 'I'm awake. I'm awake. What . . .?'

'Good.' Les looked at her and smiled. 'Listen, DD, I've got a sensational idea.'

'Mmmhhh?'

'I'll be finished this dinner thing by about eleven or so. I might call back here around then. Do you reckon you could have the fiance kissed good night and out the door by then?'

Desilu smiled up at Les. 'Yes. I think I could get awfully tired or develop a splitting headache by then. Plus I do have to get up early in the morning.'

'Okay. Now you're only staying here to get a few hours' sleep on that daggy little bed till you get the bus at seven — right?'

'Yeah. That was the idea.'

'When this dinner thing's finished I'll tell Kramer to shove it. I'm sick of the pair of them anyway. I've hired a Ford LTD. I'll call back here, we'll load your stuff up and piss off. Drive for an hour or so then book into a good motel and get a good night's sleep. And have a champagne breakfast or whatever. Then we'll just take our time driving back to Taree. What do you reckon?'

Desilu still smiled up at Les as her mind flashed to the bag of dope she had stashed in her room. She had figured on a quick trip home and getting rid of it. But a couple of nights with Les shouldn't be a problem. It'd be quite nice actually. And a lift home in a new car would be a heap better than a bumpy eight-hour trip in a bus. And what Les didn't know wouldn't hurt him. He'd be pretty cool anyway, if he did find out.

'Yeah, all right,' she answered. 'Sounds like a good idea. And I haven't got much gear.'

'Okay. Well, I'll see you back here around eleven, eleven-thirty.'

'All right.'

Norton slid his hand between Desilu's legs, stroked the silkiness of her little pussy for a second or two, then pinched a few pubic hairs and gave them a bit of tug. 'Just one thing before I go, DD.'

'Oooohhh!'

'Just make sure the fiance only gets a kiss goodnight too.'

'Oooohhh!'

221

'If I come back here at eleven-thirty and find this has been tampered with in any way, shape or form, Miss Donaldson, there'll be trouble.'

'Oooohhh!'

'Big trouble. You got that?'

'Oooohhh!'

Norton let go of her ted and ran his hand gently through her hair, tidying it up just a little. 'So what are you going to tell the fiance tonight, when in the way of polite conversation, he asks you what you've been doing today?'

Apart from a little flutter of her eyelids, Desilu managed to keep a straight face. 'I'll... tell him I've been packing my gear.'

'And that's all? I don't even get a mention?'

'Well, what do you expect me to bloody tell him?'

'Well, I think the truth would be nice, wouldn't it?'

DD's eyes narrowed a little. 'Jesus, you're good.'

Les nodded. 'Yeah, I have to agree, I'm not bad. But there's one thing I definitely am not.' He tapped DD lightly on the tip of her nose. 'I'm not a liar.'

Les let DD go, put his boots on then sat on the edge of the bed. He grabbed Desilu tightly around the waist and kissed her full on the mouth. DD kept kissing him back until Les let her go.

'I'll see you tonight,' he said, and moved to the door.

'And don't let anything happen to you this time either — boofhead.'

Les winked and smiled and then he was gone, closing the front door as quietly as he closed the one to Karen's bedroom.

Well, what about that, Basil? Les couldn't help but smile at himself in the rear-view mirror of the Jaguar. The Elastoplast over his eyes was just holding on, the strip on his arm had been torn off and his hair was just one big mess. I managed to lie my way out of that all right and I wasn't quite expecting the end result. Norton's smile got wider. Not a bad effort for a Monday afternoon. Now a pleasant couple of days or whatever driving back to Taree

222

with DD in that LTD. Bloody DD. Jesus! What a woman. Norton's smile started to turn into a laugh. And what a weird relationship. She's out with another bloke tonight and I'm going out to get into a monstrous fight. At least she's the one cheating. Not me. But what a babe. Les winked up at the sky. Thanks, boss, I knew you hadn't forgotten me. Just be in our corner tonight though — if you can. Les hit the ignition and the big car purred into life. It was all right sitting there full of love, karma and ideas, but there were things to be done and much dirty work afoot before he knocked on Kramer's door at eight-thirty to take them for a quiet drink at the Boulevarde. Les hit the blinker and eased his way onto the highway, then drove straight back to the flats.

Norton pulled up on the driveway to find a light grey Ford sedan parked there with two people in it, a man and a woman. The man stayed behind the wheel while the woman got out. Les at first thought they were journalists, but their sober clothes, sober appearance and the woman's polite smile told him different.

Norton got out of the car and smiled back at the woman. 'Don't tell me. Let me guess. You're from the car rental company?' The woman nodded. 'Mr Kramer was expecting you and ordered me to have the car washed.' Les made a gesture with his hand. 'There you go. Good as new. The keys are in it.'

'There was really no need,' said the woman. 'The . . .'

Norton held up a hand. 'Mr Kramer insisted. Anyway, I have to go inside. Thank you. I'll see you some other time.'

'It was a pleasure. Any time Mr Kramer . . .'

Les waved from the door and disappeared inside.

Norton left the lights off in the flat when he stepped inside. The first thing he did was to toss a cushion on the loungeroom floor. Bloody women, he laughed to himself. The afternoon's intense porking had left him a little more tired than he thought. He kicked his boots off and lay down on the carpet with his head on the cushion, his arms

223

by his side. It was a trick Eddie had taught him that he learnt in Vietnam. Crash sleeping for thirty minutes at a time. A kind of self-hypnosis. If you set your mind to it and do the right breathing exercises to start with, you could crash out for half an hour and wake up feeling fresh as a daisy. The idea was to put your mind completely at ease but don't make your body too comfortable.

Les checked his watch and started a rhythmic breathing cycle, sending out relaxing signals to his feet and legs, working his way up to his neck and head. Finally he lay there, staring into the blackness of his mind, completely devoid of thought but not sound asleep.

Eventually Norton's eyes snapped open. The flat was quite dark now and he checked his watch. Exactly thirty minutes. He took a few deep breaths, stretched his legs over his head a few times then stood up, did a few more stretches and switched the lights on. He blinked a couple of times then smiled; he felt as if he'd been asleep for hours. Without any further ado, Les stripped off and got under a cold shower; though it was still that hot a cold one was all you needed.

A minute or so before seven, Les was seated in front of the TV in his Speedos with a cup of coffee. He spread some sheets of newspaper on the floor and started trimming and shaping the piece of sponge rubber with the scissors and the kitchen knife. On the lounge next to him were the pages from the Spanish magazine with the photos of topless Crystal. Les kept smiling at it as he trimmed away and the ABC news came one.

Richard Morecroft looked even more sober and exact than normal. Superimposed behind him was the United States flag, the Australian flag and the seal of the President of the United States. Almost sadly, he announced that the forthcoming visit to Australia by the President had suddenly been cancelled due to illness. The screen then flashed to an official dinner in Hawaii and there was the President, surrounded by flunkies, throwing the best drama imaginable, clutching at his throat and collapsing at the dinner table like he was dying. As if on cue, his wife

224

raced to his side and began wiping his face. Then as if on cue, the Secret Service raced to his side and carted him off with his loving wife in attendance. Norton stared at the TV screen, shaking his head at the President departing, looking like a dingo that had just swallowed a bait. It was pure Hollywood. It couldn't have looked any better if Steven Spielberg had scripted and directed it. Norton wouldn't have been surprised if he had. Then Norton started to laugh out loud. If you're not an actor, pal, he mused, you should be. And your missus too. The screen flashed to one of the President's doctors saying the President had food poisoning, the rest of his trip was cancelled and he would be kept under observation for a few days at least. Then it was the Australian Prime Minister's turn, saying how much he regretted the President's tour being called off and hoped he'd be all right.

Norton continued to stare at the TV and laugh. Yeah, food poisoning my arse. Possible radioactive poisoning'd be more like it. And don't thank me and my brother either, will you. You pair of gooses. Les watched the Australian Prime Minister for a moment or two more, then turned the TV down; the news was pretty dull after that and Norton wasn't all that interested. He went back to cutting and shaping the piece of sponge rubber, smiling at the photos of Crystal spread out next to him. The scissors did most of the job, and before long Norton had the sponge rubber in the shape he wanted; or close enough. He held the piece of rubber up, had another look at the photos, and thought about Crystal standing out on his rear sundeck. Yeah. Close enough. Now for the tricky part.

With the scissors in his hand, Les walked to his room and the en-suite and started looking around, finally settling on the bag of clothes he'd brought along. For some reason he'd thrown in a thick pair of track-suit pants, dark blue cotton and rayon. Seems like a shame to stuff up a good pair of track-suit pants but these are the things you do for your brother. He dug the scissors into one leg of the pants and cut out a piece about two inches

225

square. Satisfied, he took it into the loungeroom and placed it next to the piece of sponge rubber. Now what?

Les stood in the kitchen and looked around. There was a small bottle of Coke in the fridge. He took it out and tipped the contents down the sink. Les snapped the neck off the bottle on the edge of the sink, then crushed it up a little with the bottom of the empty Coke bottle. Les picked out a few pieces he thought would do, flushed the rest down the sink and went back to the loungeroom.

Carefully he folded the pieces of broken coke bottle into the piece of track-suit and placed it on the lounge. With the kitchen knife, Les just as carefully cut a small pocket in the piece of sponge rubber, checked it with his index finger then, equally carefully, placed the folded-up square of track-suit in the pocket. The tube of Super-glue was new; Les soon had it open and squeezed a thick smear across the top of the hole in the rubber, binding it tight. He gave it a few moments, just to be sure. Yep, that couldn't be any firmer. Tighter than a finger in a bum — like they say. Les held and lightly bounced the piece of sponge rubber in his huge hands. Well, I don't think I can do any better than that. Let's just hope I'm right.

By now the news was well and truly finished, not that Les had taken much notice, and now it was almost the end of the '7.30 Report'. Something caught Norton's eye. For some strange reason, Quentin Dempster had decided to ask Rampaging Roy Slavin and H.G. Nelson for their comments on the President of the United States cancelling his trip to Australia. Les had missed the first few seconds, and turned the sound up. It was over to Roy Slavin, all po-faced, saying he'd recently been at the White House discussing world policy with the President and giving him some advice on his forthcoming trip to Australia.

'And I distinctly remember saying to the President, HG,' intoned Slavin, 'I said to him, Mr President I said, when you're in Hawaii, don't eat the poi. Don't eat the poi, I said, Mr President. It's off. Been off for years. Never really been on.'

'Well, Roy, it's a funny thing you should warn him

226

about the food in Hawaii,' chimed in H.G. Nelson, 'but I was only on the phone to him the other night myself.'

'On the hotline, HG?'

'On the hotline, Roy, yes. And I was warning the President about various trendy, so-called upmarket Eastern suburbs restaurants to avoid like the plague. Trendy restaurants with their so-called nouvelle cuisine.'

'Well, HG, you and I have always been on the same wavelength. And like myself, the President is a personal friend of yours also.'

'But viewers,' H.G. Nelson's voice rose as the camera came full in on him, 'as well as the President's visit being cancelled, Roy and myself have had to cancel a dinner for the three of us at Harry's Cafe de Wheels. That's right, viewers. Rampaging Roy Slavin and myself were to have had a formal dinner with the President of the United States of America at Harry's Cafe de Wheels.'

'Australian cuisine, HG,' cut in Slavin. 'That's what I tried to tell him. Stick to good old Oz cuisine and none of this would have happened. But would the Secret Service listen to me? Would his wife listen to me. Would . . .'

Les laughed and switched the TV off. Not bad, boys, not bad. But if only you knew the fuckin' truth. He shook his head. Christ! Wait till Price and Eddie find out. I wonder if even they'll believe me? I reckon Eddie will.

Satisfied with what he'd done, Les placed the piece of sponge rubber on a chair in his bedroom. Back in the loungeroom, he painstakingly wrapped up all the pieces of sponge rubber, plus the tube of Super-glue and the broken Coke bottle in the sheets of newspaper, placed the bundle in the plastic bag he'd brought his Nikes home in and stuffed it in his clothes bag. Les then spent the next twenty minutes packing all his clothes, his shaving gear and his ghetto-blaster. Bad luck he had to leave the rest of the beer and food, but he packed the still unopened bottle of Jim Beam. He didn't bother to tidy his bedroom or clean what mess there was in the kitchen. If all went well this would have to have, if not all the signs of a hasty departure, at least an orderly retreat.

He left a blue T-shirt sitting on one of his bags on the bed and had a last look around. Everything seemed in order. Norton then got into his jeans, the denim shirt he wasn't all that worried about getting ripped, his now completely broken-in R.M. Williams riding boots, and made sure he had all his money together and the car keys in the small overnight-bag. The last thing Les did was to go back to the kitchen, get the same knife he'd been using and put it out on the back sun-deck. Then he went and tapped on Kramer's door.

Kramer answered the door and even though it was barely open, Les could see the little conman was wearing jeans, a brown button-down-collar shirt and good old white shoes.

'Hello, Les,' he said, blinking slightly behind his glasses.

'How are you, KK?' replied Les brightly. 'You still coming out for a couple of drinks?'

'Yeah, okay. Crystal said not too late though.'

'No. As soon as you want to leave I'm with you,' said Norton.'

'All right. We'll see you down the front in about fifteen minutes.'

'Righto,' smiled Norton. 'See you then.'

Kramer closed his door. Les went inside and sat in the kitchen sipping the last of his orange juice: thinking. Not necessarily about the ensuing fight; something else besides. He took his orange juice into the bedroom and had another look at the piece of sponge rubber. He'd done about all he could with that. Now there was just one hurdle to overcome. A bit of a tricky one, but if he couldn't do it, he'd just abort the mission. It was all a bit of a long shot, a real long shot and he was only surmising. He knew he was right about one thing. The other was just an educated guess. The bottom line was though, he had nothing to lose if he was wrong. Only his brother's earn. Les swallowed the last of the orange juice. So let's just hope for Murray's sake I'm right. A couple of minutes later Les was down the front of the flats about the same time as the stretch limousine.

Well, nice to see we're all going out in style on our last night in Surfers, Les thought to himself. The limo was facing towards Cavill Avenue with Tony behind the wheel. Les gave him a smile and a bit of a nod as he walked across the driveway. The driver nodded back, noticing Les was wearing sunglasses, and if Les wasn't mistaken there was a bit of a smirk in Tony's eyes. Fair enough, thought Les, leaning against the back door. If it was the other way around I'd probably do the same thing, and aren't we all entitled to a bit of a laugh in these troubled times?

Les had just got comfortable when KK and Crystal came out the front door. Kramer was wearing what he had on earlier, Crystal was wearing jeans also and the same white chef's kind of jacket she had on when they went out to dinner some night or somewhere. Now there was a bit of a smirk behind Norton's sunglasses. I'm glad you chose to wear white tonight, Crystal. I'm not quite sure why, but I'm just glad you did.

'Hello, Crystal,' said Les, his voice dripping with politeness. 'How are you? Nice top you have on.'

'Not bad, Dempsey,' replied Crystal, also noticing Norton's sunglasses. 'Where's your white stick?'

Norton still kept smiling. 'I just thought I'd wear these. You know how people like to stare.'

'Yeah,' nodded Crystal. 'That's about all there is, down here in this neck of the woods. Rubber-necked geeks.'

'Something like that,' answered Les. He opened the back door, they all climbed in and the limousine moved off.

'Kelvin says you're actually gonna take us out and buy us a few drinks,' said Crystal, making herself comfortable. 'Shout? Is that what you hillbillies call it?'

'Yeah, that's about it,' nodded Les. 'You've both been that nice to me, I thought it's the least I could do. And it is your last night in Australia.'

'Yeah. And ain't I just broken-hearted having to leave.' Crystal turned to Kramer. 'What's this place like he's taking us to, Kelvin?'

229

'Nice,' answered KK. 'It'll probably be a bit quiet tonight. But the Boulevarde's a nice place. Even though I haven't been in there for yonks.'

Crystal shrugged. 'I don't give a rodent's much what it's like, so long as Joe Palooka here's paying for it.' Crystal smiled incisively at Les. 'So what's your story, Dempsey? You looking for a bit more trouble tonight?'

Norton shook his head. 'Not much chance of that,' he replied.

'Guess you're just gonna have to learn to tap-dance a bit faster this time, if there is, ain't you?'

Norton smiled back. 'The only dancing I'll be doing tonight, Crystal'll be a bit of Balmain folk dancing,' he purred.

Crystal turned back to Kramer. 'Balmain folk dancing? What's with this fuckin' Balmain folk dancing, Kelvin?'

Kramer shrugged his fat little shoulders. 'How would I know? I'm from Melbourne.'

The stretch limo cruised comfortably on into the night. Next thing they were in Begonia Avenue, alighting amongst the people walking past or standing outside the Boulevarde.

There was a solid bouncer standing out front behind a kind of roped-off partition. He didn't say anything as he let them through, though he appeared to be thinking about something. Les smiled from behind his sunglasses and opened the front door.

Inside was considerably more crowded than when Les had walked through the place earlier, even for a Monday night. There were a few couples on the dancefloor and two or three girls hanging round a DJ wearing a floral shirt who was playing some track by Simply Red. Naturally everybody stopped to look at Crystal, and naturally KK basked in it, although he seemed a little more subdued than normal.

'It's a bit crowded in here,' said Les. He indicated with his head. 'Why don't we go down that bar at the end?'

Crystal and KK exchanged glances and shrugged. 'Yeah, okay', said Kramer.

230

With Les leading the way, they eased their way through the crowd down to the end bar. It was a bit quieter, maybe fifteen or so people standing or sitting around or grouped around the bar next to the balcony. And sure enough, there was Stinnett and Jasper and the team, casually dressed in jeans, T-shirts or loose fitting shirts, seated or leaning up against the wall-length mirror near the window in the corner. Although he couldn't help the tremor in his body, Norton pretended not to notice them; especially Stinnett and Jasper. One thing Les did notice: instead of six, there were eight and all pretty fit looking. The team couldn't help but notice the trio walk in, they were onto them in a flash; Les felt like it was sixteen surly eyes drilling straight into them.

Smiling and acting completely oblivious, Norton made room at the bar on their left, even managing to find a stool for Crystal. 'Righto,' he said brightly. 'Now remember, this is on me. What are we having?' He gave his hands a little clap and rubbed them together.

'Les,' said Kramer apprehensively and suddenly looking a little pale. 'You see who's sitting against that wall over there?' Carrying on completely blase, Norton had a quick look around then turned back to Kramer. 'That team that gave you the hiding at CJ's.'

'Is it?' Still acting blase, Les had another quick look through his sunglasses. 'Oh well, I don't think they'll want to cause any trouble. Not in here, surely?'

'I think we should leave,' said Kramer.

'Ahh we're here now,' said Les. 'Have one drink. If they look like causing any bother we'll stall.'

Crystal soon twigged to what was going on. 'Yeah let's have a drink,' she said, adding a cynical smile. 'We've got Dempsey here to protect us. I'll have a George Dickles on the rocks, Killer. Make it a double.'

'You got it,' beamed Norton. 'What about you, KK?'

Kramer thought for a second. 'All right,' he said reluctantly. 'A Jack Daniels and Coke. Plenty of ice.'

'Good idea. I might have the same. Wait here, I won't be a sec.'

Norton walked over to the bar opposite, checking out the team and the other punters on the way over. He noticed most of the team were watching him; Les was also stuffed if he could see Murray. They were mainly couples and a few girls and overdressed men out on the run. But no sign of fuckin' Murray. Les checked his watch. Shit! The cunt should be here. Where is he? Now it was Norton's turn to be a little apprehensive. He eased himself up against the bar next to some bloke reeking of aftershave lotion, wearing white pants, white shirt, white belt, white shoes, a white hat and white-rimmed sunglasses, trying to put work on two women sitting next him. Christ! Who does this mug think he is? thought Norton, now feeling a little irritable at his brother not turning up. Boz Scaggs, Elton John or the secretary of some North Shore bowling club? Nice flip. Norton ordered the drinks and tried to check out the team in the mirror behind the bar. But it was on too much of an angle, which added to his irritability. Norton was wondering what to do when Boz Scaggs tapped him on the arm.

'Excuse me, mate. You wouldn't have the time, would you?' he asked.

Still feeling testy, Les held up his arm and bent his wrist so Boz Scaggs could see his watch.

'Thanks, mate.'

'You're welcome,' replied Les.

After those few brief words, Les completely ignored his brother. He just smiled as a wonderful feeling of relief went through his body while he waited for the drinks, then quietly slipped his watch off and tucked it in the front pocket of his jeans.

The drinks arrived. Les walked back to the others to find K K had found a stool and was sitting next to Crystal. Smiling away, Les put the drinks on the bar, picked up his own and clinked their two glasses.

'Well, here's to . . .' Les turned to Crystal. 'Here's to the South. The South's gonna rise again. Ain't that what they say?'

'They sure do, boy,' answered Crystal. 'To the South.'

232

'Whatever,' muttered Kramer.

Les swallowed almost half his drink in one go and felt it burn the back of his throat as it slid pleasantly all the way down to his stomach. Ahh, good thing I got doubles, he thought to himself. Out the corner of his eye he watched the team against the wall, now going into a bit of a huddle.

'Well, Crystal,' said Les, 'apart from cleaning up at the casino and seeing me get my head punched in, I suppose it's been a pretty quiet old trip to Australia? Still, as long as you got those other things sorted out, I guess that's the main thing.'

'Oh we got all the other things sorted out, Les.' Crystal still had the cynical smile on her face as she turned to KK. 'Didn't we, Kelvin?'

'Yeah. I suppose we did,' answered Kramer.

Kramer's eyes were still darting nervously around behind his glasses and his face still looked decidedly pale. It paled even further when Stinnett and Jasper peeled themselves away from the team and sauntered over. Les was standing facing the others, his back to the room. Stinnett came over on Norton's right, Jasper moved round to his left. Just like old times, thought Norton, continuing to sip his drink. He caught Stinnett's eye and smiled.

Stinnett ignored Les. Unsmiling he turned to KK. 'Listen Kramer, you greasy little Jew cunt, you're fuckin' lucky we have to drink in here. Otherwise I'd kick your stinkin' little reffo arse straight out the door and halfway up the fuckin' street.' Stinnett paused to take a breath and his face coloured a little more. 'What I said the other night still goes — you fuckin' little shit.'

Les stood there, calmly drinking his Jack Daniels. 'We're not looking for any trouble, mate,' he said with a shrug. 'We're just having a drink.' There was a mirror behind the bar in front of him and Les noticed the bloke in the all white gear move away from the bar and the two girls he was talking to. He very easily took off his sunglasses and still holding his drink moved just as easily to the middle of the room.

233

Stinnett glared at Les. 'If I want to talk to you, shit-for-fuckin-brains, I'll rattle a slop bucket.' He turned back to Kramer. 'Tell your piss-weak barrow boy here to keep his mouth shut, before he gets it shut for him. Only this time for good.'

'Les,' said Kramer. 'I think . . .'

'Trouble,' continued Les blissfully. 'Christ! Have a look at this.' Les placed his drink on the bar in front of Crystal who was looking up at him like he either had rocks in his head or he was the greatest suck-arse God ever put breath into. Les took his sunglasses off and placed them next to his drink. 'Have a look at this,' he said, pointing to his two black eyes.' Does that suggest to you I want any more trouble? Jesus! Give me a break, mate.'

Stinnett screwed his face almost as if he was in pain. 'Why don't you just fuckin'. . .'

'Trouble? No sir,' interjected Les. He turned to Jasper sniggering on his left then back to Stinnett. 'No sir. The last thing I'm looking for is trouble.' Then the almost apologetic look on Norton's face turned into one huge diabolical grin and a definite glow seemed to emanate from Norton's two brown and horribly reddened black eyes. 'But a bit of fun'd be all right. What do you reckon?'

Crystal was still gaping up at Les, still wondering what sort of a dill he was, when Norton dropped slightly to his right, his body and shoulders swung round like a gate closing and he king-hit Jasper with a short right that had everything in it. It wasn't so much a king-hit, Norton's massive fist nearly took Jasper's head off. All his front teeth caved in, his mouth was smashed to pulp and a thick spray of blood spattered across Crystal, K K and anybody else who happened to be close by. Jasper couldn't believe what hit him. His eyes rolled and his knees started to buckle when Les slammed two left-hooks into the side of his face. The first one shattered his jaw, the second one squashed his ear like someone stepping on a bug. He fell forward straight into Norton's right knee coming up which spread his nose all over his face. Jasper hit the deck and Les stepped back about half a pace and sunk the toe of his right R.M. Williams riding boot into what was left of Jasper's face: twice. Jasper lay on the floor face down, blood pouring out of him and gave up interest in the rest of the evening and the rest of the week for that matter.

That was one down, but Les knew what to expect next: Stinnett's big right coming over. He tucked his head into his shoulder, moved in to Crystal and KK against the bar a bit as it landed and skidded off the top of Norton's head, whistling past, a by now screaming Crystal's chin by a whisker. Les got under Stinnett, pivotted and slammed a left rip up into the tall hood's solar plexus. Stinnett grunted with pain and shock as it stopped him dead in his tracks. Norton stepped back slightly and banged a big right into Stinnett's jaw followed by a left hook into his mouth that missed KK by a little less than a whisker too. Stinnett's jaw swung all over the place, his mouth burst open and he slumped on his backside almost next to Jasper, blood bubbling down his chin and onto the carpet.

Stinnett was in an awful lot of trouble. However, by now so was Les. Although initially taken by surprise, the rest of the team made a mad scramble off their stools or from where they were standing and all six men charged at Les, ready to tear him to pieces. And they would have too, only the Boz Scaggs look-alike standing in the middle of the room had taken off his hat by now and intervened.

Murray pinged the closest one to him with the sweetest left hook that took the man's feet from under him and left him on his back, out cold, blood pouring from his nose. Murray sunk a withering right into the next one's jaw, rattling his brains around in his head along with most of his fillings. Two of the team didn't see what happened and charged into Les, the other two hesitated for a second, one decided to help the others with Les, the other decided to help his mate, who was still on his feet with Murray.

After that it was just on, a horrible, noisy, blood-drenched bar-room brawl. What women there were started screaming and men cursed out oaths of shock as drinks went everywhere and stools and tables were

bowled all over the place. The bar staff dropped everything in horror; the people on the balcony gaped as Les
and Murray and the six hoods punched, kicked, kneed
and cursed their way all round the back bar. Crystal and
KK got in the alcove next to the bar they were seated at,
along with the other customers, giving the brawl a wide
berth as the back bar got wrecked around them in a
whirlwind of spilt booze, blood and filthy language.

Although it was five on to two, Les and Murray were
giving out more than they got. The second one Murray
had pinged was just on his feet, and with a back-up he was
holding onto Murray while his mate did his best. The
three Les was fighting were fit and strong and it wasn't the
easiest, but with plenty of solid punching, head-butts,
knees and gouging, slowly the Norton brothers were
gaining the upper hand. Les went down a couple of times
in the melee, so did Murray, and the others too, then
they'd all bounce back up, lashing out with kicks and
punches. Les copped plenty, along with his brother but
they were bouncing and rolling around that much most of
the blows were skidding off or landing on their arms and
shoulders. Like some wild, rampaging scrum they
knocked over the cigarette machine, ripped down the
railing running along the wall-length mirror and sent a
stool through the folding glass door.

They kept fighting till Les ended up standing alongside
Murray up against the bar next to the balcony. Norton's
denim shirt was ratshit, with not a button left on it, and
his nose and the cuts above his eyes had opened up again.
Murray's white hat had been ground into the mess on the
floor and the rest of his all white ensemble was in tatters;
what wasn't looked like it had been taken to Bali and tie-
dyed a rich crimson. Les and Murray smiled at each other
and shaped up to the four men across the room who were
left standing, like a Mexican stand-off, only the Nortons
were keen to carry on and finish the job. The others knew
they were beaten but they were going to go down fighting.

One of them reached to pick up a bar stool and Les was
about to kick him in the groin when a movement coming

out of the crowd on his left caught his eye. It was the fair-haired bouncer Les had seen out the front earlier along with another one; taller, muscles everywhere and carrying bugger all fat and with dark hair and a sallow face pretty much like Stinnett laying on the floor. Shit! Thought Les, and it suddenly hit him. What did that mate of Jimmy Martin's say down the beach? 'One of the team's brother works there on the door.' Stinnett's brother. You could bet your life on it, and that would be another reason why they drank here. A big Uh-Oh! went through Les. Now they weren't only facing four blokes, another two had arrived on the scene; big, fit and ready to go. And the way the tall bouncer looked at Stinnett, blood all over him, still trying to get to his feet, it wasn't hard to figure out whose side they were on. Shit! Norton cursed to himself again, as the six men paired off ready to get stuck into Les and Murray. This could be very fuckin' dicey, and there was no chance of talking your way out or making a bolt for it. What have I done? So much for Murray's earn and so much for two days' driving down the coast with DD. If I do, it'll more than likely be in the back of an ambulance.

Les turned to his brother, a Jesus-I'm-sorry-mate look on his face and expected Murray to be glaring at him. Instead, Murray had this wild look on his blood-spattered face and he was laughing. He winked at Les, stuck his tongue up against his front teeth, turned to the open balcony and let go this ear-piercing whistle — *Pheew-ooo-eet*! It was that loud it stopped everybody in their tracks. The bar staff, the onlookers, even the six blokes were somewhat taken by surprised. So was Les. Then, like his brother, Les smiled too. No, it couldn't be . . .

Faces set, the two bouncers loosened their ties as they teamed up with the other four men and advanced towards Les and Murray, fists at the ready. It was three onto one, the Nortons had taken some punishment and the six heavies were more than confident of giving them some more. They were just about to start when the full-length

237

window in the corner literally disintegrated in an explosion of shattering stained glass and splintered panes crashing onto the floor and against the wall alongside. To everyone's absolute shock, horror and astonishment, right in the middle of all the broken glass skidded a snarling, bristling black dog about a metre and a half long and the same wide with a white blaze down the front of its chest. It was a fearsome sight standing there, with the hairs right along the middle of its back standing on end, its massive head and jaws moving from side to side. The weirdest thing about it, though, was it had a rubber mask around its head and across its snout, something like a burglar. But there was no mistaking those two pink, piggy eyes glowing beneath the black rubber. Norton's face lit up like a Christmas tree. You fuckin' beaut, he grinned to himself. The cavalry's arrived. Murray, you are a dead-set genius.

It took Grungle about one and a half seconds to work out who the good guys were and who the bad guys; about the same it took him to work out that coming straight through the window was the quickest way to Murray's side. The first bloke he went for was the one closest to his master. With a hideous growl, he latched straight onto the bloke's calf muscle and started tearing at it like a shark, right through his jeans. The bloke gave a scream of horror and pain as he watched a piece of his leg, about the size of a lamb's fry disappear down Grungle's throat; blue denim and all. Grungle gave another growl and clamped his jaws around the elbow of the bloke next to him, dragging him to the ground; even with the screams and shouts from the crowd you could hear the bones crunching as Grungle bit deeper, shaking his head from side to side. The bloke howled in agony as he gripped his elbow, trying to hold together the sinews, tendons and arteries hanging out and stem the blood splashing onto the floor. Like a big-league basketball player taking a slam-dunk, Grungle leapt up off the floor and bit into the face of the fair-headed bouncer. The bouncer screeched in terror and pain as Grungle chewed off his nose, half his chin and one side of his face; this all went down the hatch too. Then Grungle stopped. He turned to Les and Murray, piggy eyes still blazing, but more a look of 'well, I'm doing my bit, are you gonna give me a hand or stand there all night?' on his face. Les and Murray took their cue.

The tall bouncer staring at Grungle was too panic-stricken to see Les walk up and slam a big left into his jaw, followed by a stiffening kick in the groin. He went at the knees and Les whacked him with a right upper-cut that nearly took his head off. He hit the deck and as soon as he did, Les stepped back and drove his R.M. Williams straight into his mouth, kicking out all his front teeth.

Murray left-hooked the one nearest him, crushing his nose, then grabbed him by the back of the head and slammed his knee up into his face. The hood hit the deck on his side and lay there. This left one standing, not knowing which way to go. Before he even had a chance to half make up his mind, Les and Murray both belted him at once: straight into Disneyland. After that it was just a slaughter, as what Les and Murray weren't punching and kicking into minced steak, Grungle was ripping and gouging great bloody pieces out of.

If the onlookers wanted blood, they got it. Litres of it. All over their clothes, the floor, the wall-length mirror, the cigarette machine and anywhere within five metres of the action. Standing behind the shell-shocked Crystal and KK, still in the alcove, Les thought he saw a grey-haired bloke in glasses, wearing black trousers, maroon shirt and red tie, who looked like he could have been the owner, give a little sigh then collapse in a dead faint. Any people that weren't too shocked to move were heading for the doors, the windows or the toilets to be sick. All that was left in the back bar now were Crystal and KK, behind the bar, too petrified to move, and any men left conscious on the floor trying to crawl under the carpet; with Les and Murray, blood from head to foot, standing over them alongside Grungle. Then it finished, almost as quick as it started.

Murray could see there was no point in hanging around any longer. He gave another whistle, a jerk of his head and he and Grungle left the way Grungle had come in, through what was left of the glass door in the corner. Les figured out it might be as good a time as any to leave also. He'd certainly got his square-up with Jasper and the boys, in spades. KK and Crystal were still standing dumbstruck in the alcove, the owner at their feet. KK had thick flecks of blood across his glasses and over his white shoes; Crystal's white top looked like she'd finished an afternoon shift in the local slaughterhouse. Both were gagging and doing their best to keep down the two pizzas they'd sent out for earlier. Miraculously, Norton's sunglasses were still sitting on the bar where he'd put them. He picked them up and placed them in what was left of a pocket on what was left of his denim shirt.

Les looked directly at KK. 'Well, what do you reckon, KK? We get going?' Then Les smiled at Crystal. 'Though I'll stay and have another one if you want, I'm still shouting.'

Crystal and KK just gaped at Les and the bloodied, moaning bodies in amongst the carnage around them. Before they had the chance to answer, Les hit the button on KK's pager and started moving them through the astonished crowd and past the bar staff towards the front. The DJ gaped too as they went past him to the strains of a track he was wishing he'd never played for some big titted brunette he was trying to sweeten himself up with: 'Trouble' — Girl Overboard. Next thing the three of them were out the door and straight into the back of the limo as it rocked to a stop in front of them. Tony's eyes hung out like party whistles as he saw the looks on Crystal and KK, the blood on Norton again and the blood going all over the upholstery for him to clean off later.

'Back to the flats,' ordered Les. 'And don't waste any time getting there.'

Tony took off and did his best to gun the big limo through any gaps in the traffic on his way to the highway. Seated in the back, Les might have been a bit more

240

bloodied and bruised, but he couldn't have been any happier. Though somehow he knew he was going to have to conceal it. KK and Crystal were both still too shocked and sickened to speak. Les turned to Kramer.

'Well, what about that, KK?' he said, sounding a little surprised. 'Those bludgers. I didn't think they'd put on another stink. Not in there. You really must have pissed those blokes off, KK.' Les shook his head. 'Got me completely bamboozled.'

Kramer was too stuffed for an answer. Somehow Crystal came to life. 'Ohh my God,' she moaned. 'What in hell happened back there? I've never seen anything like that in my life.'

'No, neither have I,' answered Les sagely. 'Bloody good thing that bloke in the white gear came along. Who was he, KK? A mate of yours?'

Still in shock, Kramer shook his head blankly, still trying to focus through his blood-spattered glasses. 'I . . . don't know who he was. I've never seen him before in my life.'

'Funny sort of a bloke,' said Les.

Crystal stared at them both, then at her blood-spattered clothes and her voice started to rise. 'Don't worry about him,' she shrieked. 'What about that fuckin' dog. Where the fuck did that thing come from?'

Les shook his head. 'Buggered if I know. It just seemed to come out of nowhere.'

'Yeah,' KK was kind of staring into space. 'Out of nowhere.'

Crystal was looking at her clothes like she wasn't game to touch herself. 'That animal. That dog, or whatever it was. Those lumps of meat and flesh going across the room. I've never seen anything like it. It was eating them.' Crystal put a hand over her mouth for a second then glared at Les. 'You're from round this fuckin' way, what kind of fuckin' dog was that?'

Les looked at Crystal yelling at him and shrugged. 'How the fuck would I know what kind of dog it was. It had a mask on.'

241

Crystal moaned and shut her eyes; so did Kramer. They slumped against the seat, still trying to keep their food and drink down as the limo lurched round the corners and in and out of the traffic. Les studied them for a few moments then decided it might be an idea to put plan B into action.

'Listen, KK,' he said urgently. 'I think it might be a good idea if I got to the shithouse out of here.' Kramer looked up while Crystal continued to moan into her hands. 'That fight back there was pretty bad and you can bet your life the cops'll be round. And the one person they'll be wanting to 'ask a few questions' will be me. You being seen with me, you'll be sort of roped in by acquaintance. You know what I mean?'

Kramer gave an expressionless nod; though the mention of the word 'cops' seemed to have struck a bell.

'I don't know whether you want the cops in your hair, KK, but I don't.' Les looked evenly at Kramer. 'I'll stick around if you want me to, I won't just piss off and leave you in the lurch. But I think it might be best if I got on the toe. I'll ring those people at Murwillumbah. I'll get a cab to Tweed Heads and they'll pick me up there. I'll find my way back to Sydney from their joint. I mean, I'm mainly thinking of you, KK. But you don't want to be held up by fuckin' cops and boofhead reporters in the morning. Get one of Black's boys to go up to Brisbane with you tomorrow. In fact I'd stay at his joint tonight if I were you. Me? I think the further I am away from here the better. And if the cops say anything to you, just say you don't know where I am. I pissed off.' Norton shrugged. 'Anyway, it's entirely up to you, KK. But what do you reckon?'

Kramer stared at Norton till the words eventually came out. 'I think that might be a real good idea, Les.'

'Me fuckin' too,' moaned Crystal.

'Okay, then that's settled. I'll piss off.' The limousine lurched on in the traffic, and Les turned his attention to Crystal. 'Jesus, I'll tell you what. You do look crook, Crystal. Are you sure you're all right?'

242

Crystal continued to moan. 'Ohh God, I think I'm going to be sick. Kelvin, when we get back to the apartment, take me for a walk on the beach. Near the water. Wash this blood off me, clear my fucking mind. Christ! Look at me.' Crystal stared in horror at her white top; something stuck on her shoulder caught her eye. 'Oh my God! What's that?' It looked like a hairy leech. 'Aaagghh!' Crystal let out a scream. 'It's an eyebrow. Ohhh get it off me. Aagghh!' Crystal slapped at the eyebrow like it was a cockroach that had just crawled up her arm, till it fell off onto the back floor of the limo.

Norton turned to Kramer. 'That might be a good idea,' he said sagely. 'Take Crystal for a walk along the beach for a few minutes. The sea air'll do her good.' Kramer half nodded a reply.

They arrived back at the flats in a kind of shocked silence. Les got out of the car and held the door open for the others. 'You be needing the limo any more tonight?' Kramer shook his head as he got out. Les caught Tony's eye. The driver didn't need to be told twice; he drove off leaving Norton to help Crystal through the front door then up the stairs to their unit.

'It'll only take me a few minutes to pack my gear,' said Les, digging out his own key as Kramer opened his door while Crystal leant against the wall. 'But I'll see you before I leave.'

'Yeah, whatever you say, Les.' Kramer helped Crystal inside and shut the door.

Inside his own flat, Norton went straight to the bathroom and switched on the light. Shit! Les was a bigger mess than he thought. In all the ruckus and with his adrenalin squirting through him he'd hardly felt anything. But his eyes were bleeding again, as was his nose and he'd copped a couple in the mouth, though it wasn't all that bad. The rest was just bruises round his ribs and lumps on top of his head and someone had given him a decent kick in the kidneys. His denim shirt wasn't worth keeping, except maybe for a souvenir, and there was blood all over his jeans. Les stripped off, threw

243

everything on the floor and cleaned himself up with a towel and some hot water, and was pleased to find that most of the blood wasn't his. He grinned at his reflection in the mirror. Don't know what the fuck I'm going to tell DD this time though? How about a meteorite hit the limo. And all these little green men with laser guns got out and shot it up? These aren't cuts or bruises, they're burns. He wiped some more blood out of his hair. After this afternoon's effort and the flowers, my mate DD'd just about cop anything. But what about bloody Grungle turning up. Despite the gravity of the situation and the thought of whether he could get Murray his earn playing on his mind, Norton had to laugh. As he had surmised earlier, the thought of the cops arriving had put a rocket up Kramer's arse, but the arrival of Grungle on the scene had made things a lot easier. Now he wouldn't have to hang around. He'd just have to move smartly and hope he was right. Les smiled wickedly as he gave his hair one last comb. At least it'll be a while before Jasper and his mates go around kicking the shit out of anybody again. At least until they're all out of hospital. Norton's smile turned into a nasty, spiteful laugh. I'm glad I'm not the one having to do all the stitching. He turned off the light and went into the bedroom.

Les got into the track-suit pants with the piece missing, the blue T-shirt he'd left on the bed and his Nikes; everything else he packed away. Leaving the rest of the lights in the flat off and moving very quietly, Les got the piece of sponge rubber, put it in another plastic bag he had in the kitchen and placed it out on the back sundeck next to the knife, noticing this time there were plenty of lights on next door and raised voices. He came back inside, waited a minute or two while he had a glass of water, then making sure everything he needed was either packed securely or on him, Les decided it was time to leave. He let himself out, closed the door behind him and knocked on Kramer's.

Kramer opened the door and blinked through his glasses, which were now wiped clean of any blood. 'Les . . .'

'Well, I'm off, KK,' said Norton. 'Sorry it had to turn out like this. But, fair dinkum, Kelvin, you want to be careful with some of the people you deal with. Like that bloke said out the front, there's plenty of dropkicks up here. Though I don't think you'll be having any trouble with those blokes for a while. I suppose that's one good thing. Anyway,' Norton offered his hand, 'thanks for everything, KK. I had a great time. Apart from my head,' he added with a laugh. 'So I'll see you back in Sydney or whatever.'

Kramer gave a sickly sort of smile and dropped his hand in Norton's like it was a dead goldfish. 'Yeah, good, Les. I'll, ah . . . see you. Have a nice trip.' Kramer started to close the door.

'Thanks, Kelvin. Oh, ah . . . before you go. Those two tapes I loaned Crystal, you couldn't get them for me, could you?'

'Wait here a minute.'

'And ah . . . while you're there. The rest of that money too, if you could. I have to get my own way back to Sydney now and I'll probably need it.'

Kramer nodded and closed the door and was back in about half a minute. 'There you are, Les.' He handed Norton the two tapes. 'And there's that thousand dollars. We're all square.'

Les took the money and his eyes seemed to brim. 'Jesus, you're a good bloke, Kelvin. I'll see you.'

Kramer nodded almost imperceptibly, the briefest of smiles flickered on his face and he closed the door. Les picked up his bag and walked down to the front door. He didn't open it. He counted to ten then went back up the stairs and knocked on Kramer's door. A few seconds later Kramer opened it. He looked at Norton but didn't say anything.

'Mate,' smiled Les. 'I almost forgot. The keys.' Norton jangled the master keys Kramer had given him in front of Kramer's face and handed them to him. 'See you, KK.' Kramer muttered something and closed the door.

Norton let himself out the front door this time and

245

walked briskly up to the LTD, carefully looking behind and around him. There were people about and cars going past, but Les looked just like any other person with a couple of bags leaving or arriving on the Gold Coast. He dropped his bags in the boot, had another look around as he closed it then walked just as briskly back to the flats.

There were still more people around and more cars going past out the front, but no one saw Les shinny up the wall separating the flats from the units next door, like a commando. And no one saw Les creep up the back stairs in the shadows to his flat and hide against the wall of the sundeck which separated it from the one next door.

Les crouched there for about five minutes. He could hear voices coming from inside. They suddenly got louder, then the back door slid open and Kramer and Crystal came out. Les couldn't see what they had on but he could hear Crystal kind of gagging and gasping and KK didn't sound like he was doing much better. They slid the door closed behind them and still moaning and muttering away, walked down the stairs to the beach. Norton gave it another minute or two, peeked over the balcony to make sure they were out of sight, then with the knife in one hand and the plastic bag containing the sponge rubber in the other, stepped over onto Kramer's sundeck.

The door had a weak latch on it just like the one on Norton's and Les was able to jemmy it open with the knife, without hardly leaving a scratch, in a few seconds. The light in the main bedroom was on and as Les had expected Kramer's unit was the same as his only in reverse. The stereo and TV were bigger, the white carpet thicker and the furniture more plush; but the same set-up.

Tiptoeing down the hallway to the two bedrooms Norton could see they had the same idea as him also; sleep in the main bedroom and throw all your junk in the other one. Les decided to check the main bedroom out first. KK's blood-spattered white shoes and clothes were strewn on the floor and a half-packed suitcase was lying on the double bed which Les recognised as the same one

246

he'd picked up for Kramer at Coolangatta airport. Norton tapped the knife against his side for a moment. No, I got a feeling what I'm looking for isn't in here. Quietly he tiptoed into the smaller bedroom.

It was in darkness, but there was enough light reflecting off the hallway to see well enough and Norton's eyes were all right in the dark at any time. The first thing he noticed was Crystal's bloodied clothes laying on the floor and her bra sitting on the end of the bed next to a pair of pink knickers. Les gave the knickers a bit of a nudge with the knife, put it on the bed with the plastic bag and had a good look at her bra. Oh grand-ma-ma. Les laughed to himself. What a big pair of tits you have. All the better to ... Norton laughed to himself again.

He put the bra back exactly as he found it. Isn't this lovely, Les thought to himself as he stood in the darkness? Going through a woman's underwear behind her back. I always knew I was some sort of a perv. Next thing it'll be breather calls on the phone, a dirty raincoat and hanging around schools and toilets. Dear oh dear. What's a man coming to? But I think what this dirty old man is looking for is in one of those two nice brown alligator-skin suitcases. And why wouldn't they be alligator skin? Ain't that all there is where yo' all come from, Crystal, honey? Gators, gumbo and grits.

The first and larger suitcase contained mainly clothes: jeans, jackets, shoes, knitted tops, the bulky top Crystal wore when she arrived at Eagle Farm. Norton ran his hands round and through the bag, making sure he didn't disturb anything, before finally shaking his head. The other, smaller suitcase contained stockings, socks, T-shirts and other odds and ends plus the rest of Crystal's underwear, which ranged in colour and pattern from black with a big, purple and red heart across the front to a bright red pair with little blue alligators all over them and white lace. Norton went through the suitcase very carefully, then his face lit up. What he was looking for was tucked against the side at one end. Even more carefully, Les eased it out and placed it on the bed. A squeeze here, a squeeze there, then a huge grin spread across Norton's face. Yeah. Just like I thought, and just like that ad on TV. Who was that artist? Reubens? Rembrandt? He wouldn't have known at the time. Well, I wasn't too sure myself. But I am now. Les had another bit of a squeeze around. Though I was wrong in the garage, he thought, KK didn't stitch things up all that much at all. Maybe just a little bit. But not to worry. Les got the piece of sponge rubber from the plastic bag, fiddled around a bit, then put what he was looking for in the plastic bag along with the knife and folded everything back up and rearranged it all in the suitcase exactly as he'd found it.

More than satisfied with himself and not sure whether he could hear voices coming in the backyard, Norton had a quick look around to make sure the coast was clear and left by the front door. He walked quickly down the stairs, opened the front door of the flats a crack and peered out; no one around. Norton was up the street and sitting in the front seat of the LTD in about half a minute, the plastic bag on the seat alongside him, the knife on the front floor.

Well, have I done it or what? Les gave the plastic bag a squeeze, then he grinned. I think I just might have. And I think I've got that loving, good-looking brother of mine his earn too. Les winked out the window up towards the night sky. Thanks, mate. Another half a minute later Norton was on the highway heading towards the boarding house.

There was a dust-covered Holden utility out the front that had to be Murray's. Les pulled up just behind it and with the plastic bag in his hand, trotted up the front steps. The front door was open, Les tapped lightly on the fly-screen. The light was on in the hallway and to the left was another soft light plus the glow and sound of a TV set.

'Come on in,' came a woman's voice.

Norton scuffed his feet on the door-mat and stepped inside, sliding the fly-screen door behind him. Mrs Llivac was sitting back on the lounge watching some old movie on TV, wearing one of those knee length T-shirts in white

248

with Mickey Mouse on the front; and an ample amount of good things were poking out the front of the T-shirt, bending Mickey all over the place. Mrs Llivac had a look of dreamy contentment on her face and a box of Darrel Lea chocolates on the end of the lounge. She also had this healthy glow pulsing from her cheeks like she might have been to an aerobics class or been out in the sun earlier.

Les looked at her and was about to say something when he stopped short and gave a couple of double-blinks. It wasn't Mrs Llivac's buxom, healthy appearance that surprised Les. Lying just at Mrs Llivac's feet, still wearing his rubber mask, was Grungle. And lying up against Grungle was this old grey cat with black stripes and green eyes. Both were asleep but looked up briefly, stretched and yawned then went back to sleep, though Grungle gave his tail a wag and seemed to keep one sleepy eye on Les.

'How are you, Mr Menzies?' asked Llivac.

'Huh?' Norton felt like he'd just been woken from a dream. 'I'm... real good thanks, Mrs Llivac. How are you?'

'Fine. Just fine. Mr Thomas said you'd be calling around. He's expecting you.'

'Yeah. I rang earlier.' Les continued to stare at Mrs Llivac and Grungle lying at her feet.

Mrs Llivac went back to the TV, next thing she screwed her face up and gave Grungle a bit of a kick in the ribs. 'Oh Blackie, no. Not again.' Grungle half moved his head as Mrs Llivac started waving her hand in front of her face. 'Lord have mercy.'

Norton stared at Grungle, then caught Mrs Llivac looking up at him. 'Blackie...?'

'Yes, Mr Thomas's dog. Oh, but he's a lovely old thing though, aren't you, Blackie?' Mrs Llivac patted Grungle on the head as if to make up for kicking him. 'But some times...'

Les continued to stare. 'He seems to get on all right with the cat,' was all he could think to say.

'Oliver? Oh he and Ollie get on just fine. Ollie's a big

249

softie, just like me. Aren't you, Ollie?' Mrs Llivac patted the cat, as if to square up for patting Grungle. 'Mr Thomas had Blackie in the back of his pick-up, and he told me how he'd been bitten by a snake and he was sick. I mean, what could you do? I couldn't let him sleep outside in the cold, with all that noise and the fumes from the traffic. So I said, oh let him stay inside, poor thing. And he's such a lovely old thing too. Aren't you, Blackie?' Mrs Llivac patted Grungle again.

'Yeah. He's a good bloke all right. Aren't you... Blackie?' Norton grinned then crouched down and gave Grungle a good pat on the stomach. Grungle rolled over on his back and wriggled his massive shoulders around exposing a huge pair of black nuts. 'Yeah, he's all right,' said Les sincerely. 'Don't worry about him.'

'It's just that every now and again, Mr Menzies, he lets one go. I swear it would strip the husks from a field of Idaho corn.'

Norton burst out laughing. Luckily his nose was that swollen and clogged with blood he couldn't smell a thing. 'Well, in that case, I don't think I'd better rub his stomach any more. He might rip another one off.'

Mrs Llivac rolled her eyes at Les and shook her head. Les stood up thinking it might be time to get down to business.

'So which is Mr Thomas's room?'

'Second on your right. He only got in a little while ago. He had to do some work on his car.'

'I'll go in and see him then. I won't be all that long.'

Les gave Mrs Llivac a smile and got one back. He looked at Grungle now totally relaxed, half shook his head then walked down the hallway and knocked softly on Murray's door.

'Yeah. Come in.'

Murray's room had a single bed, a wardrobe and dressing table and was spotlessly clean. There was a writing desk and a small sofa at one end, a bathroom and toilet ran off to the right. Murray's blood-spattered white gear was in the bathroom and a familiar pair of blue overalls hung on the door of the wardrobe. Murray was sprawled along the bed in a pair of white boxers and a clean white singlet, very casually sipping a bottle of beer. Apart from a bit of a fat lip, a small mouse under each eye and a bit of bark missing here and there he looked all right.

'So how are you feeling?' said Les, closing the door behind him.

'Not bad,' shrugged Murray. 'Laddered a stocking, lost an earring. But apart from that I'm all right. What about yourself?'

Les shrugged back. 'Absolutely ruined my hair, but other than that I brushed up okay. You got a beer in the fridge?' Without waiting for an answer Les went to the small bar fridge next to the TV. 'Hello, Eumundi.'

'Yeah. It's not a bad drop. I like the long neck. I can shove a slice of zucchini in it, or whatever it is you and all your poof mates in Sydney like to stick in your beer.'

'Hey, don't talk to me about poofs. What about you in your all-white gear? You looked like Sydney Greenstreet in Casablanca. Where the fuck did you get that outfit?' Les sat down on the sofa, put the plastic bag next to him and had a long slurp of beer.

'I dunno,' replied Murray, 'I thought I looked pretty good myself.'

'For a while there I didn't think you'd turned up. I was starting to shit myself.'

'But I did, didn't I?' grinned Murray.

'Yeah, you sure fuckin' did all right,' acknowledged Les.

There was a deafening silence between them for a moment or two, then Les banged his bottle of beer on the floor, leapt off the sofa and grabbed his brother in a bit more than a brotherly hug. Murray put a headlock on Les, then they both started shaking and bashing the shit out of each other. Laughing uproariously and giving out with plenty of those Queensland yee-hahs and hoo-ees while they slapped each other silly. Finally Murray shoved Les off the bed and Norton fell back on the sofa, tears of laughter trickling from the sides of his eyes. His brother was in much the same condition.

251

'Well, did we flog those cunts or what, Les?' said Murray, picking up his bottle of beer and sitting on the edge of the bed.

'Flog them? Jesus Christ! Captain Bligh couldn't have flogged them any more than that.' Les reached over and clinked his brother's bottle with his. 'I've been in a few stinks but that was a ripper. I never seen so much blood. Best part about it, bugger all of it was mine.' Les threw back his head and roared again.

'Those poor mugs. They didn't know what hit them.'

'Hey, I'll tell you something though. Even though I snotted those two mugs first up, they were no slouches. It wasn't all peaches and cream. And when those two big bouncers lobbed, I thought, hello, we're in a bit of strife here.'

'Yeah. I was getting a bit worried myself,' Murray winked as he grinned at his brother.

'The next thing Grungle comes in through the window.' Les roared again. 'I don't know who got the biggest shock. Me or the mugs.'

'Didn't take the old bloke long to sort out whose side he was on, did it?'

'No, it sure didn't.' Les had another slurp of beer. 'So what's the story there, Muzz? How come he lobbed? And what's he doing out the front with the landlady? And what's this Blackie business?'

'Well,' Murray sprawled back along the bed, 'I didn't really feel like leaving him at home and giving Elaine another chance to poison him with her cuisine. And knowing what a dill you can be at times, I decided it might be an idea to bring him along.'

Les gave bit of a self-conscious shrug and looked down the neck of his beer. 'Yeah. I have been known to get things wrong now and again.'

'Ohh when fuckin' don't you, you big goose?' Murray gave a bit of a chuckle and continued. 'Anyway, I got here about nine this morning. Settled in and all that. Went up and checked that joint out, bought that clobber so I'd blend in with the natives. Hey, and don't knock the

252

clobber. I was doing all right with a couple of school-teachers from Adelaide at the bar till you fucked things up for me.'

'Sorry about that, Boz Norton.'

'Anyway, the... ah landlady's a bit of a friendly old bird. And when she saw Grungle with that rubber mask round his eyes and when I told her he'd been bitten by a taipan, she said to let him stay inside. I'd just as soon leave him in the ute in case some cunt tries to knock it off. And when she asked me his name, I didn't feel like saying Grungle. So I told her 'Blackie'. I'm incognito, so I thought I'd do the same for the old bloke.' Murray grinned. 'It's not a bad name for a dog. Suits him.'

Les shook his head. 'No way, Muzz. He's fuckin' Grungle.'

'Call him what you like,' winked Murray, 'but don't call him late at meal times. I forgot to feed him this arvo too.'

'Yeah. I noticed that in the Boulevarde.' Les shook his head and laughed. 'Fair dinkum, Muzz, what's going to happen when those mugs arrive at the hospital? And how are they going to explain all that to the cops when they lob on the scene?'

Murray shrugged. 'Fucked if I know. Fucked if I care either for that matter. It wasn't my dog.'

'Yeah. How would they recognise it anyway. That's what I said to that silly fuckin' Yank sheila.' Les told his brother about the trip back to the flats in the limo, with KK and Crystal all covered in blood and Crystal finding the eyebrow on her jacket. 'Fair dinkum, Muzz, you should've seen them. They looked whiter than you did in your Boz Scaggs outfit. He's got her down the beach now spewing her heart up. And fuckin' good enough too. Smart-arse bitch.'

Murray was laughing and shaking his head at the same time. 'What about that bouncer Grungle jumped up and grabbed on the moosh. I saw him on the floor as we were leaving, and his face looked like Freddie Kruger's.'

'That's probably whose eyebrow it was.'

The boys laughed and sipped their beer, then the conversation died away a little. Les sat there looking at his brother who'd driven all that way to back him up without question and in doing so had saved Les's neck. Certainly Les had jumped in and helped Murray against the terrorists. But that was just a slaughter and Les was there, he would have done it anyway. There was something different about what Murray had done for Les and now it was time to repay the favour.

'So Muzz, loving brother of mine and head of the family during my absence. Earlier in the piece I mentioned something about there might be a bit of an earn in this for you.'

Murray nodded sagely. 'Yes, you did say something, now that I come to think of it.'

'Well, Muzz,' Les had a grin from ear to ear, 'here it is, mate.' Les threw the plastic bag onto the bed.

Murray opened it and pulled out a piece of sponge rubber much like the one Les had been shaping in the flat only a lot neater. Murray looked at it, squeezed it, then looked at his brother. 'What is it?' he said, screwing up his face. 'It looks like a tit.'

'That's pretty much what it is, Muzz. A tit.'

Murray gave it another squeeze. 'Well, what the fuck do you want me to do with it?'

'You can play with it, put a love bite on it, take it to bed and tit fuck it if you like. But let me tell you the whole story. Then I think you'll know what to do with it.'

'I can't fuckin' wait.' Murray looked at the piece of sponge rubber with disdain. Les was about to speak when there was a knock on the door. 'Yeah, hello,' called Murray.

The door opened and there stood Mrs Llivac, all smiles. 'Oh I'm sorry to disturb you but I've just brewed some fresh coffee and I was wondering if you and your friend would like some, Aubery. And a piece of my pie. I'm sure Aubery would like some more of my deep-dish apple pie, wouldn't you?'

'Yeah, righto, Kay,' answered Murray. 'I'll be in that.'

'What about you, Mr Menzies? Would you like some coffee and pie?'

'Ahh ... I don't know, Mrs Llivac,' replied Les. 'I have to get going soon.'

'Well, I'll put a little extra on the tray in case you change your mind.'

Mrs Llivac left, giving Les a smile and Murray a look that almost scorched the pillows behind his head. Les stared for a moment at his brother, who was still nonchalantly sipping his beer but who also seemed to go very quiet all of a sudden.

'Aubery eh?' said Les. 'Would you like some coffee, Aubery. And some of my deep-dish apple pie, Aubery. Not bad room-service for this time of night. The dog's sitting out in front of the TV farting its head off. She's sitting there with a box of chocolates, her eyes spinning round in her head like two bubbles in a piss-pot. And the look that old auntie gave you when she left, it's a wonder the bed didn't catch on fire. What the fuck's going on between you and the landlady, Muzz? Or is it Kay?'

Murray gave a bit of a shrug and sipped his beer. 'It's short for Kalita. Means 'sweetheart' in Arabic.'

'And?'

Murray stared back at Les. 'Oh all right, Dick Tracy. You needn't worry about the landlady's deep-dish apple pie. I've been givin' her deep-dish Queensland pork sword since about an hour after I got here. And on the hour ever since.'

'You dirty low bludger.'

'Hey. Don't worry about the fourth of July. That old seppo goes off like that bomb we fired off last night. Only a bit louder.'

'What about your wife and kids, you low dropkick?' demanded Les, although it was all he could do to keep a straight face.

'Well, what's a man supposed to fuckin' do?' said Murray. 'I get in here this morning full of speed. And it's all smiles and "Oh hello Mr Thomas. I was expecting you. And I do so love your outback accent. It's just so cute."

And I said to her, "Don't worry about my accent, gorgeous. You talk sweeter than whitebox honey yourself. In fact, Mrs Llivac," I said, "your voice is the rain that'd break the drought and make the flowers bloom in the garden of my heart." She said call me Kalita. I said call me Aubery.'

'You're suave, Muzz. I gotta give it to you.'

'Anyway, about an hour or so later, I've got cleaned up and I'm sortin' things out and she comes in on the pretext of changing a light-bulb. I give her a hand and while she's up on the chair, somehow my hand slipped up her dress.'

'Right on her old deep-dish apple pie, Muzz.'

'Don't worry about her apple pie,' winked Murray. 'The crust was firm, it smelled all right, and it was that hot I reckon she just got it out of the oven. So rather than let it cool off, I slipped her one. And I've been slippin' her one ever since. In fact the only times I managed to get away was to buy the white clobber and leave Grungle in the ute outside that bar. Where, I might add,' said Murray pointing his now empty beer bottle at Les, 'I got a bluey for parking. I didn't see any of those meter-maids come round and fix it up for me either.'

'Oh, I think I might be able to cover that for you, Muzz,' Les gave his brother a dry smile.

'So that's the story anyway, Les. Say what you want, but I dropped a heap of Green Arrows I got off a truckie and they sent me old boy into a frenzy.' Murray scratched vigorously at his balls. 'I'm still speedin'.'

Les shook his head, still trying to keep a straight face. 'Fair dinkum, Muzz, you disgust me. Illegal drugs. Extra-marital sex. You're good.'

'Elaine's sweet. I rang her earlier. All the family's still out St George, I told them I was down here with you, giving you a hand and it might take a bit longer than I thought.'

'Yeah, I'm sure it will.' Les wiggled his eyebrows at Murray. 'Won't it, Aubery?'

Murray gave a bit of a shrug. 'So what's with this tit anyway?' he said, picking up the piece of sponge rubber. 'What am I supposed to do with the fuckin' thing?'

Les was about to speak when there was another knock on the door. Mrs Llivac walked in carrying a tray with a plunger of coffee, cream, sugar and several slices of apple pie. She smiled pleasantly at Les, scorched another one at Murray and placed the tray on the dressing table.

'If there's anything else you want, Aubery,' she breathed, 'just call.'

'Oh I will, Kalita,' smiled Murray. 'Don't you worry about that.'

The landlady smiled at Les again and closed the door behind her. Les smiled at his brother. 'Just call, eh. Yeah righto, Kalita, my little artichoke heart, I'll do that.'

'Leave me alone, will you.'

The coffee smelled good, bloody good. So did the apple pie. Les was now glad Mrs Llivac had brought an extra cup. He and Murray poured themselves a cup each, got a piece of pie and settled back.

'Righto, Les. Now where was I?' said Murray, making himself comfortable on the bed. 'You told me a few things going out on the SPATV about the Yank sheila rippin' off the casino and this other one you're porkin' just up the road. But what's the story on this tit. And where's my earn come in?'

'Okay, Muzz, you want the whole John Dory, do you. Well, here it is.' Les settled back on the sofa and looked at his brother over the top of his cup of coffee. 'Murray, this whole thing has been one giant con since the minute I left Bondi. In fact since the minute I met that shifty little KK. I'm supposed to be minding him and Crystal Linx while she's out here promoting this record and doing all these publicity shots, and topless and all that. Yet when I get here, the swimming pool in the flats is drained. Now it's funny how things stick in your mind. I have to admit I was a bit disappointed because I fancied sitting around the pool on my arse while I was here. But I just thought it a bit strange, because if you're going to do all these topless shots, in the backyard next to the pool would be the simplest and easiest place to do them with, no mugs around getting in the road. Plus I also got to admit, I wouldn't have minded having a look at those big boobs myself.'

'Yeah, I wouldn't blame you,' agreed Murray. 'Bob Telfer's got them all over his garage. They're rippers.'

'Then there's these blokes call round in a van with 'Mermaid Pool Service' on the side who know Kramer. Now they could fix the pool in five minutes. On top of this, Crystal never goes down the beach, never wears anything too revealing and gets around almost looking like one of those Muslim sheilas. In fact, you'd have more chance getting a look at the Queen Mother's ted than you would at Crystal's set. Then for a sheila that's supposed to be out here drumming up publicity with the media, all she does is abuse them. She's the most foul-mouthed tart I ever come across. The press hated her from the word go and wouldn't piss on her if she was on fire, let alone give her any decent publicity. I ended up belting a couple of journos one night trying to get pictures of KK drunk and spewing out the side of the car. I almost wish I had now. But for someone who's trying to promote a record, it just seemed a pretty weird way to go about it. It was almost like she was avoiding the press. In fact KK told me that if any reporters came around I was to tell them to piss off. The whole thing just didn't seem... kosher, I suppose you could say.'

'Yeah, it does a bit,' nodded Murray.

'Now, in amongst all this rattle arrives this South African rooster called Meyer Black and his two gun-toting heavies — who it turns out aren't a couple of bad blokes. Black's supposed to run the record company in Brisbane that Crystal's putting out her record through. Yeah bullshit! I ring up Price, and Black's in charge of a record company about as much as old Darcy Dugan was in charge of the Commonwealth Bank. He's a smuggler and an arms dealer amongst other things. And him and KK are as thick as pig shit; they're always pissing off together and they go out on his boat. Very pally.

One day early in the piece, one of Black's heavies comes round in that pool van with an overnight-bag and leaves

258

about ten minutes later. And he definitely didn't put a drop of water in the pool. So I'm just about positive KK's up to something. Yet on the other hand, why would you put something on in the middle of all this media bullshit and lairising around Surfers? You'd think that'd be the last thing you'd want? Mind you, Muzz, while all this is going on, I'm just acting the big, dumb minder. Not saying a word to no one, just doing what I'm paid for. But the whole thing didn't make sense.'

'Yeah, it's a funny one all right,' agreed Murray. 'Hey, what about the landlady's apple pie? It makes sense, don't it?'

'Yeah, you're not wrong,' said Les. 'If her hair pie's half as good as this, Muzz, you're on a good thing.' Les reached across for another slice of pie and continued.

'Okay. So I meet DD, it's out on the run with KK and I watch Crystal fleece the casino. And Muzz, it was one of the best things I ever seen. So between that and talking to her earlier I figure Crystal might be a dropkick. But she's got a heap of balls. I'm trying to fathom this out when KK's mates gave me that serve. So it's out to get brother Murray for a square up. Hah! Wasn't that a good move?'

'Get out. You loved it. When was the last time you saw an atom bomb go off?'

'Yeah, terrific, Muzz. When I get back to Sydney the CIA'll probably be knocking on my door. Anyway, while I'm in town, I take your advice and have a feed at the Spanish restaurant. And what do I find? This.' Les pulled the double page from the Spanish magazine he'd found out of the back pocket of his track-suit pants and handed it to Murray. 'Check that out, Muzz. Crystal Linx in all her glory. And that magazine's about three weeks old.'

Murray unfolded the two pages, spread them out on the bed and grimaced. 'Bloody hell! Compared to the ones in the little photo they look like a couple of Tai-Chi slippers.'

'Yeah. Harry the barber could strop his razor on them. Now, Muzz, they're definitely not the two giant gazonkas I've been perving on all over Surfers since she got here.

259

And when she arrived, some journo in Brisbane yelled something out to her about whether she'd been in a clinic in Europe, having a go at her. They're photos of the lovely one, drying out or whatever in a health spa, probably in Spain or the South of France. Some paparazzo snuck them off and flogged them to that magazine.' Murray stared at the photos and slowly shook his head. 'Now either she's changed her pill or taken enough anabolic steroids to arm wrestle Hulk Hogan to get into shape like that — or something else.'

'Yeah, you're right,' nodded Murray. 'There wouldn't be enough silicone on Ninety Mile Beach to get them back together again.'

'So I'm mulling all this over in my head driving back from Dirranbandi. And when I arrive half knackered — and probably suffering from radioactive poisoning' — Les gave his brother a thin smile — 'I blunder into the wrong garage, and what do I find? A big lump of sponge rubber, just like that on the bed, and tubes of Super glue. Now, Murray, you don't have to be Albert Einstein to figure out what's going on.' Les looked directly at his brother. 'Kramer's got Crystal to come into Australia as a mule.'

'A mule?' Murray looked at Les. 'I'm still trying to work out what a fuckin' paparazzo is. I think we had a feed of them in Goondiwindi one night.'

'They've done a run, Muzz. Crystal's smuggled a great swag of dope in, in a pair of false tits. It all falls into place. Flying out of New York in the middle of winter all rugged up. Abusing the press the minute she gets off the plane. Kramer drumming me all the time to make sure no one goes near her tits. All the lairising and running around. It was just a big smother. With boofhead Les caught up in the middle. Though I gotta give it to the little bludger — and her — they were bloody good.'

'Yeah,' Murray looked at the piece of sponge rubber. 'If what you say is true, they've sure got some front. What do you reckon it was?'

'I'd say coke. I was watching them when we were going

260

out of a night and they were pretty erratic. For a little bloke KK was putting away heaps of piss. And the night Crystal brassed the casino, she was ripped to the tits. So I'd say it'd be the old okefenoke.'

Murray had another look at the sponge rubber. 'How much do you reckon she's brought in?'

Les shrugged. 'Going by what her tits looked like before they hit droop city, I'd say about half a ton. No, I'd reckon at least a kilo, possibly two.'

'Shit!'

'Okay, like I said, you don't have to be a genius to work out what their scam was. But what about the earn, Muzz. The old switcheroo. Where were the chops? And the whole time KK wasn't exactly flush with cash. He had plenty, but he wasn't pulling out great stacks of it. In fact he had to snip Crystal after they left the casino. So I get to thinking about KK's South African mate Meyer Black again. Now what do they have in South Africa, Muzz?'

Murray gave a bit of shrug. 'Fucked if I know. Zebras? Winnie Mandela? Those gold things — Klingons?'

'No, they're the cunts always trying to kill captain Kirk and nick the *Enterprise*. You're thinking of krugerrands. But something else too Muzz. You got a knife?'

'Yeah, in my overalls.' Murray got up off the bed and took a fold-up knife from a pocket in the overalls hanging on the wardrobe. 'I got changed after the stink. I told my girlfriend out the front I had to do some work on the car.' Murray sat back on the bed and opened his knife.

'Now feel around that false tit and you should find a thin, hard line, just up near the back. And unlike that ad on TV, it ain't a breast tumour.'

Murray felt around the sponge rubber a lot more carefully now. 'Hey, there is a kind of hard piece.'

'Right. Now cut underneath that, Muzz. But very slowly.' Les sipped his coffee as he watched Murray deftly cutting into the sponge rubber.

'Hey, you're right,' said Murray enthusiastically. 'There is something in here.' Murray made a couple more cuts then slipped his fingers into the hole and pulled out a

261

small envelope of folded blue velvet tied with a thin white cord. 'Well, I'll be...'

'Put it on the bed and open it up, Muzz. Carefully now.'

Murray did what Les told him. He undid the white cord, opened the blue velvet and six brilliant white stones, about the size of cherry pips, glittered almost magically in the light. The sheer beauty of them captivated both brothers for a moment or two. 'Well, I'll be...'

Les put down his coffee. 'Yeah, Muzz. Diamonds. That was the bloody scam. Kramer brings in the coke through Crystal. She's game enough, her modelling days are over and she couldn't carry a note if she piggy-backed it on her shoulders. She needs the dough. They swap the coke with Black for diamonds. She takes them back to New York. There's a heap of Jew diamond merchants in New York. Kramer, the good Jewish boy, joins her. They'd move them over there quicker than you can say gefilte fish. And in American dollars.'

Murray stared at the diamonds and shook his head. 'Well, I'll be stuffed. But. I mean... how...?'

'Murray, you got to remember this was all a big guess. A punt. But I figured with this smuggling rort he's going to have three pairs of falsies. One to bring the coke in with, which he'd get rid off. Another pair he's made for her to get around in and for me to make sure no one puts their hands on. And if it was diamonds, another pair to take them out in, all rigged up and ready to go. Either he or Black made them up out here; they might've figured on doing a couple more runs. But whoever it was, they left all that junk lying around the garage. So I got a piece of that sponge rubber, made a false tit and swapped it over while they were out of the flat. I guess you could say, Murray, I guessed right.'

'So what's Crystal taking back to America? Just a lump of sponge rubber?'

'Ohh yeah. And that's not all.' Les pulled the leg of his tracksuit around and showed Murray where he'd cut the piece out. 'That, with a few bits of broken Coke bottle rolled up in it. A different sort of coke, I suppose you

262

could say, Muzz.' Les grinned at his brother. 'See how they go trying to flog that back in the Big Apple.'

Murray threw back his head, slapped his leg and roared, almost knocking the diamonds. He settled down and stared at Les. 'But they're gonna have to know it was you?'

'No.' Les shook his head emphatically. 'I'm just the poor dumb minder, remember. Crystal's convinced I've got an empty biscuit tin for a head. And Kramer thinks I couldn't pick my nose and read a newspaper at the same time.'

Les told his brother about how he washed the car, admitted it was his own fault he got his head punched in, never complained once, even took them out for a drink to show his appreciation. And when he left, stopped to say goodbye and pick up his tapes, plus his wages. Then come back with the keys. Anybody that had just nicked a swag of diamonds wouldn't be sticking around and worrying about a thousand dollars. 'Okay, they might have smelled a bit of rat in the Boulevarde. But those blokes did come over. I'd already copped one hiding. I decided to get the first one in. Big deal. Kramer might think I'm a dill, but he knows me and Billy don't stand out the front of the Kelly Club selling ice creams. The bloke in the white gear with the dog? How many nutters are there around this joint, coming and going. I don't know that the cops would be all that interested in that team of dropkicks getting a good serve either. They'd probably be laughing. In the meantime, poor Les, all battered and bruised once again, has left town to wend his own way home, still trying to do the right thing. It's kind of sad, really.'

Les watched his brother still slowly shaking his head, still looking at the diamonds. 'Ahh fuck 'em anyway. You've got yourself a nice little stack of diamonds, Muzz. Put that towards those SPATVS and you and Elaine and my nephews can all live happily ever after.'

Murray looked up at Les. 'Christ! How much do you reckon they're worth?'

Les shrugged. 'I dunno. But I have a drink with these cops in a bar in Sydney every now and again. One of them

263

comes from up the Central Coast. He's in the Major Crime Squad. These mates of his up there knocked off some cocaine cowboys at Long Jetty. He was showing us the photo on the front page of the local rag. They got just over an alleged couple of k's with an alleged street value of half a million.' Les nodded to the diamonds that seemed to sparkle more beautifully than ever against the blue velvet. 'I don't know how much dope she's brought in, Muzz, but looking at those alleged diamonds there, I'd say we're looking at — bottom line — an alleged quarter of a million.' Les winked and smiled at his brother. 'You think that might cover your parking fine?'

Murray whistled softly. 'Reckon. Stone the bloody crows, Les! You're not bad.'

'I get by,' agreed Les. 'I mightn't be able to work a computer, but I can sniff out a rort. And it doesn't take us Nortons long to work out when some prick's conning us. Not too long, anyway.'

'You're right there. So what's the story? How many can I have?'

Les shook his head when his brother looked at him. 'You take the lot, Muzz. I don't need anything. I'm sweet. But if I were you, I'd sit on them for a while. Say six months. Just to be on the safe side. Then I'll see Price about moving them. Or you might know someone in Brisbane. What ever you reckon.'

'No. I'll sit on them. I won't tell no cunt.' Murray grinned at his brother. 'Except maybe Grungle. And I know he won't say much. Then it might be a nice surprise for the family around Christmas. Won't the boys hate a nice big swimming pool in the backyard. Might even shout Eel's a bottle of perfume and a new iron. God bless her scrawny arse.'

'Come on, tell the truth now, Muzz. You've always loved that woman. You didn't steal her off Cement Head Bailey, then have to fight him three times, just for her cooking.'

Les watched his brother carefully fold the diamonds back up in their velvet envelope, carefully tie them up

264

with the cord and just as carefully place them in the pocket of his moleskin Dryza-Bone Brumby jacket hanging in the wardrobe. Suddenly there were a lot of things Les wanted to say to Murray over more than just a cup of coffee. It had been a while. But deep inside him, Les got this feeling that shortly they'd be saying goodbye again; for who knows how long? Les got another feeling that this time it shouldn't be too long.

Murray sat back down on the bed and looked at Les. His brother's thoughts were reflected in his eyes. 'So what's doing about our drink, Les?' asked Murray.

'That's entirely up to you, Muzz. What do you want to do?'

'Well, to tell you the truth, Les, I might piss off back home.'

Les nodded slowly. 'I thought you were going to say that.'

'Not just yet.' Murray gave his balls another scratch. 'I might slip the landlay another length or two. Those pills are still running around in my brain. Then I'll grab Grungle, we'll fold up our swags and disappear into the dawn. I should be home around lunchtime. Just when the gang gets back from St George.'

'Good idea, Muzz,' agreed Les. 'I don't think there's much point in hanging around here.'

'What about yourself, Les? What are you doing?'

'Well, I've met someone pretty special myself. And I'm driving her home to Taree.' Les gave his brother a wink. 'I've got plenty of dough and I don't care if it takes me two weeks to get there.'

'Half your luck, mate.'

'So I s'pose I'd better get going.' Les got to his feet. 'Don't want to keep her waiting.'

'No. If she's half as good as you say she is, I wouldn't.'

Murray looked up at his brother for a moment, then leapt off the bed and grabbed him in a bear hug, lifting Les up off the floor. 'Fair dinkum, you big ugly goose, what am I gonna do with you?'

'I don't know, Muzz.' Les grimaced and managed to

265

laugh as he held his brother's shoulders. 'But take it easy there, mate. I copped a few round the ribs tonight.'

Murray put Les down, then the two brothers gripped each other's hands. It wasn't so much a handshake, it was a bond. A bond of friendship and love, between two men who would put their lives and safety on the line for each other, no questions asked. And for the rest of the family as well. And now it was time to go their separate ways once more. Both brothers stepped back and looked at each other, each searching for the right words to say.

Finally Murray spoke. 'Well,' he said, smiling at his brother, 'I suppose it's been a bit of a funny one, you could say.'

'Yeah,' agreed Les. 'It sure has. But it all worked out all right.'

'Yeah,' nodded Murray. 'It could've turned out a lot worse. That thing could have landed on Chinchilla. Sure would've stuffed up their chances in this year's grand final.'

'Yeah. You're not wrong there, Muzz.'

Murray and Les stood back looking at each other. What could they add to that? It had been a bit of a funny one. Could've been a lot worse. But it worked out all right. They'd shot six men. Let off an atomic bomb. Almost killed another ten men. Then ripped off a fortune in diamonds. A bit of a funny one, but the weird, crazy, almost insane part about it was if Les and Murray hadn't intercepted those six terrorists, and they'd shot down the President and the Prime Minister, the whole course of world events would have changed. The Americans would have retaliated, possibly with a nuclear strike of their own. Australia would have had to join in. A third world war could have started in the Middle East. Who knows what would have happened and how many people would have died? Two Australian brothers, just country boys from Queensland, sticking up for each other, had indirectly changed the history of the world. Now they were off to see their women and carry on as if not much had happened, then catch up for a beer one day and talk about it as 'a bit of a funny one, but it worked out all right'. They talk about easy-going Australians, having a bit of a joke now and again and taking everything in their stride. There wouldn't be enough l's in laconic to describe Les and Murray Norton.

'Before you go though, Les,' said Murray, giving his brother a wink, 'there is something I would like to say.'

'Yeah, what?'

'When it's all boiled down, we are a couple of low dropkicks.'

Les stroked his chin. 'How do you work that out?'

'Well, apart from that rattle back home, the bottom line is I'm rooting some sheila behind my wife's back and you've ripped off some bloke who's done the right thing, given you a holiday and a chance for a bit of an earn, taken you out for all those grouse feeds, even his girl slung you a few extra dollars. Nice way to repay the favour.' Murray shook his head. 'So you can say what you like about me but you're not too bad yourself.'

'Hah! Hah! That's something I might like to bring up before I do bloody go. Done me a favour eh?' Les's eyes narrowed. 'Done me a favour. Say that thing had gone wrong, Muzz, and Crystal had got nicked along with Kramer. They'd be that worried about saving their own fuckin' skins they'd've wiped me like a dirty arse. I'm up here as a minder eh? Accomplice'd be more like it. I've got form back in Sydney — not counting the team I run with. I'm sure the Drug Squad, or who ever, would say, "Yes, we believe your story, Les, but we'd just like to ask you a few more questions. No, sorry, but we can't see you getting bail at the moment." I might've got bail. And I might've beat it. But it'd cost me an arm and leg in legal fees. And the stigma sticks. Ohh yeah. Les Norton. Always keen for a dollar. Involved in a major dope bust. Of course he had nothing to do with it. Nudge, nudge, wink, wink. But what say I got charged and I didn't beat it. What say a jury said, ohh yeah, bullshit! A nice ten years, all for that little dropkick. It could've happened, Muzz.'

Murray had to agree. 'Yes,' he said, nodding slowly, 'that is another way of looking at it. I hadn't thought of that.'

'But Murray, that's not the thing that shits me.' Les's eyes narrowed even more. 'That's not what burns my arse. That's not the thing that hurts — apart from all the abuse. Remember how I told you about Kramer telling me to lay off the white shoe gags when I was up here. His friends don't appreciate them. Knock up on the white shoe gags, Rodney Rude. And all that.' Murray nodded. 'And me, like a big mug, said, Ohh yeah, righto, Kelvin, and kept my mouth shut. And he's stepping out in his white St Louies all the time. And I'm breaking my neck to say something. But no, I cop it sweet.'

Les pointed an angry finger at the two pages from the Spanish magazine laying on the bed, with Crystal's boobs either flopping around or thrusting out. 'Turn that over, Muzz, there's an ad on the back for Spanish clothes. Get a dictionary or something and work out what zapato blanco means. And I've been walking in and out of that fuckin' block of flats with it right above my head for nearly a week. You don't mind being conned, Muzz, but that's jamming it right up your salmon.'

Les had his fist round the door knob. He let go and turned back to his brother. 'In fact I'll tell you what, Murray, if I wasn't driving this sheila back to Taree, and I didn't know about his brother, I'd go back round that block of flats and kick him right in the nuts. The rotten little . . . mockey bastard.

How was it?

V-man

268

Robert G. Barrett
Davo's Little Something

All easy-going butcher, Bob Davis, wanted after his divorce was to get on with his job, have a few beers with his mates, and be left alone. But this was Sydney in the early eighties. The beginning of the AIDS epidemic, street gangs, gay bashings, murders.

When a gang of skinheads bashed Davo's old school friend to death simply because he was gay, and left Davo almost dead in an intensive care unit, they unleashed a crazed killer onto the city streets. Before the summer had ended, over thirty corpses had turned up in the morgue, leaving two bewildered detectives to find out where they were coming from.

Robert G. Barrett's latest book is not for the squeamish. Although written with lashings of black humour the action is chillingly brutal — a story of a serial killer bent on avenging himself on the street tribes of Sydney. *Davo's Little Something* proves conclusively why Robert G. Barrett, author of the Les Norton series, is one of Australia's most popular contemporary writers.

Robert G. Barrett
The Boys From Binjiwunyawunya

Les Norton's back in town!

There's no two ways about Les Norton — the carrot-topped country boy who works as a bouncer at Sydney's top illegal casino. He's tough and he's mean. He's got a granite jaw, fists like hams, and they say the last time he took a tenner from his wallet Henry Lawson blinked at the light.

Lethal but loyal, he's always good for a laugh. In this, the third collection of Les Norton adventures, Les gets his boss off the hook. But not without the help of the boys from Binjiwunyawunya.

Having got over that, Les finds himself in a spot of bother in Long Bay Gaol then in a lot more bother on a St. Kilda tram in Melbourne...

Robert G. Barrett's Les Norton stories have created a world as funny as Damon Runyon's. If you don't know Les Norton, you don't know Australia in the eighties.

Robert G. Barrett
**Between the Devlin and the
Deep Blue Seas**

Okay, so it looks like the Kelly Club is finally closing
down — it had to happen sooner or later. And it isn't
as if Les Norton will starve. He has money snookered
away, he owns his house, and his blue-chip
investment — a block of flats in Randwick — must be
worth a fortune by now. Except that the place is falling
down, the council is reclaiming the land, there's been
a murder in Flat 5, and the tenants are the biggest
bunch of misfits since the Manson Family. And that's
just the good news, because the longer Les owns the
Blue Seas Apartments, the more money he loses.

This time Les Norton's really up against it.

But whilst he's trying to solve his financial problems, he
still has time to fight hate-crazed roadies, sort out a
drug deal after fighting a gang of bikies, help a
feminist Balmain writer with some research she won't
forget in a hurry, and get involved with Franulka,
super-sexy leadsinger of an all-girl rock band, The
Heathen Harlots.

And with the help of two ex-Romanian Securitate
explosive experts, he might even be able to sort out
his investment.

But can Les pull off the perfect crime? Of course —
and why not throw the street party of the year at the
same time?

Robert G. Barrett's latest Les Norton novel is probably
no more outrageous than his previous ones.

But then again . . .

Robert G. Barrett
The Real Thing

Les Norton is back in town!

It all began in *You Wouldn't Be Dead For Quids*... And now there's more of it in *The Real Thing*.

Trouble seems to follow Les Norton like a blue heeler after a mob of sheep.

Maybe it's his job.

Being a bouncer at the infamous and illegal Kelly Club in Kings Cross isn't the stuff a quiet life is made of.

Maybe it's his friends.

Like Price Galese, the urbane and well-connected owner of the Kelly Club, or Eddie Salita who learnt to kill in Vietnam, or Reg Campbell, struggling artist and dope dealer.

But, then again, maybe Les is just unlucky.

Robert G. Barrett's five stories of Les Norton and the Kelly Club provide an entertaining mix of laughter and excitement, and an insight into the Sydney underworld; a world often violent and cynical, but also with its fair share of rough humour and memorable characters.

Robert G. Barrett
You Wouldn't Be Dead For Quids

You Wouldn't Be Dead For Quids is the book that
launched Les Norton as Australia's latest cult hero.

Follow Les, the hillbilly from Queensland, as he takes
on the bouncers, heavies, hookers and gamblers of
Sydney's Kings Cross, films a TV ad for Bowen Lager
in Queensland and gets caught up with a
nymphomaniac on the Central Coast of New South
Wales.

In one of the funniest books of the past decade you
will laugh yourself silly and be ducking for cover as
Les unleashes himself on Sydney's unsuspecting
underworld.

Robert G. Barrett
The Godson

'I wonder who that red-headed bloke is? He's come
into town out of nowhere, flattened six of the best
fighters in Yurriki plus the biggest man in the valley.
Then he arrives at my dance in an army uniform
drinking French champagne and imported beer like
it's going out of style. And ups and leaves with the best
young sort in the joint... Don't know who he is. But
he's not bloody bad.'

Les Norton is at it again!

Les thought they were going to be the easiest two
weeks of his life.

Playing minder for a young member of the Royal
Family called Peregrine Normanhurst III sounded like a
deadset snack. So what if he was a champagne-
guzzling millionaire Hooray Henry and his godfather
was the Attorney General of Australia? Les would keep
Peregrine out of trouble... So what if he was on the
run from the IRA? They'd never follow him to
Australia...

Robert G. Barrett's latest Les Norton adventure moves
at breakneck speed from the corridors of power in
Canberra to the grimy tenements of Belfast, scorching
the social pages of Sydney society and romping
through the North Coast's plushest resorts to climax in
a nerve-shattering, blood-spattered shootout on a
survivalist fortress in the Tweed Valley. *The Godson*
features Les Norton at his hilarious best, whatever he's
up against — giant inbreds, earth mothers,
Scandinavian au pair girls, jealous husbands, violent
thugs and vengeful terrorists.

If you thought Australia's favourite son could get up to
some outrageous capers in *You Wouldn't Be Dead For
Quids, The Real Thing* and *The Boys from
Binjiwunyawunya*, until you've read *The Godson*, you
ain't read nothin' yet!

312 Dan Pyke
404
7923